A SCOUNDREL'S SEDUCTION

"Open," he muttered.

She did—to bite him. Her teeth nipped his lower lip.

He swept inside.

He tasted surprise, indignation. Then he tasted *her*. If he were given a blindfold and a hundred women to kiss, he would always know Alanna. Tart, frightened, excited against her will. He held her firmly, but he kept the kiss gentle.

Lifting his head, he looked down at her. "Leave your door unlocked tonight."

"You can't come to me without the wedding!" she whispered.

"I can," he boasted. "I can slip through your window on a breeze, enchant you with a spell."

"If you're the wind, then I don't have to leave my door unlocked for you, do I?" she countered.

He smiled, slow and sure. He *was* the wind, and he *would* be with her.

Other Avon Books by
Christina Dodd

A WELL PLEASURED LADY

CHRISTINA DODD

A Well Favored Gentleman

AVON BOOKS ◆ NEW YORK

AVON BOOKS
A division of
The Hearst Corporation
1350 Avenue of the Americas
New York, New York 10019

Copyright © 1998 by Christina Dodd
Excerpt from *Forever After* copyright © 1998 by Adeline Catherine Anderson
Excerpt from *Sealed With a Kiss* copyright © 1998 by Pamela Morsi
Excerpt from *The Night Remembers* copyright © 1997 by Kathleen Eagle
Excerpt from *Stranger In My Arms* copyright © 1998 by Lisa Kleypas
Excerpt from *One True Love* copyright © 1998 by Barbara Freethy
Excerpt from *That Scandalous Evening* copyright © 1998 by Christina Dodd
Cover art by Fredericka Ribes
Inside front cover art by Victor Gadino
Inside back cover author photo by Nesossi Photography
Published by arrangement with the author
Visit our website at **http://www.AvonBooks.com**
Library of Congress Catalog Card Number: 97-94308
ISBN: 0-380-79090-4

First Avon Books Printing: March 1998

AVON TRADEMARK REG. U.S. PAT. OFF. AND IN OTHER COUNTRIES, MARCA REGISTRADA, HECHO EN U.S.A.

Printed in the U.S.A.

WCD   10 9 8 7 6 5 4 3 2 1

To Scott
my well favored gentleman

ACKNOWLEDGMENTS

Thank you to everyone who helped with this book. My fellow plotters, Jolie Kramer, Heather MacAllister, and Susan Macias—we miss you, Susan. My critique group, Joyce Bell, Betty Gyenes, Barbara Dawson Smith, and Susan Wiggs—we miss you, Susan. My editor, Carrie Feron. And a special thanks to Connie Brockway, who, when I called and said, "I need you to be brilliant *now*," was promptly brilliant.

A Well Favored
Gentleman

Chapter 1

Scotland, 1800

Someone held a knife to his throat.

Ian Fairchild snapped out of his deep slumber and held himself perfectly still, eyes closed and breathing even in a parody of sleep.

Someone held a knife to his throat, and it wasn't the first time, but this time he'd been caught by surprise. He hadn't had time to make enemies in Scotland. He'd arrived only today, and had found his father, the only person here who would gladly kill him, too sick to leave his bed.

So who was it who had slipped into his bed-chamber as the hour struck midnight?

Carefully he opened his eyes a slit—and stared into the face of a ghost.

A lovely, feminine, fiercely determined ghost, if her expression was anything to go by.

His eyes widened. "You're an idiot, Ian." He spoke aloud, seeing no harm in addressing a phantom and finding the sound of his own voice vastly reassuring. "It's only a dream." And he tried to move to prove it.

He couldn't. The ghost sat on his chest, the

dream held him in thrall, and he couldn't bloody move.

A normal turn of events in a dream, he supposed. If only that steel pressed against his windpipe didn't feel so cold and so real. If only he didn't feel so . . . odd. More than sleepy, he was drifting, illogically relaxed beneath the threat of violence.

He blinked, bringing the phantom into focus. Wisps of hair sprang defiantly from her hairline. Her features were angular: square jawline, sharp cheekbones, wide mouth. Her eyes slanted up, her brows slanted up, her snub nose rose to a little point. A fascinating face, one filled with character and lively convictions. Not ghostly at all. "I know who you are. You're dead. You're Lady Alanna."

Both of her hands gripped that knife. He could see them in his peripheral vision, and they shook a little at the sound of her name.

Fear cleared his brain for one brief moment. The tip of that imaginary blade seemed so very honed. "Careful, there. We wouldn't want a bloody accident."

"No accident at all." Her voice was husky, touched by a defiant Scottish accent, and it sounded real, too.

This was the most vivid dream he'd ever had. "Lady Alanna. I didn't think I'd get to meet you. You're prettier than your portrait."

"A compliment from a Fairchild." The dream knife nudged close to his jugular. "I value that as it deserves."

Sharp-tongued and prudent as well as pretty. The portrait had portrayed her as a girl balanced on the cusp of maturity, looking eagerly toward the day she would inherit Fionnaway Manor. But she had disappeared on the eve of her seventeenth birthday, never to be seen again.

In a bit of dream magic, she now appeared to him all grown up. The night candle in the headboard illuminated her piquant features and her generous curves. It found a companion flame in the red of her hair, and her large eyes were the color of the sea before an encroaching storm.

Yet she watched him as cautiously as one watches a trapped wolf.

With justification. He could be a dangerous man, but she didn't know that. Her wariness came from having known his father, and from the Fairchilds' well-deserved reputation. His family were as famous as the Borgias, and for much the same reasons. The desire for money and power ruled them; no crime was too heinous when committed in the name of the Fairchild pocketbook.

Everyone he had met this day had watched him, waiting for his pleasant facade to peel away and show him to be as despicable as his father. For today, at least, he had managed to recall the values his mother had taught him. But Lady Alanna and the residents of Fionnaway were right to treat him gingerly; sometimes the Fairchild blood prevailed.

For instance, right now the temptation to shout "boo" was almost irresistible. Only that nervous, two-handed grip on the knife stopped him. "You seem worried. What's wrong, sweet lady?"

"You weren't supposed to be awake."

"I'm a light sleeper."

"Yes, but the smoke was supposed to . . ."

"To what?" His mind suddenly sharpened, and he noted the haze around her figure. He noted, also, an odor he had not smelled since India. Hashish. Someone had tried to drug him.

He considered the woman leaning one knee on his chest. *She* had tried to drug him, and she had done a very good job. He *was* drugged.

But in a clear, analytical corner of his mind he knew several things. He had experienced hashish before. Soon he would recover the use of his limbs. Even sooner, he would recover his ability to tell between fantasy and reality. And as the air cleared, so would his head, and as the ghost stayed, so she would breathe in the remaining fumes and get groggy.

A question occurred to him, and he asked, "Do ghosts inhale?"

"No."

But her chest rose and fell. So she was not a ghost. The recovery of his logic pleased him, but with it came another inescapable piece of information. If she wasn't a ghost, then that knife she held to his throat was real. With a drug-induced astonishment, he said, "You're trying to kill me."

Her gaze was frigid and steady. "It seems a good idea."

"To who? Not to me." He tried to gesture, and found movement had returned to the tips of his fingers. Information he kept to himself.

When he'd gone to bed, he'd pulled the covers up to his chin to shut out the inevitable drafts and pulled the bed-curtains tight. Now the curtains stood open to let in the light and smoke from the hearth, and her weight kept the covers tight against his body. Still, she was small-boned and light, and would not be a deterrent—if his muscles would work. "Why would the good, sweet Lady Alanna of whom the servants sing praises want to murder anyone?"

"*You're* a destructive, wastrel Fairchild who has come to steal Fionnaway. *I'm* the mistress of Fionnaway, responsible for its care, and I cannot allow you to desecrate it."

He stared at her, and she twitched backward. As

she should have, for if she could read his thoughts, she would know the danger she had stirred with her condemnation.

He expected her scorn, but he still despised people like her, who had grown up knowing where they belonged. For the past seven years, he'd searched the world for a home, yet never had he settled for more than a month or two before the spur of discontent moved him on. To London, when business summoned. To India, to the Americas, to places increasingly exotic.

And now his father's summons had brought him to cozy, prosaic Fionnaway, where old castle walls clutched a precipice thrusting into an arm of the western sea. What had once been the keep wherein the noble MacLeods had dwelled had evolved slowly through the ages into a manor house, neither as fashionable or as comfortable as Fairchild Manor in Sussex, and certainly not as warm. Fionnaway Manor's windows oversaw all. All the fields, all the meadows, everything to the edge of the distant forest. Ian knew this, for he had looked.

Ian had looked, also, to the west, and seen the miles of sandy beaches separated by great crags of granite. There the breakers pounded in an everlasting rhythm that called his name. *Ian, Ian . . .* He heard the echo of his mother's voice in the waves.

He hated the sea, yet despite its overwhelming propinquity, he knew his long search had ended. Fionnaway satisfied the fitful longing of his soul, and soon it would be his.

Not Lady Alanna's, be she ghost or living, breathing woman. This land would be *his*. "You abandoned Fionnaway," he taunted.

"That's not true!" Deliberately she bounced her weight against his sternum.

Her bony knee knocked the air out of him, but

he didn't care. The drug still tumbled through his bloodstream, and as soon as he got his breath back, he spoke the truth without a thought to the consequences. "You were weak. You *died*. If you were still here, you could have your Fionnaway, but to the victor go the spoils." He grinned, utilizing all his rakish Fairchild charm. "I am the victor."

"Never!" She leaned forward into his face, and the blade nicked his Adam's apple. "I'll never leave Fionnaway to you or any of your kind."

As the cut stung and the blood trickled down his neck, he realized he'd better shut up. If her indignation burned any hotter, he'd be singing in the choirs of heaven—or maybe burning in the fires of hell.

With a faint moan, he closed his eyes and concentrated on relaxing. Somehow he didn't think Lady Alanna, or her ghost, had the guts to kill a sleeping man. If he was lucky, she wouldn't have the guts to kill at all—although if he kept spouting off as he had, she might make an exception.

As he lay there, motionless, the pressure of the blade eased, and she shifted uncomfortably, releasing some of the burden on his chest. "What's wrong?"

"My head aches."

One of her palms flattened on his forehead. "You're not running a fever."

"It's the smoke." He coughed pathetically.

"Take some willow bark in the morn—" She caught herself, apparently remembering he wouldn't be alive in the morning.

"Why kill me?" Feeling had returned to his toes. He flexed them, and surreptitiously flexed his hands. "My father's been here for five years. Why not Leslie?"

With a bluntness he thought the lingering smoke

encouraged, she asked, "Why waste murder on a man who's dying?"

"Dying." Ian tasted the word and found it true. He had been shocked by Leslie's appearance when he'd seen him. The old man had barely been able to sit erect. The sound of fluid rattled in his lungs, and he was so swollen the skin was peeling back from his fingertips. Ian had never imagined he would see one of the gorgeous Fairchilds in such a condition—especially not his father. His omnipotent father, whose cruelty was legend.

But for this ghost, this woman, to say so with such certainty . . . ah, that was food for thought. "How do you know that?"

"Rumors circulate among the . . . angels."

She sounded so sure. Opening his eyes, he stared at her. Her mouth was too wide for her face, inviting a man to explore it with his lips, to find out whether her acerbic tongue could be sweetened by passion. Her outgrown, tattered gown nipped at her tiny waist, and a creamy swell of breasts pressed above the neckline. Most of all, her eyes snapped with challenge and fire.

Heavenly? No. Lady Alanna was no angel. Deliberately, knowing if he was right, she would certainly kill him, he asked, "Did you poison him?"

She reared back. "No!"

Good enough. He believed her. But—"Did someone else do it for you?"

"No one's poisoned your father. He's dying because . . ."

Her hesitation captured all of Ian's interest. "Because?"

"Mr. Fairchild visited this part of Scotland years ago." She seemed to know that without question.

"Thirty-five years ago." Thirty-five years since

Ian had been conceived. "Surely you're not saying he contracted a disease then!"

"I don't have to tell you anything. *I'm* holding the knife."

True enough. But she knew—or suspected— something about his father's illness. And his steady gaze was making her squirm guiltily.

"I've got to kill you. I've got no choice." She sounded as if she were arguing with herself. "Mr. Fairchild said you were a bigger villain even than him."

Stunned, Ian stared at her before laughter, uncontrollable laughter, erupted from his throat.

"Sh." Her lower lip stuck out like a sulky child's. "What's so funny?"

"It's just that"—he sputtered again, took in air, and laughed again—"I've never met anyone who actually believed a word my father said. Now it has to be someone who wants to kill me because of it."

"Sh." She flushed bright red, but glanced toward the door. "Someone will hear."

She didn't like being laughed at, he could see that, but nothing could contain his incredulity. "My father's the biggest liar in all the British Isles," he hooted, "and you believe him!"

"Be quiet!"

His amusement died a sudden death. "For a ghost, you're certainly concerned with being caught." The laughter had cleared his lungs and invigorated him, and with a swift movement he knocked her off of him. "When it's me you should be concerned about."

She tumbled off the bed. The knife went flying. Throwing back the covers, he came to his feet on the mattress.

"You're naked!"

He looked down at her and wondered how he

ever could have thought this petite and ruffled minx anything but flesh and blood. Certainly she sounded as shocked as a maiden, an occurrence he hadn't expected from a woman intent on murder. Yet she sat on the floor, skirt hiked to the knees and two very shapely calves extended straight out in front, and stared at his towering form—and his towering erection—with every imitation of offended astonishment.

"Yes, I am."

"You're . . . you're . . ."

"Aroused?" He didn't mind showing off, but standing ten feet high while the girl sat on the floor seemed a bit self-indulgent. Testing his muscles, he gingerly climbed off the bed. "You may claim to be a ghost, but I am not, and I cherish every physical desire known to man."

She edged away on her rump. "I was just surprised that a Fairchild *could* indulge in physical desire."

What did she mean by that? What did she mean, mocking him with her smile?

Infuriated, he launched himself at her—and found he had not recovered quite as much as he hoped. One knee buckled, and he caught the edge of the night table. It fell with him, clattering harshly in the still night.

She ducked and rolled. Standing, she tried to run toward the door.

"No more pranks, little one. Come here at once." He caught her skirt, and found himself holding a handful of shredded cotton. Good God, did the girl wear rags?

He lunged again, but she snatched up her knife and swiveled to face him. Balancing it expertly on her fingertips, she said, "If you come near me, I swear I'll stick this through your heart."

She hadn't been able to murder him in cold blood, but she looked frightened and desperate enough to kill him now, and she handled the knife like someone who knew how to aim and throw.

"All right." He held up his empty hands as she backed toward the door. "I won't do anything."

"Damned right." She groped for the doorknob behind her back and opened it. "You'll stay right where you are." As she prepared to step across the threshold, she looked at him one more time. At the sweep of his body, and then into his eyes.

Without words, he promised—*he would find her. Somehow he would find her.*

She shivered and slammed the door.

With a curse, he grabbed up his robe and ran, jerked the door open and looked down the hall.

Like the ghost she pretended to be, she had disappeared.

He started down the corridor, yelling for the steward and the housekeeper. "Mr. Armstrong! Mrs. Armstrong!" He entered the great hall. The lights were coming on all over the manor as servants stumbled out of their beds. Doors slammed, feet pattered. Ian waited to hear the cry that someone had seen her, that Lady Alanna had returned, but heard only a bewildered chatter. Frustrated, Ian bellowed, "Armstrongs!"

The steward hurried into the hallway, tugging a shirt over his head. "Mr. Fairchild, what's wrong?"

"I saw Lady Alanna. Did anyone else see her?"

Mrs. Armstrong stood behind her husband in her nightcap and a morning gown, and behind her the servants appeared in various stages of dress. Ian saw them exchanging glances.

"I tell you, she was in my bedchamber." He used his most reasonable tone.

Still he heard a swift murmur of disbelief. "Drunk," someone said.

"Sir, Lady Alanna is no longer with us." Armstrong used a soothing tone. "You saw her portrait today, and perhaps dreamed about her—"

"I tell you, she was there." Ian shook the handful of skirt at them, but they only stared uncomprehendingly.

"'Tis her ghost, then," Mrs. Armstrong said. "I wondered when it would return."

Armstrong swung on his wife. "Don't be daft, woman. There's no ghost here."

"And if there is"—Ian touched his neck and held out his fingers, stained with his own blood—"she's done a good job of trying to slit my throat."

Behind him he heard a gurgling gasp and a heavy thump. Turning, he saw his father sprawled on the floor in a stupor. As Ian hurried toward him, he heard Leslie wheeze, "Don't let her come back for me. Please, for pity's sake, don't let her get me."

Vast, restless, and overwhelming, the sea tears at the western coast of Scotland. Fingers of land reach into the water, trying to grasp eternity and losing to the constant grind of the waves. The wind lifts the brine and carries it up, into the Highlands where mist drifts over tall standing stones like silk draped over the finest ladies. Men and women, strangers to the rugged hills, have been lost in that mist, never to return, and around the fires of smoky peat, tales are recounted of mystical creatures who delight in confusing the chance-met travelers. Fairies live in the Scottish Highlands, and elves.

And so, it is said, do witches.

Chapter 2

"She's a witch, Mr. Ian."

A bluster of air off the sunlit sea swirled in the capes of Ian Fairchild's greatcoat as he strode toward the stables. It ruffled his hair and disarrayed his cravat.

"I'm na a man given t' fancies, but I would be derelict in my duty if I didna tell ye some say she's an *evil* witch." Armstrong's short legs scrambled to keep up with Ian's long gait. "Her face withers the barley in the field, she'd just as soon cause a wart as cure one, and what she did t' Kennie!"

Ian cast a diverted glance at Armstrong. "The blacksmith?"

"Aye. He threw a bit of iron at her—witches abhor iron—and she cursed him." They reached the stable yard. "And my wife claims Mrs. Kennie says he hasn't been a true man since."

Ian understood immediately. "Got a horseshoe where his rod should be, eh?"

Sadly, Armstrong nodded his head. "Badly bent."

Ian heard shouting, and saw two boys clinging desperately to the reins of his horse. Striding forward, Ian caught the reins and looked into Tocsin's face. "If you want a fight, pick on someone your own size. For instance, I'll be glad to oblige you."

The horse snorted, and quieted, and both boys scrambled onto the fence.

Ian rubbed Tocsin's nose. "You're a beauty," he crooned, and in a swift motion mounted the horse. "Armstrong, the first night I arrived at Fionnaway, I saw a ghost."

Armstrong flinched at the reminder of Lady Alanna's midnight appearance. "Aye, and the maids have na dared go alone int' the cellar since."

"And I've seen evil at work every day since I took up residence with my father. I know how to handle a mere witch."

"I dunna doubt ye, but if ye must seek a favor from her, Mr. Ian, please promise ye'll hie yerself back before the dark."

"What brew does she stir at night?" Ian pulled on his gloves, controlling the horse with tight-held knees.

"At night—that's when she changes her shape. She transforms from the hideous old crone int' a bonny woman who enslaves all men who behold her."

"She'd best keep her evil eye off my rod, or I'll be no good to her as a slave," Ian said. "I've been told she's the best healer we have at Fionnaway, so she'll come to ease my father's pain."

"What fool would send an Englishman t' a Scottish witch?" Armstrong muttered.

"Ah, Armstrong"—Ian leaned out of the saddle— "it was your own wife."

He grinned at Armstrong's dismay, then with a word to Tocsin, he raced out into the summer day. In his memory he carried explicit instructions to the witch's house. In his heart he carried the exaltation of a man escaping a prison.

The moon had come to full and waned again

since his arrival, and in that time Leslie Fairchild had proclaimed Ian his heir, and Ian had inspected every inch of Fionnaway. Yet now Ian dreamed of a moment away from the manor, away from the wary servants, and most of all, away from his father.

For that moment, Ian would do anything, even visit a witch.

Her hut nestled deep in the wood, with a thatched roof and drifts of moss all around. The garden sparkled with flowers, and a shed at the edge of the clearing held stacked wood and well-tended rabbit cages. Chickens pecked in the grass. A fire crackled in the fire pit outside, and a rich scent wafted from the iron cauldron. Stones ringed the well—a magic well, perhaps. Ian stared and wondered if he had found the wrong hut in the wrong wood.

Then the witch stepped out of the open door.

She wore dirty brown homespun. A hump deformed one shoulder and her bosom drooped over the belt that circled her thick waist. A large spoon and wickedly sharp fork hung from the rope and clanked as she walked, and the sheath beside them contained a knife of a size to gut a man. Her long hair, dry and gray, caught in the smears of green unguent on her face.

Her face. Good God, it looked like a parched meadow in a drought. Her complexion was gray, too, with furrows between her black brows and beside her red mouth and above her upper lip.

The sight of that countenance would wither a man's rod, Ian admitted.

She didn't seem to see him as she hobbled to the kettle. With the spoon she tasted the steaming brew, shook her head, and opened one of the leather pouches that dangled by her hip. Taking a handful, she sprinkled it into the cauldron.

Ian half expected to see colored steam rise and form some ominous shape. Instead the odor of marjoram filled the air.

Oh, an evil, awesome witch indeed. She used herbs in her brew. Dismounting, he led his horse to a shady patch of grass. "Old woman, I have need of your services."

His presence caused her no obvious consternation. After a single sharp glance, she picked up a wooden bowl from the stool beside the fire pit and filled it. With a tilt of her head, she invited him inside her home and entered, never looking to see if he followed.

He did, of course, tracking the sumptuous odor of vegetables and broth. Ducking his head beneath the doorframe, he said, "The lord of Fionnaway desires succor."

"I cannot think of any man who deserves succor less," the old woman said in a creaking voice.

Ian fixed her with a stern and commanding look. The crone stared right back, neither cringing nor remorseful.

So. He could not intimidate her. "Or needs succor more."

"And why should I do as Ian Fairchild demands?" the witch asked.

So she knew who he was. "No doubt you've heard the rumors about me," Ian said coolly. "That's a good reason to obey me."

"Rumors." She snorted with disdain. "Rumors." Placing the bowl on a sturdy, well-worn table, she ordered, "Eat."

He shouldn't. But Ian had been constantly attending Leslie for the past week, catching a bite only when he could. Now the odor of food made his stomach growl. Stripping off his leather riding gloves, he placed them on the table, seated himself on the stool, and picked up the spoon. Discreetly he poked at the concoction.

Stew. It looked like stew.

The witch stood in the shadows in the corner, her arms crossed over her stomach. "Eat! Eat and become my slave forever."

In a trick he'd been taught as a child, he looked toward her and blurred his vision. He could see clearly when he observed more than the physical, and he knew this woman was lying. With every breath she took, with every movement she made, she was lying.

But more important—today, at least, she had no plans to poison him.

"If you won't be my slave, eat for your own sake," she said. "You've a lean and hungry countenance, and it's not comfortable being in the same room with a wolf."

He sampled the stew, redolent with herbs and garlic. He took another bite, and the flavor convinced him of one thing—the witch should supervise the manor house kitchen, not lurk in a hut in the woods. Fionnaway's cuisine left much to be desired. "It's good."

She smiled, and he wondered what spell she had cast to retain all her teeth, white, sturdy, and young. "It's enchanted," she answered. Taking a cloth-wrapped package off the shelf above her, she tossed it to him.

Ian opened it and found a flat piece of bread. Breaking off a chunk, he dipped it in the sauce and chewed it thoughtfully. A fine, nutty flavor spread across his tongue, and he agreed, "So it is."

The witch moved to the far corner, picked up a pestle and mortar off the shelf crowded with bags, jars, and loose leaves. Holding the bowl against her stomach, she began a steady grinding of stone against stone, leaving him to eat.

When he had satisfied the keenest pangs of hunger, he pushed the bowl away and looked around the room. Climbing roses nodded into the windows. A finely carved chest stood in the middle of the far wall. A rope-and-stick bed hung in one corner, covered with luxurious furs. They provided a comfortable spot for the huge brindle cat snoring in the square of light, which opened one disinterested eye and viewed him with contempt, then stretched and fell asleep once more.

He carefully wiped his beard with his handkerchief, and wished his valet had accompanied him on this trip rather than quitting in a huff, but English servants were quite sniffy about traveling to Scotland. "You'll come to Fionnaway with me."

With elaborate care she placed the mortar on the shelf, then hobbled over to remove the bowl from the table. "What do you want me to do about Mr. Fairchild?"

"I want you to ease his suffering."

"Do you not want me to cure him?" She fixed him with the unblinking stare of the peregrine falcon.

"If you can, but the hand of God is heavy on his neck—"

"The hand of the devil, more likely." The witch touched her mouth as if she regretted her outburst, but then her hand fell away. "Do you know what Saint Peter will do to Mr. Fairchild when he sees him?"

Ian suspected he did, but he could scarcely believe the witch had the brass to tell him.

"He'll open the trapdoor and drop him straight into hell." She struck her chest with her fist. "I recognize your father as one of Beelzebub's demons, because I'm evil, right to the bone."

"I'm quaking in my linens."

"You'd better be." Then she realized he ridiculed her, and in an ominous tone she asked, "Have you heard what I did to the blacksmith?"

"Kennie the Eel?"

She thrust her head forward and rubbed her palms together. "They used to call him Kennie the Goat."

"I've heard the tale." He lounged in an attitude of abject boredom. "Is that the worst you can do?"

She gaped indignantly, then snapped, "I can wither your man-parts so small you have to tie them in red yarn to find them!"

He couldn't help it; he laughed. "You'll be a welcome entertainment when you come to the manor." She'd been too spoiled, this evil witch, by men groveling in fear of their virility. He'd take his chances against her sorcery, and enforce his will as the lord. "You *will* come to the manor."

The old woman clasped her hands under the long sleeves of her gown. She didn't want to obey him. Neither did she want to fight him. Witch or no witch, withered love apples or not, she would lose. "Aye," she said grumpily. "I will. But why seek help now? He's been ill since your arrival, and before."

"Yes, but now he screams and sees things that aren't there—and he's afraid."

Somberly she concentrated on his words, and Ian realized why Mrs. Armstrong had suggested he come here. Perhaps the witch was evil, but her interest soothed Ian. "The Edinburgh doctor who saw my father had never observed agonies such as my father is suffering, and he left me with a bottle of laudanum and instructions to make him comfortable before . . . the end."

Shuffling to the stalks of dried herbs hanging from the rafters, she grasped one and yanked, and dried leaves showered her. Crushing a little in her palm, she sniffed it thoughtfully. "Should old Mr. Fairchild die, you think you'll be the new laird."

"I *will* be the new lord." He fought the base desire, but it burrowed beneath his skin and teased the edges of his mind. He wished his father dead. He wished for the day when he would be free of the taunting, the cruelty, the lacerations of the soul Leslie so skillful applied.

And then . . . ah, then Fionnaway would be his.

As if she read his thoughts, the witch asked, "What about the good and sweet Lady Alanna?"

Some grievous emotion vibrated in the old crone's voice, a personal interest he couldn't place. It gave him an advantage, for after all, a man such as Ian sharpened all his senses in pursuit of nothing more than a continued existence. "Lady Alanna?" He studied his fingernails. "She doesn't matter."

"Doesn't she?" The witch's peculiar anxiety increased. "But don't the farmers talk about her? Haven't the fishermen spoke to you of her? Haven't the servants told you stories about her, and all with tears in their eyes?"

She was right. The people of Fionnaway wished for, hoped for, the return of the mistress. It was as if they hoped that telling their tales would bring her back. Worse, they acted as if *he* could bring her back. As if *he* could right injustice. He, Ian, bred half a Fairchild and tainted with that ancestry.

"Didn't you see her ghost?" the old woman whispered.

Slowly he lifted his gaze to hers. Her ghost. No, he'd not seen her ghost. He'd seen her. He had the scar on his throat to prove it. She had been in his bedroom, taunted him, threatened him, been willing to kill him ... and why? Because she wanted her heritage back.

Ian didn't know where Lady Alanna hid. He only knew she was a threat to him, and to these lands that filled the desolation of his soul.

The witch read his thoughts, and echoed them with uncanny precision. "She's alive."

"So what if she is? She abandoned her inheritance."

"Nay, not so! If you knew why she left—"

"Tell me, then. What made the girl run away?"

The witch thrust her ugly face toward his, and the scent of mint clung to her. "Your father, Mr. Fairchild. Your father."

"Don't call me Mr. Fairchild," he said. "That is my father's name. I am Ian."

Retreating to her dark corner, she placed the mint on the shelf. "Lady Alanna didn't want to share that name, either." Gathering up her mortar and pestle, she looked down at the already ground leaves with surprise, as if she didn't remember doing them. "Your father announced he would make her his wife."

Ian barely contained his astonishment. "Leslie? He wanted to marry Lady Alanna?"

"She is an heiress." She emptied the contents of the mortar into a leather bag, spilling some. Her hands were shaking, and she stared at them as if they were not her own. "As her husband, he would have complete control over her and her fortune."

"He was—is—her guardian. He already *had* complete control over her fortune." And for a guardian to try to wed an underage girl in his care was the lowest of acts—and nothing less than Ian expected.

"But she had no respect for him, and child that she was, she showed it. Her people followed her example, and Mr. Fairchild found himself losing control. So he thought if he took her to his bed . . ."

A sad state, when a woman as ugly as the witch trembled with revulsion at the thought of Leslie, but Ian understood. Something about his father repulsed, something that grew more vile as the years progressed. "How old was she?"

"She had lived fifteen years when her father died. Leslie arrived on the eve of her sixteenth birthday." The witch hugged herself and rubbed her hands up and down her arms, reciting the facts in a soft voice quite unlike her previous creaking tone. "He would have wed her on her seventeenth birthday."

Deliberately he leaned forward. "She's been gone four years."

"Aye, four years."

Slowly he settled back, arranging his elbows on the table behind him and striving for a casual pose. "Four years." And no matter how he counted, seventeen plus four was twenty-one.

"The gracious Lady Alanna declared she would refuse Mr. Fairchild at the altar, so he thought to ensure her cooperation," the witch said, oblivious to the direction of his thoughts.

Still dazed by the realization Lady Alanna would soon reach her majority, he fumbled to grasp the witch's meaning. "He raped her?"

"Not . . . quite." The witch smirked at him. "Your father was unable to perform."

Soon, he would wager, Lady Alanna would return from hiding to toss the Fairchilds off her land, and nothing Ian could do would stop her. "Was that your fault, too, Granny?" he mocked, furious at this turn of events.

She looked startled, then gave him a genuine smile. "Aye. As a matter of fact, it was."

She wasn't lying, and he eased one leg across the other.

"That'll do you no good, sonny, if the witch of Fionnaway decides to peel your family apples," she said gleefully.

One moment she was a menace. The next she was only an obnoxious old woman. An obnoxious old woman who knew more than she would say. "Where is Lady Alanna now?" he demanded.

"I don't know."

"Come here." She obeyed, as he knew she would. When he used that tone of voice, everyone obeyed. Holding out his hand, he allowed the sunlight to strike his ring, and her gasp filled him with the deepest satisfaction. "Beautiful, is it not?"

He turned it so the silver filigree reflected the light. The stone, however, did not. The sea opal created its own light deep within, and the witch stared as if the gleam entranced her.

"Touch it," he commanded.

Her withered-looking fingers stretched out toward the stone.

"You want to," he said softly. "It's calling to you." And when she touched it, he would know so much about her . . .

The sunlight struck her ash-slathered hand. She focused on it and seemed to come to her senses. Leaping back, she cackled. "Nay, dear lad, I've dwelled here all my life. Do you think I don't know the legend of the sea opal? Although I wonder how you learned of it. Why do you think you can use those powers? And where did you get that ring?"

"It was my mother's." He answered the last question with no intention of answering any of the others. She had a strong will, this witch, and he'd have to depend on nothing more than his canny good sense to ferret out the secret of Lady Alanna—before he'd lost Fionnaway completely.

Lady Alanna, and the witch, were in trouble.

Yet the old hag wasn't afraid. As she plucked leaves into the mortar, her gaze clashed with his. "How can you live with yourself, knowing you will inherit that dear, sweet girl's lands and fortune?"

He wouldn't, if he wasn't careful. "I'm preferable to the English buzzards."

"Are you not an English buzzard?" she asked, her Gaelic accent stronger than he'd noticed before.

He hated to divulge the truth, but he had sworn long ago never to be ashamed. "My mother's family has lived near here since time eternal."

The pestle screeched as it slipped in the bowl, and Ian shuddered at the sound, so like fingernails across flint. The crone's gaze flew to his ring.

Before she could question him, he distracted her. "I'll treasure the lands and the people, Granny."

"You'll treasure them, you say?" With an old woman's impudence, she snorted and neighed. "Treasure them as Leslie does? Tax the farmers on a failing crop? Demand the children hunt the sea caves for precious stones where there are none? Seek the chance to destroy the lands and the beaches for a silly whim?"

"Is that what you expect?"

"Of course," the witch muttered, pushing back the gray hairs that hung over her right eye in an ungainly cowlick. "Mr. Fairchild has no more honor than a billy goat. No more than you, I suppose."

"I suppose." He grinned at her chagrin, but before she could retort, a light rap on the outside wall of the hut brought both heads around.

"Miss Witch?" called a timid voice.

Ian recognized the voice.

"Miss Witch? Excuse me, but are you home?"

Ian whipped around and glared at the evil one. "Wilda?" Grabbing the old woman's shoulders, Ian set her aside and stepped out. "Wilda, what are you doing here?"

Wilda, golden-haired, sweet-faced, innocent-looking Wilda, jumped and winced as if he made a regular habit of beating her. "Ian! What are *you* doing here?"

"I asked first."

"But, Ian, I never thought to see you here. I mean, I can't imagine you coming to consult a witch for anything like you have an excess of toad-stools or your voice is too high or anything. Not that it is. Too high, I mean. It's a pleasant voice, really, and I like the way you sound even when you're galled by me"—Wilda peeked at him from under the round brim of her velvet riding hat— "like I guess you are now?"

"Very galled." He kept firm control of the voice she praised. With Wilda, if one didn't take command immediately, she galloped away with conversation, good sense, and sanity. "Why have you come here? Who told you about this place?"

"I heard my maid talking to Mrs. Armstrong about the witch. You know, she's a very good maid. When you brought me here, I never expected to have a good maid. I mean, they serve *oatmeal* and it's cold all the time"—Wilda shivered in her well-tailored blue riding costume that so brought out the sapphire of her eyes—"and I think a country that can't even work up a decent summer leaves much to be desired in the way of civilization, but the servants are lovely to me. In fact, everyone has been lovely to me." She smiled at the witch. "Don't you find the people here lovely?"

The witch, when Ian turned to her, wore the same battered, stupefied expression most of humanity wore when subjected to Wilda's babble for the first time. "Lovely," she mumbled.

Wilda nodded with satisfaction. "I wanted to talk to you, but I can't talk while Ian is here. It's girl talk, and you know how men hate girl talk. Mama says that most men are worried that women are smarter than men, but I've never found it so. Most men I know seem positively sure they're smarter than me, which is silly, because most men are so stupid they can't even look above a girl's bosom to look at her face, much less review her intelligence. Don't you find it so?"

The dirty, ugly, disgusting witch looked from Ian to Wilda in bemusement.

Ian had seen that reaction before. She didn't know if Wilda was serious or mocking her, and he wasn't in the mood to explain. "Wilda," he said. "Do you see my horse?"

Wilda glanced around the yard until she saw the stallion grazing peacefully in the shade of the forest. "Oh." She dimpled. "There's Tocsin. Is that how you got here?"

"That's how *I* got here." He took her arm. "How did *you* get here?"

"I rode." Wilda nodded, and the feather on her hat bobbed in his face.

"Where is your horse?"

"I left him right over—" She pointed, then her finger drooped. "Well, I thought I left him over there."

"Did you tie him?"

She clapped her gloved hand over her mouth.

"You must remember to tie your horse," he reminded her gently, as he had reminded her so many times before.

"Yes, Ian."

"I'll take you back to Fionnaway." Pushing her toward Tocsin, he said, "Go on, now. I have to finish my business with the witch." He waited until Wilda walked out of earshot, then pitched his voice low. "Old woman, if you ever harm Wilda, you'll discover the rumors are true."

She gaped at him. "Which rumors?"

"The ones that say I'm a force to be reckoned with."

Her mouth snapped shut. "What will *you* do when you discover rumors are true?"

"What rumors?"

"The ones about the rightful heir's return."

They had gotten to the truth with a vengeance. "If you know something which might interfere with my claim on Fionnaway, then you should confess it to me. For witch-burning is an old and honorable pursuit, and very, very painful for the witch." As he towered over her, thunder boomed from the clear blue sky.

Nothing else he had said had intimidated her, but the threat of fire worked. She cowered almost to the ground and whimpered, and for one bitter moment he wondered if it was the Fairchild heritage that made him so proficient at terrorizing this old woman.

But she deserved it, damn it, with her innuendoes about the rightful heir. If it weren't for Wilda's inopportune appearance, he would get to the bottom of this matter right now. Instead, he stared threateningly into the witch's eyes . . . They were large, and as he gazed into them, he fell into their depths—clear to her lonely soul.

A witch? No. He didn't believe in witches. Evil?

She was defiant, frightened, and determined—and if that made a spirit evil, then Armstrong would have to tie Ian to the same stake.

Bound by some unholy fascination, they stared at each other, and a sensation of mystery deluged him. There was something here, something peculiar, something familiar . . . He would have sworn he'd looked into her eyes before.

If he could only see this old woman as she really was, without the mask of old age and wickedness, he would discover the truth. He strained, traveling through layers of deception, toward the center of her essence.

Close, he was so close—

"Ian," Wilda called. "Tocsin won't let me mount him."

The witch blinked, and a shutter fell over her mind.

Ian stepped back, released by the spell of her lure, and reeled like a man after a three-day drunk. The giddiness had been wonderful while it lasted, but it left him disgruntled and irate.

Wilda squealed. "Ian!"

Glancing over, he saw her hopping with her hands clasped on the saddle and one boot stuck in the stirrup. With hardly a thought, he abandoned the old woman and her mystery. "Wilda, you can't manage a stallion!" He caught Tocsin's reins and brought the indignant animal to a standstill. Lifting Wilda away, he mounted, then held out his hand.

Guilelessly Wilda placed her palm in his. The saddle's well-tanned leather creaked as she settled sidesaddle in front of him, and only then did Ian allow his attention to return to the old woman by the hut. Guiding Tocsin close, he said, "I'll send someone to fetch you to Fionnaway."

Ducking her head, she muttered, "I'll come on my own."

He hesitated. Should he trust her? But where else had she to go? "Don't lose your way."

His warning lingered, as did Wilda's artless "Farewell!"

The witch rose slowly from her obeisance. Stepping into the June sunshine, she watched Ian, and his strange passenger, ride away.

Then her metamorphosis began. Her spine straightened into the tempered sword of youth. She shook her hair back and coughed as a cloud of gray ash enveloped her. She tossed the wads of padding out of her gown and tightened her belt around her slim waist. With a shrug, she shed her woolen hump and used the corner of the material to wipe the grease from her face. As if she were a delicate butterfly who had escaped from the dull cocoon that bound her, she stretched and twirled.

Like the shape-changer the steward called her, she had transformed herself into a young woman. She wore the rough woolen clothes of a Highland villager and a necklace of polished rune stones; she lived alone in a hovel in the woods, but only a fool would fail to recognize her—and although he had not seen through her disguise, she didn't make the mistake of thinking Ian a fool.

His parting words disturbed her, and his strength of purpose confounded her. The cat prowled out the door and rubbed her ankles. Without thinking, she hoisted the husky feline and scratched his neck. "He's clever, Whisky," she told the animal. "More clever than his father. And polite." She held the cat up and looked into its golden eyes. "More polite than his father, but that goes without saying. And bonny . . . he is the bonniest man ever I saw, and it's obvious he attracts women—beautiful, chatty women—like the thistle attracts the bee." Whisky kicked in disgust and she put him down. "Now it remains to be seen—is he as clever as the witch of Fionnaway? Is he as clever as Lady Alanna?"

Chapter 3

"Ooh, she was ugly." Wilda shivered in the saddle in front of Ian. "I don't know if I can talk to her without staring, and Mama says it's rude to stare, although some people I just have to stare at. I mean, my eyes just go to them, and if I try to look away, I feel all embarrassed, so I look back and then I just stare. Of course, if she took all that gunk off her face, she'd look better."

Caught in that whirlpool of illogic Wilda created around her, Ian asked, "Your mother?"

"No, the witch! Isn't that who we were talking about?"

"Of course." *Several moments ago.*

Wilda sighed in exasperation. "Witches are scary, don't you think? I mean, I've always been frightened of them, although Mama told me they weren't real, but if a witch lived on the Fairchild Estate, she wouldn't reveal herself to Mama, now would she? It just wouldn't make sense to walk up and say, 'I'm a witch,' just like that, because Mama wouldn't believe her, and even if she did, she wouldn't allow a witch to live there, and I can't imagine a witch defying Mama, can you?"

He didn't know whether to shake Wilda until she ceased her rattling, or run so far away he didn't have to hear her anymore. But she was his cousin, twenty-nine years old and still unmarried. He'd brought her to this godforsaken country where people spoke incomprehensible English and ate a mixture of sheep's lungs, hearts, and liver mixed with the everlasting oatmeal and boiled in the slaughtered animal's stomach. They called it haggis. He called it revolting.

"Ian, are you listening?" she wailed.

Schooling himself to patience, he guided the horse up the hill toward the manor. "Of course, Wilda. I always listen to you."

She twisted around and stared up at him, her countenance innocent and her blue eyes wide. Then a ravishing smile transformed her from a silly widgeon to one of the most beautiful women in the civilized world, with the inborn seductive grace of a Helen of Troy—or a Fairchild of Sussex, from which family she indeed hailed. Patting the arm wrapped around her, she confided, "That's what I like about you, Ian, you never make me feel stupid."

He stared back at this artlessly kind woman. She loved him, treated him as if he were no different from anyone else, and for that notion of normalcy he would have done a great deal more than lend an ear to her babbling. "Only a fool would think you are stupid, Wilda, and no one calls me a fool."

"Well, except your father, but he calls you all kinds of things."

He stiffened, the old wound always ready to bleed.

She giggled. "He's trying to make himself better than you, poor thing."

Facing forward again, she rubbed the rippling-smooth stone of his ring with her finger, and he felt the familiar warmth he associated with Wilda. She *wasn't* stupid, exactly, only unschooled, and despite her upbringing, naive to the point of absurdity. Because of her astounding affection for him, he would protect her against any threat. And for that reason he asked sternly, "What were you doing at the witch's hut?"

"Well, it was a beautiful morning and I thought I would take a ride because it's almost warm, although I must tell you, Ian, my feet are solid chunks of ice inside my boots because you've got your feet in the stirrups and mine are dangling."

"Wilda," he said. "What did you want from the witch?"

"The horse they gave me in the stable was a nice horse, one of those female ones, so I am surprised she wandered off. Do you think she'll be unharmed?" Wilda was stalling; unusual behavior for her, for she usually chattered on with no ulterior motive.

But he answered patiently, "That horse was picked for you specifically because she always wanders back home." He indicated the stable, now in view. "I'm sure she's there." He had little time to finish his interrogation, and with Wilda, a little time was seldom enough. "Now—what were you going to say to the witch?"

Wilda slumped in the saddle and with one finger traced the ornate embroidery on her skirt. "I wanted something."

"From a witch."

"Well, who else could get this for me?" To Tocsin's distress, her booted foot swung back and forth. "I need a spell."

Ian soothed the animal with a pat on the neck. "For what?"

"I can't tell you that! It would ruin the magic." He hoped the witch helped his father enough to warrant the trouble she was creating. "That witch doesn't have any magic."

"That's not true!" Wilda twisted around to look at him again. "Haven't you heard about Kennie the blacksmith?"

Lifting his hand, he rubbed his eyes. "Innumerable times."

"There you are!" she said triumphantly.

"Who told you?"

Her generous mouth pouted. "No one."

"Then how did you know about the witch?"

"My maid and Mrs. Armstrong were whispering about her." She brightened. "I have silver. I can cross her palm."

"The witch's. Yes, you could, but I think that's for Gypsies, dear." At the sound of Tocsin's hooves in the gravel outside the stable, one of the stableboys stuck his head out of the door. He grinned, a smile that showed a decided gap between his two front teeth, and Ian nodded in return.

In a low tone he said, "Wilda, listen to me. It's dangerous to go wandering in the woods, and it's even more dangerous to go seeking a witch. She might not be magic, but she's a crafty old woman and could use you for harm. You must promise me you won't go seeking her again."

"But, Ian—"

"Promise me, Wilda."

As he drew Tocsin to a halt, she whimpered.

"Or I'll send you back to Fairchild Manor." It was the ultimate threat, and cruel, but as he well knew, trouble would find Wilda. Wilda didn't have to go looking for it. "Cousin."

She capitulated as he knew she would. "Fine. I promise I won't go seeking her again. But you're mean, Ian." Before the stableboy had even caught the reins and secured Tocsin, she slid off the saddle onto the mounting block. "And I don't like you anymore."

She flounced off.

The boy glanced at her, smiling. "Ach, she's as sweet a Sassenach as ever I've met."

"Yes." Ian dismounted. "Sweet."

"Ye came back!" The boy congratulated Ian. " 'Tis a good thing t' have escaped the witch's coils."

"I'd agree with you there, Shanley." Ian loosened his cravat, already crumpled from a day in the saddle. "It is Shanley, isn't it?"

Shanley kept his eye on the stallion as he spoke. "Aye, Mr. Ian."

"You're one of Armstrong's brood, aren't you?"

Shanley nodded again. "Right again, Mr. Ian." Cautiously he walked toward Tocsin's head.

"When you see your father, reassure him all my man-parts are still in working order."

"He wouldna ask!"

"I'd hate to have him wonder." Ian handed over Tocsin's reins. "The horse has had a pleasant ride. Rub him down, brush him, and I promise you he will give you no trouble." Tocsin huffed, but Ian stepped around to Tocsin's head and looked into his eyes. "Will you, my lad? Will you?"

The stallion's nostrils flared, but Ian held his gaze. Finally the animal conceded with a grudging nod, and Ian scratched his nose. "You're a beauty," he crooned.

"Aye, Mr. Ian, that he is." Young Shanley ventured to stroke Tocsin's neck. "Has anyone ever told ye ye have a way with animals?"

"A few people." The horse swung his head toward Shanley, and Ian watched as the boy scratched under Tocsin's chin. Tocsin stretched out his neck. "You have quite a way with them your-self," Ian observed.

" 'Tis in the blood," the boy answered absently.

Startled, Ian asked, "What do you mean?"

Shanley glanced at Ian almost guiltily. "Nothing. Just a saying we have in these parts, that's all."

Tocsin laughed, a great horse-snigger, and the boy stood on tiptoe and whispered toward his ear, "Dunna be telling tales on me, great one." With a click of the tongue, Shanley turned Tocsin toward his stall.

Brow knit, Ian stared after him. Many people claimed to have a way with animals, but few truly did. Odd to find the two of them in one place at the same time.

Following Wilda's course, he made his way up the ragged stone path to the manor. Ironically, the witch's garden was better kept than this place. Since his father's advent, and probably before, the manor's maintenance had been neglected. The dairy's roof sagged. The scraggly trees hung branches low enough to strike a man in the face. One of the manor windows had been broken and patched with a wooden shingle.

Yet for all that, the manor delighted Ian's eye. The compact building seemed comfortable on its high perch, accustomed to the wind off the sea and proud of its view. Two wings had been added at various times and in various styles, giving a bird-like resemblance to the manor. The gray stone tur-rets were quaint replicas of a bygone age, and the broad stairway to the entry doors invited Ian to walk in.

He did, into a capacious corridor lined with doors. One led to the study, one to the library, one to a sitting chamber, and one went down the stairs to the kitchen and laundry. Straight ahead of him lay the great hall, with two corridors that led off in circular routes to the bedchambers. In one of those bedchambers his father rested, and there Ian should go.

Should. He leaned a hand against the ornately carved table.

Should. Duty.

Since he had arrived in Scotland, those words had ruled his life. He enjoyed performing his obligations to Fionnaway, but the neglected estate consumed hours of his time and demanded more. He dreaded the hours spent caring for his father, knowing that nothing he did could ease him and that, in Leslie's eyes, he never did enough. Now he also had to consign time to overseeing Wilda, and that was time he didn't have.

"Ye're looking fagged still, Mr. Ian." Mrs. Armstrong, tall, stout, walked toward him with an armload of dirty linens. "Didna the ride refresh ye?"

"The ride, yes." He squared his shoulders. As always, he would do what he had to. The days of dissipation were long past. "The witch is on her way, although your husband's none too happy about it."

"So he told me." An undemonstrative woman, was Mrs. Armstrong, and she had been at Fionnaway all her life.

"The witch spoke to me of Lady Alanna," Ian said. "She seems convinced the young lady is still alive."

Mrs. Armstrong shifted the laundry to her hip. "If that were true, then 'twas na a ghost ye saw."

"I never doubted it. Her knee left bruises on my chest and her knife slit a hole in my throat."

"We didna know ye when ye staggered out screaming of a ghost that night. We'd take ye more seriously now."

That was as close to an apology as he was likely to hear. It was also a testimonial to his character. Mrs. Armstrong, whose judgment he valued, had declared him a man to be trusted.

Another confirmation he belonged here. "The witch said she knew Lady Alanna well."

"Did she now?" Mrs. Armstrong's voice rose as if she were surprised, and she dropped a towel.

When she bent to retrieve it, Ian placed his foot on it. "What do you say about that?"

Reluctantly she straightened and looked at him. "I dunna remember this witch ever meeting Lady Alanna. The old witch, aye, but na this witch."

"I don't understand."

"We always have a witch here in Fionnaway, always living in that hut in that clearing. There's some who say 'tis the same witch, just growing older and uglier, but that is clearly nonsense. A witch grows old, another witch appears."

She sounded so matter-of-fact Ian forced himself to remember this wasn't England. There witch-hunting had ceased and learned men laughed at superstition. These were the Highlands of Scotland, virtually untouched by civilization. Mrs. Armstrong, who seemed so sensible, obviously believed in some kind of magical transfer from one witch to the other. He couldn't scoff, not without offending her, so he politely asked, "From where does this new witch come?"

Mrs. Armstrong slapped down Ian's insolent assumption. " 'Tis na that she's really a witch. If ever any magical creatures lived here, they must have died years ago." She chuckled, inviting him to do the same.

He could not. He could only produce a strained smile.

"The new witch who appears is no more than an

old woman thrust out of a less compassionate village. The old witch teaches her the medicines so when one dies, we have another t' tend our illnesses. Now, Lady Alanna *did* spend time with the old witch. Her mother died too early, you ken, trying t' bring forth a son, so the witch taught Lady Alanna the arts of healing. The chatelaine of a great estate must know these things."

Slowly Ian leaned down and picked up the towel. "So the witch I met today is the new witch. Fascinating. You've given me something to think about." A piece of Fionnaway's puzzle. Tucking the towel into the center of the laundry, he looked Mrs. Armstrong in the eye. "You might be a little more careful what you say around Wilda. Although she doesn't have even ordinary sense, she has very acute hearing."

Mrs. Armstrong raised her brows in query.

"I found her at the witch's today."

A life as the manor's housekeeper and as the mother of seven children seemed to have inured Mrs. Armstrong to shock, but she still gave a murmur of anxiety. Patting his arm, she said, "Ach, Mr. Ian, that could have been disaster. She must have heard Agnes and me when we thought she was toasting her toes before the fire. Very well, I'll warn the others."

He lingered for one more moment. Mrs. Armstrong had been his father's attendant during Ian's absence today; she was the only servant who dared. "How is he?"

She didn't ask who *he* was. She knew. "Mr. Fairchild has been blaspheming against ye again."

"There's nothing new in that."

A howl of unearthly proportions sounded down the corridor, and the imperturbable Mrs. Armstrong shuddered.

"The witch had better hurry." Ian tugged off his coat and rolled up his sleeves. "He needs help, and I do not know how to render it."

"Dunna fash yerself, Mr. Ian. There's naught can be done for him," Mrs. Armstrong said. " 'Tis the ancient disease he suffers from, and he brought it on himself."

She sounded almost callous, and Ian asked, "What do you mean?"

"The sinner will be punished, and the lost lamb redeemed." She nodded and gathered the load of laundry tight against her belly. "Remember that, Mr. Ian, when he's shrieking his curses on you."

"Yes." Ian had no idea what she was talking about, but he had little to do with God. God had no compassion for creatures such as Ian, although he wouldn't distress Mrs. Armstrong with such sentiments. As she turned away, he said, "Oh, one more thing."

She stopped. "Aye, sir?"

"How old would Lady Alanna be if she were here?"

"How old?" Mrs. Armstrong faced him and looked him over doubtfully. "Are ye a wee bit more tired than ye want t' admit, Mr. Ian?"

"How old?" he insisted.

"Twenty . . . nay, almost twenty-one."

So his computations were correct. And—"Do you know the date of Lady Alanna's birth?"

"I suppose I do," she said indignantly. "I was her mother's attendant! 'Twas in the summer, in the month o' July. The twenty-first, I think." Mrs. Armstrong's brow crinkled as she pondered. "Aye, 'twas the twenty-first, the day before I gave birth t' my Jamie."

"Thank you, Mrs. Armstrong. You've been of great assistance."

As she walked toward the laundry, he stared at the stone of his ring. The twenty-first of July. Lady Alanna's birthday was only a fortnight away.

He had less time than he thought.

The elderly folk of Scotland smile tolerantly when the young ones ask about their enchanted heritage. 'Tis not a thing they have time for, they reply. The mere effort of scraping a living from the harsh soil or netting it from the hostile sea requires all their time.

Some of the young ones listen, and bend their backs to the work as they should.

Others see only the romance of magic. They hope to ease their lives with its assistance. They want potions. They want spells. They seek aid from charlatans and old women who call themselves sorceresses.

They are the fools, for everyone knows there are no such things as witches.

Chapter 4

Dressed as the witch, Lady Alanna eased open the door of Fionnaway Manor. Night pressed in behind her, and before her the glow of the night candle beckoned. With elaborate care she shut the door, and stood to listen to the silence.

No one was awake. No one greeted her, but as she entered her home, joy almost brought her to her knees. Only once since the day she had run away had she dared come, and then to commit murder.

She couldn't do it. She should have known better. But the news that Mr. Fairchild's son had arrived had shaken her to the core, and she'd panicked. She'd grabbed her herbs and her sharpest knife and sneaked into his bedchamber in the night.

She still groaned when she remembered the mess she'd made of that, and she'd taken care to stay well away from Fionnaway since.

But he'd come to her today. Despite her uneasiness, he hadn't reconciled Lady Alanna with the witch, and she'd been ordered here by the man who fancied himself Fionnaway's new master.

So she arrived blissfully, and stood listening to the sounds of the manor. She had missed the creaking of the shutters in the wind. The scent of sweet wood in the fireplace. The texture of stone beneath her fingertips.

Yet at the same time, she arrived reluctantly. She didn't want to treat Mr. Fairchild. Although he couldn't die soon enough to please her, still she knew herself well enough to comprehend she would help him if she could.

But more important was the realization she dared not see Ian Fairchild if she could help it.

Mr. Fairchild had lied about his son, of course. The old blackguard would tell a lie when the truth would do as well, and she should have suspected it. Ian stood tall and proud, his shoulders muscled and broad, his legs long and powerful. His short black hair and beard displayed no gray, none of the signs of age his father had described.

And Ian's eyes—she shivered and clasped her necklace of rune stones in her fist. Ian's *eyes* were as his father described. Large and darkly lashed, the kind of eyes foolish girls melted over, although why, she certainly didn't understand. They were brown. Just plain brown. Yet . . . his gaze could never be called ordinary. Piercing, impatient, amused by her as if he could see right through her disguise and down to the solitary woman beneath it.

For the first time in too long, someone had looked at her, really looked at her.

Why did it have to be a Fairchild?

And why now, when her goal was in sight?

A fresh layer of ash coated her face and sifted from her hair as she slipped along the corridor. Hung with shadows, the great hall opened up before her, but she couldn't linger. She had been too long already. Unerringly she headed for the master's bedchamber. Mr. Fairchild had appropriated it as his own immediately after his arrival, and nothing she had done had dislodged him. She had tried, of course; it was her mother's room.

But Mr. Fairchild had sneered at her in his superior way and proceeded to redecorate with velvet hangings and gaudy furniture, and he had tossed every bit of MacLeod history in the dust bin.

The servants had rescued it and brought it to her, and thus the battle had been joined.

In the shadowy corridor, the master's door was open and light spread from it. She crept toward it, wishing she could turn back.

But she didn't make the mistake of thinking Ian would let her fail in her duty. He'd made himself clear on that account, so she clutched her bag of herbs and stepped within.

Nothing moved except the wheezing figure on the raised bed. Mr. Fairchild breathed, then sighed and halted, making her hold her own breath until he gathered the strength to inhale once again.

She walked forward and stepped up on the dais, and stared. "By the stones," she whispered, "what can I do to help him?"

The fat that he had restrained with whalebone corsets had been melted away by the disease that ate at his body. In its place, an unhealthy bloating distended his belly beneath the bedclothes. His flamboyant rings had been cut from his swollen fingers. His wig was gone, no longer an adequate disguise for his bald head. He had chewed his lips until they were bloody, their fine line ragged from pain. "Poor Mr. Fairchild," she said. "All your vanities are vanquished at last."

"You took your own sweet time in getting here."

The voice from the doorway made her jump, and

she turned on her heel. "Ian." She bowed, unwilling to make excuses to her usurper.

"I expected you this afternoon." Striding toward the bed, he loomed above her.

Too proud to step back, Alanna strained away and snapped, "The herbs retain their magical qualities when gathered fresh, and gather them, I did." She reached into the bag hanging on her belt and thrust a handful in his face. "Houseleek for ulcers, and to assuage the soreness of the mouth. Cicely for the debilitated stomach. Egrimoyne for a liver tonic—and to lay under his head to induce sleep. And betony as a panacea for all ills."

"Whew!" Ian waved his hand and backed away from the odors, off the dais and toward the roaring fire laid in the massive fireplace. "Betony? Isn't betony endowed with a power against evil spirits?"

She raised her eyebrows in mocking surprise. "A knowledgeable man? I'd believed the words were mutually exclusive."

Ian didn't slap her as he should. He didn't snarl and he didn't scold. As he had earlier, he ignored her insult as if it, and she, were of no importance.

She didn't know what to make of that, but she didn't like it.

"Can you make him more comfortable?" Ian warmed his backside before the hearth. "He frightens the servants when he screams, and they'll not enter even to save their own skins."

"Who's cared for him?"

"I have, for the most part."

Magic pervaded this part of Scotland. She'd heard tales her whole life of elves and dwarves, wizards and werewolves. Fionnaway survived because of magic, yet Alanna had never seen a magical creature in her whole life.

Until Ian. *Handsome* was too weak a word to describe him. He moved like part of the night, dark, sleek, sweeping in like a black storm off the sea. His body formed a force of nature, moving gracefully yet with the power of the wind. He sought to conceal his wildness beneath his glossy, well-trimmed beard. The severe cut of his hair couldn't disguise its ebony gleam.

His eyes narrowed as he watched her watching him, and he demanded, "What's your name?"

Not Alanna, she reminded herself. Not to him. Carefully she said, "At Fionnaway we've always called our witches 'Mab.' "

"Ah." He rubbed the warmth into his rear. "Then you've not always been Mab?"

"I took the title when the old witch died."

With the pleased air of a man making a deduction, he said, "So you weren't always an old witch. You were, perhaps, a lady."

Consternation made her bump against the bed, but Mr. Fairchild didn't stir. "Why would you think that?" she asked quickly. Too quickly.

"You speak English well to be a peasant."

She challenged and distracted him with a question in return. "How old are you?"

"Four and thirty. And how long ago did the old witch die?"

"Six months. Have you always lived with your father?"

"Since I was twelve. How long have you lived here as witch?"

"Four years. Where is your mother?"

"She abandoned me. Are you lonely?"

"She abandoned . . . ?" she began. Then his second question made its impact, and she stuttered, "Lonely? Well . . . aye." Seeking to put him back on her level, she asked, "Are you?"

He laughed, a deep and pleasant laugh. His eyes

crinkled at the corners, his lips smoothed and quirked. This man, the one she thought so dangerous, fairly purred with charm. In that he was, perhaps, more dangerous than she had realized.

"What can I do to help you take care of my father?" he asked.

"I need . . ." She took a breath and tried to calm her racing heart. He wasn't seducing her. To him she was only an old hag. Any stirrings she experienced were figments of her own desolation. "I need a kettle full of boiling water and some maids to help me move him." She glanced at his doubtful face. "I'm the witch. They'll come if I tell them to."

"How long will they be needed?"

Alanna turned a long, considering look at the motionless figure of Leslie. "Like your physician, I've never seen anything like this, although . . . well. That's of no matter. I've never seen this. Tell me, how long has he been so stricken?"

"He wouldn't say, but I assure you, he sent for me only because he knows he is dying. So"—Ian thought—"at least two months."

She turned her gaze to the rotting hulk on the bed, and she tried to still the rush of hate and guilt Leslie Fairchild brought forth in her. Hate because he'd run her away from her home, forced her to grow up and become self-sufficient when she would rather have remained the immature lady of Fionnaway. And guilt because she hated a man doomed to die, and painfully, if the legends were true. "The rumors of his illness have circulated for longer than that."

"As I thought." Ian examined her, his eyes roving her shape with persistent curiosity. Then with a nod, he walked toward the door.

Her curiosity overcame her good judgment. "May I ask one more question?"

He swung back and raised a mobile brow. "You haven't needed permission before."

"Why have you answered my questions at all? Why have you not slapped me for my impudence and ordered me to mind my herbs?"

"Because you're an intelligent woman." He grinned, showing sharp teeth that gleamed through his clipped black beard. "An intelligent woman. I'd believed the words were mutually exclusive."

Chapter 5

"*Miss Witch?*"

Wilda's muffled voice brought Alanna's head around, and she stared through evening's shadows toward the closed door of the master's chamber.

"Miss Witch, are you busy?"

Alanna looked down at Leslie's slumbering features, then up at Mrs. Armstrong. Busy? Alanna had been tending him for three days, through raging fits and deathlike stupors, and she thought that qualified as busy.

But the door creaked open anyway, and Wilda popped her head in. "Isn't that a silly question? 'Are you busy?' Of course you're busy. Even I know that. But Uncle Leslie isn't yelling right now, so I thought you'd like to take a walk. Would you like to walk with me?"

Alanna stared at Wilda, and all she could think was, *How beautiful she is.* No woman had the right to have hair that glowed golden in sunlight and candlelight. It wasn't fair, when ash smothered Alanna's face and rough wool swathed her figure, that this creature should have a silken complexion and wear a gown of amaranths cotton that accented her petite, curvacious figure.

And what Alanna hated—really, really hated—

was that sensible Mrs. Armstrong beamed at Wilda with great fondness. If Alanna had to contend with a beautiful woman in her home, then at least that woman could have the grace to be rude to old ladies and contemptible to the servants.

"Walk?" Alanna asked in a not-particularly-patient tone. "The sun has set."

"Not really. Not quite." Wilda smiled engagingly and fingered the buttons of her woolen pelisse. "I thought you'd like the darkness, anyway."

Alanna was tired. Her mind moved sluggishly, so she asked, "Why?"

"Well, you're a witch. Witches like the darkness. I always thought it was because they wanted to do mean things, but you're being kind to Uncle Leslie, so that can't be the truth. I mean, anyone who is nice to Uncle Leslie must be either insane or good, and while I am a Fairchild, and as awful as the rest of them, I can still recognize goodness when I see it."

"A Fairchild?" For the first time Alanna realized what Wilda was saying. "You're a Fairchild?"

Wilda blinked, her dark lashes fluttering. "Didn't you know?"

"Nay, why should I?" Alanna asked churlishly.

"Miss Witch." Mrs. Armstrong used the sobriquet Wilda had given, but in an admonishing tone.

Alanna slanted a look at her dear old retainer. Mrs. Armstrong had been wary of her at first, watching to see what demonic behavior the witch exibited.

Until she'd seen Alanna's necklace. Her mother had placed the silver chain around Alanna's neck on the day she turned three, and on her birthday every year thereafter, she had drawn a square stone from the bag offered her. Her mother strung the stone on the chain, and Alanna wore it all that day.

Then the necklace was carefully removed and put away until the next year.

At first she hadn't understood the ritual. The square, tawny stones were carved with indecipherable scratches that meant nothing to her. But the servants had always waited breathlessly as Mr. Lewis examined her choice, and she'd come to realize they believed their prosperity depended on her. It was a silly custom, really, and in her adolescence she had been quite scornful of it.

Yet when she'd run away, she'd placed the necklace around her neck, under her clothing, and she had never taken it off. Every year she had gone to Mr. Lewis and drawn another stone from the bag. And once Mrs. Armstrong had heard her speak and noticed the clink of the stones, Alanna's secret was known to one, at least. But Mrs. Armstrong did not tell tales.

Unfortunately, Mrs. Armstrong had strong convictions about how the lady of Fionnaway should act. The lady of Fionnaway should be kind, diligent, and hospitable.

Alanna didn't want to be, but Mrs. Armstrong assumed the privileges of one who had attended Alanna's birth, and she did not hesitate to make her opinion known.

Forcing cordiality into her tone, Alanna said, "I did not realize you were a Fairchild."

Wilda's eyes widened in surprise. "We all look alike."

Alanna glanced down at Mr. Fairchild, his countenance lit by branches of candles and by the sun's fading rays. There, to her surprise, she could see a similitude to the beautiful Wilda in the ravaged features.

Relief swept her. Relief she had no right to feel. Ian was this woman's cousin, not her lover, and that easily explained his protectiveness.

But—"Ian does not resemble you."

"No, poor man, and he was teased unmercifully about it when he lived at Fairchild Manor, although I think it would be easier to be a Fairchild and look like Ian than be a Fairchild and look like the rest of us, because all of the *ton* positively recoils when they see us coming." Wilda tapped the dimple in her chin with her index finger. "Except for the men, of course."

"Of course," Alanna murmured.

"But I don't think slobbering is attractive in a gentleman, do you?"

Wilda appeared to be serious, and a great, unexpected laugh bubbled up in Alanna. She turned it into an old woman's cackle, and when she could contain herself, said, "I wouldn't know."

"Why not? You were pretty once."

Alanna jumped.

Wilda stepped closer and peered at Alanna. "Very pretty. In fact, you could look much better now. Perhaps I could help you with your appearance and you could help me with my problem."

Alanna stared at her in horror.

Stepping back from Alanna's concentrated glare, Wilda tapped the pocketbook that hung off her arm. "Maybe you'd be happier if I just crossed your palm with silver?"

"That would be better." Alanna stepped out of the candles' light and hustled toward Wilda, planning her route through the shadowy corridors. "Let us walk while you tell old witchie what she can do for you, Miss Fairchild."

They left the master's chamber and strolled along, Alanna keeping close to the wall. But Wilda said nothing.

"Miss Fairchild?" Alanna prodded her gently.

"Oh! I suppose you think I'm silly, don't you? Waiting to speak to you all this time, trying to make sure Ian wouldn't see me, and now I can't think of a thing to say. That is, because Ian was so cross when I came to see you. He made me promise I wouldn't go seeking you again."

"Did he?"

"He said you were a crafty old woman."

"He's at least a little bit right," Alanna said with a fair amount of humor.

"But I didn't really go seeking you, because you were already here, so I didn't break my promise, and oh! Miss Witch"—Wilda clasped Alanna's hand between both of her own—"I have wished for my heart's desire for so long, and I don't know who else to ask."

Wilda's clasp startled Alanna in its warmth and kindness. This girl—no, this *woman*, for she wasn't as young as she first appeared—touched the old witch without hesitation, without fear. It incongruously reminded Alanna of her mother, and the way she would stroke a cheek, or lay an arm across shoulders, and wordlessly convey affection. "You can ask me anything."

Alanna could scarcely believe the words had come from her. She'd intended to brush Wilda off with a little medley of magic-sounding words, not offer commitment.

After all, Wilda expected real witchcraft.

"Thank you!" Wilda's blue eyes glowed sapphire. "I knew Ian was wrong about you. When you came here, I was afraid he'd be hanging about every day and every night, and I'd never find you alone."

"Instead he couldn't wait to abdicate the duty he owed his father," Alanna snapped.

"Oh, no." Wilda dropped Alanna's hand. "Not Ian."

For a woman who talked all the time, she seemed satisfied to say just that.

Reluctantly Alanna admitted Wilda was right. At first Ian had checked on his witch and her progress frequently, but as she proved herself, he had taken the opportunity to render his duties for Fionnaway. She hated to see the servants come to him with questions, hated to hear him answer the cottagers' queries with wisdom, yet at the same time, she was glad when he left the manor to roam the estate on Tocsin. His presence close by her shoulder made her uncomfortably aware of her real identity, and his dark gaze made her feel he had stripped away her masquerade.

Now he was gone all the time, and she was grateful. The estate desperately needed tending, and Ian had a competent manner that inspired trust in the servants, and more important, in herself.

Alanna didn't want to think how he would react when she appeared on her twenty-first birthday and demanded the return of Fionnaway. Nor did she want to think she owed him for his management, for she knew the coffers were—had to be—empty.

She comforted herself she would make it up to him eventually. Somehow. And she didn't dwell on his anger when he discovered her deception. When he discovered all the deceptions.

One more step and Wilda and the witch would be in the great hall, with its lights and its comforts, and Alanna didn't want that. Doing an abrupt about-face, she said, "Tell Granny your heart's desire."

"You promise you won't laugh." Wilda's voice wavered.

"I won't laugh."

"I want—I forgot to cross your palm with silver!" Wilda fumbled to open the string to her pocketbook. "How much for a spell?"

Fascinated, Alanna watched Wilda's fingers shake. "That would depend on the spell."

"I think it's a big one." Wilda pulled out a coin and immediately dropped it. "Oh, dear." Falling to her knees, she crawled after the spinning coin, leaving a trail of new coins in her wake. "Well, not a really big one. Not like moving someone's eye to the middle of their forehead or sending a plague of those disgusting insects with the wiggling things on their heads, but it's bigger than turning a frog into a prince."

"I usually send them the other way." Following Wilda, Alanna stooped and picked up coins as she went. "I usually make princes into frogs."

Wilda sat back on her haunches. "Really?"

"No." Alanna handed Wilda the dropped coins, and laughed at her palpable disappointment. She decided to relieve Wilda's anxiety. "Miss Fairchild, let old Granny tell you want you want."

Clasping her hands together, Wilda said, "You *know*?"

Of course, Alanna didn't know, but the longer she looked at Wilda, the more she realized this was not an extremely young woman. She had to be approaching thirty, and she wore no ring and she lived with her cousin. Alanna thought she made a fair guess when she said, "You want a love potion."

Wilda's face fell so far Alanna felt guilty for disappointing her.

"No! Wait. Granny really needs her cyrstal to see into your heart." Alanna rubbed her forehead with her fingers. She'd been so sure she was right.

"Money," she mused, keeping an eye on Wilda.

Wilda's disappointment deepened.

Love. Money. What else could Wilda want? "A place all your own?"

Wilda shook her head, and wisps of hair bobbed around her heart-shaped face.

Lowering her hands, Alanna blinked as if she were coming out of a trance. "Miss Fairchild, your mind is complex and fascinating."

Wilda brightened.

"Old Granny is having trouble understanding your thoughts. Perhaps you should tell me what kind of spell you want."

Slipping the coins into the purse, Wilda stood and looked earnestly at Alanna. "You are so good-hearted. I want—"

A gust of wind slammed the front door against the wall. The crash echoed through the manor, and Ian's voice called, "I'll eat dinner, and then I'll go to the stables. One of the mares is foaling, and Shanley's uneasy about her progress."

The two women looked at each other, and without a word spoken they fled in opposite directions.

"Treacherous viper." Alanna nursed her rapidly purpling eye and stared at Leslie as he raged, barely conscious. "Worm of corruption."

"I dunna know where he got the strength t' land ye that blow." Mrs. Armstrong moved toward the night candle. "Let me look at it."

"Nay!" Alanna said too vehemently, and she regretted it. "Nay."

"Ye'll bruise if we dunna put a cold rag on it," Mrs. Armstrong insisted, not at all impressed by Alanna's anger.

"Witches don't bruise." Alanna dabbed at the red trickle that etched her cheek and wished it were true. Her body ached with the tiredness caused by long hours of nursing. Her soul writhed from the fragments of malevolence Mr. Fairchild unloosed, even in his delirium.

"Nor do they bleed," Mrs. Armstrong retorted. "But if ye've a mind t' be stubborn, so be it. Don't walk into any walls with that eye swollen shut."

Alanna squinted at the women she had chosen for their levelheaded good sense. Two of them had wrestled Mr. Fairchild into submission and given him the dose of betony, and stood now on either side of the bed. Mrs. Armstrong stood at the foot, forming the point of their skeptical triangle. All wore identical stances: their hands on their hips, their elbows akimbo.

"Thank you for your help. You've been more friends to me than any since old Mab died last winter. I just had it called to my attention that I've . . . been lonely." She smiled tentatively, trying to bestow gratitude where she couldn't give more. "I don't know what I'd have done without you these last two days." Stepping aside, she shooed them out. "It's the dead of night, and you need your rest. I'll care for him now."

Clucking and protesting, the women made their exit. They would go to the servants' quarters to wrap blankets around themselves and sleep until she called them again. As their friendly warmth vanished from the room, Alanna's sense of isolation returned to swamp her. With trembling fingers she wet a cloth in the ceramic bowl on the bedside table and dabbed at the bleeding cut. The rag came back smeared with scarlet and ash, and her shaking increased. Swishing the rag in the water, she wrung it out and dabbed again—and muttered, "Oh, I don't care."

Taking the bowl with her to the full-length

cheval mirror, she placed it on the floor and sat beside it. With firm strokes she wiped the coating from her face. Painstakingly she lifted the camouflage from the bruise and from her eyelids.

As the water turned black, her ministrations became less successful, and she blinked away the tears to confront her own reflection. What she saw there made her sob again. Her eye swelled and turned purple. Crying always made her eyes puffy and her nose red and misshapen. And traces of ash and charcoal lingered regardless of her care.

But who would see and who would care? Certainly not the man on the bed. Rising, she walked to the bedside. Mr. Fairchild might never wake again.

For four years she had dreamed of coming home. Now she had, only to find changes. The newer servants were sullen and uncooperative. No improvements had been made to the manor. Mr. Fairchild had tainted her home with his very presence, and she didn't know how she could ever wash it clean.

This was Fionnaway. This was hers! And she could no longer allow strangers and Englishmen to savage the lands as a hound would savage a fox.

She'd watched her mother attempt everything to please the irresponsible, sullen man she'd married. She'd watched her die in this chamber trying to bring forth a son for him, and Alanna had sworn never to allow a man such control over her life. On her twenty-first birthday she would take the position of lady of Fionnaway. She would have a husband, aye, but only after a year. Only after she had secured her status as undisputed mistress of *her* lands, *her* wealth. She would interrogate all possibilities, and chose one who would be meek and biddable. He would know his place, and during the years of her exile she had planned how she would bring Fionnaway to greatness once more.

Yet now, when Mr. Fairchild died, his son would remain. She did not make the mistake of thinking he would easily relinquish command.

All of Fionnaway depended on her. As the lady had done for countless years, she guarded Fionnaway's secrets. Now, because of Ian, she experienced the compulsion to swim out and verify the safety of the pact. She wanted to sneak into her old bedchamber and confirm that the stones still rested, warm and unharmed, in their box.

Too many secrets. Too many responsibilities. Too many dangers.

A gasp from the dais brought her head up. Conscious for the first time in three days, Mr. Fairchild gazed at her with a wild gaze. She took a step back, but recognition distorted his face and he whispered, "Alanna."

She took another step back, muttering, "Nay. Shh."

His voice grew stronger. "Alanna." And then a bellow. "Alanna! It's her—Alanna."

He struggled up on the pillows and Alanna leaped at him. "Nay! Lie still!" One knee on the bed, she grappled with the violent man, knocking his elbows out from under him as he sought to rise.

He snatched her wrists. His call echoed louder through the night, seeking an answer in the emptiness. "It's Alanna. Seize her!"

"Be quiet!" She wrenched back to loose herself— into the arms of an attendant.

He jerked her off the bed. With a shove at her shoulders, he spun her around and stared. Gawking, she saw Ian's face hovering above her. She called on whatever magical powers she possessed to help her disappear.

She did not.

Instead, he gasped and released her as if she burned his fingers.

From the bed came the winded demands, "My ward. Catch the little slut." Then louder, "Get her, you stupid bastard!"

Grabbing her arms, Ian shook her. "Witch! If you're the shape-changer they say you are, you'd better change yourself into someone who can ease this man's death—or I'll order the English courts to convict you of witchcraft, and I myself will light the first faggot beneath your feet."

Alanna ran, escaping as if all the bears of England snapped at her heels, and Ian watched her go before turning back to the bed where the sick man wrestled with his delusions.

The very stones along the coast of the Highlands sing with magic. The lone traveler can hear it lingering like the melody of a time long vanished, can smell it in the heather's spicy scent, can catch glimpses of it through the mist. Magic moves irresistibly into the inner reaches of the soul with each change of the moon, with each rise and fall of the tide.

For the selkies decree that it be so.

When left in peace, selkies live serene lives. They fish the seas, raise their young, and swim with the grace and ease of a seal. For that is what they appear to be. Humans who watch them from the shore exclaim on their manlike antics, smug in the conviction they are superior to those lesser creatures. Yet selkies have gifts humans cannot imagine. They can see feelings. They can control the storms.

And they can take a different form.

Chapter 6

Ian had sworn he would never look directly at the ocean again. When he did, memories of monstrous waves and choking fear overwhelmed him. Yet always the sound of the surf drew him, and this morning he was too weary to resist temptation.

Resting his forehead on the west-facing windowsill in the great hall, he stared out. Rocky inlets and tiny beaches dared the breakers to carve at the land. The waves accepted the challenge, striking, spraying, retreating to try again. The wind brought the salty scent to his nose, and in the air above, black-headed gulls wheeled and gannets croaked their deep-throated song. Yet the vista gave him no relief from his thoughts.

Damn it, that crone did not have powers.

After he'd given up his useless quest for respectability, he'd traveled the world, working for Sebastian Durant, viscount and merchant, and making more money than he believed possible. At no time and in no place, he was proud to say, had he ever seen a ghost. He had never met a fairy or an elf and he'd certainly not had any run-ins with witches.

So why now? Why here, where the sea sang lullabies in his mother's voice, did he see an earthbound, ugly shape-changer? He had known from the first time he saw the witch she concealed secrets. But he also knew—knew, damn it!—she was as human as . . . well, as human as everyone else he'd met around here.

Down in the waves, a movement attracted him. The sea was the light turquoise of rare sunny morning, decorated with flecks of foam and segments of . . . Ian grabbed the arm of a passing serving maid. "What's that?" He strained to see whatever frolicked on the swells.

Agnes followed Ian's pointing finger toward the creature. Then she lowered her eyes. "Well, Mr. Ian, it might be a seal."

Ian ignored the chill that swept him. "But that . . . that thing has arms. You've lived your whole life here. What *is* that?"

"A log?" she suggested hopefully, digging her toe into the nap of the woven wool carpet.

"A fair log with a head of copper-colored hair?" Ian snorted. "What is the matter with you? Can't you see—"

"My eyes are na what they used t' be, sir," she said.

Hands on his hips, Ian looked at Wilda's maid, her lips stubbornly sealed. But he could be stubborn, too. "Who would know what that is?"

"Armstrong."

"Then send Armstrong to me."

Although Ian's voice sounded neither too loud nor too harsh, Agnes skittered backward. Ian had that effect on some people. Some people detected the savagery that lurked just below the surface. Other people, like Wilda, saw only kindness.

Ian had never had the heart to disillusion his cousin.

Agnes returned in less than a minute. "Armstrong has just returned from the fishing village, Mr. Ian. He begs ye wait while he tidies himself."

Ian nodded; he'd smelled that particular mix of fish and smoky peat before, and he would gladly wait while Armstrong washed.

But to his surprise, Agnes lingered, staring outside as if the antics of that creature fascinated her. As if to herself, she said, "Do ye think there's a tempest a-brewing?"

Ian didn't think. He knew. With a little concentration, he could bring it onshore or make it linger off the coast. It was a talent he had, although he didn't admit to it. "The haze on the horizon bespeaks a rough night."

"I wonder where she hides on such an evening."

"She?" Ian queried.

Agnes glanced at him sideways, then bobbed a curtsy and hurried across the vast expanse of floor in the well-appointed great hall.

Ian coveted Fionnaway for this great hall. It had at one time been the main room of the castle, and though it had changed through the ages, still the rugged stones of its medieval past made up its walls. Huge tapestries hung in lordly splendor, and two tremendous fireplaces roared in an attempt to heat the room. Rough-hewn beams jutted boldly forth across the ceiling, blackened by fires long dead. History steeped the very walls of this chamber, and if Ian could secure Fionnaway Manor, *he* would be part of that history. He would have a name of his own—he would be a lord of Fionnaway.

Now Armstrong's stubby legs carried him across the great hall to Ian's side. "Sir? How might I assist ye?"

Ian turned from his contemplations and again searched the waves. Glimpsing that living thing that appeared and disappeared in an irregular cycle, he demanded, "There. Can you see it?"

"Oh. She's back, is she?" Armstrong chuckled, then stiffened. "Aye, I can see it. How can I serve ye, Mr. Ian?"

"What is it?"

"It could be a seal—"

Ian bent his knees and put his face close to Armstrong's. "I've already had this conversation with Agnes, and I don't expect to have the same one with my steward. You said 'she.' Now, who the hell is 'she'?"

Armstrong examined Ian doubtfully. " 'Tis a superstition, Mr. Ian."

"Like the witch?"

"Ach, nay. I've seen the witch with my own eyes. Nay, that thing in the water . . . some of the more ignorant whisper she's a"—Armstrong dropped his voice—"selkie."

Shock, denial, anger, shot through Ian, and his head throbbed in time with the waves. He had come to Scotland with trepidation, and found a refuge. Now he discovered his presentiment of tragedy would not be denied. And not for the first time, he wondered—how could he escape the thing he feared if that very thing was inside him?

Yet he remained perfectly composed, and he kept his voice level. "A selkie."

Armstrong obviously read Ian's reaction as confusion. " 'Tis only an old Scottish tale, Mr. Ian, of a magical sea creature."

For only a moment, Ian lost control. "I know what a bloody selkie is!"

Startled, Armstrong straightened and said with offended dignity, "Most o' our English visitors dunna."

"I am not most of your English visitors. I am a

damned—" Ian stopped himself. He was hovering on the verge of being stupid.

Jerking at the window lock, he swung the casement open. A fresh breeze rustled through the hall, and he stood within it, eyes closed, letting it blow away the cobwebs in his brain.

When he felt he had regained control, he turned back to Armstrong. "I'm sorry I snapped at you. It's just that . . . a ghost? A witch? And now a selkie?"

"Ye dunna have t' believe, sir," Armstrong said with dignity.

"But she's there!"

"Aye, but blame Lady Alanna."

"Of course. Everything comes back to Lady Alanna." The woman was haunting him more completely than any mere phantom.

"Lady Alanna loved the sea, just as all o' the MacLeods have from time eternal. She would swim in the waves, never fearing the currents or the cold, and when she disappeared, we feared the sea had claimed her. Some o' the old ones, the ones who watch the sea . . . they say the selkie has Lady Alanna's features."

"Her features?" Ian stared at his steward.

"Aye. They say the selkie has the same long braid down her back, that same fair skin. Silliness, I know." Armstrong pulled a long face. "But ye asked me t' tell ye."

Pulling up the lapels on his black coat, Ian leaned out past the casement and strained to see the form bobbing on the waves below. As the wind cleared his mind, he repeated, "A ghost, a witch, and a selkie." He stared at the flash of bare skin above the whitecaps, and appalled conjecture blossomed in his mind. He pulled himself back in. "Mrs.

Armstrong said Fionnaway used to have two witches."

"Mrs. Armstrong talks too much." Armstrong sighed like a man long tried. "But aye, we did. I first saw the new witch in the spring on Saint John's Day—the day young Alistair fell from the hayloft onto a pitchfork. The witches patched him up, with old Mab telling new Mab what to do. So that was nigh on to five years ago."

"What a coincidence." Ian grinned as the puzzle pieces fell fully into place. "When did you good men decide this young witch was a shape-changer?"

"Some o' the villagers were in the woods at night ... er, drinking ..."

Or poaching, Ian thought.

"And they saw a woman washing herself at the brook. They gave chase and she fled ... Well, at the brook they found the witch's clothes, and realized she'd turned into a hind. How else could one lass outrun three hearty men?"

Ian heard the note of derision in Armstrong's voice, and risked one more question. "So within the space of one year, Lady Alanna ran away, a selkie with her features frolics in the surf, and a witch who turns into a young woman comes to live in Fionnaway. Tell me, my man, did this fleeing young woman have hair the color of new copper?"

Armstrong's mouth worked. "Ye're na telling me ... Nay, it couldn't be." He marched a few steps away, rotated on his heel, and marched back. "'Tisn't possible for a young, gently bred woman t'—"

"Not even with a guardian like my father?"

Pacing away and pacing back, Armstrong argued, "Well, with a guardian like *him*!" He stopped, appalled. "Excuse me, Mr. Ian. I never meant t' offend ye."

Ian waved it away. "No offense taken."

Armstrong went back to pacing. "But the lass couldn't have kept it up with nary a soul who has exposed her."

"No doubt there is an explanation, even for this. Certainly the serving women who flew to my assistance the night he woke me screaming for *Alanna* . . . " Ian bent the force of his gaze on the agitated man. "The women calmed Leslie with no concern for the witch's bizarre appearance."

"Ye are saying my own wife knows about this infamous charade."

Ian chuckled at the man's open indignation.

Armstrong pinched Ian's sleeve between two fingers and shook it. "But Mr. Fairchild is better! Mab—or whoever she is—eased his agony!"

Ian eased himself around so his back rested against the wall, and remembered the sensation he'd experienced while gazing into the witch's eyes. No wonder he'd felt a link, a common ground of feelings and desires. They both wanted the same thing. They both wanted Fionnaway. "She'd not harm my father, or probably any other living soul."

Nodding, Armstrong agreed, "No matter how much it benefited her."

"No, there's no need for murder." Ian remembered what she said that night she'd held her knife to his throat. *Why waste murder on a man who's dying?*

Indeed, it seemed to Ian that Leslie's days were inexorably counting down to a single moment of destiny, and nothing could be done to prevent it.

A bustle at the doorway made Ian look up, and he scrutinized the gentleman who walked in. The fellow wore a single-breasted jacket of finest buck-

skin. His snowy cravat, tied in a deliberately careless knot, offset his pea-green waistcoat. The loops
on his tricot breeches hung over his black, calf-high
boots. The young fashion plate looked about with
a proprietary air, allowing his gaze to sweep past
Ian disdainfully.

That indifference did not gull Ian, and his hackles rose like a deerhound's at the sight of a bear
marauding in his garden. "Who's that?" he demanded softly of Armstrong.

"Brice MacLeod." Armstrong kept his expression
as carefully neutral as only a good servant's can be.

Brice removed his leather riding gloves, then his
beaver hat, and Ian saw for the first time the fall of
copper-colored hair.

"He is Lady Alanna's cousin," Armstrong continued, "and the current heir t' Fionnaway."

Aye, selkies can transform themselves into humans.

When the world was young, selkies and their magic fit into the landscape of wonder. In those days men gave thanks for the sun and cowered at an eclipse of the moon. They greeted the marvels of nature with awe, and blessed any selkie who shed his skin and walked among them.

Chapter 7

Ian straightened away from the wall. "There's an heir?"

"Aye, and for these past two years he's been petitioning the courts t' have Lady Alanna declared deceased."

A wave of unexpected betrayal swamped Ian. "I've been here more than a month. Why has no one thought to mention this to me?"

"Seven years she has t' be gone before she is declared dead, and we hadna given up hope for her," Armstrong said harshly.

That put Ian in his place. He had imagined he would have this estate when his father died. He had thought the servants liked him. But he had been here but a little time when compared with the Clan MacLeod; worse, he was an interloper, an Englishman. They would never give up hope for their Lady Alanna until they saw her dead body, and then they would turn to this Brice.

Ian had viewed Alanna's return as an obstacle to his inheritance. Now it was clear she constituted only the first in a series of hurdles. Hurdles he would leap, for this only strengthened his determination to have Fionnaway.

"We both know she's na likely t' be declared

dead now. But we'll na tell this MacLeod o' that particular fact. I dunna trust him, ye ken."

Another gentleman walked in, younger than the other, but crowned with the same red hair and sprinkled with a boisterous display of freckles. He wasn't nearly as fashionable, or as disdainful, but Ian swore softly.

"Mr. Brice's brother," Armstrong explained before Ian could ask. "Mr. Edwin is under his older brother's thumb, dependent on him for everything. Yet he's a bit o' a fool, too amiable t' be troubled by much."

"How lucky for me. Is this a MacLeod invasion?"

"There's no more t' come. And, Mr. Ian . . ."

Ian turned back to Armstrong.

"Remember, the man in possession holds the high ground, and ye're the man in possession."

Ian drew one thankful breath. He was wrong about one thing, at least. Armstrong might have never given up hope for Alanna, but he would not happily turn Fionnaway over to Brice. Ian had secured that much loyalty in his sojourn here.

After sharing a curt nod with the steward, Ian sauntered across the floor to greet Alanna's cousins, the interlopers. Holding out his hand to Brice, he used his best British upper-class accent. "Ian Fairchild, sir. Welcome to Fionnaway. So good to have visitors."

"Brice MacLeod." He took Ian's hand and shook it heartily. "Good to visit the old pile again! Hasn't changed a bit since my childhood romps here."

The opening shots had been fired. Ian had established himself as the man in residence. Brice had established himself as the man whose past intertwined with Fionnaway. Ian would call the battle even so far. And as he sized up Brice, he would have guessed they were evenly matched in age, height, and weight, too. But this MacLeod would lose to Ian just as assuredly as Alanna would. Ian would make sure of that.

The younger brother cleared his throat with great importance. "Edwin MacLeod, at your service." He bowed curtly.

Ian bowed back, noting Edwin's freckles positively glowed when he stood this close. It matched the glower Edwin gave Ian.

"Won't you take tea with me?" Ian invited. "Armstrong, ask Mrs. Bridie if she's made any of her delicious scones."

Armstrong played the part of dedicated retainer to perfection. "Aye, master, ye know Mrs. Bridie has scones. She's made them every day since ye said ye liked them."

A score for me, Ian thought as he and Brice settled beside the fire. Edwin chose to prowl restlessly around the small grouping of chairs and tables nearby. He stopped occasionally and tapped on the wooden panels in one of the most annoying habits Ian had ever noted. Ian guessed his age was no more than twenty-five, and he was totally without finesse, an enemy who made his sentiments clear.

Brice, on the other hand, displayed nothing but a glow of wariness.

"As soon as I heard Mr. Fairchild's son had arrived, I came at once. As the laird of the Fionnaway MacLeods, it's my duty to give you an official welcome." Brice stretched his boots out to the heat, treating Ian to a view of their high gloss and tight fit.

Ian ran his gaze critically over the rest of him, too. The fellow had been visiting London tailors recently, for every stitch he wore reeked of faultless fashion.

"Laird of the clan? Are you really?" Ian managed to inject a measure of surprise into his tone. "I thought Lady Alanna was laird."

Brice tried to smile, but the curve of his lips looked more chagrined than pleasant. "The title goes to a male descendant." The smile grew malicious. "Much to your father's dismay. I had heard he was ill. I hope it's not serious."

He's dying, but damned if I'll let him go until I have somehow secured my position here. "Not at all."

"Will we be dining with him?"

Who invited you to dinner? "He's still recovering from the physician's last visit. You know what an ordeal that is." Ian leaned forward and put his elbows on his knees. As earnestly as he knew how, he said, "I'm embarrassed to say I don't understand Scottish law. If you could explain to me. You have the title of laird of the Fionnaway MacLeods?"

Edwin stopped pacing and said fiercely, "As prestigious a title as any English lord's."

"Of course, of course." Ian nodded agreement. "Yet Lady Alanna inherited Fionnaway."

"The title must go to a man, but only a direct descendant of the original MacLeod can inherit the estate." Brice allowed himself a tight, triumphant smile. "Or at least until there is no one else to inherit. Or if that direct descendant breaks one of the rules governing the inheritance."

"Rules?" Ian didn't have to fake confusion this time. "Don't you mean laws?"

Edwin said eagerly, "No, Fionnaway is special. It's bound by a pact that states—"

"What he's trying to say," Brice interrupted smoothly, "is that Fionnaway is so old that laws aren't as important here as tradition."

Ian looked at Edwin. "Oh, is that what you were trying to say?"

A dark flush streaked along Edwin's cheekbones. "Aye. So it was."

Edwin was lying. He did it badly, then retreated toward the fireplace where he stood tapping on the mantel.

"So . . ." Ian concentrated his attention on Edwin. "If Lady Alanna had a son, he would be laird?"

Brice answered for his brother. "That branch of the family has only daughters." He allowed himself a smug little smile. "My branch of the family has never failed to produce sons."

I could get a son on Alanna. The thought surprised Ian in its clarity.

"And anyway," Brice said, "Lady Alanna is no longer with us."

"You seem to have coped with your bereavement quite well," Ian observed.

Grasping the arms of the chair in his fists, Brice leaned forward. "After Aunt Keven's death, my family visited often."

"Aunt Keven is Alanna's mother," Ian surmised.

"Aye. A lovely lady, but with little wisdom in her choice of husbands." Brice glared as if Ian were to blame, and in tones of doom said, "She married an Englishman."

"And lived to regret it," Edwin said with priggish delight.

"We all regretted it," Brice said harshly. "Alanna most of all. I know. We used to play together. Talk together. Fight together. When she disappeared, I prayed for her safe return. But it has been apparent for some time that that was a futile prayer, and someone needed to take charge of Fionnaway before—" He stopped his impetuous rush of words.

"Before your father ran it into the ground," Edwin finished scornfully.

Brice glared at his brother.

Edwin subsided. "Sorry." He shrugged and grinned repentantly at Brice.

Irritation etched Brice's face, yet he settled back into his chair with a fair assumption of ease. "Edwin lacks diplomatic skills. I hope you will forgive him."

"Of course," Ian murmured.

Swinging his booted foot, Brice said, "What an interesting ring you wear."

Ian glanced down at the middle finger of his left hand. "More interesting than you know."

"May I look at it?" Brice asked.

Ian extended his hand without hesitation, allowing Brice to grasp the ring and twist it gently.

"Beautiful." Brice betrayed envy and amazement. "Where did you get it?"

"I've always had it." It was true. Ian couldn't remember a time when it hadn't encircled his finger.

"Family heirloom, then."

"You might say that. Rub the stone." Ian remembered the witch's quick refusal, and wondered if Brice would be as well informed.

Apparently not, for he rubbed his finger across the rippling-smooth stone, and gave an exclamation of delight. "It changes color! Look, Edwin."

Edwin hustled to Brice while Ian struggled to control a sudden, dark revulsion. Foreboding welled in him, and he barely refrained from jerking his hand from Brice's grip.

Then Edwin grasped Ian's hand, and Brice rubbed the stone again. "The stone turned from blue to green. And look—it's turning again."

"How unusual." Edwin shoved Brice's hand

away and rubbed it himself. "It's turning black."

Ian struggled to read the two brothers and fought to understand the looming sensation of disaster.

"Edwin, is this like the stones Uncle Darnell showed you?" Brice asked.

His brother scowled. "He didn't show me anything."

"But you said—"

"I said no such thing."

Ian extricated his hand. Then both brothers lurched, straightened, stared, their jaws dropped open.

Wilda drifted toward them across the great hall. *Good. The men would be busy.*

The thought hovered in Ian's mind. Then he felt nothing. Nothing but the hideous supernatural scourge of his dark gift. Cold raced from the stone and ripped through his bones like a doctor's amputating knife. Cold so violent he almost fell to his knees. He fought it; eyes closed, jaw clenched, left hand wrapped around his right, ring clasped in his palm.

For just a moment, the room and Fionnaway Manor faded completely from his consciousness, and he hovered above an abyss so deep and stark that if he fell, he would shatter. His heart stopped. Death captured him, and all the angels fled from the monster he was. He was sliding down to—

"Ian, who are these handsome gentlemen?"

Wilda. Wilda spoke to him.

"Yes, sir, won't you introduce us?"

And that boy. What was his name? Edwin. Edwin MacLeod. He wanted to meet Wilda. Slowly Ian opened his eyes.

The chamber remained as it had been. The fire still gave off warmth. Light still streamed in the windows. The men stood before Wilda with those love-stricken expressions, much like deer hypnotized by a flaming brand. No one had noticed Ian's distress. He need give no explanation.

He only wished he could explain it to himself. He'd used his ring for years as a way to discover a man's true nature, and always before it had simply involved the ring changing to cool green or heated red or coy peach. Never had it turned black. Never had he experienced such emotions. He scarcely recognized them, they were so intense. He only knew they twisted his gut and brought him close to insanity.

And wasn't insanity always just a chance away for a creature such as he?

"Ian?" Wilda prompted, her gaze flitting from Edwin to Brice.

Ian performed introductions without really knowing what he said, but it must have been right, for Wilda extended her hand to each of the MacLeods, and each of the MacLeods carried it to his lips as if it were a sacred icon.

"Will you be staying?" she asked.

"Aye, aye," they stammered together.

They were violently in love with her. Ian knew that, for he'd seen it happen hundreds of times. Every man who ever laid eyes on a Fairchild woman fell in love.

Turning away, Ian squeezed his fingers to his temples. He had learned so much today. His father was dying, but Alanna was alive. Alive! And ready to return as the lady of Fionnaway. A chill swept him. She could return, and Ian would once more be what he had always been—a man without name or place.

Yet he could do something. A way existed in which to secure his position.

He looked again at the MacLeod men as they

fawned over Wilda. For this evening, at the least, Brice and Edwin would be dazed and overwhelmed by Wilda's every utterance. They would vie with each other for her attention.

And they would not notice when Ian slipped away to seduce a witch named Alanna.

*The legend tells that selkie and MacLeod first formed
their alliance during one of Fionnaway's harshest win-
ters. On land, MacLeod's people were dying of starvation
and cold, and the MacLeods could do nothing. They had
nothing to trade to their more affluent neighbors for
food or fuel. The selkies couldn't bear the sound of the
children's crying, so they brought up stones from the
deep—precious stones of mutable colors and mystical
qualities. The humans accepted them, took them to the
South where the sun shone warmer, and to their amazement they found they could feed their babes off the profit.
But being MacLeods, they insisted on repayment.*

MacLeods, selkies say, do not accept gifts readily.

*The selkies also knew that, although they were crea-
tures of the sea, they had to have the air to breathe. They
had to come on land to mate. So years upon years ago,
the MacLeod and the selkie laird came to terms. They
wrote down their agreement, and so the pact was
drafted.*

Chapter 8

The breeze turned colder as the sun slipped behind the clouds. Alanna dove one more time into the frigid waves, then swam toward shore. The currents were tricky and she had stayed in too long. She was cold and tired, but how the sight of the pact had exhilarated her!

Treading water, she scanned the tiny beach and the cliffs surrounding it. Nothing unusual stirred; only the shore plants swayed in the stiffening wind.

As she thought. No cottager had ever dared to come down to the sea at dusk when the selkie of Fionnaway gamboled in the waves. She glanced behind her into the open water of the Minch. No selkie had ever come, either, not even in her childhood when she had implored them for a glimpse. Yet she believed they were here; after all, she'd just seen the proof.

Scampering up the beach on tiptoe, she snatched her rough linen towel and dried herself briskly. She wrapped the cloth around her hair and flung on her cape. With dusk gathering, the disguise was sufficient to assure her she wouldn't be recognized by any chance-met fisherman.

It always made her nervous, this scramble up the bit of a cliff and out into the flat open greenery the sea had created. There existed no cover for a selkie who wished to conceal her limbs; the ever-blowing breeze prohibited the growth of any but the most stunted of shrubs.

And this evening, as she skipped toward the hills rising at the edge of the plain, she thought she heard the wind moan her name.

"Alanna. Alanna."

Swinging in a wide circle, she could see no one. This beach was far beyond Fionnaway Manor. The village huddled on the far side, and no one could have hailed her from there. If someone crouched beneath the edge of the cliff and called her, the wind could have carried it to her . . .

Or the creatures of the wild Atlantic Ocean, the selkies of legend, might be anxious for her companionship.

Maybe she didn't really want to see them.

Wrapping the towel tighter around her head, she ran to the path that wound up over the fell and home, ignoring the whisper that again sighed, "Alanna. Alanna."

She really couldn't hear it.

In the enveloping shadows of the trees, she paused. Nothing was there, she assured herself. Only the wind, rising with the coming storm. The setting sun illuminated the woods with an eerie glow. Its indirect rays spread above the clouds, behind the clouds, creating a world of castles in the air and silent limbo below. Hurting her eyes, the golden light bathed the branches in precise detail and traced the dust motes as they danced in the air.

"Alanna. Alanna."

Was someone behind her? She whirled, but there was no one.

Walk quickly, she advised herself, but with dignity.

A twig broke. A cloth snapped. Feet scraped on the trail.

She abandoned dignity and scurried off, almost at a run.

Don't look back, don't look back—but she did, and in that instant the boiling clouds clabbered in the air above her, plunging the world from twilight to night. Almost as if a sorcerer ordered the transformation.

Gulping in air, she calmed herself. Then she hurried. Unpierced by any moonlight or starlight, the dark strained her eyes. She knew the way to the cottage well, but tonight it all looked different. Stories of fairies who moved the paths and trapped unsuspecting mortals flitted through her mind.

Not that fairies scared her. It was the other stories that rasped at her good sense. Stories of goblins who preyed on innocent women, plucking at their clothes and poking their ribs with bony fingers. Stories of ghosts, those briefly animated corpses stained with earth and wrapped in tattered shrouds, who followed the living with envy.

Most of all, stories of great wizards haunted her. Stories of wizards who resented mortal challenge; who directed hordes of corrupt spirits and commanded the sea and the air. Sorcerers who might seek revenge on one lone woman who dared to pretend familiarity with the powers of the ancient world. Sorcerers who were weatherworkers, brewing wind and rain into a tremendous stew to pelt the presumptuous human below.

The simultaneous flash and boom of the storm pushed Alanna into flight as surely as a hand in the middle of her back. The thunder deafened her, the lightning blinded her. She could smell sulfur, charcoal, a whiff of fire and of brimstone. She could feel something watching her: eyes in the dark, observing her flight with relish. Her scramble up the path on the mountain became an undignified tumble over protruding roots and through clawing branches.

The trees were alive, holding her back, ripping her skin. She lost her towel, snagged by the fingernail of a malevolent tree nymph. The rain roared down with abrupt disdain for her footing on the grassy trail. The deluge washed salt from her hair as it washed chill into her bones.

Her cape flapped open as she scrambled up the incline, and water drenched her body. She reached the peak above her wee valley. She could see her cottage illuminated in the eruptions of lightning. She could feel those eyes boring into her back. In one last courageous stand, she whipped around and peered into the forest—and saw, rising up on the path, a bat-winged monster.

The brightest bolt of all cracked the sky. In the moment before the explosion shook the mountain, Alanna glimpsed its terrifying countenance. Its eyes were blackened sockets, its teeth gleamed. It expanded up and up until—

She broke and ran.

She dodged off the trail, with its easy slope, choosing instead the fast downhill route to her hut. She vaulted over shrubs and around trees. Her foot slipped in the sloppy mud. She skidded to the bottom, somersaulting the last few feet to the fence marking the boundaries of her garden. Leaping over the fence, she raced to her door.

For one dire moment she fumbled with the latch, unable to loosen it.

But it gave. Flinging the door aside, she dashed in and slammed it behind her. Safety.

Her eyes strained in the dark of the hut. Safety.

The last flash of the storm, the biggest flash, illuminated the room as the thunder exploded in its finale. From her own table rose a miniature version of the specter on the hill. Up and up it rose, mouth wide, fangs bared, eyes glaring.

With a petrifying yowl, it streaked across the room toward her.

Alanna screamed at last, a full-bodied shriek that released all her fears in the forest, all her fears on the hill.

The monster skidded to a stop under her cloak and meowed pitifully.

"Oh." She clung to the support of the door for one more moment, then reached down. "You idiotic cat." Her trembling hand petted his fur, erect with electrified terror. The snap of static shocked them both, and she scooped him up with a flimsy admonition. "Don't fash yourself. The storm's almost done."

Something—not her words, surely—brought abatement of the pandemonium. The lightning subsided, the thunder growled good-night. High clouds scuttled across the sky, leaving straggling wisps to foretell another squall. Moonlight, like a trickle of liquid sea opals, leaked through the cracks in the shutters to burnish the furs on the bed.

Alanna passed one hand across her forehead and felt the grains of dirt grind into her skin. Stupidly she brought her hand before her eyes and stared at it. The dark patches were only mud, and yet—

Setting the cat on his feet, she flung the shutters open, wet her hands in the runoff from the eaves, and rubbed them together. She winced at the pain and examined her palms again, cleansed now. Dark spots remained. Spots that grew as they oozed blood. Alarmed, she looked down at herself in the luminescence of moonlight.

Mud coated her from head to toe. Leaves and bits

of branch protruded from her earthy wrap, mud encased her foot like a cast. "Ah, Alanna, what have you done?" she murmured with disgust. She stripped off her cloak, tossed it in the corner, and snatched the bucket from its place by the table. Her feet carried her to the door, her hands reached for the latch—and belated caution struck. After all, she had seen that bat-winged thing on the fell . . . hadn't she?

Easing the door open, she inspected the bit of yard she could see through the crack. It was moon-bright and very still. Opening it still wider, she leaned her shoulder on the plank.

Nothing. The stars sparkled with effervescent fervor. The three-quarter moon sailed through the new-washed blackness. Water dripped into shallow puddles. The air smelled fresh and potent. Her herbs shook off the heavy beads of rain and released their savory scent.

The sylvan clearing around her home appeared normal; so distressingly normal she derided herself, *Some witch you are. Cowering from a storm.* She stepped off her threshold, armed only with the bucket, and strode to her rain barrel. She dipped out wash water—but prudently kept her back to her hut and her eyes on the encroaching woods.

Wrapped in his cloak and holding Alanna's towel, Ian stood and watched as she bathed. Audaciously bare, she splashed herself with the chilly rain water. Her body, he was pleased to see, bore no relationship to the body of the witch she professed to be. Her delicate breasts sat high and firm on her chest, nurturing the swell of pride inside his drawers. Her hips blossomed from her tiny waist, and her legs . . . Normally he'd have been thrilled with a glimpse of those ankles, and now he could view the whole long, lovely length of her legs. Stripped of her masquerade, she looked more like a nymph than a crone. She looked like her portrait, and like the ghost who'd tried to slit his throat that night not too long ago.

She loosed her long braid and dunked her mane in the bucket, all the way to her scalp. He could hear her scolding murmur up as far as the tree trunk where he leaned. Chuckling, he listened—the lady wasn't pleased with herself.

When he'd risen from the path behind her and raised his cloak wide, he'd given her a scare. Even now he couldn't suppress a grin at her panic-stricken flight. He'd owed the little witch for the tricks she'd played on him.

But he hadn't meant for her to hurt herself.

When at last she turned away from the rain barrel, her leg gave way and she landed on her knee in the grass. He started forward, but she fumbled for the edge of the rain barrel and hoisted herself up. He halted. Holding the affected foot up, she twisted it from side to side and he heard, "It's swollen!" spoken in tones of heartfelt surprise. Again she started back, cautiously this time, and he watched anxiously. Still, his concern didn't make him blind to the slender beauty of her back, or to the pride that carried her limping into her hut.

No light illuminated the room. The lingering damp extinguished any hope she had of setting flame to candle, but he strained to watch as she passed the open window. Back and forth she walked until she leaned from the casing, still gloriously nude, and pulled the shutters closed.

Ian sat down on a boulder and considered his next move.

If he were a good English gentleman, he would go away and never would she know what he had seen. But he wasn't a good English gentleman; that had been made amply clear to him many times by many people. For one thing, he was only half English. The other half was . . . well, he didn't often speak of the other half. And there was the little matter of the wedding license his parents hadn't bothered to procure.

He didn't think bastardy made him different from other men, but apparently it did. He was good enough for a woman to take to her bed—indeed, they seemed to enjoy that quite well—but not good enough for one to marry. Not his cousin Mary, who had fallen in love with Sebastian Durant so quickly Ian hadn't had a chance. Not an impoverished viscount's daughter desperate for the money he'd made working as a merchant. Not even Nell . . .

Pain squeezed his heart at that memory. Nell had been a Quaker, kind and not given to judgment. She'd adored him and returned his kisses so sweetly he'd thought he had gone to heaven. He had thought . . . he had thought she loved him. They had been betrothed, but slowly, gradually, her affection had turned to caution. Then to fear. When he couldn't stand her little shivers of revulsion any longer, he'd gotten drunk and confessed the truth about his mother.

That had been the end. Nell had sent him a tear-stained note begging his forgiveness, but she couldn't wed a creature such as he.

An owl hooted and swooped out of the trees, hunting for its supper. Hunting, talons out, an opportunist like himself.

Ian focused again on the hut below. The woman inside was the heir to an estate. Not the biggest estate in the British Isles. Not the richest estate, either. But it was a place of belonging. A place that called to him like a siren's lure.

Leslie had failed to win Alanna. His own wickedness had worked against him. Now she lived in the woods, waiting to take her lands back on her twenty-first birthday, and by some mischance should she falter, Brice MacLeod came after her in the line of succession, and after him, Edwin, and after him ... Who knew how many MacLeods waited in the wings?

Perhaps Ian was even doing her a favor. He shuddered at the memory of the cold that had swept from the MacLeods to him through the medium of the ring. If Brice knew she still lived, what might he do to secure the estate?

Yes, Ian could do only one thing—fall back on his Fairchild heritage. He would go down to the hut and visit Alanna's bed.

Alanna's hands trembled as she measured the herbs into the heated wine. Ground willow bark for her pain, chamomile to relax her, self-heal for her sprained ankle, and cinnamon to mask the flavor. The old witch, Mab, had taught her to prescribe for herself frugally, but Alanna put a generous dollop of laudanum in the wine to help her sleep. If she didn't, she knew, pain from her injuries and worry about Mr. Fairchild's handsome son would keep her awake.

She stirred the potion, then took a sip. Really, it tasted quite good. Sitting on the bench, she took another sip. Really good.

Ian's bonny countenance was not what haunted her. His *eyes* haunted her. They were so large and brown, direct and measuring. Almost mesmerizing in their intensity.

Stirring the potion again to bring the powders to the top, she took a healthy swallow and ignored the gritty sensation it left on her teeth.

She felt as if she might fall into his gaze and never come out. Storms brewed in his eyes. Insight marked his face. And magic, she feared, dwelled in his touch.

Of course, she'd never find out, for who would want to love a witch?

If only there were a way Ian could gain these lands without molesting the lady . . .

There was not.

If only there were somewhere else he could live . . .

There was not.

So he would claim Alanna and her lands in the primitive manner so many men before him had used. This was Scotland, after all, a primitive place, and Ian came back to his lifelong circumstance: alone, with no one to depend on. For the respectability of a place of his own, for the right to father children, and for Alanna's own safety, he had to have Alanna. And after all, there was a kind of pleasure in revenge, and a greater pleasure in belonging—to the land, and to the woman.

He shivered. The damp crept through the woolen cloak, up his legs from his soaked shoes, and the freshening breeze drove it into his bones. Stepping beyond the shadow of the hill, he examined the horizon. Another cluster of clouds roiled over the crest from the ocean. Soon it would storm again. With a shrug, he trod on noiseless feet down to the witch's hut. Thus were the great matters of life decided: not by logic, but by the chill of a damp cape.

The hut stood quiet. He hoped she lay abed, already quiescent in sleep. It would make his plans easier.

He laid one hand flat on the door planks and pushed. The door swished open on leather hinges, and he slipped into the room. He heard her breathing; she almost snored. The faint rasp bespoke her exhaustion, and now he meant to tire her all the more.

Stalking deeper into the room, he laid the towel across the table to dry next to the silver drinking cup and fluted bottle, incongruously elegant against their simple surroundings. Groping for the shutters, he opened them wide. Moonlight rushed in, pooling on a square of the floor, lending a faint iridescent glow to every object in the cottage.

He glanced warily at the bed, but Alanna rested on her back, one arm flung out, one arm tucked at her waist. Her copper hair lay unbound around her, coyly hiding and revealing her fair shoulders, her slender neck encircled by a chain threaded with stones. The furs rested across her belly, and he winced to see the scratches that marred her chest— winced, too, at his reaction to the pale breasts she unconsciously flaunted. The fading bruise at her eye confirmed her identity and sealed her fate. The little witch. *His* witch.

He ought to feel ashamed of himself for securing his heritage in such a manner. Instead he fought a rush of anticipation. Alanna wasn't like any other woman he'd ever known. She wasn't afraid to take destiny by the horns. She wasn't afraid of him. And he knew he could make her love him.

A firm brush against his ankles startled him, and a meow identified Alanna's pet. Catching the tom cat beneath its belly, Ian lifted it even with his face. The feline stretched his muzzle out and sniffed delicately, then pressed his nose against Ian's. Ian accepted the blessing, then placed the hefty animal on the sill. It leaped into the grass and scampered toward the village.

Unclasping the brooch that held his cape, Ian

slipped it off. Draping it next to the towel on the table, he freed the tie at his waist and pulled his shirt off over his head. Thirst drove him to the bottle, and he sniffed the contents. Wine! He raised the goblet—undoubtedly a remnant of her manor life—and with a flourish, he poured it full and dipped it toward the bed. "We share the wedding cup, my sweet," he murmured, "although you are unaware."

He drained the full-bodied, spicy wine. The dregs lay bitter on his tongue, and he shuddered as he swallowed the grainy stuff. Then, fortified, he stripped off his trousers. Bare-chested, he leaned over the bed and softly called, "Alanna."

She gave no response at all: not a flutter, not a sigh. With gentle fingers he traced the outline of her face, traced the thin dark brows and the accented cheekbones. The unmasked countenance fascinated him.

What interest had he in the pretty little virgins of the nobility? He savored the strong, the diverse, the clear-minded, and these traits he knew Alanna embodied.

Fingering the stones that hung around her neck, he squinted, trying to read the carvings that decorated them. In the sharp edge of moonlight and shadow, he saw indecipherable markings, and realized he had seen them before. They were rune stones, used by the skilled to foretell the future.

He was not so skilled, nor did he even care, right now, why she wore them. He found himself smiling amiably at the girl. "We shall deal with each other very well, once you learn your master."

He blinked. The sound of his own voice surprised him. It seemed louder, harsher, than he expected. "Strong wine?" he suggested, and grasped her shoulders. "Pretending sleep won't save you."

He shook her lightly, and her head lolled back. He peered at her. "Pretend well." Easing her back, he turned to sit heavily on the bed. The ropes beneath the frame groaned, and he floundered on the feather mattress. He wrestled his muddy boots off, and as he stood to release his hose, the floor moved.

Staring stupidly at his feet, he repeated, "Pretend well. Can't sleep that hard. Did you . . ." He raised his head and glared at the woman. "Did you take a sleeping potion to ease your pain?" His eye fell on the silver goblet. Pointing, he continued, "In that cup?"

A deep sigh answered him as she turned on her side.

Putting his hands in his hair, he rumpled it wildly. With the unsteady dignity of a drunken man, he enunciated, "Witch, you won't get the best of me, you hear? I'm claiming you"—he swayed— "now . . . I swear it . . . now . . ." He untied the hose and dropped his linen drawers, crawled into bed, and collapsed beside Alanna.

Blocked by the thickening clouds, the moon ceased to illuminate the two bodies tangled together on the narrow bed. Thunderheads towered higher and higher over the fell; then with one swoop they flung themselves across the valley. Jagged bolts of lightning transferred the heat from the earth's surface into space. The roll of celestial drums shook the tiny cottage. Wind blasted through the open window, dragging rain in its arms: rain that woke Ian from his drug-induced slumber.

"What the devil?" He rose into the driven water, and struggled to close the shutters. Shaking his head to clear it, he glanced at the dim shape still reclining on the furs. His body retained her warmth, his subconscious mind the desire to know her, and the potion released its hold on his senses. A tiny laugh cleared his throat, and he let the rain drench him. Sealing the shutters, he locked them with a clink of the crossbar, and turned back to the bed.

To his witch.

Chapter 9

Hands. Hands smoothed hair from her face. They held her close to a marvelous silken warmth as thunder rumbled and lightning flashed so brightly it blasted behind her eyelids. One hand blocked her ear as she flinched from the cacophony. Her other ear listened to the steady rhythm of a strong heart, unfrightened by nature's vibrant display.

Hands caressed her lips when she whimpered, when horror of a woodland monster resonated in her dreams. Hands directed her chin as light kisses fell on her mouth, and then they held her more firmly as some *thing*—some warm, wet thing— tested her teeth and swirled in and out like a feather maddened by the rising wind.

Those callused hands reassured her with their stroke. Hands offered succor, comfort, solace, as she shied away from the accompanying intimacies. At the same time, hands taught her to forget her memories, taught her new responses and new pleasures. They didn't plunder, they enticed. A tracing of her shoulder blades, a touch at her breast, a pressure around her waist as they measured its span. Hands sliding her necklace aside. Hands soared shy and alluring from point to point on her body until she moved to hearten them with her response.

Then the hands changed.

Hands slid up her throat into her hair, holding her thrashing head still for a kiss—a kiss that probed and questioned and answered its own query. Hands laced fingers with her own and held them while a body taught her the weight of a man, the blend of muscles and hair and velvet hardness like no other.

Breath sighed in her throat under the skill of those hands. She shivered and tried to escape, and the hands brought her back again and again, ever more willing to yield secrets at their behest.

She had been lonely, isolated from human contact for so long, and each touch fed a long-suppressed hunger. The hands sought a gem, and she wished—nay, longed—to give it to them.

Hands slid up the inside of her thigh, and at her resistance, they petted and adored her. Relenting, she allowed them all they delved for.

Hands rested on her belly; hands ruffled the curly hair at the apex of her thighs and slipped through the niche when a warm moisture blossomed. Hands urged wantonness, hands originated passion, hands invented response as they caressed deep within her and she bit back amazed cries.

Murmurs of encouragement rose from the faceless man above her, murmurs broken by the nourishing kisses he pressed on her body. He coaxed and teased and provoked until her toes tingled and her fingers clenched and the cries could no longer be contained.

Then she was one with the rising wind and the tumultuous thunder and the shocking lightning. A quick pain as she broke through the clouds, and

then she was one with the storm and one with
Ian—

Alanna sat up in bed.

Sun shone through the slats of the shutters on
the eastern wall and striped her legs with light. She
blinked, tense with incredulous emotion. Was she
alone?

Her gaze darted about the room, seeking, fearing
to find—whom?

No one was there. The room looked the same as
always. There was no reason for her heart to ham-
mer in her chest as if it sought escape. There was
no reason to perspire in the cool morning air and
certainly no reason to feel self-conscious about her
clothing—or lack of it. She was naked, the blanket
kicked away in a fantasy fervor. Her hands
clutched the furs and brought them up to her
shoulders, gathered around her like a shield against
her . . . nightmares.

Surely that was what they were. She'd dreamed
about . . . a man. A faceless man close to her, touching her, doing unspeakable things in an enchanting
manner.

She probed her mind delicately, afraid of uncovering some gibbering emotion that would defeat
her. But nay, she seemed alive in a new way, tin-
gling with curiosity. For the first time in her life,
she was almost convinced God had not been a fool
to create women with such vulnerable bodies. Pleasure still flowed through her veins, leaving her
amazed and languid and embarrassed.

A dream. By the stones, it had to be a dream. She
was just so tired of being alone. This self-imposed
exile wore on her more each day, and she wished
she could discard her disguise and again become
Lady Alanna.

Lowering the blankets, she glanced down—and gasped. Scratches trailed across her chest and limbs, welts marred her pale skin. Her fingers flew to caress a bruise on the inside of her thigh, and ready wit returned.

To the cat who slept on the rug, she said, "How could I have forgotten? The way I raced through the wood last night, I'm lucky not to have broken a bone."

Whisky didn't respond. Didn't even lift his head.

"It couldn't have been a dreamweaver. No man's touch resembles . . . silk. No man can create comfort in a kiss, and at the same time create such . . . heat." What an illusion! Of kisses pressed on her lips. On her breasts. On her belly, and lower. An illusion, indeed, that a single kiss could comfort and inflame.

Yet it seemed so real that even now her body throbbed. She pressed her thighs together tightly to rid herself of the sensation of fullness, and tried not to remember the ruggedness of his callused palms cupped around her buttocks.

His palms. Their calluses. Such a detail!

Most dreams were formless, contradictory, unassociated with physical substance. This dream she remembered for its specifics. Brown eyes lit by a fading flash of lightning. A man's voice reassuring, cajoling, murmuring of her beauty, of his pleasure. The clink of her rune stones as he fingered them, then pushed them gently to the side. The goose bumps that raised her skin when he suckled, not like a child, who took, but like a man, who gave . . . passion. His fingers, caressing her arms, her hips, sliding inside her and creating wetness. His hands separating her thighs so her body could enfold him. His hands holding her in place when she struggled with a virgin's final defiance. His hands stroking the hair away from her face when he had pushed himself deep inside her.

Alanna took a deep breath as she recalled her bewilderment. All her senses had been saturated, overwhelmed. She hurt—a little. She experienced pleasure—a lot. She had wanted to move, to cry out, to shrink into herself and become the girl she had been before.

But her dreamweaver would have none of that. She had moved, and cried out, and behaved like a woman in the thrall of desire. Like every ancestor before her, she had given everything.

Like her mother, she had embraced disaster.

In a fury, she tossed the cover aside. "Fool." She leaped from the mattress and stumbled, grabbing the bed frame as her ankle gave way. The joint throbbed and flecks of light danced before her eyes, but she steadied herself and limped to her herb shelf. Selecting the bag containing the bitter sleeping potion, she hobbled back to the window, threw open the shutters, and with a long sweep of the arm, scattered the mixture in the grass. Whirling to face the room, she spied the goblet. The dregs at the bottom went out the window, then for added measure, she threw the goblet, too. It clattered against a bench, but not even that grandiose gesture made her happy.

"No more potions," she lectured herself. "No more apparitions who make love to you. You're sore and bleeding because you tumbled down the mountain. You're dreaming because you know you're going to take Fionnaway back. Then you must choose a husband, but not one such as Ian. Find yourself a meek man, one who knows his place." Leaning heavily on the sill, she faced into the room again and lifted her chin. "One who doesn't make you dream dreams."

Her gaze wandered from bed to bench to table to chest—and back to the table. A frown puckered her brows. One trembling hand reached up to touch her hair. "I would have sworn I lost my towel..." Her voice faltered. "Lost it in the wood..."

She shut her eyes, then opened them again. It was still there.

Limping to the towel, she picked it up and ran it through her hands. It was dry. It had been hung off the end of the table sometime in the night.

She couldn't believe it. She *couldn't* believe it. "I was so frightened last night I didn't know what I did. I had it with me all along. Unless this towel sprouted legs and walked, and while it was a very odd night, I doubt..." She weighed the towel in her hand, then shook her head at her own credulity. "You've been alone too long, lass. You're going crazy. You're talking to the cat, you're talking to yourself, you've got an imaginary lover..."

The stripes of sunlight blinked out abruptly. Turning to the window, she observed a storm sweeping across the sky.

A darkening cloud. A rain-spattered ground. Lightning to burn the skies, thunder to convulse the earth. She knew what that meant, and she took heed.

Hurrying, she fixed herself in her disguise, stuffing the straw-filled hump on her back, flinging ash into her hair and coughing when she breathed the fine powder. "It isn't him. It can't be him. No man can command a tempest," she chanted as though words could keep him away.

When she heard the warning clatter of a horse's hooves, she ran to the door, opened it, and peered straight into the brown eyes of her nemesis.

Ian. He was here, dressed in a gentleman's riding

outfit of black superfine cloth. He really seemed to bring the storms—and there had been a storm last night. But she'd better not think of that now. She'd be better off if she never thought of it.

She knew how she looked, with her gray hair hanging about her cheeks. She knew that ash covered her face, and she worried about the sharp lines of charcoal she'd had no time to blend in. Unanchored lumps of cloth shifted beneath her robe when she moved, so she moved cautiously. To the casual eye, she was the witch—but she never made the mistake of believing Ian's eye was casual.

Ian swept her from head to toe with a disappointed glance. "Well, well. The witch of Fionnaway in all her regalia."

"The interloper of Fionnaway in all his splendor. What a surprise. Come in; the weatherworkers are busy again." As if to confirm her words, thunder rumbled and lightning flashed its beacon over the rapidly darkening morning. She added, "Bring your horse—he's too fine a beast to be left out."

Surveying the sky, Ian agreed. "He is too fine a beast to be left out, but I can tether him in your shed. The rain will hold off for a few more minutes."

As if to confirm *his* words, the wind died and the storm paused in its march from the sea. Disgruntled, Alanna stood in the doorway as Ian tended his horse. She'd hoped the horse would enter her home and distract them with his nerves and his demands. Any diversion would serve her until she had control of *her* nerves and the demands of her body.

Striding toward her, Ian seemed part of the elements. His unbuttoned jacket billowed open, the renewed wind ruffled his beautifully tied cravat. The muscles of his thighs bulged as he fought to maintain his balance, and his feet trod firmly through the shallow puddles. His ring gleamed with a light all its own. His short hair whipped and his teeth bared in an exultant grin as he struggled to her door. He looked, she noticed with chagrin, like a lone wolf facing a twelve-course banquet.

In a futile moment of bravado, she wanted to stand before him and refuse him entrance, but sanity prevailed. She shuffled aside, her stoop more pronounced than usual, her limp a painful reality. She turned and Ian walked right on her heels, observing her with unnerving intensity. His huge hand reached out and squeezed her unpadded shoulder—hard—and as she winced he caught the bench with his toe and dragged it toward them. That same ungentle hand thrust her onto the seat. He lifted one of his legs over and sat astraddle, leaning toward her with well-communicated aggression.

"Well." He peered under her straggling hair to stare directly into her eyes. "How do you feel this radiant morning?"

A blush dyed her face beneath the ash. The tips of her ears and her nose and the skin of her chest burned. She knew he couldn't see it, for the caliginous clouds enhanced the dark in the cottage, but that secretive smile split his face as if he were well pleased.

"Radiant morning?" she croaked, and for once she didn't fake the quaver in her voice. "Summer storms aren't radiant."

"I think they are. I was born in a storm. Storms attract me—or I attract storms." The clouds above the cottage rumbled in agreement, and he glanced up to acknowledge their statement.

"Too much rain in the summer is bad for the crops."

"It'll stop by noon," he assured her.

Discomfited by his confidence, she bent away from him, turned her eyes from him, and noticed her hands. In her hurry, she'd failed to complete her disguise. She hadn't rubbed grease and ash into the nail beds and over the skin, and they glowed with the sheen of a healthy young woman. Self-consciously she tucked her hands into her sweeping sleeves.

He continued, "I want to talk to you. I feel close to you—"

Her gaze flew back to him.

"—in a way no one else in Fionnaway can claim."

A shiver of dismay ran up her spine. What did he mean? Could this man command dreams, too?

"What do you hear from Alanna?" he asked.

"Alanna?" she choked. "They say . . . she's dead. They say the selkies—"

"The selkies stole her away, the selkies can return her," he rejoined callously. "Lady Alanna is alive, you know it, and she'll return as soon as Leslie dies. She'll claim the lands and I'll be dispossessed."

The suddenness of his attack left her stunned and uncomprehending, and she had to think carefully before she replied. "You have custody of Fionnaway; how would Lady Alanna gain possession?"

"She is the heir. If she chose to go to the courts, they would throw me out without a pence."

Anger flashed through her. "In return for an ample portion of her inheritance."

"Are the courts so corrupt in Scotland?" he asked with feigned innocence.

"Courts are corrupt always," she said bitterly. "The courts made me take—" She barely stopped in time. The courts had made her take Leslie as her guardian because her father, as foolish a man as ever lived, thought Leslie a rollicking good friend and had given him jurisdiction in his will. The courts hadn't agreed or disagreed, they'd only said her father had the right to name who he would as guardian to his minor daughter. When she had protested she had virtually run the estate since her mother's death, they had chuckled indulgently and held out their hands for the inheritance tax.

Now she said, "The courts are run by men, and men always favor men."

"Surely she has no need to worry," he said coolly. "She'll celebrate her majority on her birthday, the twenty-first of July."

"Not long now," she said faintly. How had he learned her birth date? And how had he fathomed her plan?

"On that day Fionnaway will legally be hers. But as you just said, the courts are run by men. Men do not easily believe that a woman is capable of handling so large a trust as Fionnaway."

He spoke aloud one of the fears she dared not admit.

"Just yesterday relatives of Lady Alanna's arrived at Fionnaway, drawn by the reports Leslie was dying," he said. "The eldest gave me to understand he was the heir to Fionnaway after Lady Alanna."

"Brice." She barely breathed the name. Brice, ever smiling, ever fashionable, ever willing to give his wee cousin the benefit of his advice. She didn't like him, but that was probably because, as Leslie had repeatedly pointed out, she didn't respond well to direction. Certainly most men seemed to think Brice a good fellow and a sportsman, and most women thought him bonny.

"Yes. I believe his name is Brice MacLeod. He claims to be the head of the clan."

"Not claims. He *is* the laird."

"Well." Ian spread his hands out, palm up. "There you have it. I had thought when my father died, Fionnaway would pass to me, and I was happy. I've always dreamed of having a place. Judging by the state of the stables and the fields, and the problems some of the crofters face, it needs a man's hand."

"There's nothing wrong with Fionnaway!"

"Nothing a little tending can't cure." With a tap on his chest, he nominated himself. "Yet the fate of Fionnaway pivots on Lady Alanna. If she doesn't return, Brice will have me forcibly removed. If she does return and seeks to dispossess me, I will fight her."

"How could you do that?"

"I would inquire where she has been these years. I would imply that a young woman who has survived on her own has undoubtedly earned her living in a disreputable fashion. I would say such a woman was inadequate to inherit Fionnaway, and at the very least I would push to have *myself* made her guardian."

He would, too. He was ruthless enough to ruin her reputation without a blink. She rubbed her forehead, then remembered she hadn't disguised her hand and hastily tucked it back into her sleeve. "Brice could do that, too."

"Yes, indeed he could, and it would be him and me, fighting it out in the courts over the guardianship of Fionnaway and Lady Alanna. Fionnaway would be the sacrifice, of course, for the courts move slowly, and until the matter was resolved, Fionnaway would be without leadership."

She wavered, afraid to ask the question that dangled between them until a flash of lightning lent her fire. "What other choice does Lady Alanna have? You say if she doesn't return, Fionnaway is a battlefield. Yet if she does return, you will fight her for her lands."

"No, I only said I would fight if she sought to dispossess me. There is another way." He searched her eyes again. "She can return and take her place . . . at my side."

"Marriage? To a Fairchild?" Shock rippled through her. Shock, horror, and . . . oh, nay, it couldn't be anticipation. "To *you*?"

He nodded. "It's a gruesome thought, I know, but she's already been betrothed to my father, and I flatter myself I'm the better choice."

Better? Better how? With Leslie, she had been repulsed, but she had always known she could remain in control of the servants, and of herself. With Ian, she had no such assurance. She clutched the bench until her knuckles cracked. "You flatter yourself."

"Do I? Yet I guarantee that after our wedding night, Lady Alanna would not think me conceited." His voice lowered to a husky purr.

The skin around her lips tingled, as if the kiss she'd dreamed of the previous night had been given by a man with a beard. A black beard, soft yet clipped to disciplined perfection. Oh, why had her dreams of the night before chosen this moment to haunt her? She felt uncomfortably hot, unwillingly soft, reluctantly shy.

"The people in the village, the fishermen, and even the servants have told me stories of Alanna's pride in Fionnaway, and I believe that. When she thought me unfit, she sneaked into my bedchamber with a knife and tried to cut my throat." His voice coaxed her. "What a woman! She will be my lady.

I will sing songs to her, I will clothe her in the finest apparel and—"

"Beat her if your dinner's burned," she said, to break the spell he wove.

"Not for such a paltry cause as that." His smile had returned, but changed, softened. "I would only beat her if her loyalty to me proves less than mine to her. Or if she willingly gives her body to another."

"And can *she* beat *you* if you stray?"

"My own fidelity will be unwavering." He touched her arm and looked into her eyes. "A marriage vow binds me forever."

"Pretty words," she scoffed.

"You have no reason to doubt my honor. You must not judge all men by your—by Leslie Fairchild."

"Perhaps not. Still I wonder . . . why do you tell me what you'll do for Lady Alanna?"

"Are you not the witch? Reach her with my message." He glanced around at the hut that had been her home for so many years. "You have a crystal ball hidden here somewhere."

He spoke so impudently, her hand itched to slap him. "You haven't told me whether you would be strong enough to retain her lands."

"A good question." He sounded approving. "I'm glad you asked. From the age of nine, I was raised at Fairchild Manor, and naturally I became as corrupt as the rest of that family is renowned to be. However, seven years ago I had an epiphany involving a young woman."

"A young woman?" That jolted her.

"Actually, the young woman's brother brought me to my senses. He used"—his gaze warmed with inviting laughter—"several sharp blows to the head. Since then I have traveled the world over, working as a merchant. There I found the knowledge of human nature which the Fairchilds taught me to be useful, and certainly pertinent. I don't like to brag"—he leaned forward and whispered—"but I can spot a liar anywhere."

She tried to swallow the guilt in her throat. "Really?"

"Really. And I have the capital to treat Fionnaway as it deserves." His face lost all traces of amusement. "But I'm tired, Mab. Tired of seeing ancient splendors, of meeting people who will always be strangers, of living in houses that are not homes. I've earned a fortune, yes, but money is nothing to a man without a place where he feels at home. Nowhere else in the world makes me feel as if I belong; Fionnaway is my only refuge, and I would die if I couldn't live here."

She tried to persuade herself he was being melodramatic. But he sounded passionate, and when a flash of lightning illuminated his body in stark shades of black and white, he resembled the stone carving in the hills. The image dissipated with the next flash, and she shook off her uneasiness. She was too hardheaded for superstition.

Wasn't she?

Then she considered the facts. She had been raised to handle the day-to-day responsibilities of the manor. That was nothing more than the right and duty of every well-bred maiden. It was the night-to-night demands of the man sitting in front of her that frightened her. He was strong, he was young, he was virile. He controlled his horse with the muscles of his thighs and he controlled people with the power of his mind—and she was afraid. It seemed when she gazed at him, she no longer thought of cruelty, but of two naked bodies wrestling on the bed until the female gave up her sweetness and her passion and her cry. The female surrendered everything: the male would never be satisfied with less.

Eyes blank with trepidation, she nodded at him. "I'll convey your message, should Lady Alanna call me from above."

He watched her as if he could read her every thought, and when he saw she had truly rejected him and his appeal, he said, "You'll call *her*, I promise you."

The hut seemed suddenly warm and close, and she fought for a breath of air.

"You know all the people who work in this village and in the manor," he said. "Who is worth keeping?"

She didn't understand. "Worth keeping?"

"Who in the village should be allowed to keep his fields? Who in the manor should be allowed to remain in their positions?"

"The peasants inherit their lands, and the manor folk retain their employment according to their abilities and their needs."

"Their abilities, aye," he agreed. "But their needs? Their needs are nothing. It's my needs that matter. Old Mary can't do more than sit in the corner and spin. She's in the way."

"What do you propose to do with her?" Alanna asked, incredulous and then furious.

He shrugged. "She's not my responsibility. She can go wherever she wants."

"Go . . . ?" She had trouble articulating clearly. "Go wherever she wants? She wants to stay at Fionnaway. She's lived here her whole life. If she left, she'd die."

"She's going to die soon, anyway. Why, the old crone must be sixty. And Robbie—he farms some of the prime strips in the village, but he's crippled and has no sons. The land would produce better under someone else's tending."

"He was crippled in Lady Alanna's service!"

"But not mine."

"You accept the land, you must accept the responsibility."

He spread his hands out, palm up. "But I don't know which responsibilities are important. I don't know if the servants are taking advantage of me. If I only had someone to guide me—"

Her fingers caught his wrists in a strong grip and she leaned forward, scrutinizing him through diminished light. "I'll guide you."

His wrists twisted beneath hers and he wrestled free to grasp her hands in his. "*You?* What would an old witch know about managing an estate? If only . . ."

She echoed, "If only?"

"If only Lady Alanna would return." Lightning flashed across his sharp features, and he stroked her palm with the pad of his thumb.

Confused by the warmth and comfort of his grasp, Alanna exhaled her hard-held breath and gazed at their joined hands. Holy Mother! Her hands! In a desperate hurry to cover her mistake, she said defiantly, "If Alanna should return and marry you, your life won't be worth a bottle of spoiled wine."

"You mean Brice will kill me? Let him try."

"Nay, I mean Alanna will kill you!"

His teeth gleamed with sharp, white amusement. "If Alanna should return and marry me, I can handle her."

She tried to wrest her hands away, but Ian gripped tighter. Raising her fair hands to his lips, he kissed them, one at a time, and placed them in her lap. Standing, he stretched, expanding himself to touch the rafters of the ceiling.

Shocked out of her wits—quite a usual by-product of being with Ian—she stared, mesmerized by his promise of faith and his promise of passion.

With one long stride he was at the door and opened it to a fresh-washed day.

Looking beyond his broad figure, she saw the sparkle of puddles, and sunshine so clear it almost hurt the eyes. He stepped out and captured a drop of rain in his outstretched palm. In the distance, the church bell tolled twelve times.

Laughing, he turned back to her as she hid in the shadows. "See? The storm fled as we spoke. I told you it would be over by noon."

The pact was sealed in the oldest manner of both man and beast, with a union between the two families.

Thus the strain of selkie blood was introduced to the MacLeods. As the years went on, other matings took place among the people and the selkies of Fionnaway. Thus it was seen that most of the offspring became fully human, having only a few minor gifts of magic that faded with the generations, and the selkies realized then the humans would conquer the earth.

Chapter 10

It didn't take an uncanny sense for Ian to know something was wrong. As soon as he set foot in the manor, he heard the abnormal, shuddering silence. The servants scurried rather than walked. They avoided his eyes. And the closer he got to the great hall, the more ominous the hush grew.

Death? He thought. Had his father died? He'd been alive, if barely, when Ian had checked on him that morning. Ian had forced another potion of betony down his throat and left him in Mrs. Armstrong's care. But surely if Leslie had gone to meet his Maker, Armstrong would have met Ian at the door with the news.

No, something else was wrong. Something was very, very wrong. Ian's stride lengthened as he crossed the corridor, and he burst into the sunlit chamber like a man racing to save his beloved. And stopped.

"What are you doing, marching in here like a lout? You should have learned better manners than that by now." Leslie Fairchild leaned out of his chair by the fire and spoke confidingly to his wide-eyed, thoroughly embarrassed audience of three. "His lesser breeding will always be a stain on the name of Fairchild."

"A stain of your making, Father," Ian replied as always, but he was stunned. In his peripheral vision, he noted the others. Wilda sat at Leslie's right hand, and as always, he had reduced her to a trembling child. Brice sat beside Wilda, and Ian saw him reach over and pat her knee quickly, then jerk his hand back as if he had dared more than he dreamed. Edwin sat on Leslie's left, lounging in a parody of relaxation.

And in the center of the web perched the bloated and grinning king spider. "You're . . . awake," Ian said.

"Alive, you mean." Leslie snorted. "It would take more than that little illness to kill me, much though that may disappoint you."

But he wasn't well. Blue stained his cheeks, his breath came with hesitating regularity, his knees wavered beneath his sumptuous velvet robe. The miasma of death surrounded Leslie, and Ian wondered at the effort of will he expended simply to keep himself erect.

"And glad we are to hear it, sir." Edwin stepped into the breach with a smile that appeared to be almost genuine. "Rumors were flying, and despite your son's reassurances, we feared the worse when we arrived."

Leslie sneered with the expertise of one who used sneers as weapons. "No, young man, you're not getting your hands on Fionnaway just yet."

The open vitriol wiped the courtesy from Edwin's face and replaced it with fear. Hastily he threw his brother into the fray. "It's not I who'll inherit Fionnaway. It's Brice."

"So he will." Leslie turned his attention to the shrinking Brice, then back to Edwin. "But he'll go off to London, won't he, and you'll administer the lands, so you'll both gain from my death. Don't just stand there at the door, Ian, come in!"

Ian didn't want to come in. He had just had his worst fears confirmed. His father had known, even before he had summoned Ian to his side, that Ian couldn't inherit Fionnaway. Leslie had known there was an heir after Alanna, and he had promised Ian something he could not deliver.

And why? Ah, with Leslie a simple answer always existed. He did it to be vindictive, because he was the worst of the wicked Fairchild family, and he reveled in it.

But—slowly Ian unclenched the fists that had curled at his sides—Ian had done what few men had done before him. He had circumvented his father's cruelty. He held Alanna in the palm of his hand.

"You're a minister, Mr. Lewis. Tell me what to do."

"I *am* a minister, Lady Alanna, and I canna tell ye what t' do. Look in yer heart. Ye know the right thing."

"But if I go back, Fionnaway Village will be without a witch."

Mr. Lewis shifted on his bench, his back moving to a new spot against the church's stone wall to gather the warmth from another patch of sunshine. As always, he wore his kilt, with his woolen stockings pulled up over his skinny legs, and a hat and long sleeves, buttoned down, to protect his parched skin from the sun. Nothing seemed to help. Liver spots dotted his cheeks, and his lips cracked as he spoke. "That's a point. We've never been without a witch before."

"I do help the people. I mix the herbs and deliver the children, but I don't make magic. The people

believe in the spells enough to cure themselves."
On the other end of the bench and wearing her
witch's garb, she petted her huge cat as he draped
himself across her lap. Below them, just off the edge
of the cliff, the sea rumbled and rocked in the af-
termath of the squall. Alanna watched it as Mr.
Lewis did, in wonder, fear, and pleasure. Wonder,
for it gave Fionnaway its wealth. Fear, for when the
storms came, they destroyed with uncaring fervor.
And pleasure, because she loved it. Loved it in all
its moods, loved the creatures that lived therein,
loved it because it made her who she was. A
MacLeod of Fionnaway.

In the summer the church bench remained available to the confused or the angry or the sorrowful.
There the farmers and the fisherfolk came to seek
advice from their aging minister, who had his feet
well planted in the mud of common life and his
head cleared by the exalted air of the Lord.

"It is fitting and proper t' have a MacLeod in
Fionnaway."

"Nothing bad has happened since I've been
gone." She hated sounding defensive, but she
couldn't help it. She had done what she had done
to preserve herself, but she'd been trained differently. She'd been trained to think of Fionnaway
first, and she experienced a twinge of guilt when
she thought of her precipitous flight and ignoble
imposture.

Whisky protested her tightening hold with a nip
at her fingers.

"Aye, and lucky we are about that. If Mr. Fairchild had done anything t' break the pact . . ."

Mr. Lewis's brown eyes turned a shiny gray, and
for the first time Alanna wondered about his family. He had none she knew of; where had he inherited that dry, cracked skin and odd gaze? "If Mr.

Fairchild had done anything untoward, I would have returned immediately."

"Word is, Mr. Fairchild's dying."

"I've seen him. He may be dying, but he still . . . frightens me." When he'd come off that bed calling her name, she had wondered if he was the devil, invincible in his wickedness and impossible to kill.

"Surely he canna hurt ye now."

She touched the faded bruise at her eye significantly.

"Is it that o' which ye're afraid?"

Mr. Lewis saw too much. He knew too much. Indeed, everyone in Fionnaway had heard the story of how Mr. Fairchild had crept into her bedchamber and tried to force himself on her. And although time had passed, the disgust lingered.

Of course it lingered. It had marked the moment she had grown up. Since her mother's death when she was six, she had been the lady of Fionnaway, outspoken, headstrong, overweeningly confident. She had known—known!—herself to be untouchable. She had said and done as she wished.

When her father had died, she had been a proper daughter and put on the mourning, but she did not lie to herself. She was relieved. Even when Leslie Fairchild had appeared and the courts had upheld his right to call himself her guardian, she had still believed herself inviolate. She had laughed at him, scorned him, made him a jest in her house. She hadn't realized a seventeen-year-old girl stood no chance against such experienced viciousness.

"Did he hurt ye so much?" Mr. Lewis asked.

"A few bruises. His wee bid for manhood might even have been amusing, if not for . . ." She hesitated, hating to admit her previous silliness. "He made me realize I was vulnerable."

"As all women are vulnerable."

"He is an old man, and he held me down with his hand over my mouth. He ripped at my clothes." Her hands shook as she remembered. "He *hit* me." And at that moment she had realized that, no matter how she fought, she couldn't force him off.

Pulling a long face, Mr. Lewis said, "Aye. I think sometimes we tended ye too closely in yer younger years. Someone should have warned ye men like that existed."

"I knew they existed." She rubbed Whisky beneath his chin, taking comfort from his purring complacency. "I just thought *I* could never be threatened."

"There are some who would say ye learned a lesson that could have been much more painful."

"I know. I'm wiser now, and glad for it. I can no longer imagine using my position as the lady of Fionnaway as an excuse for . . ."

"Tantrums?" he suggested when she hesitated.

She didn't answer.

"For sarcasm and mockery?"

She looked at the ground.

"For saying what ye wished, regardless o' the consequences?"

Her face burned, but she couldn't deny the truth of his accusations.

"Ye have always done what is good and right. Now ye're just a wee bit more mature, and I canna say that's a bad thing." He watched her through half-closed eyes. "Have ye met Mr. Fairchild's son?"

She jumped. Had Mr. Lewis read her mind? "Aye."

"He's come by the church several times since he's been here." The minister watched her unwaveringly. "If I were a woman, I would say he was braw."

Brave and splendid, the Scots word meant, and Alanna agreed. "But not kind."

"Kind?" Mr. Lewis whisked that away with a sweep of his hand. "Ye mean he willna let ye ride roughshod over him. At the same time, he willna hurt ye. He seems an honorable man, and I believe he will protect ye."

"Honorable?" She remembered the threats of the morning. "Honorable is not the term I would use for Ian Fairchild. He wants to marry Lady Alanna so he can own Fionnaway."

Mr. Lewis did not look shocked and dismayed, as she had hoped. Instead he nodded. "Ah. So if ye go back, ye'll wed young Ian." The priest stroked his overhung eyebrows with the blunt tip of his index finger and contemplated her with a thoughtful gaze. "Would that be so bad?"

"Would that be so . . . ?" Like a spring coiled too tight and suddenly released, Alanna flung herself to her feet. Whisky sprawled on the ground, complaining with a deep-throated yowl. "That would be dreadful. He's no better than his father."

"Isn't he?" Mr. Lewis watched her pace before him. "I quite liked him. Na at all toplofty."

She remembered the banter between her and Ian when he'd thought her a lowly witch. He *had* thought that, hadn't he?

"And I thought his perceptions superior," Mr. Lewis said.

"Maybe." *Probably.* "He thinks I can send a message to Lady Alanna."

"*Quite* superior."

When Ian spoke to her, when he looked at her, she thought he knew the truth and toyed with her like a badger with a mouse. But he didn't. Oh, please, he didn't, because if he did, she had made a rare fool of herself. "I can't believe you're taking his part," she said to Mr. Lewis.

Like a seabird on a stroll, he cocked his head back and forth. "Well, ye've got t' wed. Ye're the MacLeod woman, and the line descends through ye. Ach, do ye want Fionnaway t' pass t' that other branch o' the family?"

"Nay . . ." She dragged her toe in the dirt. "But Ian Fairchild is not the kind of man I wished to marry."

"So you're afraid o' him."

"Pshaw! Afraid of him." Afraid of the dreams he brought her, aye. Afraid of the softening she experienced when she watched him walk, like a conqueror who had his choice of women. Afraid of this wanting to be *the* woman. But not afraid of *him*.

"That's good," Mr. Lewis said, smiling cryptically. "I wager there's good in Ian Fairchild, if ye just dig deep enough."

"He threatened to turn out old Mary from her sewing and Robbie from his fields."

"I might wonder if he had an ulterior motive." Before she could sputter a response, he held up one hand. "But either way, this is na the end o' the world. Ye go back t' Fionnaway, ye look over young Ian, and if he suits ye well enough, ye wed him. If na, ye claim Fionnaway as yer own on yer birthday."

"He intimated it will not be so easy as that. He said that he would go to the courts and claim I must have lived as a fallen woman to survive these four years. He said Brice would do the same, and they would fight over the guardianship of *my* lands."

"He is determined, isn't he? He's left ye with no recourse but t' return and marry," Mr. Lewis said. "But while I might be wrong, lass, I dunna think he's like his father. He wouldna force ye."

"Won't he?"

"There's the sadness o' yer misfortune." Mr. Lewis sighed. "Ye dunna trust any man, do ye?"

"You."

"And I'm only half the man."

She looked at him, startled.

He offered an explanation. "As old as I am, I scarcely could be called on t' pleasure a woman."

"As if that is what makes a man. My father pleasured dozens of women, yet he lacked steadfastness. My cousins have proclaimed themselves quite the profligate gentlemen, yet they're weaklings both."

"Unfortunate in yer experiences," Mr. Lewis repeated. " 'Tis too bad, for ye'll na love until ye trust."

She stiffened and declared loudly, "I can exist without love."

He laughed and picked up the cat that rubbed his ankles. "No living being on earth can exist without love. 'Tis the cause o' much foolishness, this quest for love."

He sounded so reasonable, so patient, she suddenly felt melodramatic and a bit like the walker she'd seen on a high rope once—dangling in midair for no more good reason than to give the farmers something to jeer at. Yet she said steadily, "There has never been a man born of woman who could entice me to take that kind of risk."

"Now, that I believe." Tucking Whisky under his arm, Mr. Lewis stood and took her hand. "Anyway, why do ye ask me for advice? Ye're a wise lass. Do as yer heart urges and ignore the cold reservations o' yer mind. Ian is a man, and when ye shed that witchy garb and show yer radiant self dressed like a lady, he'll react as a proper man should."

She didn't bother to wonder how he had divined her plan. She only grinned. Mr. Lewis saw her through the eyes of an old affection. She doubted Ian would have been charmed by her freckles and her carrot-top if she were poor. But she did have to marry. She would go back to rescue her people from Ian's threatened injustice, and watch him carefully. If he proved worthy . . . She wiped her palms on her skirt. If he proved worthy, would she wed him? Would she take a chance on a man who had the capacity to make her weep for his love? To try anything to capture it? To reduce her to a woman of sorrows, as her mother had been?

For it wasn't only the men she didn't trust. Now that she'd seen Ian, she dared not trust herself.

"I've secured a ride for ye," the minister said. "The woodcutter and his oxen await ye."

For one last moment, she clutched Mr. Lewis's hand tightly.

"You'll take care of Whisky?"

"Ye know I will."

She broke free. She was putting her life of liberty behind her, and taking on one of obligation and restrictions. Tying the hood of her ragged cloak tightly over the bright sheen of her clean hair, she hobbled toward the timber-laden cart.

Mr. Lewis's call stopped her. "Did ye know yer cousins are visiting?"

She halted. "So I heard."

" 'Tis uneasy I am." Mr. Lewis sounded harsh and uncompromising. "They care nothing for the pact. Dunna even believe in it."

"Brice says he's a modern man in a backwater of superstition." Alanna smiled as she quoted her cousin. "Edwin is nothing but Brice's tag-tail. Don't worry. I can handle them."

"We put our faith in ye, mistress."

Mr. Lewis didn't call her by that title often, and she understood both the intensity of his concern and the depth of his dependence. "I understand better than anyone what will happen if the wrong ones take control. I will take care."

Alanna trekked to the ox cart and climbed the small, clear space at the side.

The woodcutter stared at her and grunted, "Witch." Then he clucked to the oxen.

Alanna clung as they jerked forward. Sticks poked her sides and back as they jolted along, and she wished she could have walked to the manor. But the swelling of her ankle hadn't subsided and she'd lose her nerve if she waited another day. She yearned, with all her might, to be going the opposite way, climbing the fells or seeking the moist scents of the forest. She was breaking her word to herself; she was returning before Mr. Fairchild had died, and she knew, in her heart, he would find one more way to ravage her.

She thought of how Brice would stare at her, how Edwin would whisper speculation with a shocked expression. She knew every noble in Scotland would speculate about where she had been, and with whom. But she tried not to concern herself. After all, she had enough to fret about without concentrating on what people would do and think.

Like Ian Fairchild.

Like whether Ian Fairchild would be satisfied if she offered him a position as her business manager.

And like whether it would snow in hell this week.

As time went on, the world became a colder place to mystical creatures such as selkies. The pact became more significant; its confidentiality of utmost importance. Fionnaway's people, isolated by the rugged fells and crashing sea, spoke but little with the rare stranger who wandered by. They earned a reputation as hospitable but reticent. They didn't care. They had the stones to help them through the rough times, and they kept their shoreline pristine for their selkie conspirators.

Chapter 11

Alanna slid off the tail of the cart as the woodcutter pulled into the courtyard of Fionnaway Manor. Her heart thumped hard as she contemplated her next actions; the actions that would change her from a witch to Lady Alanna in the most picturesque way possible. It had to be done. She knew it did, but once she had begun, there would be no going back. She would never be anonymous again.

"Come on, now, whatyer doing?" the woodcutter nagged. "Ye canna just stand there in the courtyard o' Mr. Fairchild's manor. He'll have ye moved along."

She glared at him. If she had needed incentive, he had given it to her. Mr. Fairchild's manor, indeed!

Spreading her arms, she called, "Good people, I call on you to see a miracle!"

The women working in the manor garden straightened. The maids in the dairy came to the door. The men replacing brick in the aging walkway stared at her. Kennie stepped out of his smithy and glared at her.

"I am well known in Fionnaway as a shapeshifter, and now I will reveal my secret!" She gestured to the children who played alongside the pond, and they cautiously crept close.

One of the bricklayers snorted and went back to work, but someone spoke from the top of the broad marble stairway that led to Fionnaway's great door.

"Stand and listen to her. You'll learn something."

Alanna looked up, right into Ian's gaze. He watched her as if he, too, longed to hear the truth about her, and pettily she hoped to shock him so much his brown eyes would turn green—turn like his ring.

But the servants were gathering, the woodcutter waited, and Kennie held a mallet menacingly in his fist.

"Sometimes shape-changing is easy." She loosened the tie that held her hood in place and pushed it back.

Everyone took a step backward at the sight of her burnished red hair. The women gathered their children close to their skirts.

Then she heard someone whisper, " 'Tis the MacLeod mop."

"Aye, it is." She blessed the whisperer with a smile. "The MacLeod mop. A head you're as familiar with as your own." Pulling a rag out of her pocket, she limped toward the well.

"Dunna let her go there!" Kennie shouted. "She's a witch. She'll curse the well as she cursed me."

"Dunna be daft, man." Mrs. Armstrong stood close to the clothesline. "Canna ye see who she truly is?"

A murmur began as Alanna dipped her cloth into the full bucket, and grew louder as she washed her face. She peered into the bucket to see her reflection, but Mrs. Armstrong spoke from beside her. "Ye've missed a spot on yer chin, m'lady."

"M'lady," one of the dairymaids said. "Grace called her *m'lady*."

"More of the miracle," Alanna proclaimed, untying the rope from around her waist and shrugging out of her cloak. She loosened her hair so it fell all around her shoulders and shook the wrinkles out of the dress. The embarrassingly old-fashioned bodice fit too tight around the bosom, but the one that suited better, Ian had torn that night when she'd tried to slit his throat. "The shape-shifter has become Lady Alanna!"

"The shape-shifter," Ian said ironically, "has always been Lady Alanna."

She turned to him on the outskirts of the circle. She hadn't surprised him. Those threats in the witch's hut had been directed especially toward getting her back to Fionnaway. Into his hands. And she had, indeed, made a rare fool of herself. "You always knew, didn't you?"

He didn't answer. Word of her return was spreading. Servants streamed out of the manor and villagers ran up the hill. Somehow everyone knew, and one of the maids shouted, "Hey, Kennie, tell us again how the witch withered yer rod."

A great wave of laughter rose in the air, and Kennie turned redder than his forge. He would have answered, blustered and threatened, but his tiny wife stood off to the side, her fists pressed on her hips, her head outstretched, glaring through narrowed eyes. "Aye, Kennie, tell us how the witch withered yer rod. Or is it a bit o' skirt ye're keeping on the side that keeps ye from performing yer marital duties?"

She started toward him. He stepped away, dropping his mallet, and ran out the gate and down the hill with his wife in pursuit.

Ian knew the news of Alanna's return would

soon penetrate inside the manor, but he hadn't the heart to cut short her triumphant return. And indeed, looking at her in the sunshine while she spoke to her people made him glad for this moment to collect his composure. What appeared beautiful in the moonlight almost blinded him in the sun.

Alanna's hair glowed like a red halo around her head, her cowlick an exclamation of independence and originality. The previously muted angles and curves and dimples of her face were radiant, and the smile she blessed her servants with roused a longing in him. That smile would soon drench him with her acceptance.

She was delectable.

She was the selkie and the witch.

She was his.

Then he saw her wince and clutch at Mrs. Armstrong's arm, and he shoved his way through the encircling crowd. "Lady Alanna, how bad is that foot?"

Only her startled green eyes and her squeak answered him as he swung her into his arms.

Into his arms. It was the first time he'd touched her since last night. Since he'd brought her from her drugged state with kisses and with tender hands. His decision to lay claim on her, and through her, her property, had been made coldly and logically. That didn't explain his bone-deep pleasure as he'd wrung whimpers from her pliant form with each caress, nor did it explain his exultation as he'd broken through her maidenhead. If a dozen men had been before him, he would have kept her, but she was his. Only his.

Now he clutched her, restrained her as she fought his hold, and reminded her with the press of his body of the night before.

When she relaxed, she looked at him through narrowed eyes. He saw the memories fighting to form. He saw her deny them, tamp them firmly down. He smiled almost benevolently. "Coward," he charged.

"I am not a coward. I'm here, aren't I?"

He started for the stairs. "So you are."

The servants broke into applause as he bounded through the door and into the entry. They approved of him, and therefore of his wooing.

Alanna realized it, too. He knew by the sullen flush of red behind her ears, the tightly drawn lips, her stiff rejection of his touch.

How did such a little thing manage to convey haughtiness? And why did she imagine he would care? He carried her into an antechamber and placed her on a bench. "Raise your skirt," he ordered.

Her mouth rounded into a perfect O.

Going to the door, he called for hot water. When he returned, she had her chin set so stubbornly it might have been granite. So he knelt before her and tossed her hem above her knee.

Her granite chin shattered, and she scrambled to cover her legs. "Ian. The servants will see!"

"The servants don't matter. This foot matters. I will not have my bride suffer."

"I haven't agreed to be your bride."

"You'd be a fool not to agree. I'm young and vigorous, have all my teeth." He opened his mouth and waved his finger inside, selling himself like a horse. "See? I sing well and I'm a charming fellow in any social situation. In fact"—with a little flip he tossed her leather slippers over his shoulder—"I can procure references. Lady Valéry, who now lives in the Scottish Lowlands when she's not setting the English *ton* on its ear, adores me. And have you ever heard of Sebastian Durant, Viscount Whitfield?"

Staring at him as if he'd run mad, she shook her head.

"Tsk. He's an important man, my business partner, and will be one of your relatives by marriage." He glanced up to see if she would challenge him this time, but she seemed overwhelmed by the sheer grandeur of his claims. Just as he had hoped. "Lord Whitfield would also write a reference. Probably not a social reference—mind you, I admire Sebastian, but a social reference from that pirate isn't worth the ink it takes to write."

"He . . . he's a pirate?" she stammered.

"According to anyone who's ever tried to cheat him, he is." Accepting the basin of steaming water from Mrs. Armstrong, he tested it with his knuckle. It had cooled sufficiently in its trip from the kitchen, and he placed it on the floor and dunked in Alanna's foot.

She recoiled from the warmth, then relaxed. "So what kind of reference will he give?"

"Financial. You'll not wed a pauper. Monetarily speaking, you'll be making a good match." Reluctantly he lowered her skirt, making sure the hem didn't brush the water. "A very good match."

Color returned to her complexion as well as that fierce vitality. "If you're such a catch socially and financially, why aren't you wed already?"

"I should have known you'd think of that." He relaxed back onto his haunches. "My father's family are Fairchilds, and I admit your in-laws will be a trial. But"—he held up his index finger—"I've met your cousins, and I can say the same."

She wondered how the events of her homecoming had escaped from her control. She'd had it planned. She would present herself as Lady Alanna, everyone would be thrilled, she would show her weasel-like cousins they weren't going to inherit anytime soon, she would look in on the dying Mr. Fairchild and express her polite commiseration on his condition and wish she could have been more help . . . she would by heavens show Ian the Interloper who was in charge.

Instead she sat in an antechamber alone with him with her foot in a basin of warm water.

And it was all his fault. Since the moment she'd first laid eyes on him, he'd done nothing but interfere with her well-considered strategies. Turning away from his handsome, watchful, know-it-all face, she tried to recover some of her dignity. "Brice is a coxcomb and Edwin is a . . . well, he's not scintillating."

"Not scintillating? You're never that polite about me."

There were answers she could give. But not in front of Mrs. Armstrong.

As if he understood, Ian ordered, "Bring us some bandaging cloth, Mrs. Armstrong." As she bobbed a curtsy and left, he said, "Speaking for the people of Fionnaway—welcome home, Lady Alanna."

He was presumptuous. He had no right to speak for the people of Fionnaway. But he didn't sound haughty. Coaxing, rather, as if he sympathized with her desire to be in charge.

He continued, "Cook is preparing a great feast in honor of your homecoming. Mrs. Armstrong has set the maids to scrubbing the floors and preparing your room."

Of course he would want her in charge. He wanted to marry her. Once that momentous occasion occurred, he would be in charge of the one who was in charge. How advantageous for him.

"This morning I went and spoke to our Mr.

Lewis. He has agreed we should make merry this evening."

She laughed shortly. All that conversation with Mr. Lewis about whether she should return, and he had already ruled on a celebration for her. "Thank you."

Bracing herself, she looked up. Ian's gaze never wavered from her face as if he judged her emotions by the expressions she couldn't contain.

"I've ordered a barrel of fine wine tapped."

Her father had been concerned she fulfill his responsibilities so he would not be forced to fulfill them himself. Mr. Fairchild had been concerned about her lands and wealth. Mr. Lewis was concerned she protect the pact. But this man, this Ian, gave the impression of being concerned about *her*.

"Perhaps we could make this a double celebration by solemnizing our wedding," he said.

Concerned about her? Nay, 'twas the familiar landlust. Feeling gullible, she reached out to box his ears.

He ducked and rebounded. "No? Later then. And here is Mrs. Armstrong with the bandaging."

Mrs. Armstrong handed it to him, curtsied, and hurried out as if she couldn't wait to leave them alone.

"May it please your lady if I bandage your ankle?"

She stared at the head bent over her foot, felt the competent warmth of his hands, and blinked back a stupid rush of tears. If she were some common man's daughter and he a lad come a-courtin', life could be so much easier . . .

He looked up, and the world dissolved in a cloud of gray. The storms of the ocean she loved originated in those eyes; wind fresh off the sea and towering clouds and waves whipped with turbulence. A deep breath gifted her lungs with the tang of seaborne air. An updraft lifted her and she soared, not free of her body but contained within it and free of the demands of earthly order. She felt the slap of the spray, heard the roar of the deep, smelled the brine, and saw, within his eyes, the sweet, passionate appreciation of a man.

His hands moved toward her slowly, giving her a chance to back away, to slap his face. She didn't. She just watched, mesmerized, as he cupped her breasts.

Her breasts. By the stones, he didn't respectfully take her hands, or brush her lips with a tender kiss. He boldly touched her *breasts*—and she let him. More than let him. Sighed as if she had wanted such a touch, imagined such a touch. Exalted in the skin left bare by the tight bodice. Closed her eyes to better savor the sensation of his thumbs, rubbing her nipples tight with the pleasure.

"Alanna." His voice sounded like a dream she'd had, almost corporeal in its sensual depth. His body pressed against her knees. His breath whispered across the expanse of her chest. His lips settled in the curve of her neck.

She shivered from his warmth, shivered from the way he tasted her, and all the while his fingers stroked her breasts. Jamming her knees together, she tried to stop the softening deep in her body, but he knew. He must have, for he crowded forward, parting her legs so that she held him between her thighs.

Flattening her open palms against his chest, she thought she should protest. She would protest.

His mouth moved up to the place behind her ear, and she felt him murmur, "Alanna." One of his hands moved to her bottom, and he crushed her closer, right to the edge of the seat. She was open to him, without defense, her full skirt riding up.

He moved his hips against her. She whimpered, a quick little sound, and she bit her lip to stifle any others.

"No." He kissed her mouth, licking the place she had bit. "Let me hear. I love to hear you, Alanna."

Her lips. Her breast. Her bottom. Her loins. He was everywhere, melting sweet and hot like honey on fresh scones. She flexed her hips, trying to get more of the seductive sensation. If she did this right, if he moved just so, she would be in flight, high above the clouds, skimming the waves, tasting and smelling freedom . . . with him.

Her hands came up and gripped his sleeves, holding on. His body gave off heat like a stove, and she was warmer than she'd ever been in her whole life. At the same time, her nipples tightened even more, anticipating . . . anticipating.

He pulled away from her so suddenly, her eyes flew open and she almost protested.

Almost, until she saw his tight, disdainful expression.

Then she fell to earth like a bird pierced by an arrow. Hot, hateful color swept her from her toes to her forehead, but Ian impersonally straightened her bodice. He pulled back, leaving the imprint of his body on hers, leaving her cold and wanting, and picked up her half-bound ankle. Acting as if these sublime moments had not happened, he bent his head once more and began wrapping her foot.

She wanted to bunch her fist and hit him, or act indifferent with as much skill as he did. But a sound at the doorway brought her head up, and she stared in disbelief at the apparition silhouetted there.

The hated, husky whisper of Mr. Fairchild struck her like a blow. "My beloved ward returns at last."

Gradually knowledge of the pact became a tale, then a legend; finally only a few of the villagers and fishermen truly believed in it, or in the existence of selkies. The MacLeod became the sole keeper of the pact, discouraging gossip and chuckling at the old stories, while all the time knowing the truth and the seriousness of the matter.

Appointed by the MacLeod, a safeguard watched over the stones and their hidden location, and when the time came, the safeguard carried the stones to the south to be sold. Then, insubstantial as a shadow, the safeguard returned to Fionnaway, taking care that no one should discover from whence the stones had come.

The MacLeod knew about the human safeguard.

No one knew of the guardian selkie.

Chapter 12

"My dear, dear ward, where have you been?" Leslie asked. "I never gave up hope during all the years you were gone seeking your pleasure. These old knees have stiffened with rheumatism as I prayed on the cold stone of the chapel for your safe return. This old heart has nearly died from lack of your nourishing affection."

What a blackguard, Ian thought. No one could better his father with the use of words. In one short speech, he'd managed to make Alanna appear guilty and soiled and deceitful, ungrateful and petty and promiscuous.

At some point her hands had clutched him. Now her fingers fell away, and she stared up and over Ian's shoulder as pale as if she had seen a ghost. "The herbs," she whispered.

Through her, Ian lived again the shock he'd felt on seeing his dying father returned to his former vindictive fervor. Had it been the herbs that had brought Leslie to his feet? Perhaps, but more likely the devil had resurrected him for one last destructive frolic.

Ian chafed her hand until she turned shock-glazed eyes on him. Then he smiled as if Leslie could be dismissed with a shrug.

She had blushed with mortification when he had pulled away from her. Now she blushed again in remembrance, and Ian could have cursed aloud. He was in an agony of wanting, but he had thought that with his father here, the condition would quickly be remedied.

Not so. Not with her cheeks flushed and her hair mussed from his fingers. He'd be lucky if he could ever stand again.

She seemed to gain strength from him, for she spoke steadily. "I've not been far, Mr. Fairchild. You could have found me if you'd looked."

Ian twisted, careful not to display his erection to his father, and looked up. The old man was held upright by two trembling servants, and his eyes were narrowed on the two of them as if he could read in their faces the events of the last glorious moments. "You've come back prepared to honor our betrothal."

Her hand jerked in Ian's. "Nay."

"No." Ian spoke even more emphatically than she, but he did so pleasantly. "She's mine, Father."

One of the men who held Leslie gasped aloud, and Alanna tried to wrench her hand from his grasp. He held Leslie's gaze, and he held on to her.

"Yours?" Leslie rapped. "By what right is she yours?"

"I take my rights, you know that."

"Take your . . ." Leslie's color fluctuated alarmingly. "You mean . . . you've *had* her?"

"Nay!" Alanna fought for her hand.

Ian wouldn't grant her even that small victory. He pressed himself against her as she sat, and said to his father, "In every way possible."

"How could you?" Leslie asked.

"I didn't." Alanna tried to claw Ian with her fingernails.

He wrapped her hands into fists and held them. "I was a thorough cad. She had no choice."

"He didn't," Alanna reiterated.

Ian believed the drugs had muddled her memory of the previous night. The drugs, and her own denial—as if denying what had happened would change the truth. But he had taken her, and he would claim her. Catching her gaze, he compelled reminiscence. *"Didn't* I?"

Her lids drooped, her lips opened; she looked for a moment like a woman recalling ecstasy.

"Damn it!"

Leslie's curse snapped her back to the present, and she glared at Ian. "I don't remember anything."

"A likely story," Leslie snapped. "You're a prosperous piece of property, but I'll have no goods used first by my son."

Alanna shoved Ian aside and surged to her feet as if temper had cured her ankle. "I am not a piece of property. I am the lady of Fionnaway, a direct descendent of the first MacLeod. I will choose the man I wish to marry, and until I've chosen, you can both hang by your toes."

From the door came a round of applause. "Brava, cousin!" Brice strolled into the chamber, Edwin on his heels. "Well said! Edwin and I are here to uphold you for as long as you need us."

Brice was smirking like a cat with a day-old fish, but his jacket was rumpled and bespoke a hurried dash to confirm the rumor of her return. He didn't demand to know where she'd been; that didn't matter as much as how her return would affect him and his fortunes.

"With succor like that—" she began hotly. Then she took a step. She kicked the basin, and warm water splashed out.

Ian watched in fascination as she took a long breath. Her flush faded and her fists loosened. She glanced at him as if remembering his admonition about Brice and his intentions—was it only this morning he had spoken to her? She rearranged her features into a polite smile. She fought for control, and Ian approved. Her temper proved her passionate caring, and it could be turned to better uses.

But Brice stepped closer and grabbed her arm so hard she bruised. "Where have you been, cousin?" he asked in a low voice. "Have you disgraced the name of MacLeod?"

"Nay!" She tried to free herself, but he hung on and glared. "I've done nothing indecorous." She raked him, and his London-style clothes, with a look of disdain. "Can you say the same, *cousin*?"

"What I do is of no concern to a woman," he said. "What the lady of Fionnaway does is of concern to us all."

"You haven't changed, Brice," she said. "You're still a pompous ass."

"Maybe so, but there's a reckoning to be had," he answered ominously.

At this confirmation of his warning, Alanna glanced at Ian, then turned her gaze away. She wrestled herself free of Brice's grip, then beckoned to the least lethal male in the chamber. "Cousin Edwin! How good to see you. Would you perhaps give me your arm? I have sprained my ankle."

Edwin beamed as he bounded forward and offered his arm. "Of course, cousin. I'd be delighted to assist you."

"I'm glad *someone* here is happy to see me." She glared at Brice, then leaned on Edwin heavily. "You always were the helpful one. Remember when we were children? When we'd fight, Brice could always beat both of us up."

She was trying to exclude him, Ian realized, placing herself in the bosom of her family and making it clear he, and Leslie, were outsiders.

Brice swaggered a little. "Aye, I was always the better fighter."

"You were always bigger than me and older than him," Alanna said tartly.

"True." Brice obviously saw no shame in either condition. "But the funny thing was, *you* could always thrash Edwin. Remember how he used to cry?"

"For God's sake, Brice!" Edwin flushed a ruddy red.

"We used to have fun, didn't we?" Alanna asked diplomatically.

"Sniveling coward, I thought," Brice said.

Patting Edwin's hand, Alanna tried to subdue her smile as she turned toward the door—and stopped.

Wilda stood framed in the doorway, her hair coifed, her dress pressed, wearing her pelisse and gloves for warmth.

Beside her, Alanna heard two simultaneous intakes of breath. She glanced at Edwin. His mouth hung open like a half-dead cod. She glanced at Brice. For the first time since she'd known him, she saw him with a man's possessiveness adjoined to a mature determination.

Then the vision opened her mouth. "I wondered where the gentlemen had gone. I mean, it's rather disconcerting to find oneself alone with the servants so suddenly when I have so much trouble understanding a word they say, although they try very hard to help me. So kind, they are, but my mother says my mind is less than brilliant and I suppose that's true, although why she keeps telling me, I don't understand, unless it's that she thinks I didn't understand the first time, which is silly, because I might not be too intelligent, but my hearing is very good." She smiled at Alanna. "How's your hearing?"

Buffeted, as always, by the flow of language, Alanna said only, "Excellent."

"Oh, good. I think that's so important for all your body to function, although, of course, I would never be unkind to those less fortunate than me. I mean, if I were a dog, I wouldn't want people kicking me just because I didn't speak English. Or maybe they do. I mean, I've never heard one speak it, but that's not to say they don't when they're private."

Ian chuckled with every evidence of delight, and Alanna glared as he smiled on his cousin.

In all her life, no one had ever called Alanna beautiful. Before meeting Wilda, Alanna had thought herself a practical woman, untouched by excessive vanity. She did not care if others saw her charm. But when Wilda was eighty, she would still have men fawning over her, and even now, Ian smiled at her, and Alanna suddenly, violently, wished to be beautiful.

But only a beast could be jealous of such a sweet woman. In desperation Alanna held out her hand. "I'm Alanna MacLeod, mistress of Fionnaway."

Wilda curtsied, then grasped Alanna's fingers with every evidence of pleasure and not an ounce of recognition. "Delighted to meet you. I'm Wilda Fairchild. I'm not a mistress or anything, but I'm a lady because my father is an earl, although you don't need to call me lady because it's so formal and I just know we'll be friends."

"Wilda." Leslie used his most annoyed tone. "Stop talking!"

Wilda blanched and dropped Alanna's hand. "Yes, Uncle."

Leslie's voice rose. "You are the most annoying—"

"To say Wilda is annoying when she talks is like saying the ocean roars during a storm." Ian strolled over, took Wilda's flapping hand, and bowed over it. "It is an injustice to the music of nature."

Alanna tried to decide if Wilda had been insulted or rescued, but Wilda clearly had not caught any subtle nuance. She clung to Ian and smiled, showing perfect white teeth and a perfectly placed dimple. "You are so sweet to me. You're always so sweet to me." To Alanna she said, "He's so nice. Isn't he nice?"

Ian grinned at Alanna as she struggled to answer. What he'd done to her in this very chamber hadn't been nice; it had been magnificent, and she could scarcely look him in the eye at the memory.

"Of course you think he's nice," Wilda said comfortably. "All women think he's nice."

Brice apparently decided the vision had ignored him long enough, for he hurried to Wilda's side. "I'm nice, too!"

"And I!" Edwin dropped Alanna's hand and shoved Ian aside so he could gaze soulfully at Wilda.

That left Alanna teetering on one foot and at the mercy of the still-grinning Ian, who abandoned his cousin quite readily to come to her side.

"Perhaps, my lady, you would allow me to escort you to the grand hall?" He presented his hand.

She looked at it. She hopped a little as her balance shifted.

"Just taking my hand won't compromise you," he said persuasively.

"No, you've already done that." With his words.

But more, he'd caressed her breasts right here in this chamber. He'd handled her as if he had the right, as if he'd done it before, as if he were confident she would enjoy it. By the stones, was she as easy as her cousin feared?

"I compromised you to save you from my father."

"You compromised me so you would have a claim on Fionnaway."

"I am the lesser of two evils, surely." Ian wasn't smiling anymore.

He hadn't denied her charge. He wanted her lands, and unfortunately, she understood. Who wouldn't want Fionnaway? Just walking through the door of Fionnaway Manor soothed an ache in her soul.

Glancing at Leslie, she saw that he scrutinized them. Slowly she laid her palm in Ian's.

"She doesn't act like a woman who's been pleasured," Leslie snapped.

Ian's reply was uncompromising. "She's mine."

Alanna tried to jerk her hand back, but he held it firmly between both of his. He warmed it, then carried it to his mouth. The touch of his lips against her fingers, the way he watched her from beneath dark brows, reminded her of a dream, and to her embarrassment a blush worked its way up to the top of her forehead.

Ian observed, and his smile returned. "Mine," he said for her ears only.

Leslie watched as Alanna limped out, leaning heavily on Ian. He watched as Wilda smiled at Edwin, as her smile widened when she looked at Brice. He saw Edwin's expression as he realized that, once again, his older brother was winning all, and Leslie called, "Edwin!"

The lad was too polite to ignore him. "Sir?"

"These servants are so clumsy." Leslie swatted them away. "Would you be so kind as to help me to my bed? I suspect I've overextended myself this day."

"Of course, sir," Edwin answered, but he couldn't take his gaze off Wilda as she laid her dainty hand on Brice's arm. Her eyes lowered modestly, then at a word from Brice, she glanced up and gurgled with laughter. Together they left the study, and Edwin's expression would have done justice to an assassin—or a Fairchild.

"Your brother and Wilda make the couple, Edwin, eh?" Leslie smiled and tottered artistically.

Edwin leaped forward, arm extended.

Leslie took it and leaned heavily. "Do you have a home of your own?"

Edwin stiffened against Leslie's side. "No, sir, why?"

"Obviously you won't be able to live with them when they're wed." Leslie turned his head and smiled at Edwin, but Edwin's shock was such he could not smile back. Leslie's smile widened. "We need to talk, you and I. We have much in common."

Alanna sat in her bedchamber, the account books in her lap, her foot propped up on a padded ottoman.

Armstrong stood before her, twisting his cap and waiting as her finger traveled down the line of debits and credits for the past three years.

"I don't know why it should surprise me that more money has gone out than has come in." She picked up a particularly galling dun from a tailor in London. "This bill is almost two years old."

" 'Tis from Mr. Fairchild's last visit t' England." Armstrong looked as dour as she felt. "He hasn't been well enough t' go since, and it's grateful we should be, m'lady."

"How does a man dare come to a thriving estate like Fionnaway and use up its resources in such a flurry it can scarcely recover?" Picking up the wad of bills, she shook it, wishing it were Mr. Fairchild's throat. "He's spent thousands of pounds on every conceivable luxury and not put one cent back into the lands." She plucked one particularly offensive charge from the stack. "Four hundred pounds on shoes in the last year when he can scarcely walk?"

"I know, m'lady, but what could I do? I canna restrain a man such as that."

Her rage had made Armstrong feel at fault, and she never meant that to happen. "Of course not. He would have discharged you, or worse. No, Armstrong, I knew before I left that with you in charge, you'd do your best for Fionnaway."

"I have tried. But begging yer pardon, there are things which need t' be done. The horse barn lost a good portion o' the roof in that last big storm o' winter. It needs replacing before winter returns or we're going t' lose some prime horseflesh."

She remembered Ian's comment that the stables needed work. It seemed he had been right—and she hated that. He'd said more, too, so she asked, "I heard there was trouble with some of the crofters."

Armstrong looked surprised. "Ye've been paying attention, haven't ye, m'lady?"

"As much as possible," she mumbled, embarrassed to be using Ian's information but not enough to acknowledge the source.

"Aye, that same storm did damage t' a lot o' our farmers who live far out in the hills where there's damned little cover. They're scarcely scratching out a living, much less able t' rethatch their roofs. And do ye remember the terracing I discussed with ye before ye left?"

Alanna did; Armstrong hoped to try terracing on some of the hills to see if they could increase Fionnaway's arable lands. "Money existed for it once. But don't tell me—it's gone for shoes now."

Her gaze dropped once more to the books, and nothing could change the grim truth. She'd told herself it didn't matter that she had left. She'd told herself that Fionnaway was just as well off as if she'd been in charge. But she'd lied, created a falsehood to lighten her guilt. If she'd stayed, she would have had to marry Mr. Fairchild, true, but Fionnaway and her people would not have been neglected.

"Fionnaway needs an infusion of capital," she muttered. "How much do we need?"

"Four stones worth," he answered, then added bluntly, "Na little gems, either."

Standing, she limped to the fireplace and counted the bricks. Twelve down. Four over. Using the poker, she pried a rough brick out of its place among the others.

Armstrong watched, as he always did; he was the MacLeod safeguard, one of a long line of serving men or women who knew the secret.

Taking the hot pad, she reached in and brought out the box. Carved of plain gray stone, it was as old as the pact, a remnant of the days when beasties walked the earth and man kept only a precarious toehold among the forests. Carrying the box to the table, she set it down.

Armstrong moved to shield her and the box from the view of any who would dare enter without knocking. "I've kept the fire burning here night and day. They should be warm enough."

Wetting her finger, Alanna lightly touched the

box. "It's cooling." While they waited, she said in a monotone, "You know what to do. Take the stones to Edinburgh. If he swears to keep quiet, sell them to the jeweler you sold them to before. Otherwise, find another man. And watch for treachery on your way back. They've tried to follow you before."

"That's why I'm the safeguard, m'lady. No one follows me if I dunna wish him t'." He started to say something, then hesitated.

"Go on," she encouraged him.

"Grace and I have the seven children, m'lady, and I'm getting on in age."

She looked at him, surprised. Armstrong? Getting on in age? But he had always been her support: strong, firm, knowing his duties and helping her with hers.

"I'm na on my deathbed yet, so ye have no need t' look at me like that." He nodded at her. "But 'tis time t' train a successor. Just as I am the safeguard who will pass on the traditions o' the pact should something happen t' the MacLeod, so there must be someone who can take my place."

She saw the gray hairs, the wrinkles around his eyes, and realized he spoke the truth. He was in his prime now; in ten years he would not be, and the pact was too important to allow sentiment to disable it. "Have you picked one of your children t' take your place?"

"Ellie. She's only eight, but she's honest and can be trusted t' keep her word." His chest puffed with pride. "And, m'lady, there's ne'er been a child who could shadow a man like she can. She's the despair o' her mother, but she's perfect for ye."

"Take her along to Edinburgh, then." She opened the box with breathless attention. "When you come back, and if Ellie desires, we'll have Mr. Lewis teach her the first of her vows." Peering inside, she saw the fiery glitter within, and as always, she gave a sigh of relief. The stones were there, they were warm, they were bonny, and they would save Fionnaway as they had done so many times before.

Gripped by the same tension that always bound her, she picked out four large, variably shaped stones. "This leaves only two," she said.

"Save them. We'll have them in case o' emergency."

The stones' smooth yet rippled surfaces glimmered as she brought them into the light, and even in the brief moment she held them, they began to change. The delicate sea-green lightened to blue, then gleamed as the fire inside danced. Carefully she placed three in the rough wool bag lined with satin which Armstrong held open. But the last she cradled in her palm, and she asked the question she had sworn she would not. "Do you know anything about the ring Mr. Ian wears?"

"No, m'lady. It's one o' ours, for sure, but I dunna recognize it."

Each stone was distinctive, so Ian's gem must have originated in some early generation. "He said it was his mother's."

"Did he now?"

Armstrong offered no more enlightenment, so she handed the bag to him, and he tucked it next to his skin.

Bowing, he backed toward the door. "I well remember my own vows. I'll na let anyone discover the origin o' the stones."

Then his head lifted like a wolf's sensing danger. Swiveling on his heel, he stalked toward the door on silent feet. He ripped it open, leaped into the corridor, and ran.

She limped to the door, but before she got there, he returned.

She could barely breathe for tension. "What was it?"

"Someone was listening. I didna catch him, but he was there, I assure ye."

Swallowing in dismay, she asked, "How much did he hear?"

"Nothing. The door's too thick for eavesdroppers, but it doesn't matter, does it?" Armstrong's face was grim. "If someone was listening, then someone knows there's a secret t' be learned. Ye be careful, m'lady, while I'm gone. Ye watch yerself, for there's treachery afoot."

Chapter 13

Ian was annoyed.

"Where do you suppose they are?" Alanna glanced at the empty doorway as the outside light faded.

"We should start eating," Ian said again. The dining table ran the length of the chamber. Polished silver gleamed and the tablecloth sparkled white. Everything was prepared for a special supper to welcome Alanna home, yet Alanna waited because Leslie and her cousins weren't courteous enough to arrive on time.

The women were in the alcove by the fire while he stood by the liquor cabinet on the other side and poured glasses of ratafia for both of the ladies. He delivered one to Wilda as she sat in a chair beside the blazing hearth.

"Put it on the end table, dearest." Pulling an embroidery thread free of a tangle, she threaded it onto a needle. "I'll get it in a minute. And you know Lady Fionnaway is right. We can't start supper until we find out if Uncle Leslie is well. He was on his deathbed only yesterday."

Alanna appeared to be at ease, but as Ian handed the other glass to her, he noted she stood by a chair opposite Wilda rather than sitting in it.

"Thank you," she murmured, not meeting his eyes.

She was very good at not meeting his eyes. But that made it easier for him, in a way, to appreciate her. She had changed, with Wilda's help, into a grass-green Grecian robe. The skirt gathered beneath her breasts, and Wilda had draped it in one of those damnable ways she knew. Not that he didn't usually appreciate Wilda's efforts. He enjoyed nothing better than to look upon an attractive woman whose assets were attractively displayed.

But this was Alanna, and he didn't look upon her. He stared.

A thin white wrap fastened around her throat, tucked into her neckline, and discreetly covered her bosom. But the wrap was almost transparent. He could almost see cleavage.

"Perhaps he overexerted himself today and he is even now breathing his last," Wilda chirped cheerfully.

Ian jumped. "Who?"

"Uncle Leslie."

Returning to the cupboard, Ian poured himself a goblet of wine and reflected he couldn't be so lucky. He couldn't allow his father to dismantle his efforts. Not with Alanna, who stood before the fire in that diaphanous grass-green crepey skirt that showed everything.

Well, not everything. Not nearly enough. In fact, he was sure she wore at least one petticoat beneath, and probably two. But the draft around the fire molded the fabric to her legs, and sometimes he saw the gentle rounding of her bottom.

He had kissed that rounding the night before. He had fondled it today. He wanted to caress her again tonight. Now, in fact, and the wanting made his trousers fit much too tightly.

Transferring his gaze to Wilda, he said, "I would venture you're more anxious about the boy cousins than about my father."

Not at all disturbed by his strained disposition, Wilda smiled, and her dimple peeked out of her cream-and-roses cheek. "They are charming." Then her tentative smile faded. "But I am, of course, more concerned with Uncle Leslie. I mean, he's not very nice or anything, but he is my uncle, and my mother always says, 'Blood is thicker than water,' although it seems to me that is self-evident. I mean, when Daisy broke that glass, throwing it against the wall in an absolutely magnificent rage when Cousin Mary wed Lord Whitfield, one of the shards pierced my neck and the blood stained my shoulder scarf and we couldn't get it out. That doesn't happen when water drips on my clothing, although it does spot silk terribly. Don't you agree, Lady Fionnaway?"

Alanna glanced at Ian, and he could have sworn he detected sympathy in her eyes. " 'Lady Fionnaway' is so formal. Please call me Alanna."

Clasping her hands, Wilda said, "Oh, thank you! You're so kind, and although my mother says informality leads to a breakdown in civilized behavior, I will call you Alanna because we're going to be related, aren't we? You're going to love Ian with all your heart."

Ian saw a breakdown in civilized behavior right before his eyes. Alanna's clear complexion flushed, and she clasped the back of the chair until her knuckles turned white. "Did you tell her that?"

He couldn't help it; her agitation pleased him. But he said sedately, "Wilda makes her own deductions."

"There has never been a man born of woman

who could entice me to take that kind of risk," Alanna said to Wilda.

Wilda smiled, and for once, was quiet.

A line of servants brought candelabra lit with beeswax candles in from the kitchen. One was placed on the table between Wilda and Alanna. One was set on the liquor cabinet. Two lit the table, already set with six places. Alanna, Wilda, and Ian waited. As the seconds ticked by on the mantel clock, Wilda's observations grew ever less logical, and even Alanna tapped her fingers on the chair's wood carving.

Then down the corridor, Ian heard masculine laughter and murmurs of conversation. Three men appeared in the doorway. Edwin and Brice stood on either side of a beaming Leslie, their arms hooked through his to provide support.

"Time to eat, heh?" Leslie sounded almost jovial. "Get me in there, lads, I've developed an appetite."

The gentlemen turned sideways and drew him through the opening while Ian stared, thunderstruck. He'd seen his father this happy only a few times in his life, and each time had preceded a disaster of tremendous proportions.

Leslie steered a course for the high-backed chair at the head of the table, then snapped, "Don't just stand there with your mouth hanging open, Ian— pull out my chair!"

It was the footman's chore, but Ian knew better than to complain. He did not need his father reminding him of his lowly antecedents once again, and in front of so many people. In front of Alanna.

In silence he pulled out the chair and held it as Leslie settled in.

Then Leslie challenged Alanna. "You are the mistress here, but you don't mind giving up your place to your old, sick guardian."

Embarrassment scorched Ian from the inside out. He hadn't experienced such mortification since his adolescence at Fairchild Manor, when every one of his mistakes—and there had been many—had been a signal for the ridicule to start. This time he had only himself to blame; man that he was, he hadn't even considered Alanna's right to sit at the head of the table.

Her cool voice stopped his self-recriminations. "That is the only chair with arms, Mr. Fairchild, and I understand you couldn't sit erect without them."

Leslie cast her a look of virulence.

She stared back, expressionless, then asked, "Would you hold my chair also, Ian?"

Stepping to her side, Ian lifted her hand to his lips and kissed it. "I live to serve you." As he looked into her eyes, her fingers trembled in his, and in a tone meant for her ears only, he added, "And to service you."

She jerked her hand back, and he let her.

"Where did you get that ring?" Leslie's voice rose querulously. "Her ring. What are you doing with her ring?"

He was staring right at Ian, directly at his hand.

"This ring?" Ian held up his hand and touched the glimmering stone. "It's mine."

"It's hers." Leslie grunted and lunged at Ian.

Ian easily moved out of reach. "Hers? Alanna's? It's mine. I've always worn it. Remember?"

"Alanna's? No, you fool, not—" Leslie glanced at Alanna, then at the other curious faces turned to him. "Nothing." He waved his hand, so puffy the knuckles sank like dimples into the skin. "Sit down, all of you."

Sanity, and memory, seemed to have returned. Ian escorted Alanna to the other end and held her chair. Four places had been set on either side of the table, spaced evenly along its length. Room existed between them, but he took the place at her right hand.

Edwin rushed to hold Wilda's chair opposite Ian. She murmured her thanks and sat, and Brice slipped into the seat beside her.

Edwin said, "Wait. Wait! That's not fair."

"Stop sniveling," Brice said coolly.

"You can sit with me next time." Wilda smiled at Edwin. "You always entertain me so."

Edwin smiled back, his lips pressed into a thin line. Then he walked around the table to the last remaining chair.

"I never saw that salt cellar before," Leslie observed sourly. "The servants must have been hiding it. Thieves, all of them."

Ian knew what Leslie meant. In their joy at having Alanna back, the servants had done what he believed they did not know how to do. They had set an elegant table. "Not thieves," he said, "but fakers."

The butler stared impassively until Alanna said, "You may begin."

Merton summoned his minions with a snap of his fingers, and the first course of two soups and the accompanying dishes was brought forth and presented for her approval.

Wilda valiantly introduced polite conversation, and Brice and Edwin listened and contributed. But no effort of the servants or the guests could ease the strain Leslie's presence occasioned. Ian ate his way through a course of venison and pickled eel, green peas and fried sole, then a course of partridge and quails, apricot fritters, custard, and jugged hare. All the while he stoically waited for catastrophe to strike.

Yet when the cheese and bread was carried in to finish the meal, Ian glanced at his father, gray with the effort of pretending health. Perhaps there would be no scene tonight.

The butler presented the steaming loaf to Alanna with a flourish. "Will ye carve, m'lady?"

And turning, Merton presented the round cheese to Ian. "And ye, Mr. Ian, will ye do the honors, also?"

It was a sign of support from the serving staff that he had been asked. Ian understood that. What he didn't understand was how the man had worked with Leslie and still did not comprehend that Leslie would make him pay—make them all pay.

Taking the small, sharp knife in his hand, Ian stood and slashed through the waxy rind, keeping his gaze fixed on his work. The even yellow slices fell to the board one by one, each rich with its sour scent.

Then the yeasty aroma of bread told him Alanna had broken the crust, and irresistibly his gaze was drawn to her hands as she efficiently sliced the bread. Her hands were broad-palmed, her fingers long—good sense and artistry combined. He didn't want to, but he looked higher and saw again those breasts . . . Oh, God, she was chilly. He would warm her. Everywhere. As he had done last night.

He stared into her face. She glanced into his.

Once again the sea breeze swept them up. He could taste the salt, smell the freshness of air untainted by woodsmoke and age. She was his, and when they touched they could dive deep beneath the waves, ride the swells, and bask in the storm's fury. Together they could do anything.

A rattling noise broke the communion and brought Ian's head around.

At the head of the table, Leslie sat, inhaling as if each breath would be his last.

Alanna murmured, "He sounds as if his lungs are full of water."

A chill crawled up Ian's spine. It was true. Leslie even had the appearance of a drowning victim, with his bloated features and the shiny cast to his skin. Ian could almost see him lying in the sand, strands of seaweed draping his shoulders and tangling his fingers . . . and abruptly he found himself gasping for air with the same intensity as his father.

"Ian?" Alanna laid a hand over his. "Are you ill, too?"

Shaking the vision away, Ian tried to smile. It wouldn't do to alarm her. He couldn't afford to lose another bride before the wedding.

Leslie coughed, then inhaled again, and the rattling this time sounded louder. His eyes stayed shut, his hand rested on his chest, and Ian shoved his chair back.

At the scrape of wood against wood, Leslie's eyes sprang open. He coughed into his napkin, then dropped it on the floor beside him. "Pass the bread," he said hoarsely. "I'm hungry still."

Ian sank back into his seat, and in silence the bread and cheese boards were passed.

"My dear Alanna." Leslie's voice sounded less labored. "I would wager you haven't told my son of *our* night of passion."

A stifling silence fell over the table.

Alanna stared down at her almost empty plate with such attention, she might have been looking into the crystal ball.

Wilda shuddered visibly. Brice leaned over and patted her hand.

Determined to protect Alanna, Ian stepped into the breach. "On the contrary, Father, she did tell me. That very event convinced her I was the better suitor."

Leslie flicked his fingers at Ian like a horse dislodging a fly. "What does a lad like you know about such things?"

"From what I heard . . . a great deal more than you."

One of the footmen had a coughing fit and made to leave the room, then leapt back in and pressed against the wall, his eyes wide with alarm.

From down the corridor Ian heard a clatter of metal and a clicking against the hardwood floor. Every head turned, staring, as around the corner came the largest dog Ian had ever seen. The creature paused and surveyed the occupants of the room with the confidence of an animal who knew himself the superior of all within.

His gaze locked with Leslie's, and with an incongruously puppylike yip, he hastened to his master.

Alanna stiffened in obvious alarm. Wilda squeaked. Brice scooted his chair away, and Edwin bumped the table with his knees as he raised his feet.

The dog leaned against Leslie, and Leslie rubbed his giant head.

"What is he doing in here?" Alanna demanded of the butler.

Merton bowed, keeping one eye on the two devils at the head of the table. "No one dares stop him from going where he likes."

Raising her voice, Alanna said, "Mr. Fairchild, that's a vicious animal. Does he still eat cats for pleasure?"

"That's right." Leslie smiled cordially. "He did eat one of your little pets once."

Ian saw her flare of distress as she crushed the remnants of her bread in her palm.

"Aye, he still eats cats, and anything else foolish enough to get in his way. He weighs more than many men. These Scottish peasants keep their brats well away from my Damon"—the dog whined at the mention of his name—"and the servants obey me with speed when he sits at my side."

Ian watched as the footmen shuffled slowly away from the table, and knew his father told the truth.

"He should be on a chain," Alanna said.

"He was," Leslie snapped. "I ordered him released as soon as that witch worked her magic."

"Witch?" Alanna stared Leslie right in the eye.

"Aye, I was dying, for all you care, but the witch . . ." His words faded as he searched Alanna's face. "The witch looked like . . ."

"Aye?" She still watched him closely.

"I dreamed . . ." His color faded as his voice failed him. In a whisper that pierced the unnatural silence of the great hall, he said, "I dreamed you were here one night, but you looked like. . . ." His hand trembled before his face as he scrambled his fingers in incoherent description of her appearance. Then with a jerk, he slumped.

Ian and Alanna both came to their feet and on opposite sides of the table, hurried toward him.

But when Damon growled, Leslie lifted his head. "Leave me be," he said.

Ian stopped short.

Alanna did not. She leaned over him and touched his cheek. "You're clammy."

"I'm well!" A blob of perspiration swallowed his eyebrow. He raised his wrist to wipe it away, but dropped his arm back down to his chair as if it were too heavy.

The dog growled again.

Alanna stepped back, and back again when Leslie looked at her.

Hell simmered in those red-rimmed orbs. "Where have you been, Alanna of Fionnaway?" Leslie asked. "Tell us where you've kept yourself these years."

"Aye, Alanna, tell us," Edwin said softly. "You've changed, and we'd all like to know why."

Proudly she lifted her chin. "I never left Fionnaway."

"You heard about the scene by the well this morning." Ian wanted to laugh at Edwin's incredulity, at Brice's confusion. "She was masquerading as the witch, but the truth was always there for those who came for more than to count Fionnaway's assets."

Brice rose and shoved his chair back. "You dare to speak to me of this. You, a Fairchild, spreading your vulture wings over half the earth!"

Leaning his knuckles on the table, Ian said, "My vulturous money can save Fionnaway. What can you do but wring it dry?"

Wilda whimpered, and Alanna took pity on her and said, "Gentlemen, this is not fitting dinner conversation."

Ian and Brice would probably have paid her no heed, but Damon growled and Leslie chortled. The combination of those two wicked voices brought silence to the chamber.

"Mr. Fairchild, we should get you to bed." Alanna's voice carried the authority of the lady of Fionnaway, and of the healer she had been for so many years. "You're overexerting yourself."

"Not nearly enough." Leslie's heavy-lidded gaze examined Alanna, then went to Ian. "Have you told her yet?"

Ian's heart began a slow, hard thumping. "Told her what?" There were so many things he didn't want her to know. So many dark secrets his father would relish exposing.

"The truth. Have you told your bride the truth about you?"

"What truth?" Brice asked. "Shouldn't we all hear this truth?"

Ian looked across the table at Alanna and wished he stood next to her. Then he could clap his hands over her ears, pick her up and run off with her, remove her from this presence which would poison them with fact.

"It's an old secret." Leslie grimaced. "One that does me no honor, I fear. But a bride should surely know of her groom's ancestry."

Ian knew now, and he closed his eyes in anguish.

"He's my son, I don't deny that," Leslie said. "But as for the rest—he's half selkie."

Despite all the warnings from the selkie elders, despite all the harshness of the air environment, still many a callow selkie rises from the waves, hoping to find a human mate.

For there is a tradition among selkies and men alike; that when the right human and the right selkie meet, and mate, they create a passion unlike any other. They glow, they burn, they love time and again until nothing matters except that they be together. It is a love, they say, to bring tears to the eyes.

What they do not say is that when the wrong human and the wrong selkie meet, and mate, the results are tragic and everlasting, and the tears that fall then are not tears of joy, but tears of sorrow, fear—and vengeance.

Chapter 14

A moment of stunned silence followed Leslie's an-
nouncement.

For Ian, the dining chamber was shapeless, filled
with auras that swirled with emotion. Incredulity,
amazement, amusement, cold calculation: Ian saw
them all from a distance. His body remained, but
he'd slipped away, joining the other world that
waited just out of sight. He hovered, so light he
floated on air, waiting in anguish to hear what
Alanna would say.

Instead, a man tittered with laughter. "You tease
us, sir!"

The room shifted. Forms took shape.

"Indeed," another man exclaimed. "Selkies! A
silly legend."

Edwin. And Brice.

"Heard of it!" Leslie slapped his open palm on
the table. "I tell you, I bred with one."

Ian's vision cleared further. He'd been lost in the
enchanted world . . . and he'd come back again.
He'd made it back again, and no one had noticed
his absence.

Edwin looked embarrassed. Brice worked to contain his amusement.

Even Wilda mumbled, "Uncle Leslie!" in tones of chagrin.

But Alanna still hadn't spoken, and Ian risked a glance at her.

She scrutinized him. Had she seen his form waver in the winds of magic?

No. She didn't look frightened. Only grave and thoughtful, as if she were weighing the possibility he might truly be a freak.

Brice laid a hand on Wilda's arm and spoke softly. "Don't distress yourself, my dear. We have our daft kin here in Scotland, too. We understand."

Ian could see Leslie's rage expanding and contracting with each breath he took, and for good reason. He was known as a liar as well as a louse. He hated being treated like an insignificant old man, dismissed and ridiculed. "I saw. I know!" he insisted.

"Shut up, old man," Edwin said in a low, vicious tone. "You'll ruin everything for your stupid revenge." Rising, he circled the far end of the table to receive his share of Wilda's attention. "There, there, dear." He knelt beside her. "Pay him no heed."

Leslie sputtered, "How dare you sit in my home and doubt me? How dare . . ." Then he saw the way Alanna considered Ian, and he stopped.

The chamber, the people, everything came back into focus when Ian concentrated on him. That other, enchanted world disappeared . . . for the moment. Bitterly Ian said, "You're satisfied now, aren't you, Father?"

"The girl should know the truth." The words were righteous. The tone was not.

"You wouldn't know truth if it raped you."

Leslie tried to retort. Tried again.

Ian leaned forward, unsure whether his father

feigned incoherence for its dramatic effect or if he truly could not speak.

Leslie drew one of those deep, watery breaths; a tremor shook him. "It's time for me to sleep," he said hoarsely. His head dropped to his chest; his eyes closed.

Alanna stepped forward. On the other side of Leslie, the dog growled deep in his throat. She stopped, but Ian said, "He won't attack you. Just move slowly."

She glanced at him, startled by his certainty, but she believed him and gingerly pressed her fingers against Leslie's neck. Damon didn't leap, but he kept his teeth bared. "His heart still beats," she reported.

A gurgling snore escaped Leslie's parted lips.

"Obviously." Keeping an eye on Damon, Ian signaled the footmen. "Pick up the chair. Carry Mr. Fairchild to his bedchamber. And for God's sake, don't make any sudden moves. If you are careful, the dog won't attack."

"Aye, but what about the man?" one of them asked, white-faced and shaking.

Ian didn't laugh. The footman obviously knew where the real danger originated. "He's asleep."

The men circled Leslie, torn between their fear of the old man and their fear of the dog. Ian watched as the dog circled, too, daring them, and when one of the men lunged toward the chair, Damon lunged back. The footmen ran, yelling. Wilda screamed and the cousins shouted. The butler crawled onto the liquor cabinet, sending glasses and goblets flying. Chairs hit the floor among the shattering glass.

Damon whirled, looking for prey. And with a huge, echoing bark, the four-legged servant of the devil flung itself at Alanna.

Ian didn't remember moving, but he found himself on the other side of the chair and in the air. With the weight of his body behind him, he kicked the dog in the head.

Snarling, the beast rose again, stalking him as if the man were a trifling prey he would rend at his leisure.

"A knife," Alanna whispered. "Use a knife off the table."

Ian ignored her, standing perfectly still. The mastiff prepared to leap. The silence in the room hummed with tension as Damon focused its savage attention on Ian's eyes.

On his eyes.

Damon froze, stiff-legged, hackles raised.

Ian watched him. Softly, gently, he coaxed, "Down. Lie down."

Still growling, the dog slipped from an aggressive, forward tilt to a defiant sit.

"That's right." Ian spoke right to the dog's feral, twisted soul. "You can trust me. Lie down."

Damon's ears drooped. Shutting its serrated black lips, it covered the teeth that shone so menacingly.

"I won't let him hurt you anymore." Ian squatted so he was on eye level with the animal and made him a promise. "You'll be my dog now."

Looking dazed, Damon slid into a quiet recline. It huddled down, its sad gaze fixed on Ian.

Ian laid his hand on the gigantic head. "Good boy."

The animal rose and, with the peace of a babe, lay by the fire.

Everybody remained silent, watching the dog, then staring at Ian. He shifted uncomfortably and wondered what the devil they had expected him to do. Let Damon savage Alanna?

Then Leslie snorted and snored.

"My God." Brice sputtered. "How did you do that?"

"Isn't it wonderful? Ian has always had a way with animals," Wilda said. "Why, I remember one time when there was this horse at the Fairchild stables—"

Edwin interrupted her without compunction. "Maybe this lad really is a half-breed." He laughed, then stopped. "How disgusting," he murmured.

No one else laughed. No one ever laughed when Ian proved he was different. So normally he took care never to show his abilities. And when he did, even now, even in the saving of Alanna's life, he knew he would be punished by coldness, fear, disdain.

The footmen edged away from him. The butler crawled off the liquor cabinet and glared as if the broken glass were Ian's fault. In the doorway, a goggle-eyed maid watched, then whisked away to carry the tale to the rest of the household.

And as always, Ian wore his detachment like a shield, not responding to the wonder or the distaste or the amazement. He let the gossip wash over him without a quiver, with squared shoulders and shuttered expression.

Indifference. It was the only way to survive.

Then someone tugged at his elbow. Alanna. He waited for her denunciation, too.

"Ian, you saved my life." She gathered her skirt in one hand, and holding her other wrist in a graceful arch, she curtsied like a grateful subject to her king. "Many thanks to you."

He couldn't believe it. Had she . . . had she deliberately saved him from being shunned? Her servants watched her closely, taking their cue from her and smiling. Her cousins shuffled as if embarrassed that a mere woman would have courage where they did not.

And for once, Ian found himself at a loss. He knew how to counter rudeness. He knew how to handle spite. But how did a man thank a woman for treating him as if he were human?

She didn't seem to expect an answer. She simply turned toward the footmen. "Do as Mr. Ian ordered now. Take Mr. Fairchild to his bedchamber."

Still keeping an eye on the quiescent dog, the men hustled over. Each grasped a chair leg and carried Leslie's wobbling figure toward his room.

Alanna and Ian followed through the dim corridors.

Ian wondered what to say. Should he lie? Should he try to reassure her? Or should he demand she recall what had happened between them, demand she admit he was a man in the ways that count? Unfeeling society had labeled him: bastard, demon, beast. But he was more than that, and she knew it. If she would just remember, she knew it.

Outside the door, she stopped him with her hand on his arm. "Your father's a sick, foolish old man. I'm smart enough to discern the truth about you."

She didn't sound repulsed. Her hand lay on his arm. She'd touched him without fear. She watched him gravely, her eyes big and solemn.

But it's true! Just once, he longed to speak the truth. *It's true! My mother was selkie. Accept me as I am.*

But shadow and candlelight softened her sharp, intelligent face, and he wanted her. Wanted her, and remembered the Quaker girl with her fears and the abhorrence she could scarcely contain.

He should tell Alanna the facts. He should force her to believe. It wasn't fair that she should have to wed a half-breed. A monstrosity. But it was too late for her. She was *his*. He'd made her his.

Only now she didn't seem to know it. She seemed to think she had a choice.

Sliding his hands around her waist, he drew her toward him.

Her hand flew to his chest and she braced herself against him. "Too much stands between us," she protested. "My lands, my past, your greed, your father."

"Your lands I want, I freely admit that, and if that makes me greedy, so be it. But your past . . . I care nothing for your past. And I warn you now"— he spoke so softly she leaned closer to hear him— "I'll not let the memory of my father and what he tried to do four years ago strip the joy from today."

"You demand I forget how helpless he made me feel?"

"When I hold you, you're omnipotent." He held her arms and let her hold his. "Feel it. Feel the mastery you hold over me."

Uncomprehending, she tried to jerk away. Or, more likely, she feared such power—and feared him.

"Alanna." Her name rasped from his throat, emblematic of everything he wanted to say and could not. He wanted to thank her for being openly grateful he'd saved her life. He wanted to thank her for hiding any dismay she might feel at his background. But the delight of her body against his pushed him beyond civilized behavior, and he nudged her toward the wall. After all, she expected no less. He was a beast, wasn't he? And a bastard. God, he ought to tell her that, too. But not yet . . .

She turned her face away. He freed one hand and caught her neck, his fingers holding her jaw, and he kissed her.

Even the touch of her mouth was good. Even the

sample of her firmly closed lips enticed him. But mostly, her resistance fed his ire. He angled his face to hers. "Open," he muttered.

She did—to bite him. Her teeth nipped his lower lip—almost.

"I'll spank you," he threatened, and swept inside.

He tasted surprise, indignation. Then he tasted *her*. If he were given a blindfold and a hundred women to kiss, he would always know Alanna. Tart, frightened, excited against her will.

He held her firmly, but he kept the kiss gentle, coaxing.

Until she began to respond. Then the blood rushed in his veins, surging like the tides. God, she was sweet. Small and sweet and beneath it all, passionate. He'd proved that last night, and again today. The drug had helped him, lowering her resistance, lulling her fears, and she'd given in to desire with so much confusion and delight he'd had trouble maintaining his control.

Control. Her breath caught now, and she moaned, a little sound he caught and savored. He leaned into her, pressing her harder against the wall, using his weight to master her. One hand stroked her bare throat. One hand molded her curves, moving from hips to ribs and back again.

Lifting his head, he looked down at her. Her eyelids fluttered as if they were too heavy to lift. Her mouth was damp, swollen, and the skin around it was slightly reddened from the scrub of his beard. She nudged her bottom lip with her tongue, and he swooped down and met it.

This time when he lifted his head, she looked at him, dazed with the same sensuality that shook him.

"Leave your door unlocked tonight."

Those green eyes dilated, and she tried to escape him by flattening herself against the wall. As if he couldn't just lean harder.

"You can't come to me without the wedding!" she whispered.

"I'm half selkie. Remember?" He never thought he would brag about it, but he did now. "I'm magic. I can slip through your window on the breeze, lay hands on you with my thoughts, enchant you with a spell . . ."

She melted, misty-eyed with the longing he induced in her.

Then he saw logic snap into place. Her mouth firmed. Her eyes flashed. And the glow of passion died and was replaced by the color of reason. "If you're the wind, then I don't have to leave my door unlocked for you, do I?"

He smiled, slow and sure. He *was* the wind, and he *would* be with her. Carefully he placed his thumb on her forehead, right between her eyebrows. Looking into her eyes, he pressed and commanded, "Dream of me."

When selkies rise from the wave to walk the land, they entice the unwary to follow them. For selkies, when they take their human form, are as beautiful as the night, with dark eyes that flash with silver highlights and black hair that shines like sable. When a human man sees a selkie woman, he feels an enchantment grow on him, and he would do anything to possess that selkie forever.

And when a male selkie wishes to possess a human female, he uses all his skills to captivate the woman, taking her on a journey of such delight she never again desires another.

Some humans, disgruntled by others' happiness, call this use of selkie magic unfair.

Selkies say something entirely different. It is the equivalent of the incantation—"All's fair in love and war."

Chapter 15

Ian came to her like a mist, materializing out of the dark like some phantom of pleasure. "Alanna." His warm voice vibrated with reprimand. "I told you to leave your door unlocked. Every night for the last seven nights I have told you, and still you disobey me. How shall I punish you?"

Clutching her bedclothes close to her chest, she defied him as she had every night for the past week. "You have no right to command me, or to punish me."

His figure glowed with a light of its own as he placed his knee on the mattress beside her hip. With the care of a sweetheart, he uncoiled her fingers from the sheets and flung the muslin toward the foot of the bed. "I take my rights. Don't you remember that night in the witch's hut?"

"I don't. I swear I don't."

"Let me remind you." His hands slid into her hair, and he held her still as he brushed her cheeks with a closemouthed kiss.

The sweetness of it brought tears of joy to her eyes. This kiss was the composition, a masterpiece, one of nature's most exquisite blossoms. Each graze of Ian's lips brought the blood leaping to her skin, and she wondered—if this was her punishment for locking him out of her room, what would be her reward for letting him in?

He kissed her forehead, the shell of her ears, her chin and neck . . . "Ian." Somehow her hands had moved to grasp his shoulders, and she twisted her head to offer her mouth. "Please kiss me."

"I am kissing you."

His lips slid along her jaw to the lobe of her ear, and he nipped it.

Every nerve in her body sprang to attention. "Why did you do that?"

"So I could do this." He soothed the sting with a kiss, then sucked the tender flesh into his mouth.

She inhaled in a startled, desperate need for air. His tongue, his lips, his teeth, worked along the lobe and up the shell, nibbling as if her ear were a tasty delicacy meant to be savored. Goose bumps started at the base of her spine and traveled outward, trying to chill an already overheated body.

Useless endeavor. He gave her no quarter. "A beautiful ear," he murmured. "Rosy and delicate, and so sensitive." The slight breeze his speech created skimmed across the dampness. "Isn't it?"

Her eyes had closed as she tried to absorb the sensation. "What?"

"Your ear. It's sensitive."

Stupid question. With him, everything was sensitive. Her scalp responded as his fingers slid through it, seeking the contours of her skull and massaging it until she relaxed, each muscle lax, each bone detached. Then his hand slid down to her shoulder blade. She tilted her head away, allowing him to stroke her; little circles of solace ranging over a body tense from work and worry. He gave her such comfort, she wished she had had it all the lonely years ago. She wished she could have it all the lonely years in the future.

"You can," he whispered.

And her relaxation vanished.

His hand no longer massaged her shoulder, but caressed the flesh her nightgown should have covered. When, and how, had he disrobed her?

She lunged for the covers, but they were out of reach.

"Embarrassed, sweet?" His dark, rich voice checked her unease. "Silly, to be ashamed of a body as grand as this. Look." He palmed her breast, lifting it from below and accenting the upper swell. "The finest ladies of the world wish for such soft, unmarked skin, for such jaunty roundness, for a nipple the color of the dawn." His voice thickened, as if he had tempted himself.

She watched as his dark head lowered and he kissed her breast. The brush of his lips against the outer arc of flesh banished modesty, and his forefinger and thumb closed around one nipple. Gently he pinched, and she moaned, a quick dip into verbal surrender.

His eyes, sable-soft in the dim light, fixed on her, and again and again his thumb rubbed gently over her. "Sensitive here, too. Look how it has puckered, so tight with anticipation. Why do you suppose that is?"

"Oh, please." She strained upward.

"Talk to me, Alanna. In your own sweet burr, tell me why your body teases me with response."

"Because . . . I want . . . a kiss." Her teeth gritted in a combination of exasperation and desire so intense she would have done anything to assuage it. Anything . . . except unlock her door to the real man.

"You're too stubborn," he chided. "But I'm yours to command. See?" Lifting his head, he pursed his lips and bussed the air. "A kiss."

"A real kiss."

"Why, Alanna. You want me to open my mouth on you." He managed to sound shocked, yet utterly content. "You want me to suckle. Why would you want that?"

Because somehow that might assuage the craving she experienced in each receptive place in her body. In the most receptive place of her body.

"Tell me, Alanna. How would it feel if I licked you with my tongue, and took your nipple between and sucked on it? Maybe even . . . bit down."

Crazed by his spoken half promises, she stirred restively.

"Not hard!" he assured her. "No, but gently, tenderly, a mere scrape of the teeth to warn you of the danger. For I am dangerous, Alanna. Do you know that?"

Her knee crooked and one foot dragged slowly across the linen sheet, as if that little roughness would give her a base of reality. "I'm dangerous, too."

The teasing note in his voice vanished. "I know that. You have the ability to send me into exile with a mere flick of your fingers."

Damn him! Why didn't he do as she demanded? "I should."

"Yes." He wrapped his hand around her throat. He exerted no pressure, but the threat was there. "Yet you wonder—would you then never be rid of these dreams, or would frustration dog you until the end of your days?"

She laid her hand across his. "And your frustration?"

His lips, the erotic lips she coveted, curved in a bitter smile. "I'll be chained against the same rock in hell as you."

How she liked that! She had always been the

lady of Fionnaway, proud, noble, and honorable, but never had she known she could hold a man in thrall. Especially not a man of such dark charm. "Kiss me," she directed, "on the lips." She didn't know why that mattered so much, but she wanted to taste him, to have him taste her. Only then would she believe this was happening. Only then would she comprehend her power.

But he didn't answer. And he didn't obey.

Instead she found his fingers gliding down to caress her belly. She forgot about the kiss. She forgot about pride. Only his unspoken, tantalizing promises mattered. "Ian." She twisted on the bed, frantic to have him press his hand to the place that throbbed with the rhythm of her heartbeat. "Please."

"Another kiss?" He nuzzled her other breast with his lips.

"Not like that." She caressed his chest, finding a light covering of hair over his breastbone. His nipples were flat and smooth until she wet her fingers in her mouth. She touched the circles of color, and they puckered, like her own, and she heard his intake of breath.

"You are innovative." Provocatively he licked the inside of her elbow. "Or desperate."

Desperate. Aye, she was desperate. Boldly she slid her hands lower. Along his hip, slender and strong. Across his belly, rippling with muscle. If she touched him the way she wanted to be touched, maybe he'd also be driven mad with need.

But he blocked her as she reached the frame of curly hair at the apex of his legs. "That is play for lovers."

"We're lovers."

His knee pushed her knees apart, and ever so slowly he lowered himself until his weight rested on her. Bringing his thigh higher, he crowded between her legs. The pressure was a flawed replacement for the delicacy of his hand, but she moved herself against it tentatively, then eagerly. The sensation satisfied her and made her want more, all at the same time. He let her use him, propel herself against him until she whimpered from desire, until she strained toward satisfaction.

Then he held her hips still. She saw his eyes glinting in the dark above her, and he said what he always said. "We'll be lovers when you unlock your door for me."

He moved so lightly, she didn't realize he was gone until she woke, clutching the pillow to her midriff.

A light sweat covered her skin. Her breath came in short pants. Her blood pounded in her veins, and desperately she touched herself, trying to relieve the tension, and knowing from experience that nothing she did would ease the damp, empty sensation.

For the first time, he added, "It's time to remember, Alanna."

She heard him so clearly, she flung herself over and stared at the door, expecting to see him.

The door was shut. Locked, and for the last three nights, bolted with an iron bar.

Her caution had been for naught. Once again Ian had done as he'd promised. He'd drifted in her window on the breeze, enchanted her with a spell, and she had dreamed of him today as she had done every damned night. *Every* damned night.

Infuriated, shaking from frustration, she rolled off the bed, landed on the floor with a thump—and tripped as her nightgown dropped to her feet. Catching it on her toes, she kicked it as far as it would go. But it drifted in a flutter of white cotton rather than slamming against the wall as she had hoped.

Stupid nightgown. She fastened every button all the way to her neck every night, and every morning she woke to find it opened, lowered to her waist, raised to her hips . . . How was he doing this?

She glared around her empty room. The room MacLeod daughters had occupied since the castle had been built. No comfort had been spared; Alanna should have been as satisfied to be housed here as the stones were with their niche in the fireplace.

But satisfaction was the last thing Alanna felt.

Frustration. Now, that was the word. Every night Ian came to her in her dreams and caressed her until she begged for completion. Every night he denied her. He would take her just to the edge. Just to where her body was wound to its tightest. Then . . . she would wake. And all day, everything that brushed against her made her think of Ian. Everything she tasted, touched, smelled, made her remember the erotic teasing of the night before . . . and the teasing hadn't really happened.

"Bother him!" Snatching her clothes off the chair, she dressed as quickly as she could. She had to get out of here before she saw him.

Nay—before *he* saw *her*. He was the hunter, she was hunted. He followed her everywhere as she took up her duties as the lady of Fionnaway. He did it, supposedly, to help her as her foot healed. Then, when it was better, he said he came because she needed a chaperon as she rode from village to croft.

He lied. He came so he could smile at her. Smile, and touch her on the elbow as he assisted her across rocky ground. Smile, and lift her into her

saddle with his hands on her waist. Smile, and rub
the knot between her shoulder blades as she spoke
with the crofters.

And he was the reason she was tense! He did not
once touch her as he had in the study. She knew
his hands were bold, seeking, knowledgeable, but
would he show her? Nay. He would just look at
her, all jumpy from those erotic dreams, and without saying a word, he let her know he knew. Damn
him, he knew, and she feared unless she got a re-
prieve from the endless stalking, she would break.
She would agree to wed Ian just so he would show
her what lay on the other side of this tantalizing
mountain of sexual yearning.

Clutching her light leather boots in her sweaty
palms, she unlocked and unbarred the door.
Slowly, quietly, she pulled it open and stuck her
head into the corridor. She glanced first to one side,
then the other, and when she saw no Ians lurked
in the shadows, she tiptoed out. Toward escape.

Chapter 16

She made it down the corridor without seeing so much as a servant. She crossed the boundless reaches of the great hall, glancing around as if she were an intruder in her own home. The passage that led to the outside door beckoned, and she had almost reached it when—

"Lady Alanna, are you going out again?"

Alanna jumped guiltily and swung toward the fireplace.

There a lone figure huddled by the blazing hearth. "Wilda," Alanna whispered.

"You're leaving earlier than usual," Wilda said.

With her hand on her thumping heart, Alanna wanted to snap, *Of course it's earlier than usual. I'm trying to sneak out without your cousin's company.* But she couldn't. If she did, she would hurt the dear girl's feelings.

Alanna liked her. She didn't want to—well, what woman wanted to like another who so completely overshadowed her with the gifts of beauty and charm?—but as Wilda had gravely confided, "I know I'm prettier than anyone else, but Mama says I'm stupid and softhearted, and I'm not likely to catch a rich man when I feel sorry for so many poor ones."

Right now that would be Edwin. A younger son, he didn't have his own fortune. He had no prospects, because his brother had only one estate and managed it well. Brice supported Edwin without complaint—after all, Edwin was a pleasant man, impossible to dislike—but Alanna knew Brice wished she would disappear so he could place his brother at Fionnaway as steward and free him of his perpetual tag-tail.

It was really too bad Wilda had no prospects, either, for Alanna thought Wilda and Edwin would make a lovely couple.

Brice and Wilda . . . Now, that was different. Brice was harder than Edwin, given to bullying, and he had proclaimed his determination to wed a wealthy woman, for he wished above all to be greater than the lady of Fionnaway. It would take a powerful infatuation to sway Brice from his chosen course, although in the last week . . . Alanna stared at Wilda. In the last week it had become clear that if anyone could make Brice love more than money and prestige, it would be Wilda.

Resigning herself to a morning chat, Alanna walked to Wilda's side. "What are you doing up at this hour of the morning? Why, it's scarcely past sunrise."

"My bed was cold." Blankets were heaped over Wilda's hunched-up knees and around her shoulders.

"I *am* going out." Alanna sat on the floor and pulled her boots on. "Would you like to accompany me?"

Wilda shivered. "No. It's *freezing* out there."

"It's the twenty-first of July!" And Alanna's birthday. If she could, she would proclaim herself undisputed mistress of Fionnaway and throw everyone out on their ear. Except Wilda, of course.

And she couldn't make a man in Leslie's uncertain health start a lengthy journey to England. And if she tried to send Brice and Edwin on their way, she would hear manly protestations. And Ian—if she tried to throw Ian out, he would laugh at her, and maybe try and press his claim on her, and she would cave in like a weak-kneed fool.

Alanna pressed the heels of her hands into her eyes. What a tangle she'd made of things!

"You've tangled your lacing," Wilda said. "You'd best start over."

Alanna looked down. She had. Impatiently she loosened them and started over.

"It's colder in Scotland than in the South." Wilda frowned at Alanna, her clear brow creasing with anxiety. "You should put on a pelisse."

"I will." She wouldn't, but she could tell that one wee lie. More and more Wilda reminded Alanna of her mother. Fussing at her to dress warmly when she was already warm. Constantly asking about an ankle already healed. Warning that riding horses astride would ruin her maidenhood. It was sweet—and maddening.

"Do you have your wool petticoats on?" Wilda asked.

"Not wool, but petticoats." Wilda wore wool, Alanna could tell. Wilda had had the seams of her dresses let out to accommodate as many petticoats as possible. She looked stuffed as a sausage, but neither Brice nor Edwin seemed to care.

"Mrs. Armstrong made me wool petticoats so I wouldn't catch a chill. And pantalettes." Wilda stuck out her foot and showed the wide band of lace that edged the bottom of her bizarre undergarments. "She made you pantalettes, too, but I suppose you're too stubborn to wear them."

"They're not something we wear in Scotland,"

Alanna said firmly, as she finished lacing her boots. Personally she thought she never would condone such silly things. They looked like men's trousers made from white cotton, and Alanna felt sure the fashion Wilda worshiped today would be passé tomorrow.

"In England, men don't wear skirts."

"Kilts," Alanna said patiently. "They're kilts."

"Anyway, the pantalettes are warm on my legs." Wilda tried to tuck the blanket around her feet. "I can't get my toes warm."

Feeling ungrateful for mocking Wilda and her girl-trousers, Alanna knelt before her. Taking the blanket, she rubbed Wilda's feet and tried, one more time, to express her gratitude. "You've been too good, to allow your own cloth to be made up for me." She touched the buttons extending from throat to hem on her new dark blue, high-waisted gown.

"But you're the lady!" Wilda replied. "The long-lost lady who has returned from the mists to marry my cousin."

Looking up, Alanna asked stiffly, "Why do you say that?"

"Because you've been gone for so long." Wilda's answers never quite fit the questions.

Alanna took a calming breath and tucked Wilda firmly in the blanket. "Nay. I mean the part about me marrying your cousin."

"He told me he was determined to have you." Wilda beamed. "He always gets what he wants, so I'm happy for you both."

Wilda would be. Wilda saw only the good things. That was why everyone liked her. That was why Alanna liked her. But what Wilda didn't see, didn't know, was her beloved Ian's Machiavellian side.

Dream of me. He'd commanded, and Alanna had

obeyed. He chased, and Alanna ran. He demanded, and Alanna . . . Nay, she wouldn't give in. When she'd come back to Fionnaway, she'd had a plan. She wouldn't wed him unless he proved himself worthy. She would not marry in a fever as her mother had, and pay the price later.

"He deserves someone besides a Quaker girl who trembles when he looks at her."

Wilda's pronouncement grabbed Alanna's wandering attention. "A Quaker girl?"

"I told him she wasn't the wife for him—"

Shocked, Alanna demanded, "He's been married?"

"No!" Wilda impatiently blew a wisp of hair out of her eyes. "He insisted she would be his wife because she was willing to put up with the disgrace."

Alanna tried to interrupt again.

Wilda babbled like a mountain stream after the winter melt. "She should have been grateful, a puny little thing like her with no title and no fortune. Oh, she pretended she would wed him for love, but I know better. She wanted the money."

Trying to interpret the flood of information, Alanna asked, "What money?"

"He's got bags. Hasn't he told you?"

"Yes, I believe he did." And Alanna thought that might explain why he wanted a crumbling manor in Scotland. Every piddling merchant in England wanted property in the country and, if possible, a title or a titled wife. Such honors lent them an air of respectability. But she had news for Ian. A hundred manors wouldn't buy such a sensual man respectability.

"Then that miserable coward wrote him a note and said she couldn't bear to go through with it because he's a wizard," Wilda said. "A wizard! Have you ever heard such a thing? Of course, Uncle Leslie claimed Ian was half selkie, but Uncle Leslie would say anything to get attention. He's the second oldest, you know, my grandfather's brother, and really my great-uncle.''

Thinking of the pinched face, the cruel jokes, the flamboyant spending, Alanna had to ask, ''Has he always been so bitter?''

''Oh, yes. He's a Fairchild. We're all evil one way or the other, but Mama says Uncle Leslie is exceptional. Mama says Uncle Leslie always thought he should have the title and the fortune. But Papa got it instead. We truly don't know who Ian's mother is. Ian just showed up at Fairchild Manor one day.''

''How old was Ian when he arrived?''

''Eleven. I was only six years old and his cousin, but I couldn't keep my eyes off him. We Fairchilds are beautiful, of course, but Ian is just *mesmerizing*, don't you think? Uncle Leslie hated that, too, that he was getting old and saggy, and the serving maids, who hated Uncle, were constantly sneaking into Ian's bedchamber.''

Wilda touched a memory in Alanna. The maids watched Ian here, too, and she wondered if he had spent his nights alone here in Fionnaway. She wondered if she would have to dismiss every hussy who smiled at him, then realized, with a pang, that she should not care.

''Mama says Uncle Leslie is the most unnatural father she's ever seen, worse than any Fairchild before him, and that's why he's trying to drive you away by saying Ian is a selkie when everybody knows it's the witch who is magic.''

Alanna froze in astonishment. ''The witch?''

''Oh, Alanna.'' Wilda leaned forward, face glowing. ''She left before you got here, but she was such a delightful woman. She promised to help me, and I've watched and watched for her, but she hasn't come back. Do you think she'll come back?"

"The witch." Alanna looked up at the animated face above her and wished she didn't have to burst her bubble. "Wilda, perhaps you didn't hear what happened that day I arrived in Fionnaway. I came in dressed like the witch, and washed my face and took off that foul robe, and showed everyone that *I* had been pretending to be a witch."

Mouth puckered, Wilda said, "Of course you did."

"Really, Wilda. That's how I hid from Mr. Fairchild all this time. I played dress-up."

"And no one ever realized you were the witch." Wilda tossed her head. "I know I'm a widgeon sometimes, but you can't fool me. The witch was old and ugly. You're young and pleasing. You couldn't be the witch."

"I put charcoal on my face and I stuffed rags in my robe to be a hump..." Alanna wasn't getting through to Wilda, she could see. It wouldn't matter, but Wilda was still looking for the witch to make a spell for her. "What did you want a witch for?"

"You're teasing me about being a witch," Wilda said, slightly miffed, "and you want me to confide in you?"

"I thought maybe if I saw a witch, I could tell her..."

Firmly shaking her head, Wilda said, "The witch will come back to help me. I know it."

Alanna could see only grief ahead for Wilda, so she tried once more. "Where do you think I've been all this time?"

"Hiding from Uncle Leslie."

What could Alanna say? Wilda was right about that.

"Because Uncle Leslie is an obnoxious old"—

Wilda stopped and glanced around, then whispered—"ass."

Wilda looked so frightened by her own bravado, Alanna whispered empathetically, "Aye, he is." And worse than he was four years ago. It almost seemed as if Leslie fed on the hatred directed at him from the servants, from Alanna, even from his own son. Each day Leslie seemed more healthy. Each day he seemed to take more pleasure in tormenting those around him.

He hadn't forgiven Ian for claiming Alanna as his own.

"You came back for Ian." Wilda rushed back into speech—obviously her greatest pleasure. "Because you're not like that Quaker girl. You're brave and strong and free, just like Ian needs. He won't ever have to coddle you, although I suppose he'll try, just because he's that kind of man. And you've got a home for him, and he can help you build it better, and you two can sit by the fire together in the long nights—even in the summer, the nights are long here in Scotland, don't you people believe in sunshine?—and you won't even have to tell him what you're thinking, he'll know."

Alanna snapped her gaze to Wilda. "What?"

Wilda seemed to realize she'd said too much, for she squirmed uncomfortably beneath the blankets. "Maybe it won't be that way with you. It's just that he always knows what I'm thinking."

Alanna smiled reassuringly, and all the while she thought, *He knows what I'm thinking, too.*

And for once, she had to get out of here before he could torment her. It was her birthday; she had the right to spend it as she pleased. Standing, she took a step backward. "You do display your emotions rather openly."

"Do I? That explains it, then." In one of those

lightning-quick changes of subject that left Alanna reeling, Wilda said, "Ian has gone with you everywhere this last week, and he has charmed all the servants and everybody likes him. He's going to be a perfect lord of Fionnaway."

"Everything he's done has been very reassuring," Alanna acceded. "In the daytime."

"He's a good dancer, too." Wilda didn't seem to notice Alanna's preparations to go. "Don't worry about that. I know you must be, but he can fulfill every one of a gentleman's evening duties, as well."

Alanna opened her mouth to correct her, and shut it. There was no way she could explain *this* to Wilda.

Then Wilda shocked her. "I imagine he'll be excellent in the marriage bed also. That will make you happier, I'm sure."

"Happier?"

Mouth pursed, Wilda glanced at her sideways. "You've been just a little cranky in the past week."

"And here I thought I'd been handling it so well," Alanna said in a daze.

"Oh, you have!" Wilda's face, usually devoid of thought, gleamed with a kind of canny wisdom. "There have just been those moments when you looked at Ian as if you'd like to knock him down and beat him to the floor, and he shakes his head at you, and that's when you get . . . a little snappish."

Groping behind her, Alanna found a chair and sank down on it. "So everyone knows?"

"No, silly!" Wilda giggled. "Men don't notice anything but themselves and what they want. Luckily, Ian wants *you*."

"And Fionnaway."

He did want Fionnaway. Alanna had seen it

when they'd visited the farm village. As he discussed the difficulty of raising crops in the stony soil with men, the women told about his previous visits and praised him to her. They'd visited the outlying crofts. He'd already been to each one. And yesterday they'd visited the fishing village.

But there Ian had behaved oddly. They'd stood right on the shore with the fishermen, discussing the currents, the fishing season, and the recent catches. Yet Alanna would have sworn Ian never once looked out at the ocean, and once when a particularly large wave had crashed against the rocks, he'd shuddered as if it had cracked his bones.

He'd wheeled around and headed toward the horses, and the oldest man had taken Alanna's hand in his own gnarled fist and patted it. "Take care o' him, m'lady. He has seawater in his veins, and most o' them come to a tragic end. But he'll protect Fionnaway, and ye, and live to tell the tale, if ye just love him enough."

She dismissed that, but she couldn't dismiss the message she'd been given. Without dissembling, each farmer, each crofter, each fisherman, had made it clear they wanted him as lord. As frankly, he indicated he coveted that position.

The truth was, Ian's heritage did not worry Alanna. What bothered her was her own intuition— the intuition that told her Ian wouldn't be satisfied with the sensible marriage she'd always envisioned. He wanted her heart; she was resolved to guard it.

Wilda broke into her thoughts. "It just makes me warm all over to think a woman is finally going to love him as he deserves."

"I am not." Love him? Love Ian?

God forbid that she love any man. She'd been betrayed enough times: by her indifferent father, by

Leslie, even by two cousins who would be happier if she were out of their way. Alanna didn't need to love a man. Not even a man who seduced mad dogs into docility. Especially not a man who had the power to touch her forehead and bring forth dreams that made her want to lie with him and sate herself.

"Well, of course you don't want to. What woman wants to fall so madly in love with her husband she would walk barefoot with him to the ends of the earth?" Wilda sounded dreamy, as if she were thinking of someone other than Alanna. "But it happens, and when it does, great happiness awaits them both."

"Or misery." Alanna repeated the vow she had made before. "There has never been a man born of woman who could entice me to take that kind of risk." Then she realized—Ian, if Leslie's tale was true, had not been born of woman.

Wilda broke into a chime of laughter. "No matter what, Alanna MacLeod, I think you're in trouble."

Was she? Alanna stood. "I've got to go now." She walked toward the door, slowly at first, then faster and faster, until she broke into a run.

The footman in the front hall hurried to let her out. The dairymaids with the buckets stepped out of her way, the gardener who trimmed the shrubs stared.

But she made it out of the front gate before anyone—any *Ian*—caught her.

In Scotland there's a saying that those men and women with a special charm "have a wee drop of selkie blood a-runnin' in their veins." Those stable men can break a horse to the bridle while reserving its wild spirit. Those milkmaids can coax the sweetest cream from the cows. Those midwives have a way of easing the pain of childbirth that has nothing to do with herbs.

Indeed, a selkie can charm every creature on this earth.

Chapter 17

Bees buzzed around Quigley's hand as he culled the queen and her court from the branch where they hung. "See the honey bags each one carries? That makes it difficult for 'em t' work that barb they carry behind. That's why they dunna sting when they're swarming, see."

Alanna shook her head in wonder. "They always sting me."

"Ye're too nervous around 'em. They can sense it, see." The snaggletoothed farmer grinned at her as he carried the queen to the woven willow hive he'd prepared. "The scouting bees already found this place. I put those herbs they love inside t' make it all scented for 'em." He placed the queen on the swarm sheet directly in front of the entrance and watched as she danced in. "Now watch. The other bees'll follow her always. 'Tis easy, see."

From a safe distance, she stood and watched as bees followed in a swift brown stream. "Now they'll settle in their new home?"

"Aye, and make the honey for yer Christmas feast." Quigley straightened from his task. " 'Tis glad, I am, ye're back in yer rightful place, see. And 'tis glad I will be t' see ye wed t' Mr. Ian."

Her smile disappeared. Why did everyone assume she would marry Ian? "You know him, too."

"Aye, the man came out t' talk t' me almost as soon as he arrived, see. The laird o' the swarm, he is."

Everyone! Ian had captivated everyone! Every single person on her lands, with the exception of his own father, liked Ian.

"A laird?"

"Aye. He talked t' me, found out about my bee-keeping, suggested t' Armstrong I be put in charge o' the bees and the honey. Had a real appreciation o' my skills, ye ken. Perhaps, after ye're wed, he'll teach ye t' handle the bees." Quigley nodded knowingly.

Her hackles rose. As if Ian could teach her anything. "Really."

"He's got a touch with 'em, see. Helped me move a hive from a windy spot; na many's the man who'll do that. And never a sting on him!"

He shook his head in awed appreciation, and Alanna wondered if she could get away from the memory and the mention of Ian anywhere. When Quigley spoke of Ian's way with the bees, he reminded her that Ian had tamed the dog. Damon no longer threatened the peace of Fionnaway Manor; he had become its guardian.

"He's a good man, m'lady. Ye've done well."

No matter how she wished to, she couldn't snap at Quigley just because he liked Ian. So with a disgruntled wave, she started along the trail. At Fionnaway, all paths ran parallel to the sea. Right now the sound of the breakers drew her up toward her hill. There she could see it, taste it in the tang of the wind; there she could think, or not think, as she chose.

She squinted; the sun took advantage of the cloudless morning to bring the waving grass to attention. Despite Wilda's concerns, she was warm, and she gave a skip along the meadow path. Without her cumbersome disguise, dressed in her chintz gown, she felt free. Although—she glanced behind her—that relentless sensation of pursuit still haunted her.

Ian wasn't there. She hadn't seen him all morning.

In the distance she could hear the crying of lambs, the shouts of men, the bleating of sheep, and she hurried toward them. The first of the shepherds came into view, hefting stones to dam the stream, and she veered toward the man-made pool where every summer the sheep were washed and prepared for shearing. They gathered in clumps to crop the grass, waiting their turn to be pushed into the steam. There men stood in the waist-deep water, grabbed the sheep, and scrubbed them with lye soap until the winter's buildup of grime floated away, to spill over the dam and down to the ocean.

She stood and watched, marveling at the complacency of some of the older ewes. They even seemed to enjoy it, floating while they were soaped and dunked. They swam to the opposite shore and shook the wet from their fleece and immediately set to grazing once more. Some of the younger sheep weren't quite so tolerant, and they required a stern hand to get them into the water. When an aggressive ram entered the pool, the men worked in pairs, washing and dunking with the efficiency of long practice.

"Ho, m'lady!" One of the shepherds in the pool had spotted her, and she came forward to greet him. The man grinned and called to her. "Ho, m'lady. Did ye come for yer summer bath?"

As if in answer to the question, the swimming ram got its back feet on the ground, reared up, and with its front feet, knocked the saucy fellow backward. He fell with such a splash and flailing of arms that Alanna bent from the waist in merriment. When he surfaced, she called, "Nay, but I can see you're getting yours."

The others laughed while he flushed. Then he laughed also, too happy to be wet and cool on this warm day to be humiliated long. "It's good t' see ye returned from the dead," he said, as he wiped suds from his eyes. " 'Tis glad we are ye've come back, and pleased ye're marrying such a fair man as Mr. Ian."

Her smile disappeared, and in a too sweet voice, she said, "You know him, too."

"Helped us with the lambing, he did. Had a nice touch with the ewes. Na too proud t' get his hands dirty."

In unison they nodded, and the head shepherd offered, "He's a good one."

Subduing her scathing reply, Alanna produced a polite smile and walked down below the dam where the stepping-stones provided a dry passage. The interested gaze of the shepherds pricked at her spine as she crossed the flat rocks and left the path to strike out over the meadow. She knew where she wanted to be, and she knew she wanted to be there alone.

The ground rose steeply beneath her feet, and she stepped to avoid the starflowers tucked into the tapestry of grass. Blazing with the bright yellow of the sun overhead, the odorless blossoms embodied spring to Alanna. They shined warmly, existed briefly, and left a bright spot of memory.

When she reached the peak of the knoll, she paused to look around at the most marvelous place on earth. Behind her rose the tree-covered fells, stepping back from the sea in glorious summer splendor. Before her the long, grassy slope descended toward the ocean in a green cascade.

To the eye it seemed the hill descended in an ever-steepening slant to the shore, but she knew that wasn't so. The mound actually descended at an even rate until it reached a cliff, then dropped straight into the sea. Along this stretch of coast, no beach softened its plummet. If anyone was fool enough to crawl to the edge and look down—and when she was younger, she had been such a fool— she would see black rocks like jagged, rotten teeth sticking out of the water. She would see the breakers rampaging over them, around them, using the rocks to grind anything in the way of the relentless sea. Then, with a sucking noise, the waves could carry it down to a hungry gullet.

Alanna loved the ocean. She walked beside it, swam in it, gloried in it, and never, ever forgot what a vicious destroyer it could be.

She bounded in the direction of the cliff. Careless, she didn't watch her step. She tripped, fell, rolled. Grasses cushioned the ground; she caught her breath easily and then rolled again. She grinned; it was a long way to the place where the cliff dropped off. She was safe, and this was fun.

Raising her arms over her head, pointing her toes, she rolled without direction and with increasing pleasure. Over and over on her side, the sky flashed blue above her and the ground circled green and brown below her. She chuckled, her lips open. When a stem slapped her in the mouth, she stopped rolling, stopped laughing, sat up, and sputtered until she ascertained she hadn't ingested a bug. Then she laughed again—at herself—and loosened her hair to finger-comb the seeds and wisps of grass from her braids.

She sat right in the midst of the plants, her chin even with their heads. The sea glinted deep blue, and she could see the swells as they rode towards the rocks. With a groan of pure mindless delight she fell back into the grass.

The stalks loomed tall enough to block her side vision. All she could see was blue sky, white clouds that puffed and expanded in the breeze, and green stalks, heavy with the forming seed. A faint wind carried the smell of summer, and the odor of crushed grass rose from beneath her. She could hear the buzzing of Quigley's bees as they searched for nectar, and from far below the faint, steady rhythm of the sea. Every muscle in her body relaxed for the first time in days.

A fine birthday, she thought as she drifted off to sleep. *Ian's enchantments couldn't find her here.*

Yet when a shadow fell across her, she came awake without surprise. No, his enchantments could not find her. But he could.

She couldn't quite see him as he stood silhouetted against the sun. Yet she could tell he was tall, broad-shouldered, and very much a man. She squinted at him, trying to see the truth. Was he magical? It was possible. She'd been raised on such stories, and sometimes when the storms pressed close and the ocean raged, she thought she could hear voices from the waves.

Foolish fantasies, surely.

Yet she couldn't accuse him of getting into her mind and creating dreams. She suspected that if he had been as earthbound as one of her farmers, she still would have dreamed of him. He had that kind of presence.

"You'll burn that fair skin," he chided, and dropped her straw bonnet over her face.

"Aye, mustn't damage the merchandise." Then, sorry to ruin the day's good humor, she lifted the hat toward him as display. "Thank you. I'll wear it on the way back to Fionnaway."

She sounded polite and meek, and her good manners irritated her, but she didn't want to goad him today. As the days slipped past, he had shed his formal clothing. His cravat had disappeared the first day. His coat the second. His shiny boots had grown scuffed as he trod through the mud and the grass, and now he wore only a white lawn shirt and dark trousers tucked into those boots. He looked casual, intimate almost—and they were alone out here.

Ever since that kiss outside his father's bedchamber, he'd restrained himself to such an extent she might have thought he'd lost interest in her.

But sometimes she felt his reserve tottering. Some night soon, she suspected she'd be sharing her bed with not just the dream, but the man, and although her skin heated and her blood sizzled at the thought, some reticence in her mind shouted caution. If she gave in to him, he might swallow her whole.

Uncomfortable with the way he studied her as she sprawled in the grass, Alanna sat up and straightened her skirt. When she looked reasonably civilized, she asked, "What have you got?"

"Got?" He looked faintly shocked. Then he followed her gaze and seemed to realize she spoke of the basket that rested on his arm. "Oh, that." He chuckled. "Soon you're going to get all of your questions answered. The ones you don't ask, as well as the ones you do."

"I don't understand you."

"Yes, you do." Out of the basket he drew a plaid

blanket, shook it out, and laid it beside her, crushing the long grass with its woolen weight. "There's luncheon inside," he said. "Cook worried you would get hungry."

Perversely, that annoyed her. "Cook worried? And here I thought you were the one who nagged about the food."

"You're not eating enough and you're doing too much." He sat on the blanket and jerked off his boots. "Ah," he sighed. "That feels better." He wiggled his toes in the grass in an endearing motion, but what he said was not endearing. "Someone has to watch over you."

"And you think it should be you."

"I have the right."

The way he said it, the way he watched her, informed her he was willing to quarrel if she wished. And she wouldn't win, she knew.

Moving slowly so as not to wake his slumbering ire, she placed the hat at her side.

He nodded. "Intelligence is attractive in a woman. Now come onto the blanket and lie next to me."

Heat raced across her chest and bloomed in her cheeks. Rolling down that hill must have addled her senses. The dream the night before had begun in just such a manner. He'd commanded she lie beside him. She had done it willingly, because in her dream she was always willing.

"Alanna." His tone demanded.

"I am comfortable as I am."

He swooped toward her, picked her up, and placed her on the blanket in one swift motion. She lay stiff as he leaned over her.

Just as he had in the dream, he grinned, his lips

soft and tender across strong white teeth. "Very good. You do learn." With a groan, he stretched out beside her, hip to hip, shoulder to shoulder, yet not touching, looking at the sky.

Barely breathing, she wondered why he lay so still, but she didn't have long to wonder.

"That's a dragon," he said.

What was he talking about? Then she saw his finger waving in the air, sketching the outline of a cloud.

"Don't you think it's a dragon?" he asked.

"I . . . uh . . . suppose it could be. But"—her gaze sharpened—"it could be a cat."

He sounded utterly relaxed. "Too long for a cat."

By gradual degrees, she let her rigid muscles relax. "Too fuzzy for a dragon."

"Well, it is now! Look at how fast it's moving! 'Tis a dragon transforming itself."

She sighed in disgust. "A typical male way to win an argument."

"A typical female denial of logic." He sounded bland as egg custard, and she turned and gazed at him.

A mistake. *Bland* could never describe the man at her side. *Heart-stoppingly, unbearably handsome* would do better. His profile loomed as rugged as the rocky fells around them. His skin toasted in the sun. Eyebrows accented the jutting brow. Eyelashes, when viewed from the side, swept upward in a ridiculous curl. His beard formed a dark shadow across his chin, and in a futile attempt to relieve her tension, she snapped, "What are you hiding beneath that beard? Tell your valet to shave you."

Curiosity brought his head around, and those brown eyes, she was startled to see, had silver sparks deep within. "My valet didn't come with me."

His well-defined lips moved under his mustache. He looked so mild and comfortable, and she wondered at how well this man fit in the open air of her home. Previously she had associated him with dark and storms, but perhaps she should associate him with the elements that made up the storms—air and water, fire and earth. "I'll find you a valet." She hesitated, fascinated with his countenance, almost unconscious of her words.

Those lips curved up, charming, rueful. "Should I allow one of your servants near my throat with a razor?"

When his suggestion sank in, she sat up, offended. "They'll not slit your throat without my word."

"Precisely my point."

She said nothing, staring out to sea. Her chin jutted, aching as she clenched it tightly. When he tugged her hair, she refused to turn, so instead he wooed her with words.

"Your servants would do anything for you. They talk about how you were such a carefree lass, wild and swift as the birds that soar. How impulsive you were, yet never cruel. How you somehow found enough money to keep Fionnaway thriving even during bad harvests."

She tried not to think of the cache of stones hidden behind the chimney in the master's chamber. Ian seemed to see her thoughts, perhaps even to sense them, and Armstrong had said someone listened at her door.

Ian? Not likely. Sneaking wasn't Ian's way. But the fact remained, Armstrong was gone to Edinburgh, and until he returned, she would worry.

About him, about his daughter Ellie, and about the stones.

She swung her head around and urged, "Go on."

"As you wish."

But he still watched her as if he were trying to divine her secrets, and she fought the panic that rose in her throat. "The servants," she prompted.

"The servants," he repeated obediently. "Should you desire to be rid of me before our wedding, your servants will gladly noose my neck."

Her sense of peril faded—about the stones, at least.

He said, "Should you wish to be rid of me during our wedding feast, they'd feed me poisoned mushrooms. Should I maltreat you after, they'd drop me off that cliff—at the least."

The wedding. Always the wedding. Always the threat of him doing with her what a man does with a woman. Ian frightened her, for Ian, she knew, wouldn't be satisfied until she'd surrendered everything. "You're an opportunist," she said. "You'll do anything to gain my lands."

Without hesitation, he agreed. "Yes. Land hunger is a powerful motive for any man."

"You'd take to wife a hunchbacked, cross-eyed grandmother to get the land."

"Or a witch."

He sounded so solemn, she slewed around and stared at him, and found an invitation to laughter in those dark eyes. An invitation she resisted—but barely. He was the composite of charm, of responsibility, of magnetism. Did he have to be amusing, too?

His hand found hers. He tucked his fingers between her fingers and squeezed gently. "I loved the witch's wit. Perhaps you could find it again."

Briefly she remembered their first conversations

and the banter they'd exchanged. Then she remembered the events that had followed, the dreams that haunted her, and she felt the stroke of his thumb across her knuckles. "I think all the wit the witch could find was contained in her hump," she said.

"Then someday soon"—he lifted her hand and kissed her fingers—"I will go on a quest and rescue the hump and the wit so we can both laugh again." Separating their fingers, he turned her palm to his lips and nuzzled it. "Here at Fionnaway, you're surrounded by your people, and they feel guilty about what almost happened with my father. They will never let you be abused again in any way."

"I can't be so sure of that, not when it concerns you." She turned sullen, which she knew and detested, but her resentment spilled forth. "You've wooed them since your arrival. All I've heard sung is the praises of Mr. Ian."

"Really?" He sounded so sure of himself, and grinned with such cocksure arrogance, that she'd have slapped him if she dared.

She didn't dare. "From the villagers. From the maids. And today from the beekeeper and the shepherds. They might throw you off the cliff, but they'd do it reluctantly."

He chuckled, deep and low and very amused. "Is that supposed to comfort me?"

She made the mistake of looking into his eyes, and found herself caught. By his gaze, and by the pure pleasure of looking at him. It seemed reasonable to wish she were as beautiful as Wilda; to wish her looks were in some small way congruous to Ian's seemed absolutely deranged.

Still smiling, he said, "You're making this wooing much too difficult."

"I don't know any other way."

He sat up and looked down into her face. She

thought he must see each freckle, he looked her over so carefully, but he said only, "I do." Putting his hands on her shoulders, he eased her down to the blanket.

"What are you doing?" As if she didn't know.

"There's no reasoning with you." He loomed over her, blocking out the sunshine. "So I am done with reasoning."

Chapter 18

Ian didn't look angry, or aggravated, just . . . de-
termined. And, she realized, he had looked much
the same since the moment he had tracked her
down and offered her her hat. The dreams she had
fled from this morning had caught up with her
with the express intention of becoming reality. And
she very much feared the siege of the past week
had weakened whatever resistance she might have
had.

Softly, trying not to upset the beast, she whispered, "Ian."

"Alanna." He gave her name an exotic intona-
tion. "Little witch. I've given you time. Don't you
remember that you're mine even now?"

"Nay." She mouthed the word rather than said
it. It wasn't true, was it? Those dreams had been
simply dreams, induced by his magic. They
couldn't be fragments of memory, replaying in her
head . . .

Leaning down, he smoothed it from her lips.
"Don't tell me 'no.' I won't allow it."

"Please kiss me."

"I am kissing you."

The echo of their voices from another time
haunted her . . . until his lips, petal-smooth, drifted

across her skin. His breath, warm and heavy with sensuality, coaxed her to try and capture it, and when she opened her lips to do so, his tongue touched her. Briefly, almost chastely, but laden with promise of more.

"More," she whispered.

He complied. In little teasing portions, he enticed her to open her mouth wider, to join him in a feast of flavor so sensual she imagined she had tasted him like this before. Her eyes drifted shut, and as they did she heard a rumble of thunder, saw a flash of lightning so bright it struck beneath her lids.

Her eyes flew open. She shoved at Ian, and when he lifted his head, she stared around, stricken.

The meadow looked as brilliantly green as it had all afternoon. A blue so intense as to be azure tinted the sky, and the clouds were white and puffy . . . She stared at one right over her head as it formed a dragon, complete with scales. She blinked, thinking it would disappear, but instead it opened its mouth and blew a wisp of smoke.

Her gaze shot back to Ian. "Did you do that?"

"Kiss you?" He smiled with slow, sentient intent. "Yes, it was definitely me."

Magic. Not that she needed reminding of it, but the man made magic. He'd caught her in his coils as surely as a dragon captured treasure, and like the dragon, he gazed at her with eyes that coveted and promised.

Briefly Alanna thought of the Quaker girl, and pitied her. Nowhere in this world would that girl find another man who could kiss like Ian, and she would always compare. Always. No woman could kiss Ian and not remember.

Remember . . .

"Nay." She turned her head away. She wouldn't remember.

The warmth of the sun struck her through her chemise, and she realized he had pushed her gown off her shoulders.

How did he always do that? Just last night, he'd stripped away her nightgown before she had realized it. But that had been a dream. A dream that seemed so real . . . She caught his wrists in her hands. "This isn't civilized."

"Civilized?" He flung back his head and laughed, hearty laughter that echoed in the open air and made mockery of her refined protest. "Civilization is the last thing on my mind right now. What I want is primitive, basic, hot and sweaty, and so good it'll bring tears to your eyes." Leaning closer, he whispered, "Let me make you want it, too."

He offered a secret. A secret no one else knew about, a secret that would change her life. A secret no well-bred lady should know, but one that she, Alanna, desired. His face filled her vision; his gaze compelled her.

"Alanna." On his lips, her mere name created an incantation.

She responded. Beneath her chemise, her breasts tightened, wanting his mouth. His beautiful, carnal mouth.

Slowly his lips formed a smile. With large, warm hands, he lifted her necklace and looked a question. She nodded and helped him remove it, placing it with care into the basket. Then he drew down her chemise. She was bared to the air, to the sky, to the sun, and when he looked on her, his wonder created a havoc of pleasure.

Then he kissed her breast, and the brush of his lips against the outer arc of flesh banished whatever modesty clung to her mind.

"Oh, please." She strained upward, wanting him to

*open his mouth on her, to suckle, to somehow assuage
the craving she experienced in each sensitive place in her
body. In the most sensitive place of her body.*

"Alanna."

She woke from the repeat of an oft-repeated
dream, and found him with her, real and strong,
caressing her breasts with his fingertips.

"You're beautiful," he murmured. "The perfect
size." He cupped her. "Skin the color of cream,
with toasted flecks to dazzle the eye."

"Freckles," she said, trying to gain a grip on reality.

"I will kiss each one." Holding her, he bent and
started on his task. "Promise me they'll lead me
down to the seat of heaven."

Deep in her belly, the familiar ache formed. From
his tempting words? Or from his skillful touch? She
couldn't say. She didn't know. With each caress, he
pulled her deeper into her own dreamworld. A
dreamworld he'd produced out of storm and wind.
Had he enchanted her, or had she conjured this out
of her own fertile imagination?

She looked down at his head, at the glossy hair
sweeping her skin. She touched it, felt the strands
between her fingers. She delved deeper, massaged
his scalp, moved to trace his ears.

This was real. He was real.

He rubbed his cheek against her chest. "You are
innovative."

Her fingers checked. "What did you say?" *He'd
said that before.*

Lifting his head, he smiled at her. "I said—it's
time to remember."

Before she could demand he explain how he
could repeat every utterance of her dreams, he
rolled her over.

"Ian, please tell me—"

"You already know." Untying her petticoats, he slid them down her legs.

She knew, yes, but she didn't dare believe. If she could, she would turn and confront him, but . . . she was almost nude. Her short chemise reached no farther than her knees. Her garters tied her stockings in the middle of her thighs. And while her boots protected her feet very well, she doubted Ian cared whether he caught an illicit glimpse of her toes. Briefly she thought of Wilda and her pantalettes, and sent a small apology toward Fionnaway. The pantalettes she'd scorned would have provided at least a little protection from his gaze.

"Lie still," he whispered, close against her ear. "Listen."

She stiffened. She didn't want to be caught half-clothed and tangled in his arms by shepherds. Frozen, she listened for voices, but heard only the swish of the waves, the call of the gulls, the faint rustle of the wind.

"What do you see?"

"The blanket, the grass," Frantically she looked around. "There's nothing here."

His hands roamed up her legs, pushing the hem of the chemise ahead. "Exactly. There's no rescue to be had. Only the birds can see, and they approve. Believe me, they approve."

Furious with him, she said, "The devil take you."

"The devil's had me. Is it any wonder I want to sleep in an angel's arms?" His fingers stroked her skin as delicately as he might stroke the feathers of one of those birds. His breath nudged the base of her spine. "You can fly me straight to heaven."

Something touched her. His mouth. Dear God, he kissed her there, and she couldn't bear it. Bunching the blanket in her fists, she demanded, "What are you doing?"

Her voice got higher, and he murmured, "Sh. I'm not hurting you." The air from his assurance melded with the breeze. "Can you identify that fragrance?" he asked.

"What fragrance? There's only crushed grass." She shut her eyes against the twin sensations of embarrassment and pleasure, and the scents of the day came to her more acutely. "The woolen blanket. The tang from the sea."

"And you. You're like a perfume, enticing me to sample you." With the flat of his palms, he rubbed the muscles of her upper back, then slowly descended along her spine. He cupped her buttocks, then lightly touched one finger at the top of her cleft. She jumped, her eyes flying open.

"Don't! That's not nice."

"Nice?" He chuckled. "I cannot think of anything nicer. Unless . . ."

That finger roved down, waking nerves she didn't know existed. She tried to close her legs against him, but somehow he'd gotten his knee between her thighs. She gave up her last tenuous hold on dignity and tried to crawl away.

He crushed her onto the blanket with his body and with his hand on the back of her neck, turned her face to the side, and brought his face to hers. She caught a flash of his intent as he commanded, "Taste this."

He crushed their lips together, and she tasted *him*. Smoky warmth and salty passion. A savor that blocked out the scents, the sights, the sounds of the day and left her wanting more of him. Just him.

Lifting himself, he rolled her over and tucked her back beneath him. The chemise was bunched under her shoulders, still draped across her front, but this time he didn't use care in raising it. This time he just grabbed and jerked, as if he couldn't wait to see, and when he could, he groaned. "You are perfect." His turbulent watching devoured her. "Let me . . ." He urged her arms up. "I want to see it all."

He flung the cotton garment away as if it were nothing but a rag, looking at her as if she were his fantasy come to life. Embarrassment burned away under the heat of his gaze, and pride and the first tendrils of desire took its place.

Desire. How could she recognize it?

"I take my rights, as any good man must. Don't you remember that night in the witch's hut?"

"I don't. I swear I don't."

"Let me remind you."

She turned her head away, denying memory, but he wouldn't allow her to separate herself from him, or from a single moment of the day.

His hand moved deliberately, and he touched a nipple with just one fingertip. One fingertip, and her nipple tightened. Her breasts ached almost as if he'd hurt her.

But it had only been one fingertip. One incredibly gentle fingertip.

His touch didn't feel alien. It seemed familiar, as if she'd experienced it more than once. Really experienced it, not just dreamed it at night. Not just imagined it in the day.

"Don't you remember that night in the witch's hut?"

He circled her nipple, watching his own movement with a fascination that seemed foolish. Foolish. She lifted her head and looked, too, and the sight of his dark hand against her fair skin captured her. Moving gradually, afraid he would stop if she made a sudden movement, she brought her arm up and pillowed her head with it.

He didn't stop. He just looked at her face, his eyelids drooping. "What do you feel?" Slowly he expanded the circles he drew. One by one he added fingers until his whole hand brushed her. "Tell me what you feel."

"I can't." He wanted her to talk, when she could scarcely drag her attention away from the growing torture deep within.

This was just like her dreams.

This was better than her dreams.

Obligingly he lifted his hand. "Does that help?"

Just like her dreams. He would take her to the edge. Then he'd stop. "Nay!" She grabbed his hand and placed it back where it belonged.

He smiled, slow and sure and hot. "This is what you want?" Cupping her, he pressed heavily.

That relieved the pressure. Not enough, but it helped. "Aye."

He held her, then lifted his other hand. He reached for her other nipple; drew back. "Would you like me to touch you there?"

Anticipation choked her, but she managed to insist, "Aye!"

"First tell me. Tell me how you feel."

Didn't he understand? She couldn't talk, much less describe—

He lifted both hands away.

"It feels good." She spoke in a rush.

"Good?" His hands hovered close to her body. "How?"

She tried to find the words. She truly did. But all she could say was, "Really good."

His fingertip touched her other nipple, and she almost came off the blanket. "Describe that," he said.

"It burns." Desperation drove her to eloquence. "Like a splash of icy rain or a winter's wave."

"It's cold?"

"Not cold. Shocking. But"—she struggled for the right word—"proper."

"Proper?" He grinned, a shark's smile. "I never do anything proper." Taking his hand away anyway, he replaced it with his mouth.

She sucked in a shocked and ragged breath as his tongue licked her delicately.

"Tell me." Air puffed across the wetness of her skin. "What do you feel?"

"All my skin is hot, and I want . . . so much."

Taking her nipple into his mouth, he suckled, wreaking such havoc she groaned. Horrified at the primitive need she'd unconsciously expressed, she covered her mouth.

Reaching up, he took her hand away. "That's one of the sounds *I* want to hear."

Permission didn't ease her embarrassment, but when he held one breast and squeezed the nipple, she groaned again.

"Tell me how you feel."

"Out of control." She tried to clutch his hair.

He lifted her arms back up. "*Tell* me."

"You're right for me," she cried. "This is right . . ."

"Because you're mine."

She didn't answer. He demanded too much.

"Say it." He shook her shoulders lightly. "You're mine."

She tried to remember she was the MacLeod. That everything and everybody in Fionnaway depended on her. That her mother had made an impulsive decision to wed, and they'd all paid. That she didn't really know much about Ian.

"I won't say it. I can't."

He drew back, framed by blue sky and drifting clouds. The wind fluttered his dark hair, teasing the locks like gentle fingers. The sun sought his face, fighting the shadow for the pure pleasure of caressing his nose, his brow, the soft, plain curve of his lips. One of his bees buzzed close, dreaming it could drink of his nectar.

And Alanna was jealous of the wind, the sun, the foolish bee.

"Is it because you believe my father? Will you not take me because I'm a"—he stumbled over the word—"half-breed?"

"Nay!" Without the protection of his body, her skin chilled. Without his wanton caress, her body suffered.

He looked away. The sun blazed onto his face, lighting him harshly, revealing his thoughts. He'd been rejected before. He didn't believe Alanna.

And to see him now, frustrated, disappointed, made her forget duty and honor for the greater delectation of making him happy. So she told him the truth that she had hoped to keep as a weapon. "I've lived here all my life, and swum in that ocean, and never seen a selkie. But I've heard the tales, I've seen the evidence, and while we don't talk about it, of all the clans, the MacLeods are the last to deny their existence. Your father's not lying, is he?"

His chest rose hard and sharp as he took a breath and braced himself against the blow. "For once in his life, he's honest."

A selkie. All her life she'd longed to see one, to have the chance to truly believe that everything about her heritage was true. Now she lay with a man who turned his face away, who expected to be renounced for his birthright, and the rightness of it sang like a chord from some heavenly chorus. "It explains so much." Reaching out to touch his face was as brave a thing as she'd ever done.

He flinched slightly as if he expected a blow.

Instead, she stroked his cheek with her fingertips,

half expecting he would transform himself and disappear like the clouds above.

Instead his jaw clenched.

Digging her fingers into his beard, she turned his face back to hers. His eyes with their mystical silver sparks looked at her deeply. Too deeply, and she found herself saying, "You're not the first, Ian Fairchild, to brag of a selkie parent. That's why . . ." But nay, she could not tell him. Not yet. That information was reserved for her husband.

More, it wasn't important right now. Right now she had to give him what he wanted. She had to make him happy. "Ian, I'm yours."

Those brown eyes watched her warily, and suspicion stiffened his generous mouth. "Truly mine?"

She found herself tugging him toward her. "Aye."

Untangling her fingers from his beard, he examined them. The short fingernails, the freckled skin, the calluses from grinding herbs. Then he scrutinized her face, wary and hopeful at once. In a gentle tone he said, "If you believe that—if you accept me as I am—then, my darling Alanna, there'll be no escape for you. You are truly mine, now and forevermore."

And taking her hand, he laid it on his ring.

Chapter 19

The stone felt cool and smooth, almost alive. Ian trapped Alanna's hand between both of his and looked deeply into her eyes. "You freely give yourself to me?"

She began to feel dizzy as around her, the world changed. Colors brightened, senses heightened; she had said she believed, and Ian now took her into a different world. One she dared not name.

His compelling gaze held her as she repeated, "To you."

"Listen to me." His warm, deep voice wove a spell. "You'll remember this day."

"Of course." The stone warmed.

"All of the day. Everything. There'll be no more forgetting between us. Whenever the scent of crushed grass drifts to you on the wind, whenever the rough wool of a blanket scratches your skin, whenever you see clouds drifting through a blue sky, whenever you hear the call of seabirds, you'll think of me."

He wanted too much, and she tried to deny him. *Nay.* But the word wouldn't form on her lips.

"Whenever pleasure is so great as to be almost pain, whenever you long for more than you can have on this earth, you'll think of me. I'll be all

218

around you, always. You'll never go a moment without knowing I'm there. I'll be part of you, forever."

Was this a claiming, or a curse?

"Do you understand?" he whispered.

If it was a curse, it came too late, for she knew he was right. Even if at this moment a great draft swept them away and set them down on the opposite ends of the earth, she would remember him. Him, this day, and her yielding. "Aye."

He let go of her hand slowly, as if reluctant to separate from the mystical bond of their souls.

Slowly she came back to the hill, to the whispering grasses, the breeze across her skin, and gleaming blue sky over Ian's shoulder.

He stripped off his trousers, tossing them on top of her chemise in some kind of symbolic dominance. His shirttail covered the parts she didn't want to see, yet still she looked him over, all over, as if knowing would diminish her fear.

He towered over her as she lay on the blanket. She knew of his height already. She knew his shoulders filled out his shirts and his hands were capable. She hadn't realized, though, that his thighs were knotted with muscle. They rippled beneath the tanned skin like an unspoken warning. With them he would control a horse . . . or ride a woman.

Kneeling beside her, he held out his shirt-clad arms. "You do the cuffs."

He hadn't mentioned she would know his aroma. But she did. The masculine odors of saddle leather and fresh air mixed with his own scent. And what scent was that? The combination of earthy odors urged her to sit up, to do as he instructed, to complete this act before heat and frustration burned her to cinders. While she still had the chance to hold back a little of her soul.

She wiggled the fastenings free and with an inattention that matched his own, discarded them into the grass. He didn't even notice, but kept his gaze fixed to her face as she opened his shirt and deliberately spread it.

A fine black mat of hair covered his chest, tapering down to a point. Then it expanded again as if to cover that which should be private. But nothing was private on this man. His body fairly shouted, "Look at me!" His erection rose, large and sculptured, drawing her gaze.

As he slipped free of his shirt, she contemplated running again. Then the full effect of the sunshine struck him, and her mouth grew dry. He was beautiful. Beautiful and menacing and—

He caught her chin in his hand and lifted her face to his. "Mine," he reminded her. "You're mine, and I won't hurt you. You will believe me."

She just stared.

"I scarcely hurt you the first time. You remember how careful I was."

She heard the echo of his voice again. *Don't you remember that night in the witch's hut?*

His hand slid down her neck, over her breast, behind her back, and he tipped her over onto the blanket. "I certainly won't hurt you now."

She was torn between shutting her eyes and leaving them open. Between touching him and desisting. Yet some instinct or forgotten memory made her slide her hands around his shoulders as he lowered himself to her.

He liked that, she thought, for he paused for a moment, hanging over her with an expression of anguished gratification. She understood anguished gratification. She'd experienced it before, and now at the pressure of his chest on hers, it swelled in her again.

The scent of the wool blanket and the crushed grass rose from beneath her as he gently kissed her mouth. Gently, until she remembered the pleasure of his kissing. Then he pressed harder, opened her more. Her breath came faster, and she clutched at him.

But he wore no shirt, no clothing at all, and her fingers clambered along his bare skin, desperately seeking something to hold, something to keep her connected to this earth.

"That's it," he whispered. "Touch me. Touch as much as you want."

She did want. She wanted very badly. His muscles contracted as she moved over them. She found his collarbone, explored the cords of his arms, wandered tentatively to his chest. He didn't move, didn't even breathe when her fingers delved into the curly hair to seek out his nipples. She stroked them gingerly, trying to imitate his earlier seduction, and all the while she wondered—did he like that as much as she did?

"You're killing me," he answered her unspoken question, speaking between clenched teeth. "I'm going to expire from frustration."

So he *did* like that. Emboldened, she slid down over his ribs, but he caught her.

"That's all I can take." He placed her hands on the blanket beside her neck. "Another time when I'm not quite so hungry for you . . . although I can't imagine when that would be."

She wanted to protest. Then he kissed the cord in her neck, sliding down it as if it were a directional arrow on a country road. He suckled one nipple, then another, and she was sure nothing could ever feel so good, yet be so frustrating.

Until he touched her. There.

A shaft of memory entered her mind. A hard,

throbbing thrust. He had done this before. *She'd* done this before.

She looked into his eyes and gasped at the flame. This would be no genteel blackmail, but a primitive claiming. If he took her now, what she feared would come to pass. He would seize control of her lands, her life. She would not be Alanna alone; she would be part of him.

In the witch's hut. Lightning. Thunder. Her lover's voice. Pleasure—and pain.

"Don't you remember that night in the witch's hut?"

"What?" she cried out as if an answer would emerge from the air.

Her cry didn't seem to startle him. He seemed to know what she was discovering, and his dark face gleamed with triumph. "Mine," he said. "Remember."

"Nay!" Caught in a riptide of panic, she shoved him so hard he sprawled backward. Scrambling to her feet, she fled. Grass slapped her thighs; she panted as if she'd run for miles. But it wasn't exhaustion that drove her, but desperation. Not physical need, but emotions.

She didn't get far. Once again he tackled her, but this time he didn't roll to catch her. This time he let her land flat on her face, then held her down as she squirmed.

"You promised," he said, and his voice shook. He spun her over, and she let out a little scream at the rage on his face. "You said you were mine."

"Aye, but—" But what? She didn't even know. She only knew that if she let those memories in, let him in, everything would change. Something waited within those memories, something frightening.

"No." Slashing the air with his hand, he said, "No *buts*. You're mine. You can fight all you want, but you're mine." He dragged her through the grass until her bottom rested on his thighs and her legs were spread around his waist. With one arm he lifted her. With the other hand he positioned himself. "Don't you dare shut your eyes." He nudged at the center of her.

She was on the ground. He sat above. Her position was submissive. His was dominant. She glared at him as she fought him, trying to buck him off.

He grinned, but not affably. This grin accepted the challenge she presented and warned of his tenacity. "That's it. Don't make it easy. Make it a war, so I can win."

She shouted then, every swear word she'd ever heard. She twisted and struggled. Nothing affected him. He just kept grinning and holding on to her carefully, allowing her to move—but not away from him.

At last she stopped, panting. She'd accomplished nothing, and he still touched her, sliding his shaft along until it was damp with her unwilling excitement.

She turned her face away.

"No." He stopped. Taking her jaw in his hand, he turned her head until she looked at him again. "You watch me. This time I don't want you to ever forget." Lifting himself to his knees, he brought her hips off the ground. Holding her thighs, he found the center of her and pushed.

"Remember."

And as she took that deliberate, deep thrust into herself, she did. She remembered everything.

Lightning flashed so brightly she saw it beneath her closed eyelids. Thunder crashed in heaven's cacophony. Her foot throbbed, but distantly, eased by the drugs she had taken. And a man's weight beside her on the bed, warming with his body as he slept beside her. Then his seduction. Kisses so sweet they lulled her old fears. Caresses that pursued her delight. Intimacies such as she'd never imagined.

And was only this morning rediscovering.

She'd tucked memories deep into her mind, but the narcotics she'd taken were no match for the reality of Ian.

"Ah." He smiled at her expression. "You know now, don't you?"

If she didn't admit it, she could save herself.

"You do." While nestled deep within her, he laughed out loud. The wind caught it and carried it up so everyone could hear.

She wanted to tell him to hush, but he stroked again, and the muscles inside her clutched at him.

"Dear Lord." His eyes half closed. "You're glorious." He wrapped her legs around his hips and lowered her to the ground, lay on her, and surged into her again. "You remember." He surged again. "You remember." Again. "Remember."

His chest against hers, his breath on her face, the rasp of his beard, the thrust of him deep inside her—it was familiar. It was good. Compulsively she curled herself around him, taking him, wanting him, claiming him in her own way.

Driven by his need, he moved quickly, then more quickly, pushing her into the grass, receiving gratification from her flesh, shaking and gasping and straining.

And when he crushed himself against her open body, the tremors shook her. This wasn't the same. This wasn't a memory. This was better than before, greater than she'd dreamed. She cried out her pleasure and he laughed as he came slowly to rest on her.

With both hands he cupped her face. "Mine." He said it as if he couldn't get enough of the word.

"All mine." Dazed and overwhelmed as she was, he kissed her, a conqueror's kiss, and smiled a master's smile. "All happiness on your birthday, Alanna. You've reached your majority today."

Now she remembered everything, and knew why she had fought it so much.

She remembered . . . she had given him all her soul the first time they'd made love. This time she'd given him her heart.

She loved him. Loved a man who wanted her so he could take control of her home. So he could usurp her place in Fionnaway.

When a selkie mates with a leg-walker, they marry, or not, and if there's a child, a protocol must be followed. First the child must be examined by the elders, and its nature determined. Human or selkie? They look to see, and if the babe is human, the selkie parent must stay on land. Twelve years a selkie is given before it must go back to the sea. Twelve years of exposure to the parching air, the malicious sunlight, the ordeal of living with aliens. Yet even the gradual withering of the body and soul is rewarded, for the children who come of these unions are always special. Always different. Always magical.

Chapter 20

"Did I hurt you?" Ian watched Alanna closely as he fed her chunks of cold rabbit.

"Nay," she whispered.

He'd dressed her in his white shirt to protect her fair skin from the sun, and because it seemed to comfort her, he replaced her necklace so it dangled against her skin.

She looked fragile seated on the wool blanket. Beneath the hat he'd brought her, wisps of grass stuck throughout the copper strands of hair. Her lips were red, too, from his kisses, and a worthy man should have felt guilty for giving her that beard burn across her chin.

Ian didn't. He felt damned good. In fact, he couldn't remember when he had felt better. "More bread?"

"Nay."

She hadn't said one voluntary word since he'd held her down with his body and forced pleasure on her. She'd just sat with her arms across her belly, answering his questions and eating his food, and all the time appearing to be a little lost.

She didn't realize it, but those dreams he'd teased her with had teased him, too. He'd gotten no satisfaction from those nightly meetings of the

mind, and his body had ached, too full and wanting for restraint. Now, with the pressure slightly
allayed, he could coax her and court her and pretend he didn't want her again right now. Which he
did.

With his thumb he dislodged a crumb from her
lower lip. Then, unable to stop, he stroked her un-
smiling mouth. "Are you going to say you didn't
enjoy it?"

"Are you going to demand I talk about it?"

"No. I suppose not. I can make that concession
to your modesty." He glanced down. She sat
crossed-legged, everything but her knees concealed
by his shirttails. He couldn't see what rested beneath, but he could imagine. "It is modesty which
stops you, isn't it?"

"You know it is."

"I don't know anything about women." *No more
than any man.* "I only know I felt every ripple."

Startled, she clutched at the shirt she wore. "Ripple?"

"Inside you."

She set her teeth and glared, but all that mattered
was her blush.

"Did you think I wouldn't know?" he inquired.

"I don't know what you know. I don't know
much about how this works." She snapped at him
like a little bitch terrier turning on her first stud,
and he was relieved to hear it. She'd been so sub-
dued, he'd started to worry. He'd been too rough,
and yet . . . and yet she'd been almost cruel. She'd
tried too hard to deny her memories, to drive him
away, and he couldn't allow her more time.

Today was her birthday. Time was what he did
not have.

He smiled at her. "Virgin."

"Not this time."

Her voice was faint, but he heard her and he remembered. The night at the witch's hut. Her drugged sleep, the seduction he had deemed necessary. Her startled response, and his own fervent desire.

Was he suffering from guilt? No, surely not. He'd weighed his options thoroughly before he'd gone to her that night, and events had proven his wisdom. However, he now found to his surprise a man could be confident and still need to employ tact with the woman he had manipulated.

Alanna looked off to the side as if something waited there that needed her inspection, but when he glanced, he saw only the windswept grasses. She avoided his gaze, so he let his hand drift down to burrow beneath the hem of her shirt. *His* shirt. She jumped at his touch, but he just stroked her ankle and imagined how she was open, available to him if he wished.

Of course, he'd make her wish, too. "I'll teach you everything you need to know about this."

"I thought you already had."

He chuckled, low and deep in his throat. "We've barely begun. We'll find a bed, and stay there all day and all night, and that'll be just the beginning for us . . . when we are wed."

She flinched.

He felt the movement in her ankle, and he almost flinched as well. Hating to know, but realizing he had to, he asked, "Do I repulse you?"

"Repulse me? Do you jest?" She gestured, a quick little movement that took her protective hand away from her body. She tucked it hastily back, as though motion indicated an ease she didn't feel. "I think it's obvious you don't repulse me."

"Because you respond to me when we—"

"Sh." She glared.

He smothered a grin and tried to explain. "There are things that can be done to a woman to make her receptive to a man."

She watched him inquisitively.

"I'm said to be proficient..." He supposed he shouldn't brag, and losing all patience and delicacy, he said, "Like this." His hand jumped from her calf and onto her inner thigh.

Muffling a shriek, she grabbed for him through the cotton, but he kept his motions tender and discreet. She had him by the wrist, pressing down as if that would stop him, but he let his fingers circle lazily along the soft skin in the middle of her thigh.

Eyes wide, she watched him, waiting for him to pounce.

Of course, he had no such scheme. She might deny he had hurt her, but he'd been too rough for an almost-virgin and he couldn't take her again. Although ... he'd donned his trousers as a sop to her modesty, and they fit too tightly again.

But regardless of the demands of the tyrant between his legs, he couldn't use Alanna so selfishly. He had truly established his claim; now was the time for wooing.

Wistfully he withdrew his fingers, trailing them beneath her thigh, beneath her knee, and along her slim, smooth calf, shaped by years of climbing the rugged Scottish terrain. She scrutinized his every movement, and responded to his charming smile not at all.

He had some work to do. Scooting over so he sat beside her, he wrapped his arm around her shoulders. Her *rigid* shoulders. She stared stiffly forward, but he lifted his knee just in case she glanced down. He didn't think his cockstand would do much in the way of reassuring her. "There's more to this than you and me. There's your estate, and the people on it. My father is still in residence. Your cousin is still your heir. I'm not like them. You know that when you marry me, I'll help you to care for Fionnaway. You can trust me."

"Why?" she asked belligerently. "I don't know anything about you."

His fingers clenched on her arm. "You know my deepest secret." Then he recalled he was supposed to be coaxing her. He loosened his grip and softened his tone. "My father couldn't wait to share that. You believed him, and you didn't say a word. Why?"

"Everyone has their secrets, Ian." She looked at him sideways.

Did she have secrets? Of course she did. He could see them hovering about her in muted soft colors.

Would she tell him her secrets? Not yet, but he could cajole her. He could make love to her. He could slip past her guard and someday know her as well as she knew herself.

"Tell me about yourself," she coaxed. "Convince me I should depend upon you to stay here."

Cautiously he slid back on the blanket and reclined on his elbows. "What do you want to know?"

She relaxed a little. "How did your father meet your mother?"

"I believe he and your father were friends. That *is* why he's your guardian."

She bent her knees, pulled the shirt over them, and hunched forward as if the mere mention of her father gave her a bellyache. "Aye, Mr. Fairchild is just the sort of man my father would have called an all-righter."

"Leslie came here to visit—to sponge, if I want to be correct—and somehow met my mother. That is, of course, all I know for sure, but I imagine he made promises he never intended to keep, got her pregnant, and fled back to England." He waited tensely to see if she would comment about the lack of a marriage.

She didn't even seem to notice, and he wasn't truly surprised. Why would a woman who dealt with his beastliness be disturbed he was also a bastard? He probably could have confessed that he dressed in women's clothing—his father's poorly kept secret—and she still would have shrugged.

She probed a little deeper. "Do you remember your mother?"

He didn't want to answer. He'd never told anyone. But this was Alanna. Practically his wife. She still clutched her legs close like a babe with a bellyache, and if he wished to convince her to wed him, he would have to concede at least a little of the truth to obtain her trust.

Besides, she wouldn't mock or laugh. He knew that. So like a man opening a long-closed and rusty door, he unlocked his memories. "I do."

"What did she look like?"

"Like a human." He squinted, trying to see his mother down the lengthy tunnel of time. "And so beautiful, with her dark hair and sweet smile. I was her son, so of course, I thought so, but I remember the men hanging around. They wanted her, each one, until she . . . looked at them. She had a way to seeing clear down to your soul. Her eyes would get cloudy, almost silver—"

"Like yours."

He paused and tensed, wondering what other half-breed manifestations he showed. "Do they? I didn't know. I suppose that's why people start stepping backward when I stare at them."

"One of the reasons. Do you, too, see down into people's souls?"

He touched his ring. He'd worn it on his hand since the day his mother had left him at Fairchild Manor. She'd taken it from the chain around his neck and told him it was time. Then she'd slipped it on his finger, and said it would help him make his way through the confusion of human emotions. It had; it was the ring that enabled him to see auras, and the stone that helped him judge others' characters. Yet without being told, he knew the stone would not work in such a manner on another's hand, so he answered Alanna. "No, but I'm only half a selkie."

She stretched out her legs and wiggled her toes, watching them intently. "People stare at you because of your height, I think, and because you give the impression of . . . I don't know . . . of dominance."

"So I would be a good husband for the lady of Fionnaway," he quipped.

"You are persistent."

"Another worthy attribute."

"You don't belong here."

Agony struck him, a hot brand to his heart. Sitting up, he grabbed her arms and forced her to face him. "I do! There is nowhere else that I belong but here."

"Ian, you're hurting me."

Her eyes were wide, and he glanced down to see his fingers biting into her flesh.

Nothing that she had ever said, none of her denials, had jolted him as did her refusal to share Fionnaway. Scrupulously he loosened his grip. "I'm sorry." He stroked the red marks he had left on her skin. Bending his head to hide the anguish he feared must show in his eyes, he tried to explain in a way she would comprehend. "But I do belong here. I have been like a stray mongrel, searching for a place that filled my soul. I have found it here. Fionnaway is like the scent of fresh bread to a starving man, or a mother's touch to a newborn babe. I do belong here, Alanna. I do."

She didn't say anything, and he realized he'd been too intense. He'd spoken too dramatically, he'd made his vulnerability known. Now Alanna, like his father, like the Quaker girl, like all of society, had the power to strike him down if she wished.

Did she wish?

Carefully she slid her arms out from beneath his relaxed hold. "I have a temper which betrays me, as it did on this occasion. I spoke unwisely. Fionnaway is indeed your home for as long as you desire."

Her hands rested beneath his, palm to palm. The fine bones, the sinews, the pads and lines of skin, were open to him, vulnerable and yet quiescent. She trusted him not to abuse her, although his violent desires seemed close to the surface and almost ungovernable when she was near. Now they bubbled in him, making a mockery of his determination to allow her time to accept him.

He just wanted a home. He just wanted *her*. She'd made no vows before the minister; he was mad to jeopardize her goodwill with a display of unwanted passion.

Yet of its own will, one hand rose and cupped her chin. The other rose and cupped her breast. "Alanna." He meant to sound seductive. He sounded imperious. "I'll have you again now, whether you will or not."

Without a hint of shyness, she looked into his eyes. "Then I'd better agree, hadn't I?"

Chapter 21

Alanna stood and discarded her hat. "Come along. I have something to show you."

Ian sat frozen with surprise as she walked up the hill, and when he still hadn't moved, she glanced over her shoulder. "Are you coming or no?"

The question might be unconsciously provocative, but that way she dipped her head and looked at him from beneath lowered lashes was not. How had the lass learned such a trick in so short a time? She'd been an innocent not a month ago, and now Mother Nature had taught her how to bring a man panting to her side.

Finding himself on his feet, he decided he was not one to challenge Mother Nature. Alanna disappeared over the summit, and he hurried, anxious to walk at her side. Then, as he crested the promontory, he slowed. What a stirring sight to see her walk among the grass. Her dainty feet scarcely bruised the ground. Her bare legs cut through the stalks, and the ripening heads slipped beneath the tail of the shirt she wore and teased her where he longed to touch.

Descending the slope toward a run of trees, she never looked back to see if he was following. She could probably hear the requisite panting, he acknowledged, for with every step his need grew stronger.

A line of trees crowned the ground ahead, and as she neared them she bent, giving him a glimpse of her pale thighs and a round curve of buttocks.

Then, as if the ground swallowed her, she disappeared.

Torn between lust and alarm, he skidded down the incline. She couldn't be hurt; she knew this area too well. Yet . . . without warning, a small chasm opened at his feet. Only a short distance below, he could hear the splash of water as it tumbled over rocks, and farther upstream, the deeper spatter of a waterfall. He tottered on the edge, then plunged off. Before he had fallen even his own height, the ground came up and met him, and he stumbled, trying to save himself. Falling, he rolled, and when he opened his eyes, he found himself staring up at a frowning Alanna as she stood by his head.

"I always thought you were so graceful," she said.

He could see up her shirt. His shirt. The shirt. He could see . . . everything. Her legs, and between them the pouting lips lightly covered by hair, and beneath those . . .

"Did you hurt yourself?" She still frowned at him, blatantly unconscious of the direction of his thoughts.

Speechless with absolute, total pleasure, he shook his head. He hadn't hurt himself falling, but God help him, if he rolled over now he would suffer a mortal wound. She was nude, utterly naked, stark, staring . . . He was staring. She would notice. She would move away. He would die of desolation.

"I thought you would like this place. It's the upper reaches of the sheep creek, and quite clean . . ."

She studied him. "You look odd. Did you hit your head?"

He reached up to touch his head, and instead found his hand wrapped around her ankle.

"Ian, what are you . . . ?" Her voice trailed off; she cocked her head and studied him. Then she spoke, using a sultry note he'd never heard from her before. "Ian, are you looking at me?"

How could he admit it? How could he not?

She inched her free foot closer to his head. The other remained firmly planted on the ground, and he could see . . . more. She opened to him, and his hand began the long slide up to bliss.

"No." As she stepped away, her voice burbled with amusement. "I brought you here to see the waterfall, not me."

As she spun away, he grabbed and caught her calf. Giggling, she went down on her hands. He lost his grip, and she scrambled away before he could catch her again. With a whoop, she scampered down toward the brook, and instantly surging with energy, he gave chase. An arch of water splashed into the sunlight as she jumped off a high rock into the pool below the falls.

He stopped, his toes at the edge. "Alanna!"

She flipped in the deep water and dove, and for the second time in less than a minute, he caught a clear glimpse of her cleft, cupped by the globes of her bottom and followed by her strong legs, kicking toward the sky.

Never before had he understood how water nymphs lured their victims to drown, but now he did. He could see her in the depths, her powerful arms stroking, her feet kicking, his shirt streamlined along her body. Her hair flowed, a banner of silk caught in the current. He wanted to join her, yet—

She surfaced at the far side of the pool. "Bet you can't catch me," she taunted.

"I'll bet I can," he murmured. If the sight of her nudity fascinated him so much, wouldn't she be likewise enchanted? Other women had been, although with them he'd been annoyed to be valued like a horse. Now, above her on that boulder, he dispensed with his trousers and stood, naked, dappled by sunshine.

Alanna's mouth opened, her teeth caught her lower lip, and she unabashedly stared.

He didn't blame her; he didn't know when he'd ever been so aroused.

With the swift elegance on which he prided himself, he made his way down to the edge of the stream, just to where the water gathered itself into a narrow channel to flow down the hill. Here the water was only knee-deep, and, he found when he stepped into it, surprisingly cold. He spared a moment of thankfulness; at least he hadn't followed her in her mad dive.

With carefree insouciance, he splashed across to the other side and seated himself on a sunny boulder.

Alanna swam a little closer. "What are you doing?"

Stretching himself out full length, he rolled onto his side. "Warming myself." He propped his head on his elbow. "Go ahead and swim."

With a shrug, she did, twisting and turning in the water with every evidence of relish. His arousal grew sharper, needier, as with each kick of her legs she enticed him to join her. But he would not, and closing his eyes, he lay back on the rock. Here the sun cradled him, and he drifted, waiting for his prey, planning how he would take her.

Instead he was jerked from his reverie by the

splatter of cold pond on his warm skin. Rolling onto his side, he saw her treading water and laughing.

"Did I wake you?" she called. Cupping her hand, she splashed him once more.

He smiled, a slow, dangerous smile. She made it almost too easy.

Sitting up, he laid his hands flat on his chest and deliberately slid them through the beads there, leaving a glistening trail of water over his skin. He skimmed first one palm, then the other, down his arms, and with his tongue caught the drop that trickled to his mouth.

Her playfulness gone, she watched him, her gaze riveted to every movement as if engrossed by the sheen of his skin.

"Alanna, splash me again." He kept his tone intimate and persuasive.

She looked into his eyes, her mouth slightly open, her eyes wide.

"I'm warm, Alanna." He shook his hair, and droplets flew. "Splash me again."

Seemingly mesmerized by nothing more magical than his body, she swam toward him. When she got the ground beneath her feet, she walked out, and with each inch that was revealed, his gratitude to his ancestors grew. They had endowed him with his form; he would pass it on to his children.

The children he would have with Alanna.

She stepped onto his boulder, the shirt hugging her breasts, nipping her waist, caressing her hips.

He was jealous of his own shirt.

"Why are you watching me like that?" Her voice was a little hoarse, and droplets of water beaded on her thighs, then glided in an erotic dance down her legs.

"You look . . . cool. Like refreshment on a hot

day." Leaning back on his elbow, he extended his hand. "Come. Let me drink of you."

Putting her hand in his, she knelt beside him, her feet tucked under her. She kissed him, as easily as if they'd been mated for years, and her lips tasted of fresh mountain water and curiosity.

He wanted to take her head, to guide her, to show her what would pleasure them both. But he waited, wanting to see where her speculation would take them.

When she sat back up, he thought she'd failed in nerve or imagination. But no; she lifted her arms to her hair, and taking the weight of it between her hands, she leaned over him and wrung the water from her tresses.

He jumped as each drop splashed against his skin. She splattered him from his chest to his toes, and when she was done, she imitated him. She put her pale hands on his tan skin and spread the water into a thin film that glistened in the sun, then evaporated.

It should have cooled him; it didn't. She started with his shoulders, smoothing them. She stroked his pectorals, swirling her touch around each nipple. If she had more experience, he might have thought she was teasing him. But her expression was absorbed as she watched her own hands moving over him, exploring the muscles beneath the skin and stroking the sprinkling of dark hair above.

He liked it. More than liked it. His heart pounded, his breath caught. If someone was performing magic here, it was Alanna. Unable to keep still, he lifted his knee and gripped it with his fist.

His movement seemed to startle her out of her absorption. She looked down at his legs, at the cord of muscle on his inner thigh, and with her fingertip she traced it.

He audibly sucked in his breath. She looked into his face and smiled.

That smile! All feminine, all knowing. How had she learned so quickly? What had he created?

Moving to his feet, she sprinkled them with water and her strong hands slid along, up to his ankles, along his calves, over his knees. She massaged his thighs, and when he tensed in a silent groan of pleasure, she pressed and kneaded each clearly delineated muscle.

His bait had worked almost too well. His body captivated her, and he in turn was being ravished by her.

He held his breath as she reached his groin, wondering if she'd ignore it in maidenly embarrassment.

He should have known better. Not Alanna. Not his wild creature. Dabbling her fingers in the water that pooled at the juncture of his hips and belly, she stroked his balls, tormenting him with her light touch. His fists clamped shut when one fingertip traveled up the length of his erection, and she fastidiously dabbed the single drop of semen her handling had forced from him. She stared at it, fascinated, then slowly brought it to her mouth and touched it to her tongue.

"Alanna!" Aroused beyond bearing, he grabbed for her.

She twisted away. "No. I get to do it!" She shoved back at him and he let her, not caring how she took him, only that she did.

She climbed on him, wrapping her legs around him and clasping him in greedy demand. Lifting herself, she wrapped her hands around him and placed him where he wanted to be. "Here?" she questioned.

"Right there."

She was ready, soft and wet, brought to passion by the sight of his body, by the touch of her hand on his flesh. She was his, attuned to his desire so acutely that pleasure reverberated between them and grew as it journeyed.

The lust to be inside her brought his hands up on her bottom. He helped her, and her muscles flexed in his palms as she brought him into herself. As her passage closed around him, it was as if he were the virgin, receiving instruction from his first woman . . . his only woman. God, the heat of her burned him, set him afire and made him want to take her now, take her later, make her know she was his and no other's.

Her eyes had closed, her expression intent, absorbing the still new sensation of holding a man within her. Slowly she lifted herself, and as his rod moved along her passage, he slammed against the hard edge of ecstasy. The shirt still molded her body, the tails tickled his thighs and stomach. She paused, hovering over him. She opened her eyes, looked down at him—and she brought her arms up to her head. Her breasts rose as she moved, her nipples hard as raspberries beneath the finest cream.

Taking her hair, she shook it over him. He could only be surprised that the droplets didn't sizzle against his bare skin.

"I'm trying to cool you." It was blatant lie, for she sank down on him again, then rose and sank again. She used the heels of her hands against his stomach, dispersing the water over the ripple of muscle there. "Are you cooler now?"

He blazed in fiery agony. He shouldn't have been able to feel anything but the tightness of her, but her hands added to the punishment. The beads of water she'd not yet captured dribbled along his ribs, and every drop of his blood fought for the luxury of being inside the part of him buried inside her.

"You're a witch."

"I know." She smiled smugly.

Too smugly. He had weapons to wield in this carnal battle, and one of his hands coasted from her bottom to the front. With two fingers he opened her folds and lovingly rubbed the hooded nub nestled there.

Her smile disappeared. She tried to close her legs, but he was between them. She came down on him hard. His finger pressed firmly. She whimpered and rose, each movement less controlled, more hurried, her haste feeding more haste. He was thrusting now, holding her tightly, being held tightly, keeping pace and wanting to finish now, now—

"Now," she said, grinding her pelvis on him in insatiable demand, her inner muscles rippling.

Putting his feet flat, he lifted his hips and lunged at her, commanding all her response, wrenching from her a high, keening cry to the heavens. She grabbed his arms and clutched them, her head thrown back, her body demanding. He pumped his seed into her, blasting through torment to prime pleasure.

Panting, she withered down to rest on his chest, and he held her with one arm across her shoulders and the other across the soft cushion of her bottom. She was his. By whatever God dwelt in the heavens, she was his, and life couldn't be better than this.

Until she stirred and said into his chest, "Tell me about your earliest memory."

She truly had learned every trick known to woman. Soften the masculine beast with sex, then dig for information while he was still compliant. He grunted and pushed the drying strands of her hair off his face. "Why?"

"I want to know." Lightly she stroked his arm.

"I thought it might be because you couldn't face me again."

"No." But her voice sounded small and questioning.

She could be moved to passion, but not without consequences. The memory of her boldness made her shy, and her shyness made him tender where he had been impatient. He could answer her question. So many years had passed; surely the memory no longer affected him. "We were swimming in the black ocean."

"Black?"

For one moment he saw the scene through the eyes of the child he had been. "Night, I suppose. I was young—three, four, I don't know. I just knew it was dark. I was holding on to Mama's back, and she was laughing and so was I." A sweat broke out on his forehead, on the palms of his hands.

She sat up a little, a concerned frown puckering her forehead.

"This huge wave came and knocked me off." He turned his head to watch a particularly interesting cloud form—and to keep his head cocked so she couldn't see his grimace.

His heart beat heavily, and he had to take a breath of air—of warm, light air—before he could speak again. "I went down into the black, and I couldn't breathe. Not that I wasn't used to that. I'd been swimming as long as I could remember, so I knew I would always come up." He had to stop talking. He wasn't getting enough air, and he inhaled again, and again.

What a stupid idea, reminiscing about something

that had happened so long ago. It wasn't important. He wasn't going to blather about it anymore, and he would have said so, but . . . he could only concentrate on breathing.

She slid off of him, but he didn't move. God, he couldn't.

Lightly she stroked him with her fingertips. "This time you didn't come up?"

"No." Under her touch, some of the constriction around his chest faded. "The ocean was too rough. I came up a few times, I think, but I couldn't get enough air."

"Your mother found you. She saved you."

"No."

With her nose inches from his, Alanna demanded, "What do you mean, *no*?"

"The storm was bigger than she'd realized, and she was weaker, I think." He smiled tightly to prove something—that his motley upbringing accounted for nothing, or that the remembrances no longer upset him. "In later years she told me that human limbs are not an efficient way to swim."

"I suppose there are better ways."

"It was too turbulent for her that night, too. Someone else got me." Why had he chosen to tell Alanna this? Before, she hadn't truly comprehended his monstrosity. Now she would refuse to marry him. "I didn't know who. I was half dead by then, anyway. It pushed me up on the shore—"

"It?"

Ian hated being such a weakling, cringing from a mere remembrance, and he snapped, "I really don't suppose it was human. Do you?"

She shook her head.

"I couldn't see. I was coughing up water. Then my mother was there, holding me as if she'd never let me go. My rescuer was scolding her. Barking at her. She understood it." He shuddered.

Deliberately Alanna wrapped her arms around his neck.

Dragons and kittens formed and dispersed in the clouds. "We never swam in the ocean after that."

Rubbing her cheek on his chest, Alanna murmured, "Poor wee lad." She strung kisses along his jaw. "But there were good times, weren't there?"

"When I was really young, she used to sing." The clouds rearranged themselves into the image of his mother's countenance, and he found himself smiling at it. "But later . . . it was as if she were aging too quickly, drying up. She used to look out at the ocean with such longing. Then she'd look at me, and she'd have the same expression on her face. That's why I didn't expect her to abandon me." Lifting one hand, he stroked Alanna's hair with it.

"Your mother lingered as long as she could with you."

He didn't know what Alanna was talking about, and he didn't understand why she sounded as if she approved of the mother who had abandoned him. His grip on her tightened. "Explain yourself."

"Didn't you know?" Again she twisted against him until she looked straight up at him. "The laws that rule us on Fionnaway would not allow her to stay on land longer. She should have told you."

"She might have." He didn't listen. She had been his mother, and he'd thought her omnipotent. That she wouldn't leave him, regardless of the price to her.

"She went back to the sea," Alanna said softly. "Perhaps she's there yet. We'll go down someday and swim, and perhaps she'll—"

"No!" That huge liquid black wave rose again in his mind, and he remembered the choking sensation of inhaling seawater. He remembered the taste, bitter, burning, and the scrape of salt on his skin.

And regardless of the explanation Alanna gave, he still harbored a grudge against the woman who had been foolish enough to lie down with Leslie and create a son, and then give that son up without a backward glance.

She was silent, and he realized tremors shook him. He groped after the discipline that ruled him, and gradually brought himself under control.

"Your father is a stupid man." Always straightforward, Alanna spoke with blunt impatience. "He's thrown away every gift he's had. Education, charm, comeliness. He abandoned his selkie bride because of fear and estranged himself from a precious son because of envy."

"I don't understand."

"You're special. He's not. All his life he's told himself his inadequacy wasn't his fault. Then you come along, and in as horrible a circumstance as he could create, you've made yourself a man people admire and respect."

He'd never thought of his father and their kinship in such a manner. Inside himself, he'd always been the lad whose mother abandoned him and whose father rejected him. But somehow Alanna twirled the world on a string, rearranging reality as blithely as a fairy—or a witch. "There are people who don't find weatherworking particularly likable or respectable."

"Mr. Fairchild could never project power." Her mouth was grave. "You, Ian, are a powerful man."

Ian stared down at the woman beneath his chin. The unruly little lock of hair waved above her forehead, bobbing in the breeze, and she boldly met his gaze.

Where others flinched from his darkness, she absorbed it, melded with it. Without conscious volition his head lowered to hers and his mouth touched her mouth. He hesitated, but she didn't try to escape, and he pressed his lips more firmly to hers. Their noses bumped—such an awkward angle—and he slid her head into the crook of his elbow and raised himself above her. Her lips were soft and rich as the butter of summer, melting and smooth. He should, he knew, deepen the contact, but he drew back.

For his own preservation, he drew back. He'd always known he could woo this little pigeon away from her fear, but for the first time he wondered— what change would she bring to him?

Her lids drooped over her eyes. "Why did you follow me out here?"

Standing, he extended his hand, and when she took it, he pulled her to her feet. "It is your birthday, and time for you to remember. It's time for you to marry me."

She watched him as if she saw in him the pain of all the years. That would, he feared, make her draw back as nothing had, for if a man wasn't strong enough to conquer pain, he wasn't strong enough to command respect.

Instead, her mouth curved into a generous, satisfied smile. "Aye," she said. "I'll marry you."

Disbelief trickled through him. Then hope awakened, stretched, gradually grew. Finally triumph was born in a blaze of purples and crimsons and golds. Incredible, dazzling triumph.

He should speak, should express his pleasure and reassure her of his good intentions. But the only word he could force from his mouth was, "Today."

Chapter 22

"About time ye two got here. If ye'd been much longer, I'd have come after ye with a gun."

Alanna didn't appear to be surprised that Mr. Lewis waited for them outside the church door.

Ian was. The hat-clad minister and his precognitions spooked Ian.

The afternoon wind pushed at Mr. Lewis so hard Ian thought the frail old man might blow away. But nothing about the look he bent on Ian was weak. It reproved and upbraided, but Ian just returned his stare. Alanna was his, he'd seduced her fair and square, so let the old man scowl if he liked.

Clearly oblivious to the undercurrents, Alanna asked, "How's my cat?"

Mr. Lewis shifted his attention to Alanna, then cupped his liver-spotted hand around his mouth and called, "Whisky! There's someone here t' see ye."

They heard a plaintive yowl; then Whisky strolled out of the trees and headed right for Alanna. He meowed as he approached, and Mr. Lewis said, "He's scolding ye. Wondering where ye've been."

Alanna scooped up the cat. "I didn't want to

leave him, but with Damon at Fionnaway, I knew I had to."

"I would back Whisky in any fight," Mr. Lewis said.

"And Damon will not be a problem again." Ian gazed possessively at the dainty woman holding the oversized brindle cat. "Bring him home."

She smiled back at Ian as if she thought he could change the cycles of the moon. He liked having her smile like that, even when she said, "No one brings Whisky. He'll come if he wishes."

Mr. Lewis drew Ian's attention. "So ye want t' marry Lady Alanna, do ye?"

"I do." The minister had better give him the chance to say those words inside the little church, because if he didn't . . . well, if he didn't, it would break Alanna's heart to go elsewhere to be married.

Mr. Lewis settled himself in the middle of the bench. Whisky struggled out of Alanna's arms and joined him. Both minister and cat surveyed them unblinkingly, and when Mr. Lewis gestured them over, Ian half expected to see Whisky do the same. Instead, the cat pressed himself against Mr. Lewis's kilt, slowly sliding into a ball of flaccid fur. The cat blinked twice, then closed his eyes.

Ian urged Alanna forward with his hand on her waist, and when they stood right in front of Mr. Lewis, he smiled at the minister challengingly. "Marry us."

Mr. Lewis paid him no heed. "Has Lady Alanna told ye all about the sacrifices ye will have t' make t' be a husband o' the MacLeods?"

"Yes, yes, I know about the responsibilities of owning a large estate, and I understand there'll have to be money spent—"

Alanna interrupted as if he were babbling. "I

thought it would be best if we both told him, Mr. Lewis."

Ian turned to her and stared. "You've told me everything."

"Oh, nay." She looked on him without her earliest scorn or her latest compassion. She wore no expression at all as she said, "It would be foolish to speak of the pact to anyone I doubted."

He couldn't believe she'd kept secrets from him. From the man she'd lain with. Yet at the same time, this meant she trusted him *now*. And about damned time. "Then you're sure of me."

"I am."

She was. He could see it in the serenity of her eyes.

Sure of him. Not afraid of him, not suspicious of him, but sure of him. Right now, winning hovered so near he could almost taste it.

Winning. What a marvelous word.

Smoothing his hand along her cheek, he looked into her eyes. "Then I need no other wedding vows."

"Ye'll say them nevertheless," Mr. Lewis said aggressively.

Taking Ian's hand, Alanna kissed his fingers, then turned on Mr. Lewis. "He isn't bound. Not until he knows everything. He has the right to withdraw even until the last moment."

Irked, Mr. Lewis said, "Aye, aye, but he'd better na. I've seen enough o' broken vows from the Fairchild family."

"I am not my father," Ian snapped. "I don't break vows."

Mr. Lewis's mouth quirked. "Then we'd best tell ye so we can do this thing before the sun goes down."

* * *

Ian had taken it surprisingly well, Alanna thought. He'd sworn to keep everything he heard secret, never revealing it to anyone regardless of the provocation. He had scooped up the cat, seated himself on the bench, and the hand that stroked Whiskey had never faltered while, in a low, quiet voice, Mr. Lewis told him the history of the pact.

Of course, it probably helped Ian to be half selkie and have memories of early days with his mother. More, it probably helped to have magical powers. Like the ability to bring storms. And to tame wild animals. And—she looked at his ring, then looked at the palm of her hand—to own a ring on which one could swear fidelity and that would leave a mark.

She touched the rippling oval imprint lightly. A mark that looked like a burn, but didn't hurt.

But she'd been marked by more than the stone. Ian had marked her with his relentless pursuit, with his desire, and, more than anything, with his desperation. He wanted Fionnaway with a need that burned him, and he would do anything to possess her lands. He needed a place he could call his own, and Fionnaway was that place.

But, manlike, he didn't comprehend how much he needed her.

Mr. Lewis absentmindedly petted the cat on Ian's lap. "The humans provide a protected place for the selkies on the shore and in the water, and the selkies guarantee the continuation of the MacLeod family and provide a special stone as a tribute." He pointed to Ian's ring. "Those kinds o' gems."

Incredulously Ian looked at the silver-set stone. "I've never seen another like this."

"They're rare," Mr. Lewis said, "found only in the deep waters. The selkies bring up a few at a time, and the MacLeods covertly sell them. We can't afford for anyone t' find the source. If one greedy person knew, treasure hunters would descend on us and destroy my seacoast."

Ian looked at Alanna as if he needed confirmation of the crazy story, and she nodded. She wanted him to listen, to accept, to know what he faced and be willing to take the burdens.

For although he thought he had seduced her, taken her, so overwhelmed her with passion that she had no chance against him, she knew mere passion couldn't force her to agree to marriage. Only love could do that.

Love. What did Ian know of love? He'd had none for years upon years and imagined that was how life should be. He didn't understand; it wasn't the land he wanted, but the affection he found with her people. When she married him, they would accept him fully into the fold and he would be happy.

She could give him that, and she would, just as she would keep her own love quiet. This man who had walked alone for so long would have to soften, to grow secure in his very existence, before he would be willing to accept that she loved him, all of him, selkie side and human side, active side and quiet side, pleasant side and grumpy side . . . and, as with all men, the grumpy was more than half.

Regardless, she loved him, and at Fionnaway his bleak existence would be bleak no more.

She looked up from her musing to see Mr. Lewis smiling at her, reading her mind as always. Wryly she smiled back at him.

He turned to Ian. "Do ye have any questions?"

With a curious twist to his mouth, Ian asked, "Mr. Lewis, you've been here years upon years, haven't you?"

The minister hesitated before admitting, "Aye, so I have."

Ian sounded intent. "Do *you* know any selkies?"

"I've seen them."

Alanna stared at Mr. Lewis. He had never disclosed that to her. He had listened when as a child she'd planned to capture one, encouraging her to seek them with amused indulgence. But he'd given the impression the creatures she'd seen in the waves were nothing but seals. "Mr. Lewis, you said selkies are not for mortal eyes."

"Did I?" Mr. Lewis said vaguely.

With a combination of reluctance and urgency, Ian asked, "Did you know . . . about me?"

"Ah." Mr. Lewis stroked his chin. "Yer father announced it, didn't he?"

"But that's not why you know. You know because you remember from before."

Mr. Lewis nodded reluctantly.

"Did you know my mother?" Ian demanded. "When she lived on land, did you know her?"

"I did."

Ian stood as if he couldn't bear to sit, and the disgruntled Whisky tumbled to the ground. "Did you know me?"

"I gazed on ye in the cradle—and after," Mr. Lewis confessed.

Stunned, Alanna whispered, "Why didn't you tell me?"

Mr. Lewis heard her. Despite the wind and the waves and her soft voice, he heard. Picking up the cat, he replaced him on the bench, and as he settled, Mr. Lewis replied, "Ach, lass, d'ye think I relate everything I know? Some minister I would be if I told others' secrets."

"Is she still alive?" The ring on Ian's hand changed from olive green to a sparkling blue. "Is my mother still alive?"

"That would be telling *her* secret," Mr. Lewis replied. "Nevertheless, I think ye know the answer."

Ian walked toward the edge of the cliff and looked out at the sea. The westering sun caught the blue lights in his midnight hair and the wind ruffled it as Alanna longed to do. He'd never looked stronger—or more lonely.

She started toward him.

"Dunna." Mr. Lewis's voice held a note of command she dared not ignore. "Ye'll cure him, I think, but for all that ye are, ye canna hurry it."

Ian turned back as if he heard him, and his tread was firm as he returned. He caught Alanna's hand, swung it in his, and said seriously, "Nothing about these conditions has so far changed my mind. I doubt anything will."

She found herself believing him, and smiling at him with the proprietary air of a wife long wed.

Mr. Lewis linked his hands and rocked back and forth with the rhythm of the waves. His Scottish accent had grown strong. "There's been a MacLeod in Fionnaway long before ye, and if ye're willing, young Ian, there'll be a MacLeod after ye."

"Not a MacLeod," Ian said. "If Alanna marries me, our children will be Fairchilds."

A shiver of trepidation shook Alanna. "Not . . . exactly."

Ian's eyes contained those silver sparks she associated with his greater emotions. "Either it is exactly, or it isn't."

"Since the first MacLeod," she explained, "it's a tradition that the male take the MacLeod name."

"So the first MacLeod was . . ."

"A woman." She nodded at him. "As was the selkie laird."

"A female laird." He seemed only mildly astonished. Perhaps all he had heard had blunted his capacity for amazement.

"Selkies know that women keep the homes, and so are the more important. And after all, that is what Fionnaway is to both human and selkie—our home."

A grin developed on Ian's face. "So to wed you, I have to give up the surname of Fairchild? Give up the name which is a shame and fetter on my spirit?" Throwing out his arms, he laughed aloud. "I take the name of MacLeod, and gladly." Flinging his outstretched arms around her, he lifted her off her feet. "Did you truly think that would be a difficulty?"

She laughed, too, as he swung her around, and when he put her down, she said, "It is frequently the stumbling block for MacLeod husbands. They fear it indicates they'll not be the man of the house. But I assure you, all MacLeod marriages are traditional, subject to the laws of Scotland. The husband is in charge. The wife is his chattel. He can do as he wishes and the wife cannot stop him." *Our marriage will be the same as the marriage of my father and my mother.*

The thought remained in her mind, but he must have read her thoughts, for he said gently, "Then I must make sure I am honorable in all things."

She was glad she had agreed to marry him. For the security of her people. For the continuation of her line. Yet she couldn't lie. She was glad for herself, too.

"Fine talk," Mr. Lewis said. "But unless a man holds something sacred upon which he can swear, I deem his vows o' little import." He challenged Ian with his gaze. "What do ye hold sacred, lad?"

"Myself." Ian laughed bitterly. "My objectives."

Alanna jerked in shock. Did he truly mean that? She glanced at God's church, which had stood forever, and at the minister who had performed God's work for as long as she could remember. "There's a greater power over us all. Do you never pray?"

Ian didn't lie. "Never."

"Do you not believe in the Lord?"

Gently Ian released her from his grip. "I believe in the Lord for you. *You're* human. God is not for creatures such as me."

"There's only one God, and He is over us all." Mr. Lewis smiled with a flash of white teeth.

"Not beasts," Ian said.

"Especially beasts," Mr. Lewis said.

How dare Ian talk about himself in such a manner? And how dare Mr. Lewis act as if Ian knew himself well? In a flash of anger, she tugged at Ian's jacket until he looked at her. "You are not a beast!"

Ian's hand lifted, hesitated, then tenderly touched her cheek. "You're the only one who believes that, and I thank you for that."

She caught her breath at his expression; he looked at her almost with reverence. The breeze slid between them, but did not separate them. The sun shone on them, but that didn't explain her warmth. Hope rose in her, a hope that had nothing to do with Fionnaway.

"Well." The minister cleared his throat and stood. "I dunna know that I believe ye have no faith, young Ian, despite yer cynical claims."

Alanna's gaze lingered on Ian, then shifted to Mr. Lewis.

He pulled a prayer book from his pocket. "So let's get ye wed here and now."

The cat stood, too, and went to stand beside Mr. Lewis as if his blessing were equally important.

Performed on the steps of the church, in the slanting light of the sun, the ceremony was both holy and austere, and, as Alanna well knew, completely, absolutely binding. She was taking the greatest risk of her life, yet when she looked at Ian, when she thought about his wholehearted acceptance of the conditions of their marriage, she could banish her doubts. She spoke her vows without a pause, and when Mr. Lewis declared them man and wife and called them "Mr. And Mrs. Ian MacLeod," and Ian nodded as if he relished his new moniker, something moved in her heart. She felt a sweet displacement. The beginning of a change that would never stop.

When Mr. Lewis shut his book, Ian kissed her modestly, only a brushing of lips, but Alanna cherished his promise of more. And she sent a fervent prayer winging skyward that blessing would come to them both.

From the church, Mr. Lewis brought forth the thin parish record, kept for this year only, and had them sign their names. He signed his own to complete the record, and the legalities were done with.

"To marry on yer birthing day, m'lady, 'tis good luck for the union," he said. "Shall we pick a rune stone for the coming year?" He brought out the leather sack, cracked with age and heavy with stones.

Alanna closed her eyes and plunged her hand within. She brought out a buff-colored rock and offered it to Mr. Lewis.

Mr. Lewis looked at the lines that slashed the granite, and his smile faded. Then he plucked it from her hand. "Ah, m'lady, 'tis a mistake ye've made. That's my stone."

Alanna opened her eyes and stood with her mouth agape as the minister pocketed it. "But, Mr. Lewis!"

"The privilege o' age." Mr. Lewis closed the leather sack. "The wedding and yer birthday will have t' be recorded and placed with the pact."

Alanna touched her necklace, heavy around her neck. He didn't wish to speak of the runes, or of his odd behavior, and Alanna didn't understand why. But neither did she want to create a scene. Not today. Not on her wedding day.

Apparently neither did Ian, for he took her hand and asked idly, "Where is this pact kept?"

"In a cave along the seashore."

His eyebrows rose, and he took a small step back. "You've seen it?"

"I am the lady of Fionnaway." She thought he understood this, but obviously they'd not made it clear. "I'm one of the two keepers of the pact. Of course I've seen it."

"Who is the other keeper?" He wasn't questioning her. He was interrogating her.

"The selkie laird."

"How does she get into a cave along the seashore? Does she don her human form?"

"I've never seen her, but nay, I would say not. She can swim in—"

"*Swim* in?"

Alanna wasn't used to being interrupted, especially in such a tone. "If you would be silent," she said levelly, "I will explain."

His lips hardly moved. "Then do it."

"The cave is located just below sea level."

"Below."

"That cave was picked for the convenience and security of selkie and human alike. Once inside, it rises and becomes dry land. Sandy, and difficult for a selkie to travel. Yet even at low tide, the entrance is just underwater. I swim in at low tide and, with luck, swim out on the same tide."

"Without luck?"

She grimaced. "It's only happened once. I lingered too long and I had to stay. It's dark." She remembered that early mistake with a shudder. "And cold."

"You stayed in an underwater cave in damp clothes. You swam alone . . ." He gripped her shoulders as if he wanted to shake her.

Remembering his memory of the night sea, she stroked him apologetically. "I only did that once. I was young and stupid. It hasn't happened since."

"You still swim in that"—he glanced toward the sea, blushing in the advent of evening—"that ocean." He said *ocean* as if it were a curse. "You do that so you can look at an old parchment?"

"Nay." She still tried to comfort him. "The pact is there. It's been there forever. I don't worry about that. But once a year I wrap the important documents from the village in an oilskin and take them there. Soon, before the first winter storm, I'll swim out with this year's documents."

"Why?"

He demanded until her patience frayed, but she tried to restrain her annoyance. After all, he'd been so good about the other conditions of the marriage. "Because we always have kept them there. Because, I suppose at the beginning it kept them safe from marauders."

"What kind of marauders would come here?"

"Vikings," she said succinctly.

With bright eyes, Mr. Lewis observed them. "Vikings burned the church more than once."

"A long time ago," Ian said. "You're not going ever again." Alanna tried to speak, but he placed his hand across her mouth and glared. "You'll get a cramp. You'll be swamped by a wave."

She pushed his hand away. "I have never—"

"No argument. When I think about you—" He took a deep breath again, like the ones that had wracked him when he had told her about almost drowning. "I can't swim anymore," he said precisely. "There would be no one to save you."

"I don't need anyone to save me." She put her hand over his heart and felt its racing. He was truly disturbed, but he needed to understand. "Ian, I'm a skillful swimmer. I go right before low tide and I return as soon as possible. You don't need to worry."

He wasn't listening; she could see that by his set mouth and angry jaw. "You say our marriage is traditional," he said. "That I'm in charge. Fine. Then my first command is that you stay on dry land."

Old vows and new vows clashed. She knew Ian wanted her. Wanted her for his sake—and for hers.

Worse, she wanted him in the same way. He was a drug. Not like the drugs she'd taken that fatal night of her flight through the woods. Those herbs had lost their effect by morning. No, Ian permanently altered her moods, her desires, her goals, changing her from Alanna MacLeod, the lady who would give anything to protect Fionnaway, into a woman who wanted more from life than just duty and property.

She turned sharply away from the sight of him. Had he cast a spell on her? He could, after all, command the weather.

But if this was a spell, why did she think so clearly? Why did she see the doubts, know the fears? No, Ian couldn't change her. She might love him, and deeply, too, but Fionnaway would always come first. It had to. She had sworn it would.

Fixing her level gaze on him, she said, "Ian, the stones. The selkies place the stones in the cave."

"I have enough money—I *earn* enough money— to make improvements to Fionnaway. *Earning* money may be offensive to your noble bloodlines, my lady—"

She interrupted hotly. "Good Scotsmen don't scorn money honestly earned like your Sassenach nobles do."

"—but anything that needs to be done, I can afford to do. We don't need those bloody stones."

She thought of Armstrong, trudging toward Edinburgh to sell the stones. Or perhaps he was returning, Ellie in tow. "But that's part of the pact, and an important secret, one you must never divulge. The selkies contribute the stones."

If Ian cared, he didn't show it. "Who taught you how to swim? Who taught you to find the cave?"

"My mother, a long time ago."

"Is that a MacLeod tradition, too? Because someday we'll have a daughter, too, and she's not going to risk her life for some louse-eaten documents." He thrust his ring under her nose. "And for a stone." He jerked the ring off.

Alanna gave a cry, and she thought Mr. Lewis, and perhaps even the cat, echoed it.

"It's just a rock. A pretty rock." Fury and some other emotion burned in Ian's eyes as he tossed the ring in his hand. "It's not worth your life."

Walking to the edge of the cliff, he threw the ring as far as he could into the ocean he hated.

The child of a selkie-human union is well favored with gifts from the other world. They're bonny or braw, mighty of bone and thew, blessed with as much magic as the dear Lord sees fit, and given bequests of silver and stone.

Yet grief can sometimes overwhelm them. They are half-breeds, torn between land and sea, between animal and mortal. They fit nowhere. Fear of ridicule or revulsion dogs their footsteps. Sometimes it seems enchantment, not love, holds their mates, and frequently not even enchantment is enough.

The half-breeds who walk the land sometimes attempt to cast off their selkie birthright, but that is impossible. That heritage is bred into the bone.

Among humans and selkies alike, it is said that a half-breed who cannot find ease in his own heart is doomed to shipwreck on the shoals of disaster, while those who love them best can do no more than watch.

Chapter 23

As Ian and Alanna stepped across the threshold of Fionnaway Manor, he should have experienced a surge of satisfaction. He owned an estate. His bride was beautiful and titled. She gazed on him without flinching, and she trusted him. Every goal in his life had been met, yet . . . Alanna wasn't happy. She didn't understand why Mr. Lewis hadn't let her keep her rune stone. She wanted to swim in that hellish ocean, and the thought of her tossed on capricious currents made him furious. Furious with her mother, who had taught her to swim. Furious with the tradition that demanded she risk her life for so little. Furious at Alanna for insisting she was the lady, and that she had to go.

He regretted her grief, but she had taken vows to obey him, and Alanna was the kind of woman who would honor her vows.

"Is the family at dinner?" Alanna asked Mrs. Armstrong as she handed the woman her hat.

"Just finished," Mrs. Armstrong said.

He could not see an aura around either of them. He knew the auras were there; he had simply lost the sight. When he'd thrown his ring away, he'd renounced his selkie heritage.

Mrs. Armstrong took the basket from him. "Was it a fine luncheon, sir?"

"Very fine." The whole world seemed off kilter, limited to physical shapes and forms.

But Mrs. Armstrong seemed unaware. "Mr. Fairchild and the rest o' the company have gone into the great hall."

"They're all here," Alanna said. "It would have been too much to hope that my cousins, at least, would have left."

Was she nervous? Yes, nervous. He could tell by the faint trembling in her fingers. He tried concentrating to bring back the sight, but all he could sense was the pull of the tides and the disturbances in the air. That part of his birthright would never fade, he knew, for those powers were not dependent on an external prop. They were knit into his very fiber.

Taking her hand, he squeezed it meaningfully. "You're the lady, and I'm your husband, and there's naught anyone can do to change that."

She gave him a troubled smile. "I know. It's done, and we're bound, but it wasn't the wedding I expected. I thought my friends and my people would be there, and there would be a big celebration, and this just feels . . . odd."

Like a greedy lad, he'd thought only of marrying her as quickly as possible before someone, somehow, snatched her away. He hadn't thought of what she might want. "When the harvest is in, we'll send out invitations to everyone we know. We'll announce we're wed and we're going to have a big party. We'll get you a wedding dress from London and you'll get a valet to shave me, and we'll roast an ox and roll out the whisky."

A smile started on her face and grew during his recitation. "We should invite the king."

"Well, he's not doing well, from what I hear."

She drooped a little.

And even though he knew she had been teasing, he offered guests like candy to make her smile again. "But we can invite Lady Valéry, and Lord and Lady Whitfield and their children. Boys, three of them, full of mischief . . ." Alanna's eyes shone, and Ian wondered if she thought of the children they might have. "We'll invite my other cousin, too. We'll mention there are selkies in the water and Hadden will be standing knee-deep in the ocean waiting for them to appear. He's so charming, they'll probably come."

"I would like to meet your friends," Alanna said.

Ian was startled. He hadn't really ever considered Lady Valéry a friend. At one time she had been more of an opponent. But he did like her; certainly he admired her scheming.

And ever since he'd met her, he called Lady Whitfield "Cousin Mary," and for years now he'd called Lord Whitfield "Sebastian." But friends? Sebastian had taken him into business only at Mary's urging, he knew. But in the time since, there had been invitations to quiet family dinners, introductions to the right people and to eligible women . . . Yes, perhaps Sebastian and Mary were his friends.

And Hadden. For all that Hadden had once beaten the guts out of him, Hadden was certainly his friend.

Perhaps Ian wasn't such an outcast . . . although it had taken Alanna to show him. "I'd like you to meet my friends," he said. "But first we'll face my father."

Together they walked to the great hall and found Leslie and Edwin, Brice and Wilda, grouped around the fire with Damon stretched before the hearth. Despite wineglasses each human held, only the dog appeared content.

Leslie's cheeks were rosy, his eyes alert. He leaned against the arm of the chair, but he gave the appearance of a man who lounged rather than one about to topple. Not bad for a man who less than a fortnight ago had been on his deathbed.

The dog rose to stretch and shake, then trotted across the floor and pushed his head into Ian's hand. Ian petted him, Alanna petted him, and Leslie said sourly, "You've ruined another dog, Ian."

Ian scratched under Damon's chin, to Damon's obvious ecstasy, and considered his father. Alanna had said Leslie insulted him because he envied him—a poor reason, in Ian's opinion, to ruin two lives. Capturing Leslie's gaze, Ian said, "All creatures need to know they are of value, Father. I simply assured Damon I valued him." Desperately he tried to convey that Leslie, too, was a creature of value. That even now, Ian could forgive him.

For a moment Leslie looked back and read the message. But unlike Damon, he had the ability to reject such comfort, and he deliberately lowered his gaze and snorted in contempt. "You always were soft. Just like your freak of a mother."

It was not better, Ian found, to know why his father hated him. Not when Leslie refused to put the past behind.

The silence stretched until Wilda hopped to her feet. Placing her glass on the table, she skimmed across the floor to them. "You're back. I tried to make them wait dinner, but your father didn't want to, Ian. He said you wouldn't starve, although if you stayed away long enough, you would. I mean, people can't go for days without food. It makes them hungry and they get skinny and their clothes hang wrong."

"We can't have that." Ian grasped Wilda's hand and pulled her closer to the fire. Her smile wavered tonight; he wondered why.

"No! That's what I said. Mama says a well-fitting costume is of the utmost importance to make the proper impression. If company dropped in and they found our clothing needed to be taken in, they would be put off and refuse to stay beyond a short visit." Wilda stopped and frowned as if she'd forgotten what she wished to say. Then in a low tone she added, "And the bills at the tailor would be tremendous."

"You're right, as always." Edwin leaped to his feet and bowed gallantly.

Glaring, Brice retained his seat.

Glancing at Brice, Wilda tossed her head.

But Ian had no time to wonder at her curious disdain, for Leslie stirred restively. "Wilda, I don't know why you're babbling about proper impressions when my ward and my son have obviously just returned from a romp. They've got grass stains all over their clothing, and they look disgustingly satisfied."

Edwin swung about, and his flailing arm caught Wilda's goblet. Crimson wine splashed out before Brice caught the glass and set it back.

"Edwin, try not to be a ass," Brice gritted.

Leslie laughed as Alanna glanced down at her gown. Then he coughed one of those watery coughs. "There's no concealing the evidence now, miss. As your guardian, I demand an accounting of your day."

"Let me tell you the important part, Father." Ian pulled up a chair and pushed Alanna down on it. With his hands on her shoulders, he looked at all of them, one at a time, and announced, "Congratulate us. We are married."

A split second of silence.

Then Wilda squealed. "Married? You got married? After what you said this morning, Alanna? I mean, Cousin Alanna. For you are my cousin now, and I'm so happy I could just scream!" So she did, short, sharp little cries that sent Damon fleeing the room. She hopped up and down, leaned down and hugged Alanna, hugged Ian, then hopped up and down some more.

Ian tried to fight the smile that tugged at his lips, but he couldn't. The men might be sitting like great stones, but he could always trust Wilda to say whatever crossed her diminutive mind, and right now she was thrilled. Alanna smiled, too, watching Wilda's display with a great deal of pleasure, and he leaned over and spoke into her ear. "What did you say this morning?"

Without turning her head, she replied, "That I was determined to marry Damon."

"Liar."

"Coxcomb."

He straightened and looked at the others. Brice and Edwin were trying to speak, but every time Wilda bounced past, they lost their concentration.

His father . . . Ah, Leslie's gaze never wavered from the sight of his son and the new bride. And worse, he was smiling.

What Ian would do right now to have that ring on his finger. He wanted to see the emotions that he knew swirled around them.

Throwing his ring away had been impulse. Yet he couldn't proclaim to Alanna she would have to renounce her ties with the selkies if he did not do the same. Even so, he wouldn't have done it if that ring hadn't turned black when Brice touched it. Ian frowned. Or had it been Edwin who influenced its change in color?

No matter. When the ring had ripped him with its killing cold, Ian had realized for the first time it had the power to drag him into the other world. The world he'd seen in the dark ocean on that night so long ago. He'd done the wise thing by rejecting the ring, and soon he would get used to the sensation of having amputated a limb.

When most of Wilda's shrieks had quieted, Leslie said, "Congratulations indeed, Ian. You have done what I could not. You have captured the plumpest pigeon in all of Scotland."

Alanna's shoulders stiffened beneath Ian's grip. He kneaded them until she relaxed again. "She's not a pigeon. She's a great lady."

"Bah. You're still a damned opportunist, and you always will be. If you can't have one woman, take another, that's your motto."

Ian had played this game with his father before. It was never pleasant, but if he and Alanna remained united, all would be well. Calmly he answered, "Alanna is the woman I want."

"With her property and her income, why not? And you've always been able to seduce the birds from the trees. What chance has a silly girl against your powers?" Leslie lost color as he lost strength. The old man was fading, but still he managed to add, "Good work, son. Good work."

Alanna stiffened again, but this wasn't the place to remind her Leslie could twist the truth to an unrecognizable wreckage. "I'm a married man now, Father, and my primary responsibility is to my wife. So having at last achieved your approval, I must say, it no longer interests me."

"But *I* don't approve!" Brice finally gathered his wits enough to make his statement. "I'm the laird of Clan MacLeod. Alanna should have come to me for permission."

"You wouldn't have given it," Alanna said.

"I might have, but not for such a hasty marriage. It's indecent!"

She shifted restively. "MacLeod women have always wedded quickly, Brice, you know that."

"And repented of it." Brice shook his finger at her. "Look at your mother!"

Did the man always have to choose the worst way of saying things? He'd infuriated Alanna with his criticism, so Ian stepped in before she could speak. "You are right, Brice." His admission brought Brice up short, and brought a sputtering admonition from Alanna. "I should have come to you and asked for Alanna's hand. But when given a choice of Alanna or the proprieties, I never even thought of the proprieties."

"Well . . . well . . . you should have," Brice stammered.

"I agree." Ian stepped forward and held out his hand. "You have my wholehearted apology."

"He doesn't have the right to give permission for my hand!" Alanna said.

Ian ignored her. Brice was now his cousin as well as Alanna's, and through bitter experience with the Fairchilds he'd learned the sense of goodwill between relations. "Let me make you a promise, laird of the MacLeods. I will care for and protect Alanna for as long as we live, and beyond."

"Oh, Ian." Wilda clasped her hands at her bosom. "That is so romantic."

"And . . . um . . ." Brice stood and shook Ian's hand. "Aye, I suppose it's all right. Someone had to marry Alanna. Has to be someone who can control her, so it might as well be you."

Ian almost groaned. Not that he hadn't thought the exact same thing—especially when she'd announced she was swimming into a cave—but did bumbling old Brice have to say so to her face? If he was trying to sabotage them, he was going about it the right way.

Edwin stood up. "If it's all right with Brice, it's all right with me." He marched over and shook Ian's hand next and kissed Alanna's cheek. "Congratulations, cousins." Wheeling, he left the great hall.

Wilda stared after him. "Poor man," she murmured.

"What's his problem?" Ian asked.

"Nothing." Wilda widened her eyes. "He's just poor."

"Without money." Alanna translated for Ian. "Wilda always feels sorry for poor men."

"When she could have a rich one," Brice said.

"Edwin is so nice. I can't hurt his feelings," Wilda said.

"You could if you wished to badly enough." Brice grabbed her arm.

She tried to jerk away. "You're hurting me!"

"Stop struggling." He dragged her toward the study. "I want to talk to you."

Leslie slapped his palms against the arms of his chair. "I live in a place where people listen to Wilda as if she makes sense. I must be in hell."

"You would know, Father." Father and son glared, locked in their old hatred.

They couldn't fight again, Alanna decided. Not when Ian had so neatly declared his independence from his father, and his devotion to her. Patting Ian's hand, she said, mildly, "I think Brice must be in love at last."

"What?" Ian glanced down at her, breaking the connection with his father.

"Brice," she said again. "He's in love in Wilda."

Ian focused on her completely. "Everyone's in love with Wilda."

"But he's always sworn to marry a woman with money, and I see him discarding that resolve without a qualm." A hint of a smile tilted her lips. "Better still, Wilda's in love, too."

"Really?" Ian looked toward the study. How did Alanna know this without seeing their auras? How could she look into the human heart and capture their emotions? "I had hoped for someone more worthy of Wilda's sweet nature."

"Brice is the laird of the Fionnaway MacLeods, with a lovely manor and extensive lands." Alanna scowled at him. "To marry into the MacLeods is an honor not often given to the English."

"He wanted your lands," Ian said shortly.

"So Edwin could administer them. Give Brice credit for being a loving brother."

"Loving is not a matter I associate with families." Ian glanced at his father.

"My mother taught me loving is a weakness," Leslie answered. "I did my best to teach you, also, but you were ever a recalcitrant pupil."

Alanna had noted Ian's attempt to mend the rift between them, and noted, too, Leslie's unequivocal rejection of him. Leslie was stupid to discard his son so rudely, for she claimed Ian now, and she would protect him as she would protect Fionnaway. Stepping between them, she said, "We'll retire to my bedchamber and have a tray there. You should do the same, Mr. Fairchild. You're looking tired."

Leslie ignored her as a thing of no importance. That had always been Leslie's mistake.

"In a hurry to renew your passions?" he taunted. "Or are you in a hurry to count your newfound fortune, Ian?"

"There's no fortune," Ian retorted.

Alanna pushed Ian toward the door, and he went willingly.

"Of course there is," Leslie called. "Hasn't she told you about the pact . . . and the stones?"

Horror brought Alanna around to stare at the grinning old man in the chair. He knew something, and he was wicked enough to use his knowledge to ruin them all.

She abandoned Ian without a qualm and walked back to Leslie. "What are you talking about?"

"There's no need to play stupid with me." Leslie smirked like a fisherman who'd hooked a siren. "I know about the sea opals, and I know where they come from."

She stood over him and wished she could squash him like a worm. "And why do you claim to know that?"

"Your father, my dear, was one of my closest friends—and when he drank, he sometimes told fantastic stories."

Her father. Her asinine, careless father had told this unscrupulous man about the sea opals. Had he betrayed their secret to other people, too?

Leslie looked around her. "So, son. We'll start mining them right away."

"Nay!" Alanna cried.

"No?" Leslie arched his brows in jeering innocence. "But why not?" He tapped his finger to his mouth. "Oh, wait, I think I remember. There's some silly tale that demands the shore be kept unsullied for those pesky selkies."

"You don't care, do you, Leslie?" Ian stood beside her now, outrage evident in every line of his body. "If you could drive her away forever, you'd be happy."

Leslie's eyes slid toward Ian with the oiled motion of bearings in a gasket. "Drive who away?"

"My mother."

A hard trembling started in Leslie's hands and traveled up his arms to his chest. From there it radiated outward until his whole body bobbed in a palsy. "Have you seen her?" he asked harshly. "Don't go looking for her. She poisoned me. She'll poison you, too."

"When did she poison you?" Ian leaned toward him.

"Years ago. So many years ago." The old man grabbed the shirt over his chest in his bloated fingers, concentrating on each rattling breath as if it were his last.

Alanna almost wished it would be.

Ian relaxed. "A slow-working poison, then."

"The stones . . ." Leslie gasped. Gradually he regained control. His hectic flush faded, and he managed to speak with only a faint breathlessness. "The stones must have a lode. We can be rich. So rich."

"Father," Ian said gently, "I'm already rich enough."

Leslie glared at his son with such malevolence, Alanna quaked. "You are so stupid. Sometimes I wonder if you're really my son. You can *never* be rich enough."

Ian went to the door and called the footmen. "My father needs to be taken to his bed."

The footmen scurried in, still obviously frightened by Mr. Fairchild, but even more frightened of Ian.

"No!" Leslie exclaimed. "I don't want to." The men lifted the chair. "Put me down. Put me down!" Leslie struck at them as they bore him stoically toward his chamber.

As he was about to disappear, Ian said, "No mining, Leslie. There'll be no mining, and that's my final word."

Alanna waited until all commotion had died down, then she turned to Ian and said, "That went well, I think."

"You're joking."

She grinned.

"You *are* joking." He sounded relieved as he wrapped his arm around her and turned her toward her room. *Their* room. "I never plotted to marry you and bring you under my father's jurisdiction," he said.

"I know that." She turned her surprised gaze on him. "Do you think I'd believe anything your father said?"

Ian hugged her closer, and she sensed his relief—and his rising passion. "I would not have him be a ghost between us tonight."

"He hasn't the power."

She thought she heard a pleased rumble as he opened the door to the bedchamber. She preceded him and glanced around affectionately. The large bed would easily accommodate her and Ian. There was a table and chairs where they could eat their repast. The fire leaped in the hearth, and no one could tell that behind one of the bricks . . . she stared . . . that behind one of the bricks . . . Surely the light tricked her eyes . . .

"It's a very pleasant chamber." Ian smiled at her meaningfully. "And I've waited long to have the right to visit it."

She walked toward the fireplace. One brick looked out of place. One brick . . . surely not *the* brick . . .

"Alanna?"

She counted. Twelve down. Four over. And with her fingers she pried the brick from its bed.

"What are you doing?" Ian strode to her side. "Why do you look like that?"

She lifted her stunned, disbelieving gaze to his. "The box is gone. Someone has stolen the stones."

Chapter 24

"*What do you mean, someone has stolen the* stones?" Ian strode forward and peered into the empty spot among the bricks.

"'Tis where we keep them, and they're gone."

He'd never seen Alanna look like this, almost wild with grief and shaking with rage. Clasping her arms, he drew her toward him, but she fought and broke free.

Most of his life he had been rejected, frequently in family moments, occasionally in hideous public scenes. Yet Alanna's refusal to accept his comfort, minor though it had been, scraped painfully into old wounds. He stood very still, watching her as she ran a slender, freckled hand through her hair, creating a wild copper sun around her head.

"I'm going to confront him." As if inactivity were the one thing she could not bear, she paced across the bedchamber toward the door and away from Ian. "I'm going to warn him I want them back, and he'd better not tell where they came from or I'll . . . I'll . . ."

"Who?"

"What do you mean, who?" She swung around and glared as if Ian were personally responsible.

So he'd been sullied with the same brush that

blackened his father. "Who is this you're going to command? Surely not Leslie."

"Why not? He's got them."

"Does he?" Long years of experience made him answer with assurance. "Yet I wonder why, if your father told Leslie about the stones, he's waited four years to mention them."

"Because he didn't know where they were hidden."

"Has he looked for them?"

"Nay," she conceded grudgingly.

Ian took no pleasure in her admission. After all, it would have been easier if the thief had been Leslie. Easier, and yet ... so difficult. "In any case, how would you threaten my father to make him keep his silence? He's dying and already terrified of what awaits him on the other side. There's nothing to threaten him with."

"He doesn't look as if he's dying anymore," she said. "He just looks a wee bit ill."

"He's dying." Ian said it without a doubt.

Her hands slid up to hug herself. "How do you know?"

"I know."

So did his father, and his father, like a crab before a massive wave, scrambled ever more desperately to get out of the way.

Biting her lip, Alanna looked away from Ian, and toward the fireplace. "But then who has stolen the stones?"

"I don't know. You tell me. How many people know of them? And of their hiding place?"

"There are only two of us." She frowned as she thought. "The box remained in its hiding place last week on the day I returned. I saw the stones. Armstrong was there."

"Armstrong?" He realized he hadn't seen the

man in the past week. "He's gone. He could have stolen the stones."

"Not Armstrong! Nay, I sent him on an errand." She hurriedly added, "He heard something outside the door, but when he looked, the hall was empty. He said I should be careful."

"Yes," Ian said, but his mind wasn't on her words. She avoided his eyes guiltily, as if she wasn't telling him everything. Oh, for the insight his ring provided! Then he would know if she blamed him for his father's misdeeds. He would know if she was regretting this marriage to a Fairchild. "Shall we organize a search?" he asked.

"Nay! We don't let anyone know that the stones exist, much less announce some are gone." She swayed as if she faced a strong, erratic wind. "I've failed in my trust. I thought I would do better than my mother, and instead I've led us into disaster. This is what comes from running away." Cupping her hand over her eyes, she said, "It's a cataclysm I've brought on us all."

Ian didn't move. He couldn't. Alanna had mourned her mother's poor judgment in a husband; now she stood before her bridegroom and complained of disaster. Maybe she didn't mean him, but maybe she did, and probably it was his fault.

He had ferreted out the witch. He had demanded she bring about Leslie's temporary revival. He had discovered her secret and forced her to unmask. He had refused to accept defeat and he had wed her, claiming a source of wealth someone else coveted.

Oh, Leslie had not stolen the stones, but Ian knew no infamy occurred in Leslie's vicinity without his instigation. So who had his father trapped in his sticky web of evil? The answer was obvious.

The one who had told him the legend. The one who had stolen the stones.

Brice. Edwin. One of the servants. If Ian had been paying attention, he would know the culprit. He would have seen the truth spinning in the air around their heads. But he had been chasing Alanna, forging dreams for her to dream, every sense intent on the woman he was stalking. He had barely noticed the others, and now, without his ring, he could not catch even the faintest stench of evil in any of them.

A faint knock on the door made Alanna jump and shudder, lower her hand, and stare at the portal with anguish.

"Expecting the devil?" Ian asked pleasantly as he moved past her to the entrance.

"Wait." Alanna touched his arm. "It could be our thief."

"Thieves don't return to the scene of the crime."

"They do if they think there's more to be stolen." The knock came again, a little louder this time.

Ian found himself reassuring her. "It's more likely our dinner." He opened the door, expecting to find Mrs. Armstrong with a tray.

Instead, a babble of words came from the petite, caped and hooded woman who stood there. "I know it's your wedding night and only a madman would interrupt you—not that I'm a man, I don't have the body and my voice is too high—but I think I've gone slightly mad and I *have* to speak to Alanna. Please, Ian, can I speak to Alanna?"

Ian's initial reaction was annoyance. He and Alanna had bigger problems than Wilda ever could. But a slightly desperate, breathless quality tinged Wilda's tone, and he opened the door wide and stepped aside.

But Wilda still hovered on the threshold, her small features contorted by unease.

"Come in, dear." Alanna cast Ian a perplexed glance before moving forward to take Wilda's arm and usher her forward. "We're glad to have you visit, but why are you dressed like that?"

Wilda moved to the fireplace and stood jiggling up and down in constant, nervous motion. She glanced at Ian, then glanced again, and asked plaintively, "Aren't you going to shut the door?"

He did.

"It's my disguise. I didn't want anyone to know who it was if they saw me."

"We have so many diminutive, slender, blond women living here in Fionnaway," Ian observed.

Pushing back her hood, Wilda cast a defiant glance at him. "I know you won't like this, but I don't care, I have to do this, so just let me alone."

He looked inquiringly at Alanna, who shrugged in bewilderment. He said, "Wilda, you are my favorite cousin. I just want you to be happy."

She didn't smile as he expected her to; she frowned and said, "I'll do it whether you like it or not. I can't be happy until—" She bit her generous lower lip. "Oh, Alanna, do you remember yesterday telling me you were the witch? I didn't believe you, of course, so silly to think a woman who looks like you could be a witch. But I said I wanted a spell, and you said you were the witch, and I knew it wasn't true, but you said you might see the witch and tell her I wanted her. Did you see her when you were out? I know you were busy getting married, but I really, really need her right now. Have you told her?"

Ian almost staggered from the shock. Wilda sought the witch, and she wanted her with a determination quite unlike his simple, easily swayed cousin. "What do you want the witch for?" he asked.

Wilda swung on him as if she wanted to strike him, and her gentle voice rose. "For a spell. I told you that. I want a spell."

Alanna seemed at as big a loss as Ian. "If I could convince you I really was the witch—"

"Then you couldn't help me, could you?" Wilda lifted her dainty chin. "I need a witch, not a lady."

Ian could see a horrifying scenario unraveling before him. Wilda talking to the servants, to the visitors, asking after a witch. Someone would know of one, of course. Someone would send Wilda chasing across Scotland on, literally, a witch-hunt. Wilda would be hurt, and he couldn't bear that shining, open-faced ingenuousness to be damaged. She'd gone through enough just because she was a Fairchild; she didn't deserve to suffer because she was Ian's cousin, too.

Ian found himself speaking before he realized it. "The witch is still in the manor."

"She is?" Wilda asked.

"She is?" Alanna collected herself swiftly. "Ah, aye, she does linger here occasionally."

Placing a firm hand on Wilda's shoulder, Ian pushed her toward the door. "Go to your bedchamber. Wait for me there. I'll find her, then come and fetch you."

"Would you?" Wilda clasped her hands.

"For you, Wilda. Only for you." He smiled at her, then closed her out and turned to Alanna.

Only to find he didn't have to explain. She knelt by the fireplace, lifting cold ashes from the bucket with the hearth spade. "There's bits of charcoal here for highlighting, but you'll have to go and find me some ragged work clothes from somewhere," she said. "Ask Mrs. Armstrong. She'll know where to get them."

A strong sensation gripped him by the throat as he watched her. The firelight flickered across her features, touching them as he longed to. Her high cheekbones brought a tilt to the changeable eyes he admired. The fractious lock of hair fluttered in the waves of heat coming off the flames. Her lips moved slightly, but unceasingly.

He had to ask. "What are you saying?"

"I'm rehearsing an incantation to ease Wilda's mind." Looking into the flames, she bit her lip. "I wish I knew what spell she wanted. It would make it easier to know what to have and what to do."

Ian couldn't help himself. Walking up behind Alanna, he gripped her shoulders in his palms. "Thank you."

His voice came out harshly, as if he were angry, but she looked up at him and smiled, then laid her cheek on the back of his hand. "We'll do it for Wilda, shall we?"

By the time he returned with a clean set of woolen garments, Alanna had made herself up with charcoal, and covered her bright hair with ash. She was the witch again, but looking at her, he wondered that she had ever fooled him—he, who had always prided himself on seeing more—and wondered more if every man saw only what he expected to see.

She swung in a circle for him. "Will I cozen her, do you think?"

"You look fearsome, but we'll douse the lights for good measure." He slipped the gown over her clothing, then helped her roll a length of cloth in a good-sized hump.

"I put the kettle on to boil, and slipped some allspice and cloves into it. Can you smell it yet?"

He sniffed. "Yes, I can. What magic does that make?"

She grinned, and charcoal flaked off around her mouth. "It gives off a sweet scent." She secured several pouches and a knife at her waist with a length of rope. "The bubbling sound and the steam are part of the act. Old Mab taught me that."

"She taught you a lot, didn't she?"

"How to care for myself when my mother died." Alanna was still smiling, but rather crookedly. "You once mocked me for saying that Lady Alanna had spent a great deal of time at the witch's hut, Ian, but it was true. Mab taught me how to care for my people. Later, when she had to, she took me in and taught me how to disguise myself. We could have been caught, and she would have been hurt, but she did it anyway." One tear tracked down the dust of her cheek. "I miss her."

Moving close, he caught the tear, then helped smear the ash back into unity. "You're doing what she would have wanted. Healing people. Helping Wilda. Mab would be proud of you, Alanna MacLeod."

"I hope so."

She said it so quietly, he knew she was thinking about the stones once more. Probably their disappearance dominated her mind. Yet they could do nothing tonight, so she made herself hideous to help Wilda make a spell. And he was happy for that. Happy to offer his cousin as a distraction. "I'll go get Wilda now."

Wilda opened the door at the first rap of his knuckles. "Alanna found the witch lurking near the kitchen," he said. "But the cook wanted to throw her out for making the stew taste too good, so Alanna is keeping the cook busy while the witch helps you."

As Ian turned away, Wilda followed eagerly. "Did she remember me?"

"The witch? Of course. She's only been waiting at Fionnaway to help you. After that, she wants to go to her hut."

"I hope it's not a difficult spell." Wilda came as close to brooding as Wilda could get. "I hope she can do it."

"She's an excellent witch," he found himself assuring her.

"That's not what you said before." Wilda glared at him as he opened the door to the bedchamber. "You said the witch had no powers."

"Kennie the blacksmith convinced me otherwise," he said smoothly.

Wilda nodded knowingly and flounced into the room, then stopped short. Stepping inside, Ian could see why. Alanna had doused the candles, giving night possession of the room. The fireplace flickered and popped, the kettle steamed with a slight hum, a swirl of smoke drifted on the air, and Alanna herself was a misshapen lump of witchly majesty seated at the table where a single candle wavered low.

"Come in, child." Alanna beckoned with a grease-covered hand.

Wilda crept forward, her gaze fixed on the witch. "Come and sit down."

One chair sat empty opposite Alanna, and Wilda pulled it out. The chair legs scraped across the floorboards with a screeching sound, and Wilda glanced anxiously over her shoulder at Ian.

Remembering her previous conviction that the magic wouldn't work if he knew of it, he asked, "Do you want me to leave?"

"No." Wilda's voice squeaked.

Taking a stool, he watched as Alanna laid her

hand in the middle of the table, palm up. "Give me your hands, dearie. Let me read the lines."

Wilda's hands trembled as she laid them on the table beside Alanna's, and Alanna pushed the candle over to light them. "The lines of your left hand and your right hand are very different. That means circumstances haven't allowed you to fulfill your talents."

"I don't have any talents," Wilda said.

"Your hands say you do. This mound"—Alanna tapped the raised area below Wilda's thumb—"is raised. That means you're warmhearted. The line of life loops wide around it. You're vibrantly alive. You have much to give, and no one to give it to."

Wilda nodded, then Ian was horrified to see a tear drip from her chin onto the table. Were all his women going to cry tonight?

"But things are about to shift." Alanna traced the life line. "Look. Here. A change comes to you now, because you were persistent and determined to see old witchy. Tell me what you want."

"I want"—Wilda took a quivering breath—"a spell. I want . . . to be good."

Alanna didn't move. She just stared at Wilda, waiting.

Wilda remained silent, evidently convinced she had explained sufficiently.

"You are good," Alanna said.

"No. No, I'm not. For a long time I couldn't understand why no one loved me." Wilda's voice trembled. "Then I realized—I'm a Fairchild. I'm evil, just like the rest of them, and I need someone to make me good."

Alanna's mouth hung slightly open, and her eyes looked glazed.

Ian spoke from his corner. "Wilda, do you want the witch to create a spell to make you good?"

"That's what I said." Wilda sounded cross now.

Leaning against the wall, Ian grinned in rueful amusement. Trust Wilda to completely undermine Alanna's preparations. He was willing to bet she didn't know one incantation that had anything to do with "good."

"Well," Alanna croaked finally. "Evil old witchy doesn't usually get a request for this."

"But you can do it, can't you?" Wilda asked.

"Of course." Alanna patted Wilda's wrist. "Just for you. I only hope I don't get struck down by lightning."

"Oh, no." Wilda half rose from her chair. "I don't want you hurt!"

"You're not good, heh?" Alanna cocked her head, then nodded at her deliberately. "I won't get hurt, and this will be easier than you think." Rising, she opened the kettle and let out a gush of steam that carried the scent of cloves and allspice into the room. With a wooden spoon she stirred wildly, and Ian could almost see her contemplating. Then, lifting a spoonful of liquid from the kettle, she trudged slowly toward Wilda, her hand cupped underneath to catch the drips. Standing before her, Alanna flicked drops of spicy water over Wilda's head, while reciting something in Gaelic.

Ian thought it sounded remarkably like the grace the crofters said before each meal.

Wilda sat with her face outstretched, allowing each drop to settle on her face like a benediction.

With a hand on her arm, Alanna gently lifted Wilda to her feet and spun her around three times. She chanted again, and this time Ian definitely recognized the words to an old Scottish planting song. Then she sat Wilda back down and pressed a kiss on her forehead.

Stepping back, Alanna said, "There you have it. *Goodness.*"

Wilda stared at Alanna. "Is that all?"

Alanna visibly wavered. "That's all the *spell*. But you have to have a memento, a token to prove you are good, something to show yourself when you remember this night and wonder if it was a dream."

From beneath her robe Alanna brought the necklace of clinking rune stones.

"My cousin has one of those," Wilda exclaimed. "Is that a sort of Scottish tradition?"

Ian buried his face in his jacket to stifle his laughter at Alanna's dismay.

But she recovered. "It is a tradition, and old witchy's going to give you one of hers." Unclasping the chain, Alanna poured the rune stones onto the table in a heap. She stepped behind Wilda and covered Wilda's eyes with her hands. "Choose."

Wilda groped on the tabletop, then buried her hands in the pile. Each square pebble had a different marking, and Wilda hesitated as she fingered the runes.

"Just choose," Alanna said in her ear.

Taking an audible breath, Wilda grabbed.

Alanna took her hands away. "Let me see."

Wilda handed over the stone, then waited, agog, while Alanna examined it.

A slow smile blossomed on Alanna's face. " 'Tis the hearth stone." Holding it between both palms, she warmed it with her flesh. "It is the symbol of home, of love, of goodness. It means the spell has already taken effect, young Wilda, and can never be undone."

Wilda's eyes grew round with excitement. "I'm already good?"

"Aye." Alanna's cleared her throat. "You're already good."

Wilda held out her palm.

Alanna placed the stone within. "Put it on a chain and wear it around your neck."

"What if I lose it?"

"Nothing you can do can break the spell," Alanna reassured her.

"Oh, Ian!" Wilda flung herself toward him. "Did you see?"

"I saw." Slipping off the stool, he hugged her, then looked at the stone with her. "But then, I never doubted you were good."

"That's because you're a Fairchild, too, and can't tell the difference," Wilda said.

"Half devil, half beastie, I am," he conceded softly.

She hugged the stone to her bosom. "I have to go now."

"I'll walk you back to your chamber," Ian said.

"I'm not going back to . . . that is . . . I can walk alone." Wilda edged toward the door, her joyful smile alight. "Go and find Alanna, and have your wedding night. And you, Miss Witch"—Wilda blew her a kiss—"thank you."

The door shut behind her, and he turned to Alanna. "Well done, Miss Witch. What does that rune really mean?"

Alanna chuckled with pure delight. "Exactly what I said."

Ian lifted his brows.

"Home. Hearth." Alanna shrugged out of her robes. "And in Wilda's case, it definitely means goodness. If you believe the old tales, by choosing that rune, she guaranteed she would wed before the year is out."

"Then I must believe in the old tales." He

propped himself against the fireplace and watched as she took a brush to her hair. "Mrs. Armstrong will come now with a bath and meal for us both."

Ash flew, and she coughed. "Thank you, husband."

She had a slight tremble in her voice, and he clenched his jaw. She no doubt thought he would not allow her to bathe in peace, but only a sod would attack a woman as besieged with trouble as Alanna.

But before he could reassure her, Alanna put the brush down and came to him. "Wilda wanted to be good. Dear, sweet Wilda was afraid to marry her love because she thought there was some evil inside her that only magic could wash away." Wrapping her arms around his waist, she looked up at him. "Can you imagine Wilda thinking that just because she's a Fairchild, she's tainted?"

Painstakingly he hugged Alanna to him, scrutinized her pure, guileless countenance, and thought—*Yes, I could imagine that. I can imagine that very easily.*

Chapter 25

Edwin gave his cravat one last touch, and smiled into the mirror as he smoothed his hand across his perfectly coiffed red hair.

His luck had begun to change at last. He'd always been the handsome brother. He'd always worn clothes with more dash. Certainly he'd always been more intelligent, although such a thing wasn't difficult. But he'd been handicapped by poverty, by his position as second to the heir. Now, thanks to his own wits, his dead uncle's indiscretion, and Mr. Fairchild's urging, he had wealth and a chance for more.

So what if he hadn't snared Fionnaway? Being Fionnaway's keeper would have been nothing but hard work and responsibility. Alanna's return had saved him from that, and given him a way to bleed the estate without effort. He knew how seriously Alanna took her duty to that ancient pact, and he would use that knowledge ruthlessly. She'd buckle under the threat of blackmail.

Of course, he might be only a second son, but even he was too much of a MacLeod to do as Mr. Fairchild wished. No one would mine the seashore, looking for the precious sea opals. Edwin would simply make his demands and know the selkies, and Alanna, dared not disobey. And he relished the power he held. God, how he relished the power.

This morning perhaps he would stop by Wilda's door and offer to take her to breakfast. He was, after all, now as great a catch as Brice. Better, for Brice had always sworn to take a wealthy woman of position as his wife, and Edwin had made no such vow.

Edwin patted the pocket he'd quickly created inside his waistcoat. She'd been watching Brice, flirting with Brice, aye, but with the two sea opals he'd stolen, a woman like Wilda would look on Edwin's courtship favorably. And Edwin would like to have a wife so beautiful he would be the envy of Scotland.

Opening the door, Edwin stepped into the corridor. He could hear two voices murmuring, and he halted and stared at the portal just down the hall. That was Brice's chamber, Brice's voice, and it sounded like a woman answered him.

The door swung open, and Edwin quickly moved back into his room, just far enough to take himself out of plain sight. He held his breath as the cape-clad woman stepped into the corridor. He couldn't see her face, but only one petite woman with flyaway blond hair resided in Fionnaway Manor. And only one woman spoke in that breathless, babbling manner.

Brice wouldn't let her speak. He kept cutting her off with kisses and soft chuckles, and finally with a push that sent her hurrying past Edwin.

She looked so besotted she didn't even see him.

Brice, disheveled, smitten, did. He leaned his arm against the doorframe and beamed. "Congratulate me, brother," he said softly. "At last she has consented to become my wife."

"Congratulations," Edwin said through stiff lips.

And he realized—Mr. Fairchild was right. There was more to this than wealth and power. There was vengeance, too.

Ian kept his hand on Alanna's waist as they walked toward the dining chamber.

Last night had been an exercise in restraint. Restraint while Alanna bathed. Restraint after they'd gone to bed and she'd crept into his arms. She'd wanted comfort, nothing else, and he'd given it to her. He'd held her all the night long, repeating—*his* bed, *his* manor, *his* bride. There would be other nights. Thousands of nights. A lifetime of nights for him and for her.

Now he inhaled the scent of rose soap and Alanna. No woman he knew would dare wear a rough rune-stone necklace with a fashionable chestnut-colored gown. But Alanna could, and did. Her face, her walk, her style, were uniquely her own, and even all those weeks ago, when she had dressed as the witch, he had recognized her confidence and delighted in it.

Now her confidence was wavering, but he would restore it, for humility did not fit his Alanna at all.

She stopped short of the door. "Ian."

"Aye, lass?" He lived in Scotland now; he would speak like a native.

"Do you really think you can find the thief?"

"If we shake the right pocket, we can." Automatically he touched the place where his ring should be. What a time he had chosen to toss it away! "Don't worry, Alanna. Whoever has taken the stones will want more, and he'll make his hand known quite soon."

Squeezing his arm, she nodded. "Aye. You're right, of course." Stepping into the dining chamber ahead of him, she smiled and said, "Good morning." Then she stopped.

He bumped into her, grabbed her waist to steady her. "What . . . ?"

Then he saw what she saw. Their families were seated at the dining table, their half-eaten breakfasts before them. Brice was staring at them with concentrated disgust. Edwin kept his eyes on his plate and refused to look up.

Leslie watched them with a great, malevolent pleasure.

And Wilda was saying, in as hostile a tone as he'd ever heard from her, "What's wrong with that? Lots of people are born on the wrong side of the blanket. I mean, it's not as if it's Ian's fault Uncle Leslie slept with Ian's mother and never had the integrity to marry her."

Alanna blundered into the room as if a great hand pushed her, and when Ian hurried to help her, she turned on him and knocked his hands away. "Tell me it's not true," she choked.

"That I'm illegitimate?" He spoke slowly, trying to comprehend why she should exhibit such consternation. "But it is."

Her voice rose. "And you didn't tell me?"

Wilda's voice formed a shrill background. "He probably promised all kinds of things. Mama says men will say anything to seduce a woman."

Ian tried to remember. "I told you my father had made promises to my mother and not kept them."

"I didn't think you meant he hadn't married her!"

Ian stared. Was this virago the same Alanna who had accepted his need to own land and married him in spite of it? Who was willing to put up with Leslie as a father-in-law? "What other promise does

a man make to a woman? I thought you understood, but didn't care."

"Didn't care?" She paced away from him, then
paced back. "Why wouldn't I care?"

"You easily embraced my . . . rather odd heritage. My illegitimacy didn't seem important."

"Not important?" Alanna trembled as if a cold
wind had blown through the open windows. "It
was the *only* important thing."

"Uncle Leslie probably promised to marry her,
then refused. It's not as if Uncle has never broken
a promise." Wilda's voice took on a note of desperation as she dared slander Leslie. "And he lies
all the time. He's a *big* liar."

"I don't understand." Ian tried to take Alanna's
hands, tried to establish contact in the manner that
had always worked between them. "Tell me what
I have done."

Jerking back, she scraped her hand through her
hair and pins went flying. It should have hurt; she
didn't wince. "You've ruined me. You've ruined
everything."

"Why are all of you looking like that?" Wilda
wailed.

Ian gazed around. Brice and Edwin were on their
feet, and Ian still didn't understand what was happening.

"What are we going to do?" Brice asked.

"What we have to do," Edwin answered.

"For God's sake, Edwin." Brice couldn't have
looked more disgusted.

"She's the lady of Fionnaway. You know the
law." Edwin argued with a seriousness he'd never
shown before.

"It's not a law." Tugging at his cravat, Brice said,
"It's more of a . . . tradition."

Alanna interrupted. "It's part of the pact. The sacred pact."

Ian watched the three cousins, not liking anyone's tone.

"Alanna, why are you saying that?" Brice demanded. "You're the one who will lose."

"I'm the lady of Fionnaway." She faced Brice grimly. "It's my duty to enforce the pact."

"It's an archaic bargain with creatures who don't exist," Brice snapped. "Are you insisting we abide by it and throw you from your home?"

"What?" Ian sprang forward. "What are you babbling about?"

Finally Leslie made himself heard. "The contract. The one the MacLeods made with the selkies. It requires only one thing of the man who marries the lady of Fionnaway. Do you know what that is, Ian?"

Of course, Ian knew. How could he not know as he faced Alanna's despair and Leslie's high spirits? But his father would tell him anyway.

"It requires he be of legitimate birth." Leslie bent his head back and burst into laughter. Fullthroated, full-bodied laughter that rang through the chamber and echoed down the corridors.

Ian would wager everyone within earshot cowered from the sound of that merriment. It was as if the devil himself loosed his glee upon an unsuspecting world.

"He's right." Edwin shuffled from side to side, like a child in need of a chamber pot. "Ian must leave."

"Why?" Ian demanded. "Why does it matter so much that the groom is legitimate?"

"Fionnaway is passed from mother to daughter, and because it is the law in England and Scotland that the lands always go to the eldest son, there was a concern that unscrupulous opportunists might try to steal Fionnaway by any means." Alanna steadied her wavering voice. "So the man the lady marries must be above reproach so that no one of lesser descent can lay claim to Fionnaway for any reason."

"This is your fault, Alanna. You were supposed to ask," Edwin said.

"I know, but I never thought to because"—she stared at Leslie—"because it seemed so obvious . . ." Leslie didn't meet her eye, and she said, "There's something curious here. I thought—"

Edwin interrupted. "Maybe we could get them an annulment."

Alanna's head snapped around, and she looked as aghast as she had when Ian admitted his bastardy. "An annulment?"

"She just spent the night with him, you *fool*." Brice glared at his brother, then turned hopefully to Alanna. "Unless you could swear nothing happened last night."

"Try not to be silly, Brice, if you can." Alanna looked longingly around at the room. Then she looked at Ian with the same kind of longing.

She wanted Fionnaway above all else. Ian understood that. Damn! Of course he understood. *He* had just lost this estate, his only place in the world. He'd held his dreams in the palm of his hand. Now, like sand, they slipped away, and he would be in exile once more.

Yet he supposed . . . No, he knew his deprivation could in no way compare to hers.

Now . . . now he would lose his bride.

No, that was wrong. Now he would perform the kind of act that always made him want to puke. He was going to *give up* his bride. "Nothing happened last night."

Edwin smirked. "Do you expect us to believe that?"

Ian paid them no heed. He could only stare at Alanna, her hair wild about her shoulders, and wonder at himself. He'd just told the truth about the night before and cast his virility in doubt with every man who would ever hear about it. He had discarded Fionnaway in the best tradition of noble asses everywhere. And what filled him with anguish? The woman. Alanna.

She was only a woman, just like so many others. Damn it, she didn't even have what he wanted anymore. Surely, with his experience, he could give her up without a qualm.

Yet her gaze locked with his, and a slow, sensual smile started on her lips.

And Ian had qualms. Many, many qualms.

Until Leslie laughed: great, ringing laughter that raised goose bumps on Ian's skin. "I knew you'd been under her skirt before the wedding. You take after me a little, at least."

Alanna's smile disappeared. She faced the tribunal around the table and said resolutely, "I took the vows of my own free will. In the eyes of the law, whether or not we have consummated the marriage means nothing beside the saying of the vows. I always keep my word—always!—and Ian is my husband. There's no solution except that I must leave."

"You're awful." Wilda pushed her chair back so hard it clattered to the floor. "You're all awful. You"— she pointed at Brice—"you're as bad as the rest of them. Ian and Alanna are *married*. They're in *love*. They're the two nicest people in the world, and you're making them seem sleazy and uncouth. Well, you're nothing but a bunch of . . . old . . . meanies!"

With a loud sob, she ran from the room, leaving

Brice clutching his chair as if, without its support, he would fall to the ground. Edwin stepped away from the scene as if he wanted to distance himself.

Alanna sighed, her color fading. She staggered as if she were exhausted, and said to Ian, "Come. We have to leave Fionnaway now."

Chapter 26

Ian stood outside the witch's hut, gazing toward Fionnaway Manor with such an ache of hatred he could scarcely breathe. His loathing grew, roiling in the air, thick, black, awesome. Soon it would burst forth with such a massing of fury the whole world would know that Ian MacLeod *hated*. Hated his father, and hated those two weaselly cousins.

They had stripped him of everything. Pride. Lands. His dream.

He glanced into the darkness of the hut. His dream. Alanna.

Just as he'd willed, she'd dreamed of him, and he'd enjoyed it. He'd loved visiting her mind, tormenting her with visions of hot nights and sweet, slow passions. He had adored seeing her the next day, worn-out with frustration and blushing at her fanciful wantonness.

Now the memory of *his* dreams tormented him. He'd dreamed for years of a place of his own, a place he could belong where no one judged him a freak or a bastard.

And beneath that dream had been a deeper dream. One he thought so impossible he'd never even tried to bring it to fruition. The dream of a woman who was loyal to him. Who wanted what he wanted. Who welcomed his loving. Who bore his children gladly.

Lately the woman in those dreams had had Alanna's face.

Alanna. His bastardy had crushed her, stripped her of her rights, ground her into the dirt when he longed to lift her to the stars.

Everything, *everything* he touched, he destroyed. And like one of the old gods, he would wreak his vengeance now.

He didn't even have to concentrate this time. The lack of his ring made no difference. His selkie birthright fed on his enmity, and together they drew the storm. The breeze gusted his hair. Great clouds raced toward Fionnaway and tumbled in the atmosphere above the castle. They rose, higher and higher, turning first grayish-green, then black, blocking out the yellow sunlight, shutting out the hope. Ian had to strain to see even across the clearing.

But the darkness wasn't enough. He demanded the terror of anticipation.

So the wind stopped. Sound died. The trees stilled, the birds cowered, the animals hunched down. Like a great cap, the clouds smothered each squeak of comfort, each groan of fear. The vapors above moved silently, capsizing on themselves, then re-forming with greater strength. Ian could see them in his mind, in his heart, and he waited. Waited until he knew the fishermen had returned to shore. Waited until the farmers had raced across the fields to home.

Waited until Leslie had noticed what his son could do and had learned to quail.

Then, lifting his arms, Ian unchained the storm.

Wrath smashed down on Fionnaway like a vengeful hand. Lightning struck in searing, white bolts and broad, shimmering sheets. Thunder crackled, rumbled, a hellish cacophony. Wind blasted brown leaves off the ground and swirled them aloft in hypnotic whirlwinds. And the rains came.

Ian stepped into the hut and with all his strength, shoved the door shut. He no longer wished to reject his selkie heritage, for it was not that which had brought him to this pass. It was Leslie and his mother and the freedom they'd abused.

With his back against the rough planks, he watched as Alanna moved toward him, a lit candle in her hand. The flame gilded her with gold. The lightning flashes kissed her with silver. Each curvaceous shadow hinted of unsolved secrets. And her hair burned with a life of its own.

"Ian, did you do that?"

To him her words sounded censorious, but he scarcely cared that he and his monstrous powers had repulsed her at last. Raising his voice against the pounding of the rain, he said, "I did."

"Good."

His heart jumped at the enigmatic smile that played around her lips.

Carefully she put the candle on the sill and stepped close to him. Running her palms from his waist to his chest, she said again, "Good."

Blood pounded in his veins as he stared down at her. What did she mean, *good?*

Lightning flashed with the rhythm of his heart, and in each flash her face drew closer to his. Her fingers wrapped in his hair. She tugged him down and stood on tiptoe—and kissed him.

Openmouthed. She sucked on his lower lip and groaned as if the taste of him excited her. She touched his teeth with her tongue, a faint hum of pleasure vibrating through her, and her breath warmed him from the inside out.

Jerking back, he grabbed her head and held it. "Alanna, do you know what you're doing?"

Her eyes opened slowly, and she licked her lower lip before she replied. "Becoming part of the storm."

He wanted her. He always wanted her. And now, here, she seemed to crave him. His fingers tightened in her hair, and he searched her face as he tried to understand her. Alanna, the woman he would never understand. The woman he would gladly spend his life trying to decipher. "You had better be very sure."

She brought her body forward until it pressed against his, her hips undulating. "Ian. Now."

His control split as surely as lightning breached the sky. Picking her up, he reached the table in one long step. He lowered her and with his hands on her legs, he pushed her skirt up and stepped between.

She watched him with warm, shining eyes, acting as if she thought him a lord in and by himself.

"On the way here," she said, "I wished I were really a witch so I could wreak vengeance on your father."

Her voice grew breathless as he massaged his thumbs in little circles on the cord that led to her center.

"Wreak vengeance on all of them."

With utmost care he caressed her on the very surface of her skin, in the place where the color changed to rose and she was damp and warm.

She stiffened. "Ah, Ian, that feels . . . " She tried to catch his hand. "Don't. I can't talk. I'm trying to tell you . . ."

"I'm listening." She yearned for him, and she

would have him. But she wasn't ready enough for an almost-virgin. "Tell me about vengeance."

Lifting herself on her elbows, she looked down at the place where he touched, then up at him. Reaching out, she touched his trousers, in the place where his erection strained against the buttons. "Vengeance"—she molded him—"can go both ways."

He wanted to rip the cloth away, plunge inside of her until he'd found forgetfulness. But he wouldn't let her off so easily. In one matter, at least, Ian MacLeod would triumph this day.

As he slid his hands toward the buttons of his trousers, her lips parted. He could see the slight gleam of her teeth as he slipped each fastener free, see her struggle to catch an uneven breath.

Outside the storm grew in intensity; the wind roared, the thunder rumbled, each bolt struck with clever intent. Inside he tormented his woman. He would take her to the edge—and beyond.

Pushing the trousers open, he bared himself to her, and she lay back and stretched out her arms to him. "Hurry."

Hurry? No, he would not. His desire was obvious, his resolution well hidden. "So beautiful." He captured one of her knees in each hand. "Do you remember"—with his foot he scooted the bench around—"when I said"—he sat down and brought her right to the edge of the table—"I would like to kiss you everywhere?"

Alanna's eyes widened. For an innocent, she understood him very well. "Ian." She struggled to sit up. "Ian."

She was going to try and talk him out of it. Talk him out of tasting her, fresh and clean and his. "Watch if you want to," he said. "That just makes it hotter."

She fell back with a groan, then started up again. "Ian . . ."

"Watch."

She did watch. She watched as he started at her ankle and kissed the inside of one leg all the way up. She whimpered when he stopped short, and he grinned at her. Her breath came in ragged bursts, her legs trembled. "I don't want you to do this," she said.

"Really?" He rested the well-kissed leg on his shoulder, then began the long journey up the other leg. "I would have said you want it badly." He looked at her, copper-colored hair above, copper-colored hair below. "As badly as I want it. Anticipation is hell, isn't it?"

With his fingers he opened her to him. Even there she was beautiful, feminine, inviting.

She tangled her hands in his hair and tried to lift his head away. "This isn't proper."

He grinned. "Who *have* you been discussing it with?" Then his smile faded. "Let me, love. It will give me great pleasure."

Her fingers loosened. One smoothed over his ear, and she whispered, "Well. Just to make you happy."

He chuckled. Chuckled with delight at her wit and a barely restrained sexual aggression. "I'm going to be very happy before I'm done with you."

Lightning struck and thunder crackled as he delicately touched her with his tongue. Her muscles tensed; he didn't know if she struggled with aversion or exaltation. Lifting his head, he looked— and saw the picture of a woman in ecstasy. Head thrown back, hands clenched on the edges of the table, breasts full and nipples thrusting through her bodice.

This was what he'd trained for in the boudoirs

of India and Tahiti and London. To drive Alanna MacLeod to orgasm. He licked at her, sucked at her, tasted her pleasure. He slid his tongue inside her, feasting on her whimpers, relishing her instinctive undulation.

She fought this climax. She exclaimed against it, raked the table with her fingers, gave in to it at last and shuddered in a desperate tide of ecstasy. He thrust his finger inside her and felt the frantic spasms.

God, she was tight, sweet, hot, and just for him.

"Ian," she called hoarsely. "Please, Ian."

"Yes." Rising, he kicked the bench over and pushed his trousers down. In one thrust, he penetrated her. She screamed, and her muscles clamped down, holding him as if she'd never let him go. And he thought he could stay like this forever.

Instead, the frenzy took them. Like the lightning outside, he struck, and struck again, each movement of his hips driving him deeper, each motion making a brighter light. Like the thunder, she echoed his desire, lifting her hips to take him, concentrating all her being on satisfaction.

His. Hers.

This time he was inside her when she came. Her legs wrapped around him, she held him to her, and she thrashed on the table in a glorious rapture. He held off, held off, held off until she slowed, then he placed his hands on the table on either side of her. Leaning over her, he held her still as he plunged so deeply she had no choice but to take his seed into her womb.

And she did it with a glad cry.

He drooped over her, his chest heaving with the exertion, his arms trembling with strain. He wanted to kiss her, exclaim over the awe he felt in their mating, caress her while she recovered.

But did he dare? He wondered if he had hurt her, given her too much, expected experience where he knew she had none. She was new, and hardly understood what she had incited. He, who should have known better, had sizzled so much he had exploded in a flash of light.

He tensed as she spoke.

"Ian?" Her soft voice dipped and wavered. "I hope you don't mind . . . but I love you."

Chapter 27

Alanna hadn't meant to confess it. She had known it would be better if Ian had the chance to settle into Fionnaway's routine before she told him. But now she didn't know if he would ever have that chance, and somehow she had wanted to make the loss up to him—and the phrase had just popped out.

I love you. Hanging between them like a noose.

To her, everything had been clarified in their coming together—but not to Ian. He hadn't tried to talk her out of loving him. In fact, he hadn't said a word. He had just taken her to the bed. He'd stripped her bare, removing each piece of clothing and revealing each new place with something that looked like reverence. He'd taken off her necklace, then strung kisses around her neck, one kiss for each stone. Then he'd made slow, tender love to her, creating such a whirlwind of passion she'd voiced nothing more than broken sounds of joy.

Now she snuggled against his back, her arms wrapped around his waist. The poor man was stunned, but she couldn't call the words back, so he'd have to get used to it, wouldn't he? For a re-silient bubble of joy had formed in her, and nothing could destroy it now. ''Husband, would you like something to eat? We've not yet eaten breakfast, you ken."

Silent, he stared out into the witch's hut, not flinching as the lightning cracked the darkness again and again. So be it. She could interpret his reticence as she wished. "Not hungry?" She kissed his shoulder blade. "Good. I have greater plans for you."

Still he said nothing. Brooding, no doubt. She'd never seen such a magnificent brooder, but she would cure him of that. "Don't you want to know what they are?"

"What . . . what are?" He sounded hoarse and more than a little dazed.

"My plans." She massaged her thumb down his spine, around each vertebra, trying to relax him.

When she reached the base of his spine, he groaned and stretched. "Plans."

She smiled at the sinuous ripple of muscle beneath his skin, then sat up and shook out her hair. "*I'm* going to shave you." Rising, she climbed over the top of him and off the bed. Going to the big valise she'd brought, she rummaged in it and pulled out a dressing gown.

He watched her with a hunger that fairly vibrated the air. A hunger that manifested itself in the constant flicker of lightning and rumble of thunder. Yet he appeared detached. "Shave me."

She felt almost sorry for him, having to deal with emotions he'd never hoped to experience. Yet she couldn't let him retreat. He was hers. The sooner he understood that, the better. "Aye." She smiled at him. "A little warm water, a sharp razor, and at last I'll see my new husband's whole face."

"Of course. Shave me." He sounded a little more enlightened as he sat up enough to lean on his elbow. "You've discovered a better way to rid yourself of an unwelcome husband than a mere annulment."

His hostility startled her, and she blinked. "What do you mean?"

"Why don't you just say you want to slit my throat?"

A flush of fury raced through her at his cynical statement, and as she grabbed for control she wished *she* could express herself with lightning and thunder. Instead, she had to make do with mere words; how inconveniently mortal. With her hands clasped at her waist, she stared at the man cloaked in shadows. "Why would I want to slit your throat?"

"Because I cost you Fionnaway."

"Fionnaway." Hope shriveled. "Fionnaway." How silly of her. She had been thinking of ethereal emotions. He had been thinking of her very substantial lands.

Digging in her bag, she pulled out a velvet robe. Its jade color flattered her hair and skin; it was no accident this robe had accompanied them into exile. But right now she wanted only to cover herself, and she hastily shrugged it on. "So I was premature in rejecting Edwin's solution of an annulment."

He froze in the process of pushing back the blankets.

She fumbled for the belt, caught it, and knotted it around her waist. "*You* wish an annulment."

Her accusation hung on the air, and he stood slowly to confront it. Magnificently male, he shrank the tiny room with his height. His midnight hair captured each lightning burst and from it spun silver. His body gleamed and rippled: molten steel and polished bronze. And his enigmatic eyes caught the candle's flame and reflected it back at her. "Never. I don't know what you're talking about, but *I* don't want an annulment."

Holding the ends of the velvet belt, one clutched in each fist, she asked, "Even though I no longer have what you desire?"

"What do I desire?"

"Fionnaway."

A muscle clenched in his jaw, and he took a step toward her. "You are not going to make it appear you separated from me because you were doing me a favor."

She swallowed and tied another knot in the belt. "You never lied to me. I always knew you wanted Fionnaway."

"No, my lady." His voice mocked her. "You accuse me of rejecting you when I am the cause of your downfall."

This time she stepped toward him until only a breath separated them. Carefully she examined him. His eyes no longer looked enigmatic. Enraged, hurt, he had been battered by life and had no reason to expect her to behave any differently from the other people who had so abused him.

She ached for his anguish, yet at the same time, that small bubble of hope expanded and rose in her. "I want you to be happy, and I know you can't be happy without . . . You desire an estate. If you want an annulment, I won't stop you."

"As an actress you have no peer." He turned his back to her. "You almost have even me convinced." Picking up his breeches, he stepped angrily into them and glanced at the window.

He wanted to leave, she could tell. Like a wild creature, he wanted to run away from her, from the situation. Yet the wind still howled around the eaves, and rain splattered on the thatching. He prowled across the room, then prowled back again.

Lightning stoked the heavens and thunder vibrated the shutters.

Ian's own storm trapped him here. With her. And maybe it wasn't just the loss of the lands that made him prowl and snarl. She had to find out, didn't she?

"Sit down," she commanded, and pointed to the bench.

Head up, nostrils flared, he glared at her.

"Don't be so dramatic," she chided him, and saw him flush belligerently. Lifting the half-full bucket onto the table, she dipped a linen cloth in it and wrung it out. Coaxing him, she asked, "If I promise not to slit your throat, will you sit down?"

"Bloody hell, but you're irritating." He flung himself onto the bench so hard it rocked on its back legs and he had to catch himself. Leaning his elbows against the table, he made a parody of relaxation.

"I don't hold the license on irritating." She heated the cloth over the candle flame until it was so hot she could scarcely handle it, then she tilted his head back and wrapped the cloth around his face. He recoiled and swore violently, but she held it tight under his chin. "Now." She put her knee on his thighs to keep him in place. "Are you always this cranky when your women declare their love?"

He pushed her hand away. "My women?" His laughter cracked like the thunder. "I don't have women."

"Your mistresses, then," she insisted. "When they say they love you, do you always flee?"

"I am not going to discuss this with you." The towel started to slip, and he caught it. Then as if he couldn't stand it, he sat straight up. "What makes you think I want to flee?"

She almost smiled, but caught herself. "Woman's intuition."

He slumped back against the table, and he wrapped the towel tighter around his face. In a muffled voice he said, "No one has ever told me before."

"Of course not." Now she mocked him as she shook out a clean towel and tied it around his neck. Digging through her valise in pursuit of the razor and strop, she said, "With a face that looks like God's grace on earth, and so much charm every one of my maids sighs for you, and you claim no woman has ever said she loves you. Pull the other bucket, if you please."

"Hell, yes, the maids like me. I made sure of that. I made sure all your people like me." His eyes glittered as he watched her sharpen the razor with long sweeps of her arm. "I was determined to do this lord-of-the-manor thing correctly. But women . . . no, women don't love me."

She tested the honed edge with her thumb, then, satisfied, she placed it on the table behind him. "So you were a virgin yesterday?"

"Women have wanted me. For the money. Or because they think I'm dangerous, and they want an illicit thrill." As she pulled off the still warm cloth, he grinned savagely. "Are you complaining my training is incomplete?"

"Your lovemaking, as you very well know, is dazzling." Leaning over him, she kissed his lips. "But if you're telling me the truth, and I'm the first to love you . . . well, then, I know why you're upset."

He steadied her with a hand to her back. Her muscles flexed beneath his palm as she straightened, and he enjoyed the sensation of her movement as much as he hated her cross-examination. "Why am I upset?"

"Because you don't like people to be too close to you."

He jerked his hand back. Not since his childhood had anyone ever been able to pierce his enigmatic facade. Now this bit of a girl "felt" his fear, his disturbance, without even seeing his face.

"There must be selkie blood in you." Thunder shook the hut in a long, shattering roll, and he waited until it had finished. "You see feelings."

"That selkie blood is back so far, it's barely a dribble in my veins." She lathered soap into her hand, and spread it on his throat. Picking up the razor, she said, "Tilt your head back." He did, and she placed the razor against the skin close to his Adam's apple. "Ready?"

Ready? If she leaned down much farther, he would catch a glimpse down her robe. Then he'd be ready.

Sounding patient, she said, "Ian, I really don't intend to slit your throat."

Of course she didn't. Alanna would never take the easy way out—nor allow him to. She would drag out this conversation until he ran away, or went mad—or until he believed she loved him.

God, did he dare believe her? "Shave me," he said gruffly.

With a long stroke, she removed the first of his whiskers—and, to his surprise, none of his skin. Carefully she wiped off the blade and started again, and after the first tense moments, he realized she was good. Very good. "You're better than my valet."

"I used to shave my father. He didn't trust anyone else to do it—there were plenty at Fionnaway who wished him dead—and he said my sense of duty was such I wouldn't slit his throat." With a clean cloth she wiped it off and leaned back to him. "Unfortunately, he was right."

He couldn't stand it anymore. He had to know. "Why aren't you angry at me about the loss of Fionnaway?"

"It was my fault. I failed in my duty to ask about your background."

"And why did you do that, when you'd been so conscious of your duty in every other way?" He waited, breath held, for her reply.

"Perhaps I didn't care about the answer." She finished his throat with tender care, then stropped the razor again. "When I was the witch, you took loving care of Fionnaway. When you found out who I was, you didn't try to kill me. You wanted to wed me instead. You didn't declare your undying love, but told me the truth. You want Fionnaway, not for its wealth of sea opals, but for the home it gives you." Again she soaped her hand, and spread it this time on his cheeks. "You're a good man, Ian MacLeod."

"You've had a hard upbringing, Alanna, if you think my determination to wed rather than kill you is evidence of a noble character."

Her dimple blinked at him as she smiled. "There are some who would not have hesitated if they had known my location."

Her suspicion of his intent, he could have understood. He could have comprehended her resentment about the marriage, about his illegitimacy and the destruction he'd wrought to her life. What he could not understand was her trust.

She seemed to know his thoughts, for she leaned against his shoulder and said it again. "I love you."

I love you. She said the words; they sliced at him

as the razor had not. And he didn't even bleed. "You can't love a scarred, crippled man."

With her free hand she smoothed his hair back and looked down into his eyes. "You're none of that. If I were a conceited woman, I would crow to the world I've wed the finest-looking man in all Scotland."

Leaning his head back, he traced her features with his gaze. The glaze of freckles melted across her nose, and her wide mouth smiled or frowned or, as now, thinned with determination. For Alanna, emotions were not enemies, but simply the best part of living, and he envied her her naïveté. But while he knew he couldn't bear it if she sought out and found all the dark corners of his soul, still he also knew he had to caution her. "You can't see the scars. You can't see the impairment. You don't love me. You love an illusion."

She laughed. Laughed at his dark warning, "Oh, Ian, do you think I can't distinguish who I love?"

With her fingertip she turned his head to the side. He heard the scrape of the razor as she bared more of his face to the air. The sun would scorch his newly exposed skin. The wind would burn him. Yet his skin would grow tough—his spirit had to be tempered by exposure, too.

"I know that compared to you I'm a green girl, but that doesn't mean you know everything and I know nothing." Leaning close, she laid her cheek against his and hummed her satisfaction. "In fact"—her breath dusted his ear—"when it comes to love, I know more than you."

Maybe he could bleed, after all. "Do you? So you've declared love to many men."

Offended, she straightened. "I can see why you're worried about getting your throat slit." Spreading the hem of her robe open, she said, "But don't be silly. No men. Until you, I haven't particularly thought well of men. Love is not only about male and female."

"Isn't it?" Right now, with his gaze fixed to the gleam of her legs, he would have sworn it was.

She straddled him, one knee against his thigh, the other foot flat on the floor. The clean scent of her intoxicated him. The restless stir of her body against his created eddies of pleasure. The wind roared outside, but inside the hut was snug and warm, and her breasts were close enough to tease his mouth. He waited in anticipation for her to open the top of her robe.

"Tighten your lips," she said. "I want to do your chin."

"Do my chin?"

"*Shave* your chin," she enunciated clearly. "I want to shave your chin. Now, tighten your lips." He did, and watched entranced as, unconscious, she imitated him. Her words came out oddly as she moved her mouth to one side, then the other side. "I love Fionnaway. I love my people. I love my cat." She gestured toward Whisky, sleeping on the rug. "Long ago, I loved my mother. She always told me what to do. She reprimanded me and forced me to take responsibility. She made fun of me when I threw tantrums." She grimaced at him. "But I still loved her."

"Why?"

"You've got a cleft," she said inconsequentially. "I think you might be the most handsome man in all the Britains beneath this thatch."

"Oh, I am." So the women said.

"Do you want any whiskers at all?" She held the razor at the ready. "A mustache, perhaps?"

"You might as well see it all," he answered, knowing that if she could successfully shave the delicate contour of his upper lip, a valet would be superfluous. Then, driven by unsatisfied curiosity, he said again, "How could you love your mother if she was like that?"

"What do you mean, how? I loved her because she loved me enough to care to tell me what to do. So don't tell me I don't know what love is. You're the one who wouldn't know it if it bit you." Bending over, she nipped his shoulder.

He shuddered and grabbed for her. She chuckled and expectantly looked down at him. She was warm in his hands, alive and vital in a way he could never be. Yet he clung to her in the vain hope that somehow the heat of her body and the depth of her passions might someday melt his heart. "I can't return your love."

"Well . . . nay. Probably not. Not now." Her chest rose and fell in a sigh, and she put the razor to his other cheek. As she scraped the whiskers away, she said, "But you can't crush my hopes for the future."

She seemed to have faith that if she just loved him enough, sooner or later he would naturally return the emotion. Yet he had spent years wandering alone; he had no such faith, and if he were a good man, he would smash such hopes now.

"I'm not a good man." He said it to himself as much as to her.

She tossed back her head and laughed, a delighted froth of merriment, while he noted her body's scent and the grace of her neck, and wondered how the woman had made a sensual pleasure of a shave and confrontation.

"Ah, Ian, I would say you are very good."

"Saucy lass."

Still smiling, she dabbed suds on his upper lip. With a delicate touch, she removed the last of his whiskers from his face. Wiping away the lingering flecks of foam, she stepped back and surveyed her handiwork. He found himself waiting for the verdict, as if her opinion could change his visage.

"Ohh." The sound was a mere exhale of admiration. As if she couldn't resist, her hand hovered over his face, then came to rest on his cheek. She traced his cheekbone, then smoothed her hand over his chin. "You're right. You are the best-looking man in all the Britains." Taking the towel from around his neck, she leaned over him, her mouth hovering above his. "The thing is—I fear I would have wed you regardless of your appearance."

"Would you?" He wrapped his arms around her. The razor clattered on the table behind him.

"Oh, aye."

He weighed her words, judged the sincerity behind them. She told the truth. Maybe not all the truth, but enough of it to make him say, "I always thought if I loved someone, I could make magic."

"I would say your magic has wet Fionnaway pretty thoroughly." She kissed him lightly, then rubbed her lips against his. "I like you without a beard."

"Good." He opened her robe and surveyed the body he'd claimed. "Because I've just discovered I like to be shaved."

Abruptly she pulled back, and he let her go, wondering why she wasn't clinging to him. Had he insulted her? Was she shy again? Capricious, perhaps? But no, she struggled to open the double-tied belt, and allowed her robe to slip to the floor.

The lightning crackled, no longer right over their heads, but still strong enough to illuminate her tentative smile. He didn't have to take, demand, seduce. She was offering herself.

He was a scoundrel, he thought, as bad an opportunist as any in all of the Fairchild family. But he had to have Alanna. He'd flaunted himself in front of her, forcing her to accept him, and like a magic mirror, she reflected back a different image. A better image.

This time he resolved to hold the mirror for her. To show her how she affected him, and why. With a shaking hand he stroked the curve of her hip and said, "If I loved someone, I could do more than just create a storm. I could make real magic."

Lightning flashed; thunder boomed as he lifted his hands. Electricity streaked along his nerves as he delicately smoothed her skin.

She flung back her head with a moan. "Aye. Magic."

Driven by some internal need, he made the declaration he'd always kept in his heart. "If I loved someone, I'd make the full moon shine from a new-moon sky. I'd make the waves die down on a windy night. I'd make the ocean clear as glass."

"Somehow"—she tilted his head back with a tug at his hair—"I believe you could do it."

He took her hand and put it to his lips so she could feel the caress of his declaration. "If I loved anyone, it would be you."

Leslie stretched his legs out to the fire. They were swollen again. When he pressed on the skin over his ankles, it was like pressing on risen bread dough. His finger would leave an indent that slowly filled again. But he was going to get better now. He'd fixed things, and all he had to do was make his move—before time ran out. Feeling almost cocky, he said, "We'll start looking for the lode of sea opals at once."

Edwin scarcely glanced up from Fionnaway's accounting books. "We'll have to import miners.

These Fionnaway peasants wouldn't know a lode if it bit them on the ass."

Leslie winced. That was exactly what this disease felt like. Like he was being nipped from behind by old, broken promises. "Doesn't matter. When they hold a pickax in their hands, they'll rip that shoreline to shreds."

"Maybe I don't want it ripped to shreds." A page rustled as Edwin turned it. "Maybe I want this done right."

Leslie's head swiveled, and he stared malevolently. "You'll do as I tell you."

"Why?" The MacLeod blue eyes, so like Alanna's, gazed back at him unflinchingly. "With Alanna married and ousted, you're not the guardian. You're not in charge anymore."

This imbecile challenged him. He, who had set this all in motion! Leslie took a deep breath, trying to take in enough air to shout out a reply, but his lungs were too clogged. He settled for an infuriated whisper. "Is that how you repay me after all I've done for you?"

"You told me your son is a bastard. This was the information I needed to get my hands on Fionnaway, and I appreciate that." Edwin turned another page and frowned. "But looking at these figures, I'd say you've had your reward. You've wasted every cent Fionnaway has earned."

Leslie snorted. As if waste mattered. He was an English aristocrat. "You have the other two stones. Sell them!"

"I intend to—so I can hire miners to do the job right." Standing, Edwin closed the book. "I'm the lord of Fionnaway now, and if you have any sense, you'll remember that."

Leslie laughed, ignoring the rattle deep in his chest. This young nobody thought to outfox Leslie

Fairchild. Well, no man had ever done that, and only one woman. "If *you* had any sense, you'd do as I say."

Arrested by Leslie's tone, Edwin turned. "Why?"

"Because, little pigeon"—God, how Leslie relished this!—"I married Ian's mother in a handfast. He's not a bastard at all."

Like the coils of a snake, evil loops through the stream of life, distorting each reflection and consuming every hope. Evil feeds on itself, growing strong on fear and madness.

Magic, too, permeates all existence. One can see it in the rainbow, hear it in a raven's call, taste it in a simple stew. Yet like evil, magic can create havoc. Every time it is used, it acts like a stone dropped in a pond. Ripples spread out to touch every shore. It effects every life, makes changes the most far-seeing cannot envision.

Evil destroys. Magic deceives.

What power on God's earth creates a balance for these mighty forces?

Chapter 28

Alanna slipped away from the hut, dressed and in her sturdiest boots, with her necklace clasped firmly around her neck. The wind still blew, but most of the clouds had dispersed, leaving only wispy rags that slid past the westering sun. She walked as quickly as she could, hoping the storm hadn't created any crises that demanded Mr. Lewis's attention. She needed him to be there in front of his church.

As he was. He stood there as if he had been waiting for her, watching her walk toward him. "I thought ye'd be coming t' me, m'lady," he called, "when I heard ye'd been chased from the manor."

Stopping directly in front of him, she put her hands on her hips. "Then you know why I've come."

As usual, the minister wore his broad-brimmed hat, his long-sleeved shirt, his kilt of the MacLeod plaid. As usual, he was discreet. "Tell me."

"Leslie Fairchild declares his son is illegitimate. Yet Mr. Fairchild shows all the signs of a man dying because he broke his promise to a selkie." Urgently she leaned close. "Is he lying, Mr. Lewis? Did he wed Ian's mother?"

"Come." Mr. Lewis gestured. "Let us walk, and I'll tell ye a tale."

He started to walk, but disappointment kept Alanna in place. "Oh, please, Mr. Lewis, I don't want to hear a tale. I just want to know if they were married."

"Ye youngsters are too impatient." He just kept walking. "If ye want the answers, ye have t' wait for them t' come."

"All right." Alanna hurried to catch up with him. "But you'll tell me, won't you?"

"Selkies, ye know, have made their homes in this part o' Scotland for as far back as anyone can remember, and just like humans, they have their good ones and their bad ones, their calm ones and their wild ones."

Selkies. He spoke about the selkies. "You *are* going to tell me," Alanna said with satisfaction, and she stepped out with more eagerness. They were taking the trail that wound along the cliffs, alternating views of the still restless sea with the more tranquil groves of wind-sculpted oaks.

She listened closely as Mr. Lewis said, "Ian's mother, Muirne, was one o' the wild ones, wanting always to see what was on the land. On her sixteenth birthday she transformed herself for the first time."

"How?" Alanna asked, waiting breathlessly for an answer. She'd always wanted to know, but her inquiries had been brushed aside.

But Mr. Lewis knew. There could be no doubt about that now.

"She'd come up on the rocks—see? Those right there, right against the shore." He pointed, and Alanna saw the black stones worn almost flat by the wind and waves. She'd seen the seals there sunning themselves on the warm days; how many had been selkies?

"Muirne struggled her way out o' her tight-fitting skin. Her head slid out first, then one shoulder, than the other. Like a child from the womb, she slid free. An arduous birth, followed by a difficult adjustment. She stretched, wiggled her toes, tested her legs, wobbling like a child taking its first steps."

A vision rose in Alanna's mind of the dark-eyed, dark-haired beauty as she staggered along the beach, gaining confidence with each step until she felt strong enough to climb the cliff walk toward the village. "Did she have clothing?"

"What babe comes into this world with clothing?" Mr. Lewis asked. "But the girl had observed the humans and knew o' their penchant for covering themselves. Without a qualm, she stole clothes from a drying line and went t' walk among the mortals. The men fell in love with her, o' course, she was that beautiful, and she taunted them."

Alanna winced. At one time she'd taunted Mr. Fairchild with his lack of power over her, and she'd been hurt by it.

Mr. Lewis saw her reaction, for he said, "Aye, ye know the trouble that causes. The men resented that, and one day a bunch o' them caught her. They were harrying her, calling her a freak, preparing t' do more, I fear, but Leslie Fairchild came upon them."

"That should have really frightened her," Alanna said sourly.

"Nay. He was visiting Fionnaway then, drinking and carousing with yer father, handsome as the devil and just as devious."

"The handsome is gone."

"So goes all earthly beauty." Mr. Lewis flicked

her cheek with his finger. "That's why, Alanna, we all look for someone t' love us. When ye're shriveled and disgusting, like me, ye'll be glad for Ian."

"He doesn't love me." She answered without a tremor, and she was proud of that.

"The day isn't over yet." Mud slickened parts of the path. Leaves paved the rest. Mr. Lewis slipped, then said irritably, "Now, do ye want t' hear this tale, or do ye want t' chat?"

Leaning down, she picked up a stout stick that had blown off one of the trees and passed it to Mr. Lewis. "I'm listening."

Halting, he examined the staff, then stuck it in the ground and leaned on it. "All the lasses were in love with Mr. Fairchild. He took his pleasure as he pleased, and I knew even then he was no good. But he rescued Muirne, and she thought he was wonderful. More, he loved her beyond anything."

"Oh, Mr. Lewis. That man never loved anything more than he loved himself."

"I didn't say that. Only, I think, he loved her as much as that warped man has ever loved." Mr. Lewis's gaze roamed over the sea. "He haunted the shoreline all the summer, begging her t' wed him, and at one time, I admit, I thought she would be the making o' him."

"So they married?"

He sighed deeply. "They did."

"I knew it. I knew it!" Alanna could scarcely contain her triumph. "Did you perform the ceremony?"

"Aye. But I refused t' wed them in anything but a handfast, because I didn't trust him."

Surprised, Alanna said, "He's English. Did he understand the handfast?"

Mr. Lewis started walking again. "I explained very clearly they could live as man and wife for a year, and if they wished t' remain together at the end o' the year, and if the union had proved fertile, then they would be wed for eternity."

She grasped Mr. Lewis's arm and pulled him to a stop. "Did you explain the conditions of wedding a selkie?"

"He knew very well the consequences o' his actions. Muirne was responsible and told him. Let's go there." Mr. Lewis pointed the staff at the path that broke away and meandered down to the shore. "She loved him, but I dunna think she trusted him. It was a union destined t' fail, and I knew it before the end o' the first winter. He hated the Highlands when the storms raged and it was so cold a man's ears tried t' hide in his hair. Muirne was unhappy, too. She wanted t' see her family, but they were gone from her until she returned t' the sea. He wanted t' go t' London; she told him she couldn't. She could never live anywhere else."

Alanna was incredulous. "Didn't he know that?"

"We told him. He just didn't believe. But for all their unhappiness, they couldn't keep their hands off each other, and before the spring, she was with child."

"Finalizing the handfast. They were married for all time."

"Aye, and when he knew that, he told her he would away t' Fairchild Manor for a visit with his family before settling down here at the edge o' forever."

Mr. Lewis didn't say more. He didn't have to. Alanna knew Mr. Fairchild had run like a rat, abandoning his pregnant wife in hopes he could break the spell. Imagining Muirne's grief, Alanna asked, "Did she bear Ian alone?"

"All alone." Mr. Lewis's sorrow echoed in his voice. "She and the child lived in a cottage on the cliffs overlooking the ocean na too far from here, and when the time came she had t' go back t' the sea, she went with Ian t' Fairchild Manor. She delivered him into Leslie's hands with the admonition the child be treated well. And she reminded Leslie he was t' come here t' her when Ian had grown t' maturity."

They reached the head of the path where the rocky descent to the shore began. Alanna went first, and the incline and the narrowness interrupted the conversation. But the trail reached its end and became a sandy beach, bracketed behind and on each side by the cliffs, and there she waited for him. When he caught up, she said, "I cannot believe Mr. Fairchild foolishly came here as my guardian."

"Staying away wouldn't have saved him."

She couldn't argue that; Mr. Lewis knew the legends better than she did.

"And anyway, the others, the people who live in a part o' the British Isles where magic died long ago . . . they dunna really believe it's possible. I think he came here assuring himself that years ago he'd had a bad dream. That Muirne was really just a woman, and he'd never have t' pay the price for breaking his word." A great, dry block of granite lay tumbled among its fellows at the base of the cliff, and Mr. Lewis seated himself on it. "He's discovered differently, and he's a desperate man now."

Alanna remembered the way Mr. Fairchild had looked when he demanded Ian excavate the shoreline. "I think he hopes if he destroys all of this"— the sweep of her arm included the granite cliffs, the shore, and the sea, all the way to the horizon—"the spell which brings prosperity and tranquillity to Fionnaway will be broken."

"Perhaps it will." Mr. Lewis gazed at her, and

she thought she saw lustrous tears wet his eyes. "That's the danger, isn't it?"

She understood. This was her sacred trust, the place she'd been raised to preserve. "So I can't wait to go get the marriage document, can I? I have to go right now."

She did have to go. This was Ian's heritage. He wasn't a bastard whom Leslie had fathered on some chance-met selkie on the rocks. He was legitimate, created by two people who loved, at least for a brief moment in time.

And she knew, because she'd heard Ian's determination, and beneath it his very real fear, that he would forbid her to go. No matter that he said he didn't love her; he would forfeit his legitimacy out of apprehension for her. He would lose Fionnaway, his heart's desire.

"The tide is low," Mr. Lewis said softly, "but it'll be turning soon, and this storm has raised great swells."

He was right. Alanna wouldn't have chosen this moment for a swim, and she stared at the distant overhang that hid the cave. The storm had died, but its effect on the ocean lingered. Breakers thundered so loudly Alanna and Mr. Lewis had to raise their voices to be heard. Froth whipped up by the storm capped every swell. Shards of driftwood and smashed bits of shell littered the beach. Some sea creatures hadn't been lucky enough to escape the storm's wrath. If Alanna was unlucky, she would end up like them.

Then, for the first time in her memory, Mr. Lewis removed his hat. His short hair was coarse and slick as a seal's, and the setting sun bit into the wrinkles on his face. He was an old man, she realized, a man made weary from tending his far-flung flock of parishioners and from guarding the integrity of the pact.

"Would that I could go with ye, but I'd be a burden, na a help." He sounded as if he were trying to convince himself.

"I can do it," Alanna assured him. She had to do it. Quickly she removed her boots and her stockings and put them high on the boulder. The cold sand pressed against her bare feet as she tucked her necklace inside a boot. "I don't have the oilskin to protect the marriage license."

Standing, Mr. Lewis fumbled in his sporran and brought out her oilskin pouch. "I thought we'd need this. And inside, I placed yer marriage license. Yers and Ian's."

"Sure I would go, weren't you?" She accepted it, grinning at him, then gestured for him to turn his back.

He did. "I prayed t' God ye would."

Taking off her sash, she used it to tie her skirt up between her legs. It wasn't ladylike, but neither was her preferred method of swimming—stripping.

"I'll pray t' God ye get back safely, too," Mr. Lewis added.

"I'll take that prayer, and add my own." Lightly she touched his shoulder. "But you've always told me to pray as if all things depend on God, and work as if all things depend on me. So I'll be back, Mr. Lewis. Don't worry about that."

As she plunged into the surf, Mr. Lewis whispered, "Ah, lass, and now I'll follow my own advice."

Chapter 29

Ian strode through the woods toward the church. The storm had worn itself out as he slept. The westering sun shone on the branches and leaves littered the ground, and in the distance he could hear the sea calling his name like a long-lost parent.

He ignored it, directing his thoughts to Alanna.

When he'd woke to find her gone, he'd been grim and determined to locate his bride and bring her back. She was angry that he'd said he couldn't love her, he supposed, and she'd run somewhere to lick her wounds. Or, worse, maybe she'd woken up to the fact that because of him, she'd lost her precious Fionnaway. God knew he would have been livid.

Probably she'd run to the church, to talk to Mr. Lewis. Where else could she go? Not back to Fionnaway, obviously. No welcome awaited her there.

She was young, and he forgave her, but she had to be made to understand that the matters between a husband and wife were not to be taken outside the marriage, not even to a minister she trusted. Ian would explain. Alanna would obey. They would go on to live their lives elsewhere . . . and he would do everything in his power to make up for the loss of Fionnaway.

Make up for the loss of Fionnaway. He wanted to roar with anguish at the thought of it. How could he make up for such a deprivation? What could he give her that would take its place? His town house in London was cold and somber, a site he inhabited rather than lived. He had no pets, and he barely knew the servants.

Not like at Fionnaway, where the people welcomed him as if they understood the torments of his soul. Not like at Fionnaway, where he recognized the very stones as his kin. Not like at Fionnaway, where a woman insisted she loved him, and with her words alone created an illusion of warmth and safety, just for him.

He paid no attention as the mud from his storm sucked at his boots, and the restless breeze ruffled his hair. Instead, thoughts of Alanna consumed him.

No, the London house would be no substitute for her home—just as *he* would be no substitute for the husband she ought to have had. A husband who had the capacity to love her as she deserved.

The trouble was, he couldn't let her go now. She was the only light in his long, dark future, and somehow he would find a way to make her happy.

Blinking, he found himself standing at the edge of the cliffs. Before him ranged the path leading down to the beach. Beyond that, the ocean stretched to infinity. And once again he heard his mother's musical voice calling, "Ian. My son."

"No!" He tried to wrench himself away. He couldn't succumb to some magical enchantment. He had a wife to fetch, two lives to repair.

"Ian." He heard his name again, but this time the voice wasn't musical. It wasn't even feminine, and he glanced down.

There, on the shore, stood Mr. Lewis, waving his

arms like a windmill. "Ian! Ye've arrived just in time. Come down. Come down at once!"

Ian didn't want to. He wanted to stay far away from that wretched, churning sea.

But if Alanna wasn't with Mr. Lewis, then he didn't know where to find her, and he might as well go down and ask advice. All his instincts nagged at him; he had to find Alanna.

The scent of fish and brine clogged the air more and more as Ian descended. Salt chapped his lips, and the roar of the waves throbbed in his head like a long-forgotten melody. Instinctively he knew the tide was starting to rise, just as he knew the storm he'd conjured had agitated creatures of the deep best left undisturbed and modified shoals long settled. Those intuitions were the part of himself he hated, almost as much as he hated the selfishness he'd received from his father.

No matter that he'd thrown his ring away; the senses of a selkie could never be denied. No matter that he'd disavowed his father; the coldness of a Fairchild could never be cured. He clung to Alanna as a drowning man clung to a raft, hoping her humanity somehow would save him.

"Ian." Mr. Lewis grabbed Ian's shirtfront as he took the last steps onto the beach. The minister's hat was creased as if he'd been wringing it, and blood spotted his parched lips. "Ian, ye have to help her."

The hair on Ian's neck lifted. He grabbed the old man back. "What do you mean, I have to help *her*?" But already his gaze scanned the horizon, looking for Alanna. Looking for his wife. "She swam out, didn't she? After I told her no, she swam out."

"She did it to save Fionnaway."

"How? Is she going to find a previously unnoticed part of the pact that says she can marry a bastard?"

"Something like that. Ah, Ian—"

Ian didn't want to hear Mr. Lewis making excuses for his wife. Bitterness rose in him as inexorably as the tide. "So she's risking her life so she can have Fionnaway back."

"Aye, and for ye." Mr. Lewis quickly defended her. "She wants it for ye."

"Of course. She is sacrificing herself for me." He sneered. "For her bloody inheritance, more likely. Damn her. Damn her for a witch and liar!" He scanned the boiling surf. Nothing bobbed among the swells. "She's like every other woman in the world. Out for what she can own, what she can *have.*"

"Well." Mr. Lewis folded his thin lips as if he were offended. "What does she have with ye?"

Ian had no answer to that, and savagely he asked, "How long has she been gone?"

"Too long. I saw her dive down to get in, but the tide is rising, and she hasn't come back out." Mr. Lewis pointed. "There. The cave is behind that rock face." He grabbed Ian's arm. "Something has happened. Ian, ye've got to go after her."

"And damn you." Ian transferred his gaze to Mr. Lewis's withered face. "How could you let her go?"

Mr. Lewis smiled faintly. "I sent her, lad. Dunna ye know yet who I am?"

Seeing the silver sparks in his eyes, Ian did know. He pulled the knowledge from the depths of his soul, along with a reverence for this creature who had given over his life for the good of all. "You're the guardian selkie, the one who makes sure the humans keep the pact."

"Aye, and right now yer father and his accomplice are up there plotting to destroy this place. Our home. So get ye into the water and bring Lady Alanna back *alive*."

Ian didn't wait to hear more. He struggled out of his boots, ripped off his shirt, and plunged in.

Coldness bludgeoned him. The deep, bone-chilling cold of an ocean so ancient and so indifferent it cared nothing for the creatures who dared to challenge it. The ruthless whitecaps struck him down like the slap of a careless hand, and as he plunged deep, propelled by ferocious currents, the darkness closed over him. It was more than the darkness of depth. It was a darkness of the spirit, a rising of the old fear to choke him.

Dear God. He was suffocating. He wasn't a selkie, he couldn't breathe. He couldn't swim. He wasn't a three-year-old boy anymore who thought the sea was his playground. He was only a *man*. He had arms and legs, and his mother had said they were ill suited to swimming. He kicked wildly, desperate to find the surface. He broke free, rising high like a breaching whale, sucking in air in great gulps. Then he submerged again, and another wave pushed him down.

The panic returned, but again he struggled to the surface. He set up a frantic rhythm, tumbling under with the whitecaps, then rising to the air. He was nothing but a bit of flotsam, tossed here and there, unable to take control ... and whether or not Alanna knew it, she needed him.

Bursting out of the water, he roared with frustration. He *was* a man, damn it, and he would not allow this endless stretch of merciless sea to direct his destiny—and take the life of his wife.

With revived tenacity, he struck out toward the cave. The swells still tossed him aside, but he thought, *Alanna. Alanna,* and doggedly he would return to his course. As he neared the cliff that housed the cave, he strained to hear a cry, but the cacophony of the waves breaking against it covered any sound.

But she was here. She had to be. Remembering her description of the cave—the overhang of rock beneath which she had to maneuver, the dry, sandy land inside—he thought she must be trapped inside by the rising tide. He hoped she was just trapped inside. He prayed she had not tried to swim out now, into a sea that allowed no mistakes.

He *prayed*. He, who didn't believe in help for one such as himself, would plead for the life of Alanna. She was human. Surely God would listen.

He would join her in the cave. Denounce her there as a grasping jade. And he would thank God she was alive.

Please, God, make her be alive.

As he approached, the ocean chewed at the rock like a hungry monster. He grappled with the breakers as he scanned the area, searching for the sight of a small, red-capped head. Searching for the opening of the cave where avarice had led her.

There! The churning surf dipped enough for him to see a place where the cliff had been undercut by currents. There. Taking a huge breath, he ducked under the oncoming wave and let it carry him down and toward the cliff. Light disappeared as he rode beneath the rocky overhang, turning the water to the black ink he dreaded. Sand swirled around him, ripped from the bottom by the frantic water. He felt the rush of current as rocks tumbled off to the side.

Startled, he opened his eyes; salt stung so badly he could see nothing. All he could do was swim with huge strokes, hoping to avoid further rock-falls, seeking the entrance, somewhere ahead and above.

Then his hand tangled in something. Seaweed.

No. Wait. He reached again.

Hair. Long, flowing hair. Hands grabbed at him. Alanna. She was coming up, rising to the surface.

Not here.

With that uncanny sense of his, he realized they couldn't reach the air. The changes beneath the ocean must have disoriented her, and if they surfaced now, they'd be directly under the cliff. They'd be trapped, dashed against the rocks.

Frantically he plunged deeper, pushing her down.

Frantically she fought him. She was out of oxygen.

Please, love. Please, trust me this last time.

She twisted against his hold for one more moment. Then, as if she'd heard his plea, she went limp. He nudged her down farther, seeking the lower current, the one that flowed away from the cliffs. She stirred again, shuddering, and he knew she was losing the battle for life. If he didn't get her out of here and back to the atmosphere soon, he might as well swallow seawater and join her on the bottom.

Then something shoved him hard. He clung to Alanna as some creature pushed him from behind. Down. Out. Up.

Ian and Alanna broke the surface into the slanting sunlight. As he greedily sucked in air, he saw a head pop up nearby. A sleek, seal black head with eyes he recognized. A face he knew.

Yearning struck him such a blow he almost went under again. Salt burned his eyes; not the salt of the sea, but of old tears long suppressed. He cried out, he didn't know what.

Then in his hands, Alanna struggled. She coughed, half drowned but still fighting. A great wave rose over them; he lifted her, keeping her above water as it broke over his head.

When the swell had subsided, he looked around them again. That other creature had disappeared.

Wrapping his arm around Alanna's chest, he dragged her after him. The shore appeared and disappeared as the sea rose and fell. He cursed the anger that had brought the storm, then imagined how he would scold Alanna. Damn her for causing this great, tearing emotion inside him.

The incoming tide carried them along almost without effort, and he was grateful. He couldn't have done it on his own. The swim out, the panic, and the cold had depleted his resources.

Then he remembered the push he'd received below the surface.

He *hadn't* done it on his own. Something had helped him.

Someone.

His feet struck sand. He stumbled erect, holding Alanna; then a wave pushed him over. She was choking when they came up again, closer to shore, and this time he let the breakers carry them as far as they could. When he struck bottom, he crawled on his hands and knees, dragging Alanna.

Above the line of wet sand, to the place where the waves couldn't touch them.

Like flotsam on the beach, they lay on their stomachs, panting, coughing up seawater. Bits of shell dug into his cheek as he stared at Alanna, covered with goose bumps, shuddering with cold, hair stringy with sand and strands of seaweed.

She looked good. She looked alive.

Turning her head, the greedy girl caught his gaze and her blue lips parted in a loving smile. Did she think he believed in that love now?

"Why did you do it?" The question burst from him. "You betrayed me."

Her smile faded. She sat up on her elbows, then dipped her head guiltily. "I know you told me not to swim out there." Sitting up, she untied the sash wrapped around her waist and carefully freed the oilskin packet. "But when I tell you what I retrieved—"

"I know about your beloved document! Mr. Lewis told me."

She halted, her hand outstretched as he eyed the oilskin disdainfully. "Then I don't understand. Aren't you thrilled?"

"Thrilled?" He rose to his hands and knees and glared at her with as much rancor as Damon at his most feral. "Thrilled? That my wife would risk her life—and mine—for a piece of paper and a bit of land? But I suppose I can't blame you for that. After all, I did everything in my power to get Fionnaway, too. But you lied to me."

She had the nerve to look confused. "What lie did I tell?"

"You said you loved me."

Her hand fell back to her side. "I do love you."

"Only if you can have Fionnaway, too."

Cocking her head, she studied him. Studied him when he thought she would be stammering explanations and excuses. Her calm manner almost made him uncomfortable, as he had been years ago when his mother confronted him about his unreasonable temper.

He turned his back to Alanna and sat down, staring out at the sun as the rim just touched the horizon.

And heard her scooting up beside him. "Ian." She wrapped her arm around his shoulder, or at least the part of his shoulder her arm could cover.

"When we left Fionnaway, I knew—or at least, I was quite sure—your father lied."

He twitched, but her arm remained in place. "Which time?"

"The last time. The time he said you were a bastard."

Ian's breath caught in his throat. "Bastard?" he croaked. "I am a bastard."

"Nay," she said softly. "You're not."

Turning his head, he stared at her. Nothing stirred in his breast. Not hope, not pleasure, nothing but the weary knowledge she was wrong. She had to be wrong. He'd been a bastard all his life.

"Mr. Lewis didn't tell you that?" Opening the oilskin, she unwrapped a series of packages until she could spread the stiff sheepskin flat. She offered it to him. "Your parents' marriage license."

He refused to scrutinize it. If she lied to him about this—oh, God, about *this*—he would die. He would shrivel and die.

"Ian." She stroked his cheek. "Look."

Sluggishly he moved his eyes. Just his eyes. *Marriage*, he saw on the top. He looked back at Alanna. "It's real. Touch it."

Coaxed by her gentle tone, he took it between two fingers and, taking a deep breath, stared at it.

Marriage at the top. A date: *5 June, 1765*. Signatures at the bottom. *Leslie Ernest Edward Hyatt Fairchild. Muirne of the Selkies.* And *The Reverend Mr. Ranger Lewis.*

Ian's hand began to shake. "All my prayers . . ." He could scarcely speak. "All my prayers, all these years, unanswered. And now . . . now . . ."

Alanna's voice was rich with satisfaction. "So God does listen to creatures such as you."

Her face swam before his eyes, and she caught the fluttering license. "Let's not lose it, shall we?"

"No." He let her have it and dashed the tears from his face. "Let's not."

The wind still blew, but it seemed less harsh as she rewrapped the license and half buried it in the sand.

"How did you know?" he asked hoarsely.

"Leslie told me." She butted Ian until he put his arm around her, then she snuggled close. "Not in so many words, of course, but it's obvious to those who are raised here. He couldn't walk away from your mother. The marriage between humans and selkies is made in the eyes of God. Just like ours."

A timely reminder.

"They marry for all time. As long as they're alive, they should be together, but because of the children, that's not always possible. So your mother stayed on land to raise you, then took you to your father. When you had grown to be a man, he was supposed to come back and join your mother in the water."

His head swiveled to face her. "How?"

" 'Tis selkie magic."

"He would have drowned."

"Why? Selkies breath air, like we do. They just swim better." She looked out over the thrashing sea. "A lot better."

It didn't take intuition to know what went wrong between his mother and father. "My father was afraid."

"He should have thought of that before he married your mother, then abandoned her and you." She condemned Leslie without compassion. "But your father's not the only coward who's ever lived, so we know about the sickness that develops when a human breaks that sacred vow. Have you noticed how your father's complexion looks shiny and bloated, as if he were a body washed up on the beach? Have you heard how he breathes, as if his lungs are full of water?"

Ian remembered a vision he'd had once, of Leslie cast up on the beach.

"He's drowning," she confirmed. "Drowning in pure air."

Of course. Leslie was dying because of the selkie curse. "That's why he was so desperate to destroy Fionnaway's shoreline. He thought that would break the spell."

"That's why I never asked if you were legitimate." She rubbed her head against his chest. "I recognized the signs of your father's illness and thought it proof. I won't lie to you, Ian. Fionnaway is important to me. Not just because I have sworn before God to protect it from all danger, but because it's mine. My place in the world, and I love it. But I think you understand that, just as I understood why you would marry a silly girl for her inheritance."

She *had* understood. She'd never reproached him, or cried that she wanted to be loved for herself and not her lands. Now that he thought about it, she was probably glad he coveted Fionnaway as he did, for his desire formed a bond between them, an assurance he would care for it as she did. "Not such a *silly* girl," he said.

"When Mr. Fairchild denied he had wed your mother, and you agreed it was true, I felt as if you had betrayed me." She brought up her knees and tucked her hands between them. "But I realized you didn't know that was the condition which would make us lose Fionnaway. And then . . . then you said we could get an annulment."

He grunted.

"Oh, Ian." She wrapped her arms around his

neck and kissed his ear. "You were willing to give up Fionnaway so I could have it."

This was making him uneasy. She was acting as if he'd behaved nobly. He never behaved nobly. "I'd already lost it. I wasn't giving anything up."

"I flatter myself it would have been a wrench to give me up." She sounded as if she were smiling.

He glanced sideways. She *was* smiling.

"I would have let you keep me as your lover," he said grudgingly.

She burst into laughter. "Thank you very much." Uncovering the oilskin pouch, she tucked it into his shirt. "There's the proof of your legitimacy, if you want it."

Groping, his hand found the bulkiness of the parcel. Of course he wanted it. He'd wanted to be legitimate his whole life, and now he discovered he was. Yet he hadn't greeted the news with unrestrained joy. Instead he'd been distrustful, and acted the bastard everyone had called him.

Alanna crawled around to face him. The ocean rumbled behind her; the wind struggled to pick up the heavy strands of her hair. She shoved them behind her ears and asked, "Ian, is it so hard for you to believe I love you? I had nothing to gain by telling you so."

He looked at her, framed by the sea, the sun, and the crimson sky. She'd said she loved him, and maybe she really did. Maybe . . . she did.

"I just don't understand why." He caught her neck in his hand. "Why would anyone love me?"

"For the same reason I love Fionnaway." She smiled. "You're mine."

She leaned toward him. He leaned toward her. Their lips met—and an incoming wave splashed around them.

He jerked her up. They ran backward while she

laughed, and he found a grin curving his lips.

He'd thought he would never grin again.

Rubbing his hands along her tightly clenched arms to create friction, he said, "It's getting dark. We've got to go get warm."

"Yes." She let him turn her away, then pointed upward. "Look. The new moon is rising."

So it was. The barest sliver of light in the purple sky of the east. He stared at it, and wondered if it was a sign. A new moon for a new life.

"Ian." Alanna wrung seawater from her skirt. "What was that thing that pushed us?"

"That thing?" He knew perfectly well what she meant, but he stalled, his emotions precarious and fragile.

"In the water." She watched him. "The creature that got us up to the surface before we drowned."

He turned back to the ocean and scanned the waves, looking for a familiar head. "I suppose it was my mother."

"You suppose?"

Remembering the face, the smile, he said, "It was my mother."

"That's what I thought," Alanna crowed. "She couldn't save you when you almost drowned when you were a lad, because she was human. But she did it this time."

"Yes. Yes, she did." His mother. For years he'd thought she had irresponsibly conceived him and abandoned him without thought. Now he knew better. Relief and bliss swelled in his chest until he thought his heart would burst. Unsteadily he said, "I suppose Mr. Lewis saved me the first time."

"Mr. Lewis? But I thought you said it was a . . ." Her voice died as she realized the truth.

Ian enjoyed her slack-jawed surprise.

"He's a selkie?"

"The guardian selkie."

"Like Armstrong is the human safeguard. Armstrong is the one who"—she took a breath—"the one who sells the sea opals at market."

Remembering her reticence about Armstrong's whereabouts, he asked, "Why didn't you say so?"

"You were so angry about the stones I thought you'd be angry about that, too. But he'll be returning soon." Her mouth curved with satisfaction. "And there'll be a decided increase in our coffers."

He touched the bulk of the oilskin beneath his shirt. "I suppose you got more stones while you were in the cave."

"The selkies didn't leave any this time. They have a way of knowing what happens at Fionnaway—well, obviously, Mr. Lewis informs them—and until we find out who has stolen the sea opals, they'll not leave any more."

"So when we have solved that mystery, you will want to swim out again."

She kicked at a fragment of shell.

"Not by yourself," he said, staring up at the moon. "I'll go with you."

She tugged at his arm until he looked at her. "But you're afraid!"

"For good reason, as we've just proved. But I'd be more afraid to stay onshore and wonder. So I'll go."

"Oh, Ian."

She was staring at him as if he were noble again, and he thought he'd better say something before he started basking like a cat in the sun. Glancing up and down the beach, he asked, "Where is the old busybody, anyway?"

"Mr. Lewis? I don't know." Alanna frowned. "I don't know."

"Damn." He scanned the rocks. "Would he have gone back to the water?"

"Forever? Not without saying good-bye. Do you suppose he's had an accident?"

"I doubt that smart old man would have an accident."

"But he *is* old. He said so. He said he would have swum with me, but he couldn't. What if a wave caught him, or he fell on the rocks?"

Ian didn't know why, but her disquietude struck him hard. "You go that way"—he pointed toward the path—"I'll go that way." The longer way. He could cover the ground faster, and with the tide coming in, they had no time to waste.

He hurried, peering among the boulders at the base of the cliff, looking for any sign of the thin man with the broad-brimmed hat. There was nothing, and Ian had just started back when he heard Alanna shout at the far end of the beach. Clambering over massive boulders, she disappeared into a crevasse at the base of the cliff.

She reappeared on the top of the rock, waving frantically. Cupping her hands around her mouth, she yelled, "I recognize him by the hat, and by my rune on his chest, but he's . . . not human anymore."

Ian saw her lips move again, but the wind and the waves washed the sound away. "What?"

This time he heard her only too well. "He's been stabbed."

She turned to go back to Mr. Lewis.

"No." Ian increased his speed. "No! Alanna, get out of there."

He saw the masculine form climbing onto the rocks above her. He ran, and knew he'd never get there in time. He shrieked a warning; she turned and raised her arms to protect herself.

Edwin jumped at her, his silver knife flashing red in the rays of the setting sun.

Chapter 30

"What do you think you're doing?" Alanna shouted at her cousin. She knocked his hand up, and followed with a punch to the face. "I could always thrash you."

As Edwin staggered backward, the significance of his presence struck her.

Edwin had a knife. Mr. Lewis was dead. And Edwin—stupid, blundering Edwin—was *attacking* her.

She tried to jump out of the way, barely avoiding the gray seal-like creature that had been Mr. Lewis. Boulders rimmed the little cleft. Her soggy skirts tripped her, and she fell. She groped for something, anything; grabbed a handful of material and rolled. Caught Edwin's deadly slash in the crown of the minister's hat. Edwin cursed and tore the tattered felt out of her hands. He lifted the knife.

In the distance she heard Ian's shout.

He wasn't going to make it in time. She lifted her arms to protect her heart.

Then from the side, someone attacked. Edwin sprawled against the boulders. Alanna struggled to her feet, and Brice shouted, "Get away! Alanna, get out!"

She hesitated. With the two of them against Edwin . . .

"He won't hurt me," Brice said.

Using her hands and feet, she scrambled out onto a boulder. Ian was shouting, running across the beach toward them, and she yelled, "Hurry!"

And heard a scream behind her. She turned. Brice writhed on the ground. Edwin stood over him, blood dripping from the blade. As he lifted the knife again, she tried to scream.

But from above her she heard, "Edwin, mercy. He's your brother!"

Wilda stood on the path, her hands pressed to her sides. She panted in great breaths, but she cried again, "Edwin, mercy!"

Edwin lifted the knife higher yet.

"Edwin . . ." Wilda sobbed.

He dropped his hand. Working the knife in his grip, he said to Brice, "You got in my way."

And stalked toward Alanna again. *Run,* she urged herself.

Edwin grabbed for her and missed, grabbed for her skirt and caught it. She fell, striking the flat top of the boulder hard. She lost her breath. She clawed for a handhold; caught a cleft in the rock. He pulled, trying to drag her back down. She kicked at him. With a curse, he pulled himself up beside her.

She heard the shout from down on the beach, and Edwin glanced up into the deepening gloom.

"Ian," she whispered.

Standing, Edwin kicked her in the ribs. "Later," he promised. Then as Ian ran up, he launched himself at Ian.

Alanna tried to catch her breath, tried to sit up, but the struggle with the sea had consumed her strength. Worse, she knew Ian had done more, swum harder, run farther, and now he rolled on the ground with Edwin.

With her gentle cousin Edwin who would kill them all to take possession of Fionnaway and its cache of stones.

Seeing movement on the path, she shouted, "Wilda. You've got to get help."

Instead, Wilda reached the beach and ran at the two men. What good could Wilda do against a killer with a knife?

But Wilda bypassed them, and Alanna, as if they weren't even there. Scrambling up the boulders, she slid down into the cleft and grabbed for Brice. "Don't die," she pleaded.

"Damn, Wilda, don't jiggle me," Brice said.

Wilda burst into tears and cradled his head in her lap.

Below Alanna, Ian and Edwin tumbled, locked together in a macabre embrace. Encroaching breakers continued to crash up the beach, overpowering all sound. Alanna strained to see in the gathering dusk, strained to stand, but could only slither off the rock onto the ground. She sat gasping, clutching her side. Each breath was agony.

She braced herself and picked up a good-sized stone in both hands. The muscles across her ribs pulled and burned, but she stumbled to her feet. Dimly she saw Ian, flat on his back, the thinnest part of the waves sliding beneath him. She saw Edwin, his dark shape straddling Ian like a giant leech. His head formed a clear target. The bloodlust rose in her. She'd see him dead. He'd threatened her Ian.

She staggered toward the two men.

In time to witness Edwin plunge the knife toward Ian. Catching Edwin's wrist in both hands, Ian slowly began to turn it. Edwin screamed in rage and punched him in the face with his free hand, but Ian ignored the blows. The muscles in Edwin's face strained as he tried to stop the knife. Inexorably it descended.

Edwin broke. Whimpering, he dropped the knife and twisted, trying to get away. Ian let him. He picked up the discarded blade and when Edwin splashed to his feet, prepared to run, Ian lay there and said, "Sniveling coward."

Two words. *Sniveling coward.*

"Bastard!" Edwin shouted, and jumped at Ian's prostrate form.

In the feeble moonlight the knife flashed, point up.

Edwin jerked as he landed on the blade. Alanna heard Edwin's grunt as it penetrated his neck. Instinctively she turned her head away.

"It's over," Ian said. "Help me get him off."

Her rock landed with a thump on the wet sand as she hurried to him. He had already levered Edwin away, and she shoved at her cousin's legs and arms without regard until the body fell facefirst in the sand.

Ian lay flat. Something was wrong.

"Did he hurt you?" he asked.

"Broke one of my ribs." She knelt in the ebb and flow of the waves. Her hands skimmed over his head, his neck, his shoulders. Why wasn't Ian sitting up?

He tried to laugh. Gasped in agony. "He killed me."

She froze. "Ian?"

"Stabbed me when he jumped off the boulder. Made it worse in the struggle." He lay limp on the sand, his voice growing fainter with each word.

"Ian?" She found the wound. A thin, deep stab

to the chest spurted blood with each of his heart-beats. "Ian?"

Then they stopped. Just stopped. No more spurts. No more heartbeats. No more breath.

"Ian?" She crouched over him, fumbling with his chest as if she could bring the life back. "Ian?"

At that moment in Fionnaway Manor, Leslie Fairchild slumped in his chair. A gush of salty water spewed from his mouth, and he died.

Alone.

"Heaven's mercy, m'lady, what's happened?" Armstrong stood on the beach, a dun silhouette against the gathering stars.

She didn't wonder why he was there or how he'd got here. She just said, "He's not breathing, Armstrong. Make him start."

Armstrong splashed into the water, dropped to his knees beside her, and pushed her hands away.

She put them back over the wound. That would keep the blood in.

Armstrong pressed Ian's neck, held his hand to Ian's lips. His voice rich with pity, he said, "M'lady, he's gone. M'lady . . ."

She couldn't hear him. "We need to drag him above the waterline. He'll get chilled. It's not good for a man with a wound to be chilled."

"Da?" A young girl spoke beside them. "What's wrong with him?" She pointed at the other body. "And him?"

Alanna could see the faint gleam of Armstrong's eyes as he looked up at his daughter. A multitude of footsteps sounded, and Mrs. Armstrong said, "In the name o' God, what's happened here?"

Alanna harkened to a murmur of voices, realized the events of the evening had drawn the servants from Fionnaway Manor. The fishermen and the villagers had followed, and now the beach was full. Full of people. Full of . . . nothing.

Crouching closer to Ian, she stared at him, trying to make out his features in the feeble light of the new moon. "Ian . . ." She called him softly. "Ian, please . . ." *She could see him better now. His strong features were peaceful.*

"What is that?" Mrs. Armstrong asked sharply. "Armstrong, what is that?"

His pale skin caught the white light and reflected it back to her.

"It's the moon."

He looked as if he could wake if she just called him. "*Ian . . .*"

"It canna be the moon. It's time for the new moon. I saw it as I ran here."

"*Ian . . .*" *She cupped his face in her hands and kissed him. Kissed him, and realized he was already getting cold.*

"What else could it be? It's the moon, and it's—" Alanna looked up. "It's full."

Armstrong stared at her. Mrs. Armstrong, and Ellie, and behind them all the villagers and fishermen, stared at her.

"He said if he loved me"—Alanna removed her clinging hands from Ian's still body—"a full moon would shine from a new-moon sky."

As if on her signal, everyone looked up, and she did, too. The full moon shone brightly, assuring her of her heart's desire. Assuring her when it was too late.

Alanna stood, her whole body aching with pain and grief. "He said he'd make the waves die down on a windy night." She gestured at the sea, now quiescent as a pool on the stillest day. "He said if he loved me, he'd make the sea clear as glass."

Babble arose as the moonlight penetrated the ocean water near Ian. Visibility spread out from him in an ever-increasing circle, displaying first the sandy bottom close to shore, then encompassing the sandbar, the broken rocks at the base of the protruding cliffs, and at the edge of the bay, the shoals and schools of fish that darted among them. And for just a moment, in a far deeper place, Alanna saw the selkies swimming in agitated circles.

"He said he'd do all that—if he loved me." Her voice broke, and she bowed her head as the reality of his death crushed her.

Someone tentatively touched her shoulder. A handkerchief was pressed into her hand. But she wasn't crying. How could she? The pain plunged too deep, too fresh. She could barely breathe, barely comprehend. How did anyone think she could do something so banal as cry? Not when Ian was dead.

Ian was dead.

The growl, when she noticed it, seemed only a illusion, a figment of a mind dazed and simple. But the ground beneath her feet began to tremble, growing in strength as the seconds passed. Gravel showered off the surrounding cliffs. The people around her muttered, their voices rising.

"Armstrong," Mrs. Armstrong said. "Armstrong, what is that?"

Alanna lifted her head and tried to see through eyes so dry her vision blurred.

"Run," Armstrong ordered. "Take Ellie and run." Grabbing Alanna's elbow, he said again, "Run!" He didn't wait to see if she obeyed, but dragged her with him toward the path, shouting to everyone, "Run, before it gets us all."

The ocean, rebelling against the constraints Ian's love had placed on it, rose in a huge wave. People were darting about, yelling, pressing close to the cliff. Mrs. Armstrong had Ellie up on a boulder, and she held the child against her chest and watched the sea with terror-filled eyes.

"Nay!" Hysteria filled Alanna as she saw Ian's still form laid out on the beach and tried to wrestle herself free from Armstrong's grip. "Ian. We've got to get Ian!"

Armstrong wouldn't let her go. He wrapped her in his arms and held on grimly as she fought him, pulling her ever farther up the shore.

Then the wave crashed down, covering Ian, filling the beach, sucking hungrily at everyone caught in its maw. Shrieks of terror rose as first one, then another, lost their footing. They came up again, caught by clutching hands, or standing on their own. Armstrong held Alanna, both wet to their knees, and braced them against the suction of the retreating wave.

When the wave had withdrawn, everyone remained on the beach. Everyone—except Ian. The place where he had rested was empty.

"Nay." Alanna couldn't believe it. How could they? How dared they? "Nay, I want him back." She broke away from Armstrong, and this time he let her go. Frenzied with rage, she ran into the surf until it slapped at her thighs. The ocean wasn't transparent anymore, but she knew the selkies were there. She knew they could hear her. "Give him back to me. He's my husband." Beating on the water with the flat of her hand, she shouted, "He's human, not selkie, and he deserves to be buried on the land. Next to me. Give me back his body."

Armstrong waded out to her. "M'lady, don't do this." Agony laced his tone.

"I want him back." She slapped water toward Armstrong to keep him away. The whitecaps were surging again, not gentle, nor overwhelming, but still big and agitated by the storm. She didn't care. She stumbled, righted herself, breathing harshly as she made her demand. "I want his body."

"Maybe the ocean'll give it back." Armstrong tried to comfort her. "Sometimes it does."

"I want it *now*."

"M'lady . . ." The night was dark again, lit not by a full moon but by a new moon. She could scarcely see Armstrong's face, but she knew he stood there, a servant, a friend, not wanting to lay hands on her again, not wanting to leave her alone, but shivering and more than a little afraid.

She wasn't afraid. What was there to be afraid of now? Ian was dead.

But inside herself, she heard a wee voice chide her. She was the lady, it said. She had duties. Duties that started with Armstrong, her safeguard. *He* still had a wife and child on the beach, and more children at home. His family did care what happened to him, and it seemed the ingrained habits of a lifetime were not easily discarded.

So Alanna turned away from the thief of an ocean and waded out of the surf. "We need to take Mr. Lewis's body and put it in the water." She sounded almost normal, she noted, and the lady's conscience approved.

"Aye, m'lady," Armstrong said.

"And is Brice dead?"

"Nay, m'lady." Armstrong pointed a shaking finger at the beach.

She saw two dim figures limping toward the path, and she stopped, her feet still covered by the sloshing surf. By the way Wilda held him, by the way Brice leaned on her, it was clear they had worked out whatever problems plagued them. The laird of the MacLeods would be celebrating his wedding as soon as his wound had healed.

Alanna turned her head away. She was the lady of Fionnaway. She had to help the sweethearts, but she didn't have to watch. "You'd better pick out two of the biggest men and have them carry Brice. He'll never be able to get up that cliff by himself." The waves were rushing up on her calves now, then falling back. "Edwin stabbed him."

"Edwin?" Armstrong said incredulously.

"He killed Ian, too."

"That other body was Edwin?"

She started walking again. "Is Edwin gone, too?"

Armstrong looked around. "I dunna see it."

She half turned toward the ocean. "I don't want that one back," she told the selkies.

The people on the beach milled about, talking in low voices, but a few of the wetter folk, the ones with children, were beginning to leave. Soon, Alanna knew, the path would be full as they climbed to their homes and settled in their beds.

Together. They would be together.

Everyone would be with their families. With the people they loved—and the people who loved them. Except her.

Walking to one of the boulders, she wearily sank down. Her ribs hurt again; she hadn't noticed them before, but now the ache was persistent—and negligible when compared to her heavy heart.

A heavy heart. She leaned against the rock. She had never realized it before, but the phrase was more than a cliché; it was the truth. Her heart felt as if it weighed her down, beating slowly beneath the magnitude of impending grief. She knew in her mind Ian was dead; soon, she could tell, she would know with her heart.

"M'lady, it's cold and dark. We should go back t' Fionnaway."

"Go ahead." Twisting her heels, she dug her feet into the sand and waved Armstrong off. "I'll come up soon."

"Then I'll stay here with ye."

She heard the uneasiness in his tone. He was, after all, the safeguard, and responsible for her as well as for the stones. But he had no reason to worry. The lady of Fionnaway understood her duty. "I'd like to be alone."

"I dunna think that's wise."

"I'm just going to sit here for a while." She looked up at his dim shape, careful to keep the hovering anguish at bay. "Go home to your family, Armstrong. They need you more than I do."

Something about her calm manner must have convinced him, for he bowed and retreated. But he returned promptly with a blanket he'd scrounged from someone, and laid it across her shoulders, then he placed her boots beside her.

"Thank you," she said faintly. The blanket smelled of damp wool, but it protected her against the breeze. She tucked it close around her shoulders as the last whispers of concern died away. Everyone was gone.

Chapter 31

She was all alone. Trying to comprehend, Alanna stared out at the ocean. It had given her so much. Fionnaway, the stones, the pact: everything about her birthright found its origin in the sea.

Now it had taken its fee. She still had her heritage, the estate that had meant so much to her. She was still the lady of Fionnaway. Before her stretched days filled with work and worry, joy and fulfillment. And she would perform her tasks alone.

Reaching for her boots, she shook out her socks. Her necklace dropped onto the sand. Picking it up, she stared at it as if she had never seen it before.

No one was left to offer her a rune stone on her birthday, and Mr. Lewis had taken the one she'd picked yesterday. She'd seen it on his bloodied chest. She had recognized it. The death rune.

So Mr. Lewis had sacrificed himself for her. Ian had sacrificed himself for her.

Lifting the necklace, she placed it around her neck and felt the chill of the stones.

Didn't these men comprehend that loneliness ate at her spirit until she was nothing but a hollow shell? She'd already been isolated when she lived at the witch's hut, but then she had subsisted on hope.

Now she had nothing.

She worked her hands into the sand, lifted it and pressed it into clumps. Some would say her responsibilities would be easier to perform without Ian. He had, after all, been selfish, cynical, and determined to have his own way.

She clenched her fist and stopped the flow of sand. He had also needed her. Needed her warmth, her laughter, her love. His last, magnificent gesture proved that.

She looked up at the sliver of a moon now high in the sky.

And she had needed him. Dear God, she needed him now.

The first sob tore from her throat, followed by a second, and a third. She wanted Ian. Tears scoured her cheeks until the skin was raw. Her belly ached, her lungs burned. She wanted her lover to hold her, but the chill of a indifferent Scottish night surrounded her. Sorrow tumbled from her, unimpeded by convention or discretion. No one heard her, no one cared, as anguish lacerated her with the dull edge of a blade.

Until she heard a feminine voice call across the distance.

"Alanna. Alanna."

She dashed the tears from her eyes, looked around frantically. Her mother. It had sounded like her mother.

"Alanna. Out here."

She stared out at the black waves. Was there someone out there?

Groping along the rock behind her, she lifted herself to her feet. There was something. Someone? Yes, a head bobbed toward shore, and in the face

Alanna glimpsed echoes of enchanting beauty.

But all her attention fixed on the large object the creature propelled in front of her.

"Ian."

Not her mother. His. Muirne had brought him back.

"Ian!" Alanna screamed his name, tossed the blanket, and ran. Water sprayed as she pounded into the surf. The waves swamped her; her movements slowed. Unsteadily she struggled on. "Ian."

Alone, he rolled toward her, still clad in his trousers, and she caught him. Was he alive? Had the selkies somehow used their magic to cheat death? "A miracle," she pleaded aloud. "Another miracle."

She dragged him to shore, onto the sand, knelt beside him, touched him . . .

Dead. Still dead.

"Please." She smoothed her hand along his face. "Please. I need you so much." She clasped his hands, touched his chest. The wound had healed, leaving only a thin line that faintly glowed; the selkies had been able to do that. "Ian, please come back to me."

She'd demanded his body back, but what she'd really wanted was his life. She'd wanted the selkies to take him into the deep and use their magic on him.

They hadn't. They couldn't. Death held reign over the greatest magic.

So now she had him, and the having was almost worse than not having. When he wasn't with her, she could delude herself. But no delusion was possible as she held him, saw his dim features, and knew he would never again smile at her, trying to charm her into his bed. Never frown at her and forbid her to do her duty. Never look over the land with the craving of a outcast. Never create dreams for her and make them come true.

Her tears dropped onto his skin, glistened in the feeble light. "I love you." She heard the call of the seabirds as they nested in the cliffs above the beach, and as Ian had commanded, she remembered that day in the meadow. She remembered the rough wool of the blanket, the scent of crushed grass, the clouds drifting through the blue sky. He had forced her to listen, to look, to absorb his possession into her every sense, and now she could never forget. He would be with her always—but only in her mind.

Dropping her head onto his chest, she pressed her wet cheek against his chilly flesh. "I'll always love you."

Beneath her ear, she heard a sound. She caught her sob, half formed.

Nothing. His heart remained silent. There was nothing but a desperate woman's longing.

But then . . . a swish. A thump.

A beat.

"Ian?" Hope tumbled in her. Desperation ignited her. Holding her breath, she pressed her ear as hard as she could against his breastbone.

Nothing.

"Please, God." If heartfelt prayer could bring a man back, then Ian would live indeed. "Please, God." Lifting her head, she shook Ian. "You can do it. Come back to me. Ian!" She put her hand to his slack mouth. No breath. "Ian!" Frustration roiled in her veins, and she smacked her fist against his chest.

And he flinched.

"Oh, please." She cried, rubbed him, begged him and God and love itself.

He shuddered beneath her ministrations. Had

her faith been rewarded? He was moving. He was alive!

Euphoric, anxious, afraid that the life that had gone so easily could go again, she stumbled to her feet. "Cold. Are you cold?" Running to the discarded blanket, she raced back and spread it over him.

He was breathing. Faintly, but breathing.

"You've got to get out of the water." She caressed his face, petted his hair, lifted the edges of the blanket and winced at their dampness. "Nay, wait." He was like a newborn, and she expected him to walk. How foolish. "I'll get you out. Don't exert yourself."

His eyelids fluttered as she grabbed his shoulders and jerked. And fell to her knees as her ribs protested. Holding her side with her hands, she fought the pain.

When she opened her eyes, she found him watching her.

His lips moved, but no sound came out.

"Try again," she encouraged him, wondering if she'd run mad, then touching his forehead and knowing she had not.

Faintly he whispered, "You brought me back."

She had brought him back? She almost laughed. What had she done but shriek and cry and adore him past the doorway of death? "Not me." She whispered, too.

"It was you who brought me the final step." His hand lifted, groped until she caught it in her own. "Your tears on my face. Your love."

She cried, dashed the tears off her face, cried some more. "Can you move?"

Stupid, inconsequential question, when she wanted to say so much more.

"Of course." He lifted himself onto his elbows. "See?"

"You're in the water. The blanket's getting wet."

Wincing, he inched back onto the beach while she hovered, wanting to help, unsure if she should.

"Sorry." As he lay flat, he apologized for his breathlessness. "I'm weak."

"Of course you are. You've never been dead before." She leaned toward him. "Let me help you sit up."

She knew it was he, Ian truly returned to her, when he used her nearness to capture her face in his hands.

"Alanna, did you see the moon, the wind, the sea? Did you understand?"

Beyond words now, she could only nod.

"I love you. You're a part of me, the best of me, and I couldn't bear to leave you."

"Thank God," she murmured.

"Yes. Thank God. My God." Pulling her to him, he wrapped her in his arms and held her. Just held her.

It was the only place in the world she wanted to be. She savored his heat, his breath, his heartbeat, as surely as she did her own. And slowly she became aware of the salt-laden breeze, the cold sand beneath them, the tumble of rocks as another wave undercut the cliffs. Loath to leave, yet knowing he should be resting before a fire, she said, "We should go."

"Yes. Alanna?"

"What?" She helped him first to sit, then stand, supporting him as he regained his balance.

"Look what I brought back."

She glanced at his outthrust hand. There, on his middle finger, he wore a ring. His ring. She caught it, lifted it to her mouth, kissed it. "I took my true wedding vows on this ring. I'm glad to see it back."

"I'm glad to have it back. And, Alanna?" He fumbled in his trouser pocket, then brought out the oilskin parcel. Opening it, he ordered, "Cup your hands."

She did, and he poured a glistening hoard of sea opals into her palms. In the warmth of her hand, they changed, grew bright, and blazed with radiant joy. Her joy.

With a deep satisfaction, he said, "There they are."

She looked up to smile at him, but he was gazing out to sea.

She stared, too, and realized he wasn't talking about the stones, for heads bobbed in the surf. Selkies. Dozens of selkies.

Ian waved an arm toward them. "They've come to congratulate us."

Faintly, on the wind, Alanna heard their cries, and among them, one special voice.

Muirne's voice.

Ian heard it, too, absorbing it with a smile. Then he hugged Alanna close and turned her toward the cliff. "Come on, love," he said. "Let's go back to Fionnaway. Let's go home."

Vast, restless, and overwhelming, the sea tears at the western coast of Scotland. Fingers of land reach into the water, trying to grasp eternity and losing to the constant grind of the waves. The wind lifts the brine and carries it up, into the Highlands where mist drifts over tall standing stones like silk draped over the finest lady. There where the land and the sea meet is a place of special enchantment, of special beings, of humans and of selkies.

Some die. Some live. Some perish from broken promises. Some are rescued by love.

One is my son. Ian is his name, and he has what I could never find. A helpmate and a lover.

He has given me what I have always longed for. A daughter I hold most dear.

Alanna.

For them I see six lassies and the first lad ever born to this branch of the MacLeods. I see success and wealth and happiness. Most of all, I see long life and everlasting love.

And what else could a mother wish for her children?

—Muirne of the Selkies, August 1800

THE WORLD OF
AVON ROMANCE SUPERLEADERS

Cross-promotion and rebate offer in the back of every book!

MEET THE MEN OF AVON ROMANCE . . .
They're fascinating, they're sexy—they're irresistible! They're the kind of men you definitely want to bring home—but not to meet the family. And they live in such romantic places, from Regency England to the Wild West. These men are guaranteed to provide you with hours of reading pleasure. So introduce yourself to these unforgettable heroes, and meet a different man every month.

AND THE WRITERS WHO CREATE THEM
At Avon we bring you books by the brightest stars of romantic fiction. Christina Dodd, Catherine Anderson and Pamela Morsi. Kathleen Eagle, Lisa Kleypas and Barbara Freethy. These are the bestselling writers who create books you'll never forget— each and every story is a "keeper." Following is a sneak preview of their newest books . . .

Enter the world of New York Times *best-selling author* **Catherine Anderson**. *This award-winning writer creates a place where dreams really do come true and love always triumphs. In April, Catherine creates her most memorable characters of all in* **Forever After**.

County Sheriff Heath Masters has a hard enough time managing small-town crime, and he doesn't need any complications—especially ones in the very attractive form of his new neighbor, Meredith Kenyon, and her adorable daughter, Sammy. But when Heath's giant of a dog causes trouble for Merry, he finds himself in trouble, too . . . of the romantic kind.

FOREVER AFTER
by Catherine Anderson

Heath vaulted over the tumble-down fence that divided his neighbor's patchy lawn from the adjoining cow pasture, then poured on speed to circle the house. He skidded to a halt about fifteen feet shy of a dilapidated woodshed. A child, dressed in pink pants and a smudged white T-shirt, stood splayed against the outbuilding. Her eyes were so wide with fright they resembled china-blue supper plates.

Fangs bared and frothing at the jowls, Goliath lunged back and forth between the child and a young woman Heath guessed to be her mother.

"Stay back!" he ordered.

At the sound of his voice the woman turned around, her pinched face so pale that her dark brown eyes looked almost as large as her daughter's. "Oh, thank God! Help us! Do something, please, before he hurts us!"

Heath jerked has gaze back to his dog. If ever there had been an animal he would trust with a child, Goliath was it. Yet now the rottweiler seemed to have gone berserk.

Heath snapped his fingers. "Goliath, heel!"

At the command, the rottweiler whirled toward Heath, his usually friendly brown eyes glinting a demonic red. For an awful instant Heath was afraid the dog might not obey him.

What in the hell was wrong with him? Heath's gaze shot to the terrified child.

"Goliath, *heel!*" He slapped his thigh for emphasis.

The rottweiler finally acquiesced with another frenzied bark followed by a pathetic whine, massive head lowered, legs stiff, his movements reluctant and abject. The second the dog got within reach, Heath grabbed his collar.

"Sammy!"

The woman bolted forward to gather her child into her arms with a strangled cry. Then she whirled to confront Heath, her pale, delicately molded face twisting with anger, her body quaking.

"You get that *vicious*, out-of-control dog *off* my property!"

The blaze in her eyes told Heath she was infused by the rush of adrenaline that often followed a bad scare.

"Ma'am, I'm really sorry about—"

"I don't want to hear it! Just get that monster out of here!"

Damn. Talk about starting off on the wrong foot with someone. And wasn't that a shame? Heath would have happily fixed this gal's plumbing late at night—or anything else that went haywire in the ramshackle old house she was renting.

Fragile build. Pixieish features. Creamy skin. Large caramel brown eyes. A full, vulnerable mouth the del-

Catherine Anderson

icate pink of barely ripened strawberries. Her hair fell in a thick, silken tangle around her shoulders, the sable tendrils curling over her white shirt like glistening ribbons of chocolate on vanilla ice cream.

Definitely not what he'd been picturing. Old Zeke usually rented this place to losers—people content to work the welfare system rather than seek gainful employment. Even in baggy jeans and a man's shirt this lady had "class" written all over her.

Nationally best-selling author **Pamela Morsi** *is known for the trademark wit and down-home humor that enliven her enchanting, memorable romances that have garnered rave reviews from critics and won national awards. This May experience the charm of Pamela Morsi in* Sealed With a Kiss.

When Gidney Chavis jilted Pru Belmont and left Chavistown, the nearly wed bride was devastated, the townsfolk scandalized . . . and Chavis was strongly discouraged from showing his face again. But now he's back, a bit older, a whole lot wiser . . . and rarin' to patch things up with Pru.

SEALED WITH A KISS
by Pamela Morsi

The cowboy allowed his gaze to roam among the customers. There was a table full of poker players intent upon their game. One tired, sort of half-pretty woman looked up hopefully and pulled her feet out of the chair next to her. He didn't even bother to meet her glance. A couple of rowdy farmhands seemed to be

starting early on a weekend drunken spree. A few other men drinking quietly. No one that he recognized for certain.

At the near end of the bar a dandied-up gentleman in a plaid coat and summer derby sat alone, his traveling bag at his feet.

The cowboy almost smiled. If there was anyone more certain not to be a local, it was a drummer in a plaid coat. Without any appearance of haste or purposeful intent, he casually took the seat right next to the traveling bag.

"Afternoon."

The little man looked up eagerly.

"Good afternoon to you, sir," he answered and in true salesman fashion, offered his hand across the bar. "Arthur D. Sattlemore, Big Texas Electric Company."

The cowboy's only answer was an indecipherable grunt as he signaled the barkeep to bring him a beer.

"Hot weather we've been having."

The cowboy nodded. "A miserable summer," he agreed. "Good for cotton."

"You are a farmer, sir?" Clearly the drummer was surprised.

"No," the cowboy answered. "But when you're in Chavistown, it's hard to talk about anything here without mentioning cotton."

The drummer chuckled and nodded understanding. He leaned closer. "You have the right of it there, sir," he admitted. "I was asked to come present my company to the Commercial Club. I've been here a week and haven't been able to get a word in edgewise. The whole town is talking cotton and what will happen without old man Chavis."

The cowboy blanched. "He's dead?"

The drummer shook his head. "Not as of this morning, but without him to run the gin and the cooperative, the farmers are worried that their cotton will sit in wagonloads by the side of the road."

"Ginning time has just begun," the cowboy said.

"Surely the old man will be up and around before it's over."

The drummer shook his head. "Not the way they're telling it. Seems the old man is bad off. Weak as a kitten they say, and the quacks warn that if he gets out of bed, he won't live to see winter."

"Doctors have been wrong before," the cowboy said.

The drummer nodded. "The whole town hopes you're right. The old man ain't got no one to take over for him. The gin's closed down and the cotton's just waiting."

The cowboy nodded.

"They had a meeting early in the week and voted to send for young Chavis, the old man's son."

"Is that so?"

"Young Chavis created some bit of scandal in this town eight years ago," the drummer explained. "Nobody's seen so much as his shadow since."

The cowboy listened quietly, intently.

"So they sent for their son and they're hoping that he'll come and save their biscuits," the little man said. "But for myself, I just wouldn't trust him."

"No?"

The traveling man tutted and shook his head. "They say he was all but married to a local gal and just left her high and dry."

"Is that what they say?"

The drummer nodded. "And I ask you, what kind of man blessed with plenty of money, an influential name, a fine place in the community and an innocent young sweetheart who expects to marry him, runs off with some round-heeled, painted-up saloon gal?"

The cowboy slowly picked up his beer and drank it down in one long swallow. He banged the glass on the bar with enough force to catch the attention of every man in the room.

"What kind of man, indeed," he said to the drummer.

*Best-selling author **Kathleen Eagle's** marriage to a Lakota Sioux has given her inspiration to write uniquely compelling love stories featuring Native American characters. She's won numerous awards, but her most gratifying reward was a note from a reader saying, "You kept me up all night reading." This June, stay up all night with* **The Night Remembers.**

Jesse Brown Wolf is a man living in the shadows who comes to the rescue of kids like Tommy T, a street-smart boy, and Angela, a fragile newcomer to the big city. Jesse rescues Angela from a brutal robbery and helps nurse her back to health. In return, Angela helps Jesse heal his wounded soul.

THE NIGHT REMEMBERS
by Kathleen Eagle

He hadn't been this close to anyone in a long time, and his visceral quaking was merely the proof. He sat on a straw cushion and leaned back against the woven willow backrest and drank what was left of the tea. He didn't need any of this. Not the kid, not the woman, not the intrusion into his life.

A peppering of loose pebbles echoed in the air shaft, warning him that something was stirring overhead. He climbed to the entrance and waited until the boy announced himself.

"I had a hard time gettin' the old grandpa to come to the door," Tommy T reported as he handed the canvas bag down blindly, as though he made regular

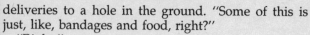

deliveries to a hole in the ground. "Some of this is just, like, bandages and food, right?"

"Right."

The boy went on. "I said I was just a runner and didn't know nothin' about what was in the message, and nobody asked no questions, nothin' about you. You know what? I know that old guy from school."

"A lot of people know him. He practices traditional medicine."

"Cool." Then, diverting to a little skepticism, "So what I brought is just roots and herbs and stuff."

"It's medicine."

"She might be worried about her dog," the boy said, hovering in the worlds above. "If she says anything, tell her I'm on the case."

"You don't know where she lives."

"I'll know by morning. I'll check in later, man." The voice was withdrawing. "Not when it's daytime, though. I won't hang around when it's light out."

On the note of promise, the boy left.

The night was nearly over. The air smelled like daybreak, laden with dew, and the river sounded more cheerful as it rushed toward morning. Normally, he would ascend to greet the break of day. The one good thing about the pain was the relief he felt when it lifted. Relief and weariness. He returned to the deepest chamber of his refuge, where his guest lay in his bed, her fragile face bathed in soft candlelight.

He made an infusion from the mixture of herbs the old man had prepared and applied it to the tattered angel's broken skin. He made a paste from ground roots and applied it to her swollen bumps and bruises, singing softly as he did so. The angel moaned, as though she would add her keening to his lullaby, but another tea soon tranquilized her fitful sleep.

Finally he doused the light, lay down beside her,

closed his eyes, and drifted on the dewy-sweet morning air.

He was so much thinner, his body lean, almost raw-boned, his heavy muscles thrown into stark prominence. His skin was so much darker, a rich bronze hue that was far too exotic and striking for an Englishman. But it *was* Hunter . . . older, toughened, as sinewy and alert as a panther.

"I didn't believe . . ." Lara started to say, but the words died away. It was too much of an effort to speak. She backed away from him and somehow made her way to the cabinet where she kept a few dishes and a small teapot. She took refuge in an everyday ritual, fumbling for a parcel of tea leaves, pulling the little porcelain pot from its place on the shelf. "I—I'll make some tea. We can talk about ... everything ..."

But her hands were shaking too badly, and the cups and saucers clattered together as she reached for them. He came to her in an instant, his feet swift and startlingly light on the floor. Hunter had always had a heavy footstep—but the thought was driven away as he took her cold hands in his huge warm ones. She felt his touch all through her body, in small, penetrating ripples of sensation.

A pair of teasing dark eyes stared into hers. "You're not going to faint, are you?"

Her face was frozen, making it impossible to smile, to produce any expression. She looked at him dumbly, her limbs stiff with fright and her knees locked and trembling.

The flicker of amusement vanished from his gaze, and he spoke softly. "It's all right, Lara." He pushed her to a nearby chair and sank to his haunches, their faces only inches from each other.

"H-Hunter?" Lara whispered in bewilderment. *Was* he her husband? He bore an impossibly close resemblance, but there were subtle differences that struck sparks of doubt within her.

He reached inside his worn black broadcloth coat and extracted a small object. Holding it his palm, he showed it to her. Eyes wide, Lara regarded the small, flat enameled box. He pressed the tiny catch on the side and revealed a miniature portrait of her, the one she had given him before his departure to India three years earlier.

"I've stared at this every day for months," he murmured. "Even when I didn't remember you in the days right after the shipwreck, I knew somehow that you belonged to me." He closed the box in his hand and tucked it back into his coat pocket.

Lara lifted her incredulous gaze to his. She felt as

if she were in a dream. "You've changed," she managed to say.

Hunter smiled slightly. "So have you. You're more beautiful than ever."

Barbara Freethy's poignant, tender love stories have garnered her many new fans. Her first Avon romance, Daniel's Gift, was called "exhilarating" by Affair de Coeur and Romantic Times said it was ". . . sure to tug on the heartstrings." This August, don't miss Barbara's best yet, One True Love.

Nick Maddux believed he'd never see his ex-wife, Lisa, again. Then he knocked on the door to his sister's house and Lisa answered—looking as beautiful, as vulnerable as ever. Nick soon discovered that, despite the tragedy that lay between them, his love for Lisa was as tender—and as passionate—as ever.

ONE TRUE LOVE
by Barbara Freethy

Nick Maddux was surrounded by pregnant women. Every time he turned around, he bumped into someone's stomach. Muttering yet another apology, he backed into the corner of his eight-by-twelve-foot booth at the San Diego Baby and Parenting Fair and took a deep breath. He was hot, tired and proud.

His handcrafted baby furniture was the hit of the show. In some cases, it would be a challenge to have his furniture arrive before the stork, but Nick thrived on challenges, and Robin Wood Designs was finally

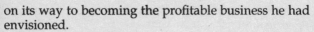

on its way to becoming the profitable business he had envisioned.

Nick couldn't believe how far he'd come, how much he'd changed.

Eight years ago, he'd been twenty-five years old, working toward getting his contractor's license and trying to provide for a wife and a child on the way. He'd kept at it long after they'd gone, hammering out his anger and frustration on helpless nails and boards.

Two years had gone by before he ran out of work, out of booze and out of money. Finally, stone-cold sober, he'd realized his life was a mess.

That's when he'd met Walter Mackey, a master craftsman well into his seventies but still finding joy in carving wood. Walter made rocking chairs in his garage and sold them at craft fairs. Nick had bought one of those chairs for his mother's birthday. She'd told Nick he'd given her something that would last forever.

It was then Nick realized he could make something that would last forever. His life didn't have to be a series of arrivals and departures.

Nick had decided to focus on baby furniture, because something for one's child always brought out the checkbook faster than something for oneself. Besides that mercenary reason, Nick had become obsessed with building furniture for babies that would nurture them, keep them safe, protect them.

He knew where the obsession came from, just not how to stop it. Maybe Robin would be proud of all that he'd accomplished in her name.

Nick felt himself drawn into the past. In his mind he saw Lisa with her round stomach, her glowing smile, her blue eyes lit up for the world to see. She'd been so happy then, so proud of herself. When she'd become pregnant, they both thought they'd won the lottery.

He closed his eyes for a moment as the pain threatened to overwhelm him, and he saw her again.

"I can't believe I'm having a baby," Lisa said. She took his hand and placed it on her abdomen. *"Feel that? She's kicking me."*

Nick's gut tightened at the fluttering kick against his fingers. It was the most incredible feeling. He couldn't begin to express the depth of his love for this unborn child, but he could show Lisa. In the middle of the baby store, he kissed her on the lips, uncaring of the salespeople or the other customers. *"I love you,"* he whispered against her mouth.

She looked into his eyes. *"I love you, too. More than anything. I'm so happy, it scares me. What if something goes wrong?"*

"Nothing will go wrong."

"Oh, Nick, things always go wrong around me. Remember our first date—we hit a parked car."

He smiled. *"That wasn't your fault. I'm the one who wasn't paying attention."*

"I'm the one who distracted you," she said with a worried look in her eyes.

"Okay, it was your fault."

"Nick!"

"I'm teasing. Don't be afraid of being happy. It's not fatal, you know. This is just the beginning for us."

It had been the beginning of the end.

Award-winning author **Christina Dodd** *is known for captivating characters and sizzling sensuality. She is the author of twelve best-selling romances, including* **A Well Pleasured Lady** *and* **A Well Favored Gentleman.** *Watch for her latest this September,* **That Scandalous Evening.**

Years earlier, Jane Higgenbothem had caused a scandal when she'd sculpted Lord Ransom Quincey of Blackburn in the classical manner. Apparently every-

thing was accurate save one very important part of Lord Blackburn's body. Jane retired to the country in disgrace, but now she has come back to London to face her adversary.

THAT SCANDALOUS EVENING
by Christina Dodd

London, 1809

"Can you see the newest belle?" Fitz demanded.

"No."

"You're not even looking!"

"There's nothing worth seeing." Ransom had better things to do than watch out for a silly girl.

"Not true. You'll find a diamond worth having, if you'd just take a look. A diamond, Ransom! Let us through. There you go lads, you can't keep her for yourselves." The constriction eased as the men turned and Fitz slipped through the crowd. Ransom followed close on Fitz's heels, protecting his friend's back and wondering why.

"Your servant, ma'am!" Fitz snapped to attention, then bowed, leaving Ransom a clear view of, not the diamond, but the profile of a dab of a lady. Her gown of rich green glacé silk was *au courant*, and nicely chosen to bring out the spark of emerald in her fine eyes. A lacy shawl covered her slight bosom, and she held her gloved hands clasped at her waist like a singer waiting for a cue that never came. A mop cap covered her unfashionable coil of heavy dark hair and her prim mouth must have never greeted a man invitingly.

Ransom began to turn away.

Then she smiled at the blonde with an exultant bosom beside her. It was a smile filled with pride and quiet pleasure. It lit the plain features and made them glow—and he'd seen that glow before. He jerked to a stop.

He stared. It couldn't be her. She had to be a figment of his wary, suspicious mind.

He blinked and looked again.

Damn, it *was* her.

Miss Jane Higgenbothem had returned.

America Loves Lindsey!

The Timeless Romances
of #1 Bestselling Author

KEEPER OF THE HEART	77493-3/$6.99 US/$8.99 Can
THE MAGIC OF YOU	75629-3/$6.99 US/$8.99 Can
ANGEL	75628-5/$6.99 US/$8.99 Can
PRISONER OF MY DESIRE	75627-7/$6.99 US/$8.99 Can
ONCE A PRINCESS	75625-0/$6.99 US/$8.99 Can
WARRIOR'S WOMAN	75301-4/$6.99 US/$8.99 Can
MAN OF MY DREAMS	75626-9/$6.99 US/$8.99 Can
SURRENDER MY LOVE	76256-0/$6.50 US/$7.50 Can
YOU BELONG TO ME	76258-7/$6.99 US/$8.99 Can
UNTIL FOREVER	76259-5/$6.50 US/$8.50 Can
LOVE ME FOREVER	72570-3/$6.99 US/$8.99 Can
SAY YOU LOVE ME	72571-1/$6.99 US/$8.99 Can

Coming Soon in Hardcover
ALL I NEED IS YOU

America Loves Lindsey!

The Timeless Romances
of #1 Bestselling Author

GENTLE ROGUE	75302-2/$6.99 US/$8.99 Can
DEFY NOT THE HEART	75299-9/$6.99 US/$8.99 Can
SILVER ANGEL	75294-8/$6.99 US/$8.99 Can
TENDER REBEL	75086-4/$6.99 US/$8.99 Can
SECRET FIRE	75087-2/$6.99 US/$8.99 Can
HEARTS AFLAME	89982-5/$6.99 US/$8.99 Can
A HEART SO WILD	75084-8/$6.99 US/$8.99 Can
WHEN LOVE AWAITS	89739-3/$6.99 US/$8.99 Can
LOVE ONLY ONCE	89953-1/$6.99 US/$8.99 Can
BRAVE THE WILD WIND	89284-7/$6.99 US/$8.99 Can
A GENTLE FEUDING	87155-6/$6.99 US/$8.99 Can
HEART OF THUNDER	85118-0/$6.99 US/$8.99 Can
SO SPEAKS THE HEART	81471-4/$6.99 US/$8.99 Can
GLORIOUS ANGEL	84947-X/$6.99 US/$8.99 Can
PARADISE WILD	77651-0/$6.99 US/$8.99 Can
FIRES OF WINTER	75747-8/$6.99 US/$8.99 Can
A PIRATE'S LOVE	40048-0/$6.99 US/$8.99 Can
CAPTIVE BRIDE	01697-4/$6.99 US/$8.99 Can
TENDER IS THE STORM	89693-1/$6.99 US/$8.99 Can
SAVAGE THUNDER	75300-6/$6.99 US/$8.99 Can

Experience the Wonder of Romance

LISA KLEYPAS

MIDNIGHT ANGEL
77353-8/$5.99 US/$6.99 Can

A beautiful noblewoman in disguise and under a false identity finds unexpected sanctuary in the arms of a handsome British lord.

And Don't Miss

DREAMING OF YOU   77352-X/$5.50 US/$6.50 Can

ONLY IN YOUR ARMS   76150-5/$5.99 US/$7.99 Can

ONLY WITH YOUR LOVE 76151-3/$5.50 US/$7.50 Can

THEN CAME YOU   77013-X/$5.99 US/$7.99 Can

PRINCE OF DREAMS   77355-4/$5.99 US/$7.99 Can

SOMEWHERE I'LL FIND YOU
                                        78143-3/$5.99 US/$7.99 Can